LIKE THE WIND

ANYDAYNOW SERIES #1

J. BENGTSSON

To Sarah
"I see you!" - Bodhi

J. B

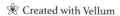 Created with Vellum

This book was written in the aftermath of the deadly California wildfires and is dedicated to all those who found themselves in the path of mother nature's relentless fury.

AnyDayNow is an American boy band formed in Los Angeles. Under the direction of famed manager Tucker Beckett, the group is composed of **Bodhi Beckett, RJ Contreras, Shawn Barber, Dane Makati,** and **Hunter Roy.**

Propelled to global success after the release of their first album, the five members of AnyDayNow are considered teen idols and, as such, are often the objects of fan hysteria. Their followers refer to themselves as Dayers.

"WATCH OUT!"

Her scream pierced the cab, commanding my foot to brake even before I knew the reason for her outburst. A tree, fully engulfed in flames, crashed to the ground two car lengths in front of us, sending embers cascading up and over the windshield. My sudden deceleration caused the back end of the Range Rover to fishtail and I struggled for control. We both screamed as the truck performed an entire rotation before coming to an abrupt stop within inches of the burning obstruction.

Breathing heavily, I looked to my passenger for encouraging words of wisdom, but she had nothing more to add to the stunned silence. It occurred to me then that the yappy dog in the backseat had actually stopped barking. Apparently he wasn't a fan of my Tilt-A-Whirl driving skills.

I placed the car in reverse to get us a safe distance from the burning blockage, but with distance came clarity. This narrow road was our salvation, and now the downed tree was blocking us from deliverance. The only way out was through the punishing flames.

Slowly I turned toward my passenger, ready to explain the dire situation, but the minute our eyes met, an understanding passed between us. We were out of options. I knew it. She knew it. The sloppy-tongued canine in the backseat knew it. If we turned around and followed the fire trucks up the mountain, we would die. If we stayed put, we would die. Our lives lay on the other side of that tree.

Incredibly, the woman seemed to absorb every word I didn't speak. Gripping my forearm, she nodded, ready to meet the challenge head-on. Even if that challenge meant driving through a stone-fire oven.

"Wait, what's your name?" I asked, suddenly overwhelmed with the urge to know this stranger beside me, the woman who faced the possibility of death with stunning courage and strength.

Her eyes softened, the fear in them temporarily abated as she answered my question. "Breeze."

I wasn't sure I'd heard her correctly. "Breeze? Like the wind?"

A tiny smile found its way to the surface. "Yes, Bodhi Beckett. Like the wind."

1

BODHI: THE LETTER

"I SEE YOU."

The microphone amplified my voice as I lifted my arm high in the air and pointed to the furthest seat in the stadium. A frenzy of activity followed, culminating in giddy screams pinging off every surface.

Jumping up and down near the edge of the stage, an adolescent girl squealed, "See me, Bodhi! See me!" I tipped my head in her direction and smiled. Such a trivial gesture, yet enough interaction to turn the girl into a free-flowing sprinkler system.

My band mate, RJ, batted his own lovesick eyes at me before shimmying on up to my side with that snarky grin on his face. Knowing his propensity for pantsing me on stage, I spun around in time to prevent his fingers from getting a hold of my waistband.

"See me, Bode-Hi," he cooed, deliberately mispronouncing my name because, well, he apparently found it hilarious. It's not like his name rolled off the tongue either - Renato Javier Salazar Contreras. Dammit, it actually did.

"Bo-dee," I corrected for the hundredth time. "The H is silent, asshole."

This little game of ours had been going on since he'd accidentally mangled my name the first day we met. Now he just said it wrong to piss me off. Pushing him away, I puckered my lips and sent him packing with an air kiss and the discreet extension of my middle finger. RJ's eyes narrowed in on me. He'd been challenged and there was no doubt I'd be paying for it later. Every part of his body language screamed, 'I'm going to pummel you.' Had we not been on stage in front of a crowd of thousands, he probably would have jumped on my back and knocked my head into a wall or something equally over the top.

RJ was the youngest child of three sons and, as such, never let a diss go without swift, physical engagement. In contrast, I'd always been a more cerebral, calculated person. Making a sound decision took time and patience. Not so with RJ. There was no thinking in his 'survival of the fittest' world. He was all blustery reaction and you either rolled with the punches or hid in a maintenance closet until he'd safely passed.

I'll admit, when I'd first met the dude, he'd taken some getting used to, and I'd done more hiding than rolling. Growing up an only child and never having gone to a traditional school, toys were my only playmates, and none of them ever beat the shit out of me.

But beatdowns and defensive training weren't the only things my friend taught me. He'd also modeled for me what it was like to have siblings and, surprisingly, I loved the brutal inclusion. I could barely remember what life was like without RJ and his hyperactivity, but I'm sure it was unbelievably boring.

Both singled out as the fan favorites in a five-man boy band, there were a whole multitude of reasons for RJ and me to dislike each other, but somehow we'd risen above the petty jealousies that came along with preteen fangirls fainting at our feet.

Hunter, Shawn, and Dane rounded out our quintet. Together we made up the members of AnyDayNow, currently the most popular boy band in the industry. We were household names... as long as those households in question had girls under the age of fifteen living in them. Okay, so maybe we were bigger than I gave us credit for. After all, our mere presence in the tour cities prompted irritated locals to bitch about road closures, ear-splitting headaches, and Salem-witch-style hysteria.

As the fan cherished 'hotties' of the group, RJ and I were responsible for much of that delirium. The other guys were popular too, don't get me wrong, it was just that they didn't have as many bedroom shrines dedicated in their honor. And even though the two of us rose to heartthrob status at the exact same time, I'd learned to harness the awesome power, while RJ was still in the process of trying not to cut his arm off with the light saber.

The band's handlers worked hard cultivating our images, although admittedly they had their hands full with RJ and Shawn, both of whom provided a steady stream of fodder for the tabloids. Me? I was on autopilot and always had been. The tale they'd spun for me from the very inception of the band had been elaborate in its details and carefully crafted throughout the years. I was the wholesome boy next door... or so it would seem. Given the fact I was a former child star who had lived most of my life out of a suitcase, portraying me as well-adjusted boyfriend material was a stretch by any means of the imagination. Not that I was a closet serial killer or anything, but I had issues that dated all the way back to my birth and no amount of whitewashing could wipe away the guilt that plagued me.

Still I was a competent enough actor to embody the character that had been created for me, and I played the part well. To all those sobbing little girls, Bodhi Beckett was *da bomb*. And really, who was I to burst their sheltered little bubbles? If they wanted to worship the ground I walked on, I was inclined to let them. After all, there were worse things in life than being adored. Besides, the fan devotion had made me a millionaire many times over and afforded me a lifestyle anyone would be envious of. As long as no one dug too deep into my personal life, I really was the perfect fantasy guy to bring home to mom and dad.

Sometimes I wished I were as fearless as RJ, who lived his life like he'd be trampled by a rhinoceros at any moment. I'd never been so carefree, not even when I was young, although it was up for debate whether I'd actually ever been a child. By the tender age of two, I was already supporting my family, although again, it was debatable whether my dad and I constituted a family. For all intents and purposes, he'd been more my manager than my father. Our dinner conversations were about business, not pleasure. The closest I'd ever come to a real family was playing the dutiful son on television.

Don't believe me? I lost my virginity to a twenty-year-old prostitute my father had hired when I was seventeen. Not that I was aware she was a prostitute at the time. Apparently he felt I was taking too long to close the deal on my own, so he did what any responsible father would do – he found me a sure thing.

We'd met at a party and one thing led to another. Suddenly the pretty girl I'd been flirting with turned into a fucking porn star before my very eyes. It had never occurred to me at the time that she might actually be one. I just assumed I was a *really* good lover. But no. It was all smoke and mirrors leading to years of anxiety over my sexual partners not being who I thought they were. Thanks, dad, for the lifelong phobia. Way to parent!

Stellar moments like that peppered my childhood, closing me off to real, honest relationships, especially with women. I never knew who to trust so, as a general rule, I trusted no one. It was just easier being alone than finding out years later the woman I married was the star of 'Debbie Does Dallas.'

It's not that I was complaining... okay, maybe I was. Even

though I'd lived my life in the spotlight, it had never really been by choice, and the older I got the more I wondered if this was truly the road I wanted to follow. I found myself looking forward to AnyDayNow's inevitable demise. I mean, how long could a bunch of twenty something guys pretend to be bubble-gum chomping teenagers? Not that getting out of my commitments would be as easy as stepping off the beaten path and walking away. I was bound securely around the man who'd made me a star, my father, and cutting myself loose from him promised to be a bloody affair.

Maybe someday, long after the euphoria faded, I'd be one of those dreaded cautionary tales of the 'former child star' struggling to find his place in the world. God knows I'd be a prime candidate for self-destruction. But I thought more of myself than to become just some footnote in history. Damned if I would meet my end overdosed on some park bench.

When the time came, I'd bow out gracefully. No point in trying to hold onto a fame that didn't want me anymore. Besides, it would give me the chance to live the quiet life that had always intrigued me. The idea of showing up at some dive bar with just my dependable guitar playing 'poor me' songs to a crowd of twelve hammered assholes was strangely appealing.

Shaking off the inevitable, I focused my attention back on task. I had a job to do. There were thousands of girls who had to fall hopelessly in love with me before the end of the show, and I aimed to please. Allowing the excitement to die down some before repeating my earlier words, I called out, "I see you - in Section H. Yes you... girl wearing the AnyDayNow t-shirt."

Squeals erupted as every female in Section H wearing a t-shirt with our band logo on it assumed I was speaking directly to her.

"The guys and I, we can't thank you enough for coming to

see us. All of you are like our family and when you're here, it feels like home."

You could almost hear the hearts bursting throughout the arena... and RJ's cynical gagging. Okay, it was a cheesy line. But this was a young crowd who hadn't fully developed the bullshit gene, so I could get away with sounding like Ferris Bueller here and no one would give a shit. Even if I might occasionally cringe at my own words, my audience gobbled it up like a bag of Sour-patch Kids.

I looked in the general direction of Section H, pretending I could see each and every person in it, though binoculars prob-ably wouldn't even do the job. These were the nosebleed seats, after all. But really, it didn't matter whether I could see them or not. What mattered was every girl wearing one of our t-shirts and sitting in that unfortunate section truly believed I'd locked eyes with her for the briefest of moments. It was all about guiding the fans through a fantasy and making them feel like they'd made a special connection with their idol. Their parents paid good money for the privilege and I'd learned long ago never to bite the hand that feeds.

Unlike RJ, I respected our fans enough to give them a perfor-mance worthy of their devotion. Yes, they were young and loud and excitable, but they were also responsible for our meteoric rise to fame. If it weren't for these girls and their moms, and the few courageous men and boys who braved the embarrassment of being seen at one of our concerts, we'd just be five guys standing on stage pretending to be something special while everyone else made fun of us.

At least now when we were ruthlessly mocked for being talentless wastes of space, we had a wad of cash in hand to make the poison go down easier. Would I like to be respected for something other than having nice hair? Sure. But that's not how boy bands worked. It didn't matter how many of our songs soared to the top of the music charts or how many shows we sold out, to our critics we'd always be dismissed as a manufactured group of minimally talented guys making a living off prepubescent fantasies. As long as we remained in the band, we'd never be taken seriously as artists, singers, and songwriters.

Five years ago, when we'd been handpicked for AnyDayNow, the distinction between performer and artist hadn't bothered us. We were all teenagers, eager for success. Our goal back then had been simple – work hard, give the best performances possible, and ride the wave as far as it would take us. We'd accomplished all three objectives, and then some.

As the final song began, the guys and I took our positions, standing side by side at center stage, belting out the words to our most popular song to date, *Wait For You*. Unlike other boy bands, we weren't dancers, even though the producers had diligently tried to make that happen. At the beginning of our rise to fame, our dance routines had been so painful to witness that in one scathing review, we'd been compared to a family of three-legged giraffes suffering from ear infections. After that, we were allowed to do our own thing, and it turned out we had just enough spasmodic moves to entertain the fans just fine, thank you very much.

Fireworks exploded overhead as we finished our final encore. Smiles plastered on our faces, we waved to the crowd as the stage descended, shielding us from view. A half a dozen tech guys swarmed around us. We stood silently under the stage while they removed our earplugs and mics, having learned the hard way that anything we said after the show would be broadcast live into a stadium filled with innocent ears. You only had to drop one f-bomb into a crowd of preteens to learn your lesson.

Now free from all devices, it was like surfacing from a deep-sea dive. We could hear and breathe normally again. In an hour's time, we'd be ushered out of the arena under heavy security to the chorus of all those little screamers damaging their vocal chords just to let us know how much they loved and appreciated us. There would be pushing and cameras flashing and middle-aged men fighting to keep the makeshift fences from toppling over in the crush of overeager fans determined to adore us to frickin' death.

But that was in an hour. Until then we were free to be the twenty-something guys we were instead of the larger-than-life perpetual teenagers our fans envisioned us to be. And with the veil of perfection lifted, we transformed into a group of frat boys trying to one up each other. In the short trek from the stage to our dressing room, I'd been shoved, punched, and grabbed in the ass. After five and a half years together, there was nothing off limits anymore.

"Can we all just take a moment to recognize our friend Dane here? I mean bravo, dude. It takes a special kind of stupid to trip over your own shoelace in front of a crowd of twenty-five thousand people." Shawn clapped for our fallen brother before acting out a step-by-step replay of the entire event by pretending to trip and fake-slam his face into the floor. The slow-motion reenactment had us all in stitches.

"It came untied," Dane grumbled, fixing us with his droopy, condemning stare. He had what was commonly referred to as bedroom eyes. You know, the kind that made a person look perpetually stoned? Even when Dane wasn't high, like right now, he still had that 'Dude, where's my car?' expression on his face. And it certainly hadn't helped his cause when the guy had a spiritual awakening last year and shaved his head. Suddenly those eyes of his took center stage and, truth be told, he creeped the rest of us out in a Steve Buscemi kind of way. "And just so you know, while you dickheads were laughing your asses off, I had blood hemorrhaging from of my nose. I think it might even be broken. So, fuck you all."

That only brought a fresh round of laughs. Certainly not the sympathy he desired but what did he expect? We'd all taken our tumbles on stage at one time or another. Dane's clumsy ass wasn't special by any means.

"You're having your face fixed with plastic surgery, you say?" RJ flashed a satisfied smirk as he patted Dane's shoulder. "I think that's probably best."

"Fuck you, dude. Your ass must be jealous of all the shit that comes out of your mouth."

RJ made a show of speaking in a low tone as he addressed me personally. "He's just upset because I matched with his mom on Tinder."

Retaliation was swift with Dane jumping over a chair to get at RJ.

Completely ignoring the combat zone behind him, Shawn formed his hands into prayer and pleaded, "Please. Please let someone have Dane's face plant on video. We could switch it to slo-mo and add a little music montage. No offense, Bodhi, but I'm getting tired of all your Barbie doll sex tapes."

Oh god, don't remind me. Shawn was referring to the special edition AnyDayNow collector set of dolls that some bigwig toy executive thought would be a moneymaker and preceded to sell the idea to our manager, also known as my father. Because we were just the hired help and had no real say in the business decisions, shit like those dolls flooded the market. Our images also adorned pillows, posters, key chains, and even toilet paper, where haters got to use our faces to wipe their shitty assholes. Sure, we got a cut of the profits, but was it really worth the loss of our dignity?

"Oh trust me, no offense taken," I said, and meant it. If I never saw another Barbie doll of any kind for the rest of my life, I'd be a happy man. "I'm more than willing to hand over the YouTube crown to Dane here."

He waved me off as if the words were beyond ridiculous. "Dude, it's gonna take a lot more than me flopping face-first on stage to unseat your dolly's gangbang sessions with Ken and GI Joe."

When the faux Barbie dolls hit the store shelves, we tried to justify their existence by calling them action figures. "My action figure this" or "His action figure that." It was our way of feeling better about the plastic, dickless versions of ourselves. And while everyone else's doll was fairly well done, mine looked like a young Steven Tyler—had he been a boobless twelve-year-old girl. Okay sure, yes, I had the surfer boy fringed, shoulder-length dark brown hair... big, damn deal. A lot of guys had long hair without looking like chicks.

Anyway, as you might imagine, my doll was a hit. For entirely the wrong reasons. It took all of two days for videos to spring up on YouTube, starring my doll in bikinis, evening gowns, and high heel shoes.

The other guys harassed me relentlessly and what could I say? Had the stiletto been on the other foot, I never would have let them live it down. Still, it sucked that I couldn't get behind my dolly the way the other guys had. In fact, every one of them had been thrilled with their likeness.

RJ scored with an Enrique Iglesias look-a-like doll.

Dane was more than stoked to discover his resembled the Dali Lama.

Shawn, or 'Blackout Shawn' as we knew him, couldn't have been happier with his doppelganger. And why wouldn't he be? For the first time in his life he had abs. His love of beer had resulted in a pregnancy pouch that was none too funny to our handlers, who expected nothing short of physical perfection from the five of us. But due to Shawn's hilarious escapades with alcohol, he didn't have the stamina in the gym that the rest of us had. Not to mention, he surely had brain damage after the many times he'd passed out in the last four years. So excuse me if I was a tad bit irritated that the guy who spent half his life draped over a toilet got a cooler doll than me.

And finally, there was Hunter. 'The Sweet One' as fans knew him. Oh Hunter. I mean if anyone deserved a pretty doll in our group, it was that guy. The dude spent more time in front of a mirror than anyone I knew. His hair alone took an hour to style, and don't even get me started on his skin care regimen. Had I known charcoal masks were such a thing, I would have scooped the black residue out of the barbeque for him long ago.

Yet, instead of giving Hunter the high-maintenance doll he deserved, the toy makers inexplicably made him look like the ultimate player, complete with bulging muscles and a sexy come-hither expression.

Let me be very clear here when I say, Hunter was no ladies' man. He wasn't even a dude's man. In fact, the oldest member of our band was as celibate as they came. Hunter was saving himself for marriage and wanted that same lofty commitment from his bandmates. You can imagine the brick wall he came up against when he explained the benefits of abstinence before marriage to the rest of us horndogs.

But a couple of years ago, after much debate, the four of us decided to open our minds to a new way of thinking... or at least humor Hunter with a stretch of celibacy. How hard could it be, right? Unfortunately, with our busses rolling through Sweden the first week of that crucial month, it was clear we'd chosen the wrong country to begin Hunter's experiment.

"I keep telling you to report copyright infringements on YouTube," Hunter lectured.

I groaned because it's not like I hadn't heard that exact same advice from his mouth numerous times before.

"It's a doll, Hunter." I replied matter of factly. "It doesn't have any legal rights. Besides, don't you think if I could prevent my Barbie from getting porked in front of a live audience, I would?"

Everyone laughed except Hunter who still seemed overly invested in the purity of my plastic clone.

"Um... excuse me... Mr. Beckett?"

I turned in search of my father before realizing that the security guard, standing in the doorway, was actually speaking to me. I didn't recognize him and, from the look of his nervous shifting, he'd never seen me in person either.

"Yeah?"

"Um... sorry to bother you, but your mom is outside. She wants to see you."

My jaw dropped open in surprise. *My mom?* Well this certainly was news worthy of interruption. Glancing to the guys, I found them sporting the same disbelieving gape.

My response required maximum clarity. "Sorry, what's your name?"

"Carter."

"Well, *Carter.*" I was just being a dick, exaggerating his moniker for effect. But Carter deserved it after the bomb he'd dropped. "That's just flippin' awesome news. I can't wait to see her again."

His face brightened. Apparently he thought he'd done good coming in here to bother me with his bogus news.

The series of words that shot from my mouth hit their intended target. "Especially since my mother has been dead for the past twenty-four years."

Poor Carter. The hopeful expression on his face was no more. Now he resembled a man who'd just been clocked in the nuts with a twenty-pound weight. "I...I, oh god."

"Exactly," I said, turning my back to him and wiping my hands of the conversation.

LIKE THE WIND 15

Much to my surprise, Carter wasn't giving up easily. "It's just she... she asked me to give you this."

I craned my neck in his direction only to find him boldly stepping forward with an envelope in one hand and what appeared to be a photograph in the other.

"Dude." Dane cut in front of Carter, blocking him from reaching me. "Not cool. Shit like this happens all the time... fans trying to talk their way in. You've been had. Next time you get something like this bring it to the head of security. Don't bother Bodhi with it. Now go. And don't bring fan stuff back here again, got it?"

Carter backed off immediately. "I ... I'm sorry. She showed me this photograph of her holding a baby and Bodhi's father was in the picture, so I guess I just assumed she was telling the truth. I'm really sorry."

What the fuck? My father? Now, I was more than just a little curious about the photograph he was holding.

"Hey," I called out to his retreating frame. "Give it to me."

Carter turned around, appearing horrified by his misstep. He knew well that I could get him fired but what was the point? I was certain the security guard had learned a valuable lesson and would never again get within fifty feet of me. After placing both the photograph and the letter in my hand, he hurried out the door as if he feared the knob would knock him in the ass on the way out.

"What was that all about?" RJ asked, leaning over my shoulder to get a look at the photograph in my hand. I shrugged him off, finding a vacant corner for this little blast from the past. After all, it's not every day a guy gets a letter from his dead mother.

The background noise faded the minute I laid eyes on the photograph. My brain struggled to make sense of what it was seeing. The woman in the picture looked identical to the woman in the photograph I kept of the mother who'd died giving birth to me. Yet here she was staring vacantly into the camera, holding a baby who looked suspiciously like me. It was as if she'd somehow checked out of the entire scene.

My father, a good five to ten years older than the woman, stood off to the side, his arms folded in front of him, a scowl hardening his disgruntled expression. It was clear by their body language that these two people didn't much like each other. None of it made any sense.

With shaky fingers, I pulled the letter out of the envelope and read the first two lines before slumping against the wall in shock. *Bodhi, I know what your father told you about me, but it was all a lie. My name is Marni Easton and I'm your mother."*

BODHI: TWINKIE ISSUE

THREE MONTHS LATER

Sitting with my back propped against the bathroom door, I pressed my feet firmly to the wall, as if that extra little bit of resistance would somehow keep my female pursuers from busting through the barrier and devouring me. Minutes earlier, alone in the aisle of a grocery store, I'd come face to face with my worst nightmare—a giddy girls soccer team.

Okay so maybe not my worst nightmare. It's not like I'd just survived a terrorist attack or anything but, regardless, my heart was pounding. Sure, my pursuers wore braces and were armed with only their unmatched enthusiasm, but that didn't make them any less dangerous. And now here I was—trapped like some hapless victim in a slasher flick who'd chosen to hide from the chainsaw masochist instead of running. I was such an idiot. When had the 'hide in plain sight' approach ever worked in anyone's favor? The world was filled with people who ran.

I know what you're thinking—that I'm over-exaggerating the threat to my person but, I can assure you, the risk was real. I, of all people, knew what little girls were made of and it wasn't sugar and spice and everything nice. Oh no, they were made of skin-shredding nails, high-pitched squeals, and impromptu fainting spells. As far as I was concerned, I was lucky to get out of the cookie aisle alive.

"*Bodhi. Bodhi.*"

The chanting and pounding were getting louder and more insistent.

"Just go away," I pleaded quietly, knocking the back of my head against the door. A few months ago, I would have handled this fan encounter very differently, but I wasn't the same golly-gee popstar I was back then. My dear ol' *not-dead* mother had taken care of that.

Twisting the cap off the Smirnoff, I took a long pull, wincing at the burn. You'd think I'd be stealthier when it came to pounding down the liquor seeing as I'd become well versed in the bottle of late. In fact, before making my Uber-led booze run, I'd been pregaming it quite effectively with the mini bottles I'd acquired on my last flight.

Honestly, you'd never know that up until a few months ago, drinking hadn't been my thing. Back then, I'd viewed alcohol as wasted calories, not worthy of the extra time in the gym it would take me to work them off. But that was before letter-gate ... before I discovered that deception really wasn't my thing either. It's not every day you find out the man you thought was your father really may not actually be, and the woman you thought was your deceased mother had been alive and kicking your whole damn life.

I mean, where does one even begin with bombshell information like that? I'll tell you where—with the bottle! And although I'd once been a vocal opponent of the evils of excessive alcohol consumption, I could now objectively say the benefits clearly outweighed the harm. How else was I going to numb my mind to the realities of what I now knew?

It was almost comical the way the bosses initially brushed my destructive behaviors under the rug. When they'd first discovered my burgeoning appetite for liquor, they'd reacted with surprised indifference. So what if their Golden Boy was blowing off a little steam? It wasn't like their mild-mannered Clark Kent was going to suddenly morph into an unrecognizable badass flying machine. But then I did. And they were left dazed and confused in my wake.

Once they understood this would not be a passing phase, the bolts were tightened on my freedom. Babysitters, disguised as security guards, reported on my every move. Mini fridges were emptied long before I ever stepped foot into my hotel rooms. And access to the outside world became a privilege I had to earn. I was twenty-four-years-old, for god's sake. When had I suddenly become a hostage to my own life? Or maybe it had always been this way and I'd just been blind to the restraints securely wrapped around my wrists.

Now that my eyes were opened wide, I didn't like what I was seeing. Not one bit. My team, the people who claimed to care about my well-being and who were supposedly committed to making my hectic life easier, had really just been prison guards milking me for every last dime I could give them. And that team included my father, Tucker Beckett, the man who made me call him by his first name in mixed company because he didn't want others to think he was playing favorites. He was my father, for god's sake, hadn't I earned the right to call him Dad? I suppose it didn't matter either way because it didn't change the fact that he was the worst of them all. Under the guise of fatherly love, he'd kept me shackled to his side since I was a child. Not because he wanted what was best for me but because he wanted what was best for *him*.

I shuddered to think of how long it would have taken me to uncover the truth had my mother not delivered her drop-the-mic message when she had. Would I have wasted even more of my life being danced around on strings by the puppet masters who controlled my every move?

That's not to say my so-called mother was some heroine coming to save the day. She had her own agenda, one I hadn't figured out yet. But I wasn't naïve enough to believe her intentions were pure. Who was to say the woe-is-me tale she'd woven was even the truth? Judging by her abandonment, it's not like the woman had my best interests at heart either.

The question wasn't who was lying— it was pretty clear they both had their secrets— but who had the most to hide. Maybe I should have hunted down the security guard and demanded he deliver my newly resurrected mother to me on the spot, but I'd been too shocked to react in any coherent manner. Instead, I'd let her go and have since been lingering in this uncomfortable state of uncertainty. Who was she? Why had she left me? And most of all, who the hell was the man I'd been living with all these years?

Confronting my father with the accusations seemed the most straightforward way to get answers, but he'd been lying to me my whole life so who was to say he'd tell me the truth anyway?

So I'd made the guys promise not to tell a soul about Carter's interruption and the unexpected message he'd delivered. I would deal with this information on my own terms but, for now, I was content to just let the man suffer, wondering what had happened to his perfectly obedient son.

Asshole! If my father thought I would continue playing by his rules, he had another think coming. How could I have been such a wuss for so damn long? My sheer lack of gumption was embarrassing. I'd allowed myself to be led around like a mindless wooden puppet. Fuck that. I wasn't some toy to be molded and manipulated. This was my life and that wake-up call was what I'd needed to finally take control. Pinocchio was going back in the drawer.

Or...okay... so maybe I was over-stating my newfound supremacy. After all, I *was* currently sitting on a bathroom floor after fleeing from The Children of the Corn, and that certainly wasn't the manly representation I wanted to project. Although, to be fair, I was in a boy band. It's not like people hadn't already formed their own opinions about my masculinity. Hell, there were blogs dedicated to it.

The minute I'd signed my name on the dotted line and become a bona fide member of AnyDayNow, I'd lost the respect of nearly every red-blooded male on the planet. And for any guys still on the fence about whether I was a spineless wimp, this little grocery store stunt should seal the deal. Not that I really cared what other people thought of me. That was a luxury I didn't have time for. Besides, growing up as a child star, you either developed a tough hide or you died young in a puddle of your own urine.

My knee-jerk reaction after receiving the letter was to quit the band and run off into the night. But I was loyal to the guys and couldn't just up and flee in the middle of a tour. They were like brothers to me. Not to mention the mountain of trouble I'd leave behind in terms of broken contracts, binding agreements, and lawsuits.

So professionally, I still showed up for every appearance, giving the most I could to my performances. But something had dimmed in me and, try as I might, I couldn't muster more than a half-assed rendition of my former self. Gone were the corny endearments and the playful stage antics with RJ. Pants me in front of a live audience now? Dude, I dare you.

The 'truth' bomb my mother had detonated had robbed me

of my sense of humor as well as my pride. When fans chanted for me now, I felt nothing. Their love and devotion rang hollow. I wasn't who they thought I was. Hell, Bodhi Beckett wasn't even my real goddamn name!

The phone in my pocket buzzed non-stop, leaving no doubt that my grocery store debacle was trending on social media. Dammit, if I'd just stayed in the liquor aisle none of this would have happened. That's what I'd come to the store for in the first place so why hadn't I just stuck to the plan? I'll tell you why, because of my father and his insane rules against sugar—the one food group I'd been denied since childhood. And since my current strategy was to stick it to the man, it only seemed right to stuff my face with as much processed sugar as possible. And maybe, with a steady stream of the stuff, I could grow some fairly impressive love handles, which would surely give the man a heart attack. Win-win.

Unfortunately, the ski cap and dark glasses I'd used to disguise myself didn't fool the gaggle of preteen girls. Moments after I'd arrived in the Hostess aisle, slinking around like some pervert in the kink section of a sex shop, the girls materialized, crowding around me in their quest for sweets. I'd grabbed the first thing I saw, a box of Twinkies, and then quickly retreated. Seconds from a clean getaway, a girl with side braids and freckles had made eye contact and I was done for.

"Oh my god! It's Bodhi Beckett," she'd screamed, and all her friends joined in the hysteria. That's how it usually played out. All it took was for one baby bird to chirp and the others began squawking. The soccer team had descended like a swarm of vultures ready and willing to rip the flesh from my bones, leaving me no choice but to flee the aisle clutching my Vodka and the box of sugary delight.

As I'd raced to the front of the store with a trail of screamers in my wake, I faced a crucial decision – die, go to jail, or give up my Twinkies. If I stopped at the cash register, I died. If I ran out of the store clutching stolen contraband, I went to jail. But if I gave up my Twinkies, my asshole father won.

I chose the Twinkies.

And that's how I ended up here, barricaded in a gender-friendly bathroom and praying for the girls' bedtime to roll around sooner rather than later. Remembering I still hadn't laid waste to my Twinkies, I grabbed the box and tore it open. Ten individually wrapped pieces of heaven called my name. For maximum effect, I tore open the plastic on the first spongy cream-filled cake with my teeth and shoved the whole thing into my mouth. Instantly my jaws tingled from the goodness and as the sugar hit my system, I groaned with pleasure.

Heads up, people. This was the shit that happened when parents deprived their offspring of sweets. Their children grew into adults with Twinkie issues. Had my dad just allowed a sampling of sweets once in a while, maybe I wouldn't be sitting on this nasty-ass floor with cream filling smudged on my lips, all while attempting to ward off a bunch of teeny-boppers in training bras.

"Bodhi! Bodhi!"

Damn. Kids this age never tired. What were these girls doing out so late anyway, and why were they stocking up on cookies and candy? It was half past midnight, for god's sake! Shouldn't they be all tucked in bed wrapped up in their favorite Bodhi Beckett blankets? Why didn't they have parents who enforced the no Twinkie rule? How was that fair to me?

The phone chirped again. My father's ringtone. Shit. That was quick. I wondered who'd tipped him off to my freedom flight. Probably the guard who I'd tricked into leaving his post with a pornographic video of my Barbie doll taking it up the butt by Buzz Lightyear. He'd laughed hysterically while I slipped out the back door to summon the Uber. Oh shit! The Uber. I wondered if he was still waiting for me. How committed was he to my cause?

The phone stopped ringing, then started up again. I checked the screen on the off chance someone else, someone pleasant, might want to chat with me, but no luck. It was still my father, and it would continue to be my father until I manned up and answered his call. My pointer finger, crusted with cream filling, stuck to the screen as I pushed the talk button.

"Yeah?" I whispered into the receiver, licking my fingers to rid myself of the evidence as if he could somehow see through the phone and bust my ass for breaking the Twinkie rule.

"You are quite possibly the stupidest human on the planet!"

Okay, so... he'd heard. I already knew the script, so I held the phone away from my ear for the rest of his tirade. He would go through the list of all my faults, verbally assaulting me until he had no more vile words to scream. Thankfully I had a quarter of a bottle of Vodka in my system to lessen the sting of his questions.

"Good god, Bodhi, do you have shit for brains?" *Yes, that must be it. Someone crapped in my headspace.*

"Do you think the universe revolves around your sorry ass?" *Well, yes, now that you mention it, I do feel partially responsible for the earth's rotation.*

"Are you just trying to piss me off?" That one was easy. *Yes, I was most definitely trying to piss him off.*

I closed my eyes, mentally devising ways to kill the man with nothing more than the power of my mind. He was ground zero - the target of all my rage. Tucker Beckett—my father... my manager— the Twinkie Nazi.

––––––

Knowing what was coming, I'd managed to finish off over half of the bottle of vodka before his booming voice and fake laughter penetrated the walls of my sanctuary. Standing up on wobbly legs, I mentally prepared for dear ol' dad. I'd learned the hard way that dealing with him head on was always preferable to weak waffling, although I wasn't sure how head on I could be when I was currently well over the legal limit.

"Open up," my father said, in an easy, conversational tone as he rapped his knuckle on the wood. There was no anger in his voice, never in front of a crowd of strangers, but I knew better. Just under the surface was a boiling volcano. My behavior reflected on him and, at the moment, neither one of us was looking real pretty. One thing I'd realized after being plunged head first into this family drama was that my father's whole identity rested on me. When I shined, so did he. But now, in my current state of destruction, he was just a shitty dad who'd raised a shitty kid.

Knowing there was no point in dragging this out, I unlocked the door. Instead of waiting for me to allow passage, Tucker pushed his way inside. He didn't say a word, nor did he have to. The look on his face was murderous. Grabbing the bottle of booze from my hand, he tossed it in the garbage, along with the now empty box of Twinkies. He humored me with the raise of an eyebrow but said nothing about my late night snack attack.

Surprisingly, the loss of my vodka hurt more than I thought it would, triggering a sudden urge to fight for its honor. I lunged for the trash. Quick as a frickin' ninja, my well-conditioned father kicked the door shut and then pushed me forcefully against the wall. The wind knocked out of me, I struggled to make sense of the sudden violence. Aside from some shoving and the occasional childhood spanking, Tucker didn't get physical with me and had never crossed the line like this before. To be fair, I'd never given him the chance, always caving to the pressure well before things got out of control.

"This ends now," he growled under his breath, careful not to let his anger seep through the cracks of the door. God forbid people think he wasn't the jovial guy he pretended to be. "You, of all people, can't afford to go down this path."

"*Of all people?* What the fuck does that mean?"

His eyes widened like he just realized what he'd said and that pissed him off even more, bringing us right back to where we started. "It means I've had enough of your shit." Tucker grabbed my shirt, pulling me away from the wall before slamming me right back up against it. "You will go through that door, smile for the cameras, and walk out of here like you own the place. If I see anything less than the charming, confident Bodhi Beckett I know you can be, I'll..."

"You'll *what?*" Challenge seeped from my core. "Hit me? Ruin my career? Well, news flash, *DAD*..." I dropped my tone to a whisper. "I don't care."

"You will."

"Yeah? Then give me your best shot. I dare you, because when I go down, I'm taking you with me."

The tiniest trickle of fear lessened the contempt in his glare. He knew what I was saying was true. This empire he'd built wasn't made of stone like he'd once assumed. His kingdom was nothing more than a cluster of sticks and I was itching to blow them all down.

Tightening his grip, he clenched his teeth and said, "What's gotten into you? I don't understand why you're willing to throw away everything we've worked so hard for all these years. This isn't you, Bodhi."

We? I was the one who'd given up my childhood to make him rich beyond his wildest dreams. It was me who got up on that stage three to four times a week while he rested in the green

LIKE THE WIND 27

room with a gin and tonic—dollar signs floating in front of his eyes. And my life he'd stolen before I could even speak. No, he was right. I wasn't the weak kid he'd groomed me to be. I was the man who was about to light up his cushy world.

Coming to his senses, my father let go of my shirt, releasing me from the wall. He then smoothed the fabric and spoke to me like I was a child. "Let's just focus on getting out of the bathroom and then we can go back to the hotel and talk in private. How does that sound?"

Did he really think I would fold that easily? Of course he did. It's all he knew.

I smiled, but felt nothing but contempt as I answered his question in my best Eddie Haskell voice. "Sure, Dad. Let's do that."

———

When the door opened, my cheering squad was gone. That would've been good news had the soccer team not been replaced with paparazzi lobbing questions at me like hand grenades.

"Bodhi, what were you doing in the locked bathroom?"

"Were you shooting up?"

"Are you being charged with shoplifting?"

"Is this a wake-up call, Bodhi? Are you considering rehab?"

Now popular wisdom dictated you never respond to the paparazzi because everything you said could, and absolutely would, be used against you.

My father nudged me as if to say, 'Smile and wave, Son. Just smile and wave.'

And yes, that would have been the smart thing to do. Old Bodhi would have rocked that fake shit, but not drunk and sugar-hyped Bodhi. Oh no, tonight's Bodhi had other plans.

My middle fingers went up before my father could stop them

and I made aggressive and sexually suggestive hand gestures as the cameras flashed around me. But I didn't stop there. As my father was hustling me out of the grocery store, I took hold of my waistband and slid it down just far enough to ensure my Barbie doll wouldn't be the only Bodhi Beckett video worth watching on YouTube tonight.

———

Like a death row inmate, bulky bodyguards flanked me on either side. My father, the executioner, walked ahead in silence. He hadn't spoken since the buttocks incident. After being liberated from the convenience store, I'd thrown up twice. Once out the skylight of the limo and a second time somewhere in the hallway of the hotel after a bumpy elevator ride riled up my stomach.

Once we finally made it to the suite, my father slid a key into the lock on my door and motioned me inside.

It occurred to me to be pissed. "You have a key to my room?"

Tucker seemed wholly unimpressed with my slurred speech and didn't bother to give me an answer. Asshole.

"Leave us," Tucker said to the guards. "Wait outside the door and if anyone lets him out, you'll be terminated of duty."

"What if there's a fire?" I challenged, my impaired mind already considering setting one myself to escape.

"There's not going to be a fire," he mumbled, shutting the door on our grinning audience. Obviously they found my drunk uncle act entertaining.

It struck me then that the security guards were only following orders. They didn't want to imprison me any more than I wanted to be trapped, but neither of us had a choice. We were all beholden to the same king.

When the two of us were finally alone, an awkward silence

set in. I took to staring at the dent in the wood table and wondering if I'd had something to do with its imperfection. Probably. Destruction seemed to be a theme with me lately.

I could feel my father's hard eyes trained on me. Finally he spoke, sounding tired and maybe even a little defeated. "What were you thinking, Bodhi? What was that stunt you pulled?"

"It's called mooning but I prefer the term 'ass flash'," I answered, burping up a nasty liquor-filled air bubble. "It's defined as the act of baring one's anus in a sign of defiance."

I couldn't stop the sloshed snickering. I mean, I did just say anus, and it didn't matter how drunk I was, the word was always hilarious.

"You think this is funny?"

"Sort of."

His jaw taut, my father could barely get the words out through clenched teeth. "Do you have any idea what I'm going to have to do to clean up this mess?"

You know, really, on the celebrity bad behavior scale from one to ten, my evening escapades scored a very mild two. I couldn't even do 'bad' with any real conviction. No domestic abuse. No driving drunk. No pissing in a janitor's bucket. I got hammered, ate some Twinkies, and bared my ass. Big fucking deal. By my calculations it might take him all of fifteen minutes to put a heartwarming spin on my evening.

But now was not the time to ponder such things as sickness began to bubble up from my gut. Without responding, I dashed off to the bathroom.

———

The pounding on my door jolted me upright, sending a wave of pain through my head. If I'd thought I would sleep off my drunken stupor and wake up a new man, I'd been sadly mistaken. It felt like a team of basketball players were dribbling in my ear.

"Oh man," I whined, rolling knuckles over my temples. Why had I thought this was a good way to irritate my father? Any plan where I also had to suffer sort of defeated the purpose. I needed to get more creative with my sabotage.

I flung the sheets off my weakened body, and shuffled to the door so I could peer through the peephole. There were only four people who could get me to open that door, and one of them was standing on the other side.

"Ah, shit," I mumbled, in no mood for company but also in no position to refuse my guest.

"Open up, dickwad," RJ demanded. "I can see your dilated eyeball."

"Fine," I mumbled, opening the door for him.

He looked me up and down a few times before nodding in approval. "You look like shit."

The half-hearted smile I offered officially committed me to the conversation. "Well, I worked hard to look this hung over, so thank you."

"I know you did. Your drunken ass is all over Twitter."

"Hell yeah. Don't get too comfortable with that bad boy title, RJ, 'cuz I'm coming for you."

"Hang on there, Howdy Doody. Learn to hold your liquor and then we'll talk."

"I hold it just fine."

"Tell that to the potted plant you barfed in last night."

"How'd you know about that?"

"Pretty much every detail of your evening was chronicled on film. My favorite part was when you tried to pet the squirrel on the way into the hotel."

"Impossible. I hate rodents."

"Not drunk you don't. You got on your hands and knees and were calling out over and over, 'come here you cute little rascal.'"

"Oh god—*no*."

"Oh, yeah."

We sat there in silence for a minute or so, me worrying about all the things I couldn't remember and RJ looking as if he were trying to conjure up the courage to dive deep into a conversation with me. Finally, he seemed to find his bravery.

"So, even though I find the squirrel-loving Bodhi humorous, I'm sort of getting worried about you. I've known you a long time and I've never seen you like this. I've come to the conclusion that you either have a tumor pressing on your brain stem or you're dealing with some shit you obviously don't know how to deal with."

"I'm going to go with the tumor theory," I said.

"Man, come on. What's going on with you?"

"Nothing. Are you the only one allowed to have a little fun?"

"No. But honestly, you don't appear to be having any fun at all."

I shrugged off the pain radiating through my head. He wasn't wrong about that. There was nothing fun about the way I was feeling right now.

"Look, if this were just about you blowing off some steam, I'd say good for you. All publicity is good publicity, right? But, dude, I'm not gonna lie, this is starting to look like a cautionary episode of *Celebrity Rehab*."

I laughed despite the misery I was in and the gesture brought fresh agony. A groan escaped my throat.

"I'm asking you this as a friend. Should I be worried?"

"I'm fine, RJ," I lied. "Really I am."

His brow rose in response. Obviously he didn't believe a word out of my lying mouth.

Sighing, I said, "I'm just working through some shit right now."

He nodded, twisting his hands together. Clearly there was more he needed to say. "What was in that letter?"

The letter. Jesus. What she'd written to me wasn't some standard 'I'm your long-lost mother' crap. She'd taken the wound that had lived in me—the one that formed the day I was born and the day she supposedly died—and ripped it wide open. I wasn't who I thought I was. My father sure as hell wasn't who I thought he was. And now, all of a sudden, the dead mother I'd idolized my entire life was just a flawed woman with demons all her own. I wanted to confide in RJ, but the deception was still too raw.

"You can trust me," he said, hopeful for more after watching the turmoil pass over my conflicted face. "You know I have your back."

I rubbed my tired eyes. "I know, but not now. Not yet."

His disappointment hung thick in the air. "Okay then, just tell me this one thing and then I'll leave you alone. Is she alive, your mother?"

The answer to that question still sent shock waves through me. She'd been 'dead' my entire life, so her resurrection was something I hadn't yet come to grips with. "Yeah, RJ. It sure as hell looks that way."

———

The second knock on the door was not nearly as welcome as the first, but this visitor didn't wait for me to open up. Tucker just let himself in... with the key card he apparently felt entitled to have even though I was the adult child who paid his damn bills. Again, I bristled at the balls of my father.

"RJ," he nodded, telling my friend in no uncertain terms it was time to leave.

We exchanged a glance before RJ dutifully exited the room. Tucker controlled the other guys too, just not with the same iron grip he used on me.

"What do you want?" I asked, busying myself with making the bed, which I never did unless I was avoiding a conversation with my father.

He made himself comfortable on my sofa. "Come over here. I need to talk to you."

"I don't have anything to say so don't bother."

He pointed to the chair opposite him before fixing his stare on me. I felt nothing but contempt for him now. My father was no more to me than my boss and the hate that coursed through me was hard to contain.

"You'll want to hear me out, I promise," he said.

I let him wait until the sheets were lined up and the pillows appeared reasonably fluffed before I walked over to the chair and slumped into it.

"Thank you," he offered, and I could tell he was in a conciliatory mood. "I'm not sure what's gotten into you lately, but I can see how tired you are. I think you need a few days' rest. As you know, I'd already arranged for the band to take a six-day break in Los Angeles next week."

I nodded. The break he spoke of was not a vacation. We were still working, just not as hard.

"Anyway, I've made the decision to cancel all appearances leading up to the Friday and Saturday night concerts."

My eyes widened in surprise as I sat up straighter in my seat. Now that was news. My father lived and died on the band meeting our obligations. He had to think I was really going to embarrass him to make such a concession.

"I rented you a place. It's secluded. Lots of trees. Plus, there's a pool, spa, sauna, movie theater, and arcade. You can take some time to yourself to regroup and get the rest you need."

"Are we talking some resort type place?" I asked. "Because, if that's the case, I'm not interested."

He smiled, humoring me. "I knew you'd say that. And to answer your question, no, it's a private residence. You have it all to yourself for five days."

I couldn't help but be intrigued by his offer. "And am I going to be imprisoned by your security cronies?"

"No. They'll drop you off, but they won't stay. There's a security gate surrounding the place so you'll be safe inside. I think it goes without saying that any outings you want to take will need to be cleared through the team first so we can take appropriate precautions. We don't want what happened last night to happen again."

Even I could agree with that. No more Twinkie freedom flights for this guy. My father watched me intently, waiting for a response. It really did sound awesome and I wanted to accept his offer more than I dared to admit. But there was only one word I could think to say to him. "Why?"

Tucker hesitated, and his bottom lip quivered for a split second. Was that sentiment I detected? A little too late if you asked me. He cleared his throat as he fought back the emotion that had suddenly overcome him. "I know I don't always show it, but I love you, kid. I'm hard on you, yes, but it's only because I know what you're capable of and I hate to watch you throw everything away. And for what—a bottle of booze? Addiction is a slippery slope, Bodhi. You start with alcohol but that can lead to chasing new highs. If there's one thing you don't want, it's to go down that path. I can see you're struggling with something and if you'd just talk to me I know I could help you."

In that moment it took everything in me not to tell him *you're the one who created the problem* and then have it out with

Tucker. He didn't have the right to suddenly care. I had to remember what he'd done... what he was accused of.

And before you start feeling sorry for my father, don't. He was the mastermind of deception, not me. Tucker had never just been 'my father.' He secured me my first modeling job at two years of age and I'd worked ever since. Even as a toddler, I'd never been allowed to be a kid. There was no time for fun when the breadwinner of the family was still wetting the bed.

"Okay."

"Okay?" He repeated, perking up. "Okay that I can help you?"

Knowledge needed to be earned and my father hadn't worked a full day yet.

"No, Dad. I accept your offer of the mansion, or whatever the hell it is you rented me. But no guards. If I see you've stationed them around the perimeter, I'll find my own place to stay. And I won't be sharing the address with you."

"I got it. No guards. Now, can we talk?"

I stood up, running my fingers through my hair. "I've got nothing to say. You can let yourself out. I'm going to take a shower."

Tucker kept his eyes focused on me as if he were willing me to change my mind. I didn't. He sighed in disappointment before finally extracting himself from the sofa and heading for the door.

"Oh, and Dad."

He pivoted on cue, the hopeful expression on his face almost comical in its need.

"You can leave that key card on the table. You won't be needing it anymore."

3

BREEZE: THE PROPOSAL

"HERE IT IS," THE WOMAN IN MY CHAIR SAID, PULLING UP A picture on her phone. "This is the hair I want."

I leaned in to get a closer look at the photo in question and nearly choked on the breath mint I'd just popped in my mouth after a particularly garlicky lunch. Oh good lord, not Gigi Hadid again. I was a hairstylist, not Houdini. It seemed everyone and their mother wanted the supermodel's hair. Of course, I wisely bit back any discouraging words. That's not how I rolled.

"So cute," I agreed.

And it was a good style ... for a twenty-three-year-old super-model! But I was in the business of making people feel beautiful —selling the dream. So, if my client wanted Gigi's hair, I'd do my best to give it to her, at least for one day.

"Although, keep in mind," I said in a sugary tone, "You don't have the same hair texture or color, so the style might be difficult to maintain. Gigi has straight hair and you have natural waves, so just be aware it will take a lot of blowing out and straight-ening to get this look every day."

There. The disclaimer. Instead of telling her I could never in a million years make her look like Gigi Hadid, I placed the bulk of the challenge on her solid shoulders. She'd have the style, but the rest was up to her.

After agreeing to my suggestions, I went to work transforming my visionary client's hair into the most glamorous version I could whip up in the two-hour time slot she'd been allotted.

We were an hour into the beautifying process, waiting for the highlights to set, when Trina, my colleague from the adjacent cubicle groaned. "Oh, not again. *Breeze.*"

My gut clenched. I didn't have to even look up to know what she was talking about. He was back. Hugh—my stalker.

"Crap!"

I'm not sure what possessed me but, before I knew it, I'd wedged my ass down under my workstation and hid like a coward.

Transfixed by the scene playing out at her feet, my client stared down at me through fantastically bugged eyes, her hands going straight to her hair. Who could blame her? That would've been my reaction if my hairstylist had a similar outburst while stripping my hair color.

"Not you," I whispered, patting her leg reassuringly. "Your hair's fine. You look gorgeous."

She didn't.

I was a liar, and a boldfaced one at that. The woman had tin foil protruding from her scalp like one of those satellite dishes extraterrestrials used to call home.

Dammit.

Hugh's timing couldn't have been worse. By my calculations, I had exactly eight minutes to get rid of the guy before chunks of hair started falling from my client's head.

"I'm not here," I whispered loud enough for anyone in the

vicinity to hear. Which sort of defeated the purpose of whispering in the first place. In fact, it might've drawn *more* attention. Now I had a rapt audience as I spun a cocoon for myself under my workspace. "I'm not here."

Ugh, I was a horrible person. No wonder I had a stalker named Hugh. Why couldn't I get someone with a cool name like Freddie or Michael? But no! I got Hugh. It hardly seemed worth the effort I put into hiding, or the discomfort of being poked in the ass by the hairdryer plug.

The door chimed and in walked my silver-haired suitor, a silk rose in one hand and a wedding ring box in the other. Like every other time he'd come in here to propose, Hugh was wearing his Sunday finest— on a Tuesday.

The confused look on his weathered face was too much for me to bear, so I reluctantly pushed to my feet and brushed myself off. People told me all the time I was too nice, as if being a congenial human being was a fatal disease or something, but today I agreed with them. I'd gotten myself into this mess by being too accommodating the first time he'd come in and singled me out. Hugh was old and cute and sweet in a newborn, hairless, long-necked, baby bird sort of way. And he was about to become my fiancée. *Again.*

"Hi Hugh," I said, smiling warmly at my suitor. Although multiple engagements had never been my dream—one solid, decent guy would do the job nicely—I made an exception for the man standing before me. "Shall we get started?"

Something must've triggered a long lost memory, and Hugh's eyes misted. His hands shook as he reached out to me. "Victoria."

"Yes," I lied. What was the harm in pretending if it brought a measure of comfort to an elderly man who lived mostly in his memories? Hugh took a step toward me before struggling to one knee.

Gazing up at me as if I were the light that kept him living, he began, "My dearest Victoria, from the moment we met, I knew you were the only girl for me…"

Though I'd heard these exact words from him many times, tears welled in my eyes. What would it be like to have a man lay himself bare like this for me? Even when I'd been in this situation for real it hadn't felt like this. Sure, there was excitement and love in the proposal. But it wasn't Hugh-level love.

The door swung open, and Joel, a staff member from the memory care facility down the street stepped in just in time to witness the end of the proposal. He opened his mouth to apologize for his charge's intrusion, but I held up my hand. Hugh deserved a beautiful finish.

At some point in his life, the old man had found *the one*—a woman who'd captured his heart so completely that in the twilight of his life, his only thoughts were of her. It took my breath away. If only I was his Victoria … or anybody's Victoria.

Presenting me with the empty ring box, Hugh's voice shook with emotion. "Will you marry me, my lady?"

Tears threaded my lashes, as they did every time we got to this point in the proposal. His face, so full of hope for a 'future' he'd already lived, slayed me every time. Had his Victoria said yes once upon a time? Had they lived the life I could only hope for? I wanted to believe so.

With tears trailing down my cheeks, I took his aged hand and stared lovingly into his expectant eyes. "Yes, Hugh. I'd love to marry you."

———

As soon as my last client left for the evening, I dashed for my car and dialed the number I did every time Hugh came calling. "So I was proposed to again today."

"Oh, Honey." My mother laughed. "I feel like I say this a lot, but congratulations."

"Thank you. And I have to say, it never gets old."

"Poor Hugh," Mom replied wistfully. "He must miss Victoria so much."

"I wonder if I actually look like her. I mean did women really have bleach blond hair tipped in pink back then, or am I just the only woman he's found who'll put up with his repeated proposals? Today's engagement was lucky number eleven."

"He's fortunate to have found you."

"Yeah? Why do you think that?"

"Because you say yes. Every single time. A lesser person would call the police or just kick him out of the salon. But not you, Breeze. I think Hugh found a kindred spirit. He knew you would protect his heart. That's what I love about you."

Ah, Mom. That's why I called her every day. Her positivity was the shot in the arm I needed. But after having acted the way I did today, I wondered if I really deserved her devotion.

"I tried to hide from him today," I admitted. "Under my work station."

"Why?" she asked, surprised. "I thought you loved his proposals."

"I do. It's just emotional for me and I feel drained afterwards. I see what love could be, the magic and passion, but I can't picture any man ever loving me the way Hugh loved Victoria. I mean, what if you only get one shot at love? What if Brandon was it for me?"

Brandon had been my universe. High school sweethearts, we'd planned out our lives well before graduation. I went to beauty school. He trained as an electrician. We were going to have two kids, a boy and a girl, and live in a modest three-bedroom home with enough space for the stray animals I brought home and nursed back to health.

Like Hugh, my man had dropped down to one knee and proposed. When he'd slipped that platinum band with the shiny diamond onto my finger, I couldn't imagine ever being happier than I was in that moment. As far as I was concerned, I had it all. Until Brandon went and murdered our dream.

"Breeze, honey, I fell in love more than once and so can you. Think of Brandon like I think of your father. He was the pinch hitter—a bench player not worthy of a starting spot. But the quarterback, now that's your guy. Maybe he's still in the dugout, but once he steps out onto the court, you're going to know he's the one for you."

"Seriously mom, you're mixing up all the sports. Pick one and stick with it. Plus, you know I'm not the girl who gets the quarterback. Sure, I'm prime real estate for the band geeks and the stoner boys. But as far as athletes go, I might be able to land a tennis player. And even that's stretching it."

"Don't sell yourself short, Breeze. I'm sure you could get a weightlifter... or even a bowler."

I laughed. "Wow, thanks for the support, Mother."

"My point with the whole sports analogy is that sometimes you have to be patient and wait for the right guy to come along. Just like my Terry. He doesn't need to be a star athlete to treat me the way I deserve to be treated."

"So Terrance is your quarterback?"

"Terrance is everyone's quarterback."

And he was. My stepfather had stepped up to be the man my mother and I had needed in our lives. He'd been more of a father to me than mine ever was.

"So, was that pep talk enough to convince you to come home for the family reunion?"

As if.

The woman never gave up. It didn't matter how many times she'd asked, my answer was always the same.

"We've been through this before," I answered, trying to keep my voice light and airy for my own sanity. "You secure me a date with Jon Snow and I'll come to your family reunion."

"*Game of Thrones*. I can work with that. Are we talking the actor or the fictional character?"

"Um... I prefer the fictional character. But not if he's wearing that big snowy outfit. It's not his best look. I like the sexy leather number he wears in warm weather but, you know, I'm not picky. Surprise me."

"Sure. I've got a call in to his agent."

"Yay."

Silence broke into our lighthearted banter and I braced for the begging.

"Breeze?"

I took a deep breath. "Mom?"

"Please come. For me?" When I sighed she was quick to add, "If not for me, then for Terrance. He misses you."

My stomach clenched. Typically I'd do anything for her and Terrance. But this was asking too much. "He'll be there. I just can't. Besides, I'll be home for Christmas a couple weeks after the reunion."

"I know, and I can't wait, but I hate to see you avoiding the family because of a man. You're letting Brandon win and that's not like you at all."

Letting him? My ex was the one with the charmed life. Married to the perfect woman. Father to a two-year-old, with another on the way. I was the one whose only legitimate suitor was an eighty-three-year-old Alzheimer patient. Maybe it was selfish of me but there was no way in hell I was going to face Brandon without, at the very least, a fictional television character by my side.

You might be wondering how my ex wound up attending our

family functions in the first place. Well, I'll tell you why. While he was engaged to me, Brandon was having unprotected sex with my cousin, Jenna. I discovered their deception a mere week before the nuptials after I took notice of Jenna's swollen belly and innocently asked who the father was.

And just like that, I'd become a horrible cliché—the jilted bride. Object of behind-the-back gossip. The last one in on the joke.

I hadn't been able to get out of town fast enough, retreating south to join my best friend Mason in the land of sun and surf. I'd managed to reinvent myself in this county by the sea. New friends, a new job... a new life. It should have been enough, but it wasn't. The stigma remained, if only in my own mind.

Not that I was still hooked on Brandon. I'd gotten over the sting of his betrayal long ago, and even moved on from plotting his murder. But the scars from his deception remained, bloody and raw, even more than two years after the fact. So yes, I'd once again be missing a family function because I couldn't stomach the idea of watching Jenna and Brandon live the life that should have been mine.

I shook my head, casting off the memories. "I'm just not ready yet. Besides, I'm pet sitting that week and I can't flake on this lady. She's one of my best customers—gives the big tips. You know, like those people who hand out the giant candy bars on Halloween?"

"How can I compete with the king-sized candy bar lady?" Mom asked, sounding bummed but resigned.

"I'm sorry, Mom. You know I want to be there for you. It's just hard."

"I get it, baby. I do. I just wish he'd picked a girl outside of the family unit to screw."

"You and me both."

"So, what exotic location should I tell them you're visiting this time?"

"Mmm... good question," I pondered, relieved to have the Brandon discussion out of the way. "Oh... how about an African safari?"

"No. That won't do. You were in Zimbabwe for Garrett and Laura's fortieth anniversary."

"Crap, you're right! Good catch. How about an expedition to Antarctica?"

"In the winter? I don't think so, Breeze."

"Yes, but is it winter in Antarctica? I don't think so."

"It's always winter in Antarctica!" Her voice rose in amusement. "Either way, it's too far-fetched. How about something more believable, like you're spending the winter in Aspen cutting hair for the rich and famous?"

"Right, but that makes me sound like I'm just there working."

"Well how else would you be able to afford to be such a world traveler?" Mom sighed. "Anyway, I can't keep up with your fictional life, so when you get it figured out, let me know."

"Alright, I'll come up with something good," I promised.

"Or plausible. I'll settle for plausible."

"Plausible is boring. No thanks. You didn't name me Breeze for nothing."

———

The power of music is a beautiful thing. Transformative.

As the song began, I tapped my boots to the beat. Kelly, a like-minded friend, tipped her beer bottle against mine before jumping from her stool and grabbing my hand. "Let's go girl. No way can anyone sit still for Luke Bryan."

Country music—my dirty little secret. One I kept from my family and friends back home. Mason was the only one from that group who knew the truth, and he wouldn't dare judge after all the crap I'd kept quiet for him throughout the years.

Listening to a specific type of music might seem like no big deal to most. But as the daughter of modern-day San Francisco hippies, I cut my teeth on the likes of Janis Joplin and Jimi Hendricks, making my preference for country a darn right sinful admission. So I kept my obsession to myself, spending several nights a week at my favorite haunt, a country western bar. It seemed like an oxymoron, country music fans in Southern California. But we did, in fact, exist. And so did a few establishments catering to my kind.

I hadn't always been a fan. But my break up with Brandon led me to the healing powers of country music. That and a glaring lack of income. The first few months in this new place were trying—living alone, struggling to pay my bills, and relying solely on my radio for entertainment. That's when I'd discovered that the only programming that came in clearly was the Spanish language channels and one lowly country western station. Since I couldn't speak a lick of Spanish, I begrudgingly tuned in to the country. And as each song filled my ears, I realized the music was slowly pulling me out of my post breakup blues. Packed with happiness, love, and persevering over heartbreak —as well as the occasional hunting and fishing story—country music got me through the worst time of my life, and I found myself clinging to its optimistic lyrics and foot stomping beats.

"I can't dance yet." I scanned the room for my best friend. "I'm waiting for Mason to get back from the bathroom. I've got to get him drunk quickly so he'll stay."

Mason was not a country music convert. Not yet anyway. He only came tonight because it was my turn to pick the place. Turnabout was fair play, and if he was content to drag me to strip clubs, it was only right that he pay his dues here. Mason and I had a long history together. We were classmates before we were neighbors, neighbors before we were friends, and friends before we were siblings. The sibling part was honorary. After a particularly nasty episode where Mason's crazy-ass mother chased him down the block with a butcher knife, he'd sought refuge at my house and never left. But one thing held true to this day, Mason had never been, nor would he ever be, mine.

Like me, Mason lived his own kind of lie. I wish I could say being gay was the biggest secret he kept, but Mason had come out years ago. No, my friend wrestled with demons few could understand, and keeping him afloat had always been my job. So if he sometimes had to suffer through music he abhorred, too damn bad. He owed me.

Kelly grew bored with the one-minute wait and pulled out her phone. Giggling replaced her impatience.

"What?" I asked.

"Damn, little Corey Waldon grew up to be a hottie," Kelly said, turning the screen toward me. I was expecting to see a face but instead an ass wriggled in my vision.

Hitting replay, I said, "Who's Corey Waldon?"

Mason slid back onto his stool and took the phone out of Kelly's hand. "You don't know who Corey Waldon is? Shame on you."

"It was the name of the kid brother on the TV show Waldon Road," Kelly explained.

I shrugged. "Well, if it aired before 2010, I wouldn't know. My parents didn't believe in television. They said it stunted growth, made kids stupid, and squashed creativity. Yet here I am standing all of 5'4, can't tell the difference between my right and my left hand, and the last time I went to the 'paint with wine' class my sunset looked like an over easy egg."

Mason laughed. "I didn't want to say anything about the painting but..." In fact, he had said something – many times.

"You do know Betsy and Terrance used to sneak to the sports bar to watch games, right?"

"What?" It couldn't be true. My parents, the two people who'd preached the evils of television, slipping away to watch behind my back? I shook my head. "No way."

"Yeah, my mom used to see them there all the time."

I didn't believe it. Not for a second. My parents hated television. I mean, *hated it.* "She must have confused them with someone else."

"Yeah, no." Mason smirked. "Maybe *you* didn't watch TV before 2010, but your parents sure as hell did."

"Oh. My. God." Gaping at Mason, I struggled to come to grips with his insider information, before adding through gritted teeth, "I'm just going to have to kill them both."

My over-exaggerated response gave Mason a good laugh.

"I mean, I was the freak in school who didn't know any of the popular television characters of the day while my parents were getting shorter, dumber, and less creative. What hypocrites."

"Anyway," Kelly broke in, oblivious to the internal pain of missing out on the Gilmore Girls. "Corey Waldon is none other than Bodhi Beckett – boy band cutie."

"Bodhi? Really? Wait, that's his butt? I thought he was the good boy of the group?" I asked. It's not like I didn't know who those guys were. I was a hairstylist, after all. I spent a lot of time flipping through the latest celebrity magazines while waiting on my clients, and Bodhi and his band mates were always somewhere inside the pages.

"Bodhi's vanilla for sure," Mason said. "But if you're looking for a wholesome, preacher boy, his band mate, Hunter Roy, is the man for you."

"Wow, Mace, you really know your boy band members." I nudged him good-naturedly.

"Maybe you forget I'm gay."

"What does that have to do with anything?"

"We like boy bands and hot men. But don't worry. You can have Hunter. Dane's my guy."

A particularly catchy tune drew the melody to my lips and Kelly and I sang at the top of our lungs.

"Dammit Breeze, you used to be so cool. What happened to you? Oh yeah," Mason motioned around the bar, frowning, "this happened to you."

"I hope I'm not detecting attitude. Because, if I am, maybe you'd like to do a little line-dancing?"

Mason shook his head vigorously.

"Okay then, shut it, because tonight, I hold the power."

It was a deal we'd brokered years ago. Whoever picked the place also dictated the activities. And Mason was one complaint away from kicking up the dust.

"Bodhi was also in the sitcom Hot and Cold." Kelly picked up the discussion Mason and I had already dropped. Either she was struggling to keep up or just not listening to us at all.

"Yep." Mason nodded. "And now his ass is all over the internet. Good for him. Actually, I'm surprised it took him so long to self-destruct. Everyone knows former child stars have a short shelf life."

One of our favorite songs came on and just singing along was no longer an option. Kelly jumped to her feet again, pulling me with her. This time she wasn't taking no for an answer. Once we were on the dance floor, I kept an eye on Mason. I was no stranger to his severe mood swings, but something was off with him and no amount of probing would get it out of him.

Mason wasn't one of those happy, fun gay guys that girls dreamed of having for a bestie. We didn't fill our days with shopping trips and gossip. Nope, Mason was sarcastic and brooding and, worst of all, he hardly ever threw frivolous praise in my direction.

With Kelly knee-deep in conversation with a forty-year-old Californian man pretending to be from the deep south, I headed back to the table, plopped down onto my stool, and laid my head on Mason's shoulder.

"You okay there?" I asked.

"I was going to ask you the same question, *Victoria*."

I looked him in the eyes. "Who told you?"

"Kelly."

I sighed. "Yeah, I'm fine. Hugh's looking pretty frail. I don't know how many more proposals he has in him."

"Well, he *is* a hundred and twelve so ..."

"Hey." I laughed. "That's my fiancé you're dissing."

Mason's smile melted. "You worry too much about things you have no control over, Breeze."

Suddenly, I got the feeling we weren't talking about Hugh anymore.

"What's going on with you, Mace? Why won't you tell me?"

He stiffened before taking a shot of whisky.

"Seriously? You're not going to tell me? What happened to us telling each other everything?"

"That was your idea, not mine." He laughed. "I never agreed to be your girlfriend."

"Yeah, well, maybe that's what you need. I can't help you if you keep secrets from me."

"Trust me, Breeze. You can't help me either way."

Mason looked into his glass, grimacing. He was a tough nut to crack. One moment we could be talking and laughing and the next he looked like he wanted to shoot himself.

"Hey," I side-hugged him. "Forget I asked. Let's just have fun tonight."

He nodded, still not meeting my eye. No matter how old he got or how confidently he portrayed himself, when it came right down to it, Mason was an insecure little boy running from the demons of his youth. He craved affection like everyone else, but sometimes I wondered if he had the capacity to fully embrace it.

That wasn't my issue with love at all. I was ready and willing to fall, but I just couldn't find a guy to do it with. And unlike other 'gay and girl' best friend pairings, Mason and I had no contingency plan. We had no baby pact at thirty or desperation marriage promise. We either found love separately, or we remained best friends who met at bars to drink to each other's failures.

"My mom wants me to go home for the family reunion, but Brandon will be there... with his baby and Jenna."

Mason downed another shot.

"Are you drinking to my pain?" I asked.

"If we have to have another Brandon discussion, I need to get drunk." He was joking... sort of. Mason had lived through my breakup and all the misery that came with it.

"It's not just Brandon, it's all men in general. I mean, I'm a fairly decent looking girl..." I waited for his affirmation, and when he said nothing, I kicked him under the table. "That's your cue, Dude."

"Yes, Breeze, you're gorgeous. You've got great hair, love the pink highlights, by the way."

"You like?" I fluffed my fingers through my dyed silver blonde locks, complete with subtle pastel pink highlights. "I was going for crazy fun."

"Yeah, well congrats, you've got the crazy part down pat but the fun?" He looked around the bar. "You need to work on that."

"Stop, be serious."

"I am. With that great hair and your killer little bod—mmm mmm— if I wasn't gay, I'd be all up in your shit."

"That's it." I clapped my amusement. "Oh my god, Mason, you have no idea how long I've waited for you to talk to me like that!"

He met me halfway for a high five. "And it only took eighteen years."

"I know, right? Anyway, as I was saying, I'm a decent looking girl, with a winning personality, so why can't I find a civilized guy who still has all his teeth?"

Mason took another shot.

"Stop drinking to my pain," I repeated, giggling.

"Hey, you complain, I drink," he said, shrugging. "Don't blame me. I don't make the rules."

"Yes, Mason. Yes, you do! You made the game up, jerk."

He laughed so I tapped his leg with my boot.

"Hey, beyotch. You kick me again, I'm going to dump your ass in an old folks' home and find me some stud to finish out the night with."

"At a country western bar? Good luck with that, my friend." He winced, knowing I spoke the truth. "Besides, what would Curtis think?"

An exaggerated eye roll came from Mason. "Curtis pees sitting down."

"Yes, but he's always there for you."

"Right, because he's a stalker, Breeze. That's what they do."

"Fine. Die alone. See if I care."

"Me?" He scoffed. "This whole guy thing clearly isn't working out for you either. Have you ever thought about switching sides? I hear tits are all the rage."

"I don't know, Mace, have *you* thought about switching sides — you know, because of the whole tit thing?"

We stared at each other for a second before breaking into matching grins.

The magic faded quickly, along with my smile. "Look," I said. "I know we made a pact never to make a pact, but that was years ago, before the two of us proved to be such failures at love. So, if neither of us is with the man of our dreams by the age of thirty-five, can I pretty please with sugar on top, borrow a vial of your sperm?"

Mason blinked down at me and, squaring his shoulders he replied, "Breeze, if neither of us is in love at thirty-five, I'll put the boys in you myself."

4

BODHI: WELLNESS RETREAT

I HAD TO HAND IT TO MY FATHER, HE'D DELIVERED ON HIS PROMISE of seclusion. The place he'd rented sat atop a coastal mountain, with sweeping views of the Pacific Ocean. I spent the first few hours just wandering around the grounds, enthralled by the Eucalyptus grove behind the estate.

Canopied by intertwined branches, the thick shade provided a welcome relief from the heat of the day and gave the grove a dusk to dawn type feel. Despite the fact that it was December, the temperature soared in the afternoon. In Southern California, seasons didn't really matter. Every day was a nice day... until the Santa Ana winds arrived, blowing in from the desert and rearranging the landscape.

Giving myself over to the beauty of my surroundings, I marveled at the incredible peace I felt amongst the aging giants. Solitude was a treat I rarely had the time to taste. Wherever I went, pandemonium ensued. My life was like being in a parade —on display twenty-four-hours a day. There was never any relief from the constant gawking. Even zoo animals got breaks from the action from time to time. I never did. But here I was, as insignificant as the dried, leafy debris discarded on the forest floor. Somehow that realization helped ease my conflicted mind.

In the next few days, a decision needed to be made in regard to my mother. She wanted to meet me and, although I was curious about her, something in the back of my mind warned me to be cautious. I couldn't shake the feeling that she was after more than just a reunion. Or maybe my father had totally warped my view of humanity. Had he taught me to be wary of the world? Were people really as he'd described—self-serving leeches, ready and willing to drain my blood the first chance they got? Was my self-imposed isolation merely a reaction to his backward teachings? My father's underlying message had always been that he was the only one I could trust. And maybe that's why I'd stayed close to him over the years. Even after everything inside had screamed for me to leave.

Taking a seat on one of the giant roots protruding from the trunk of a particularly twisted tree, I ran a hand over the bark and wondered what had happened in its lifetime to become this disfigured version of itself. Did the tree mind carrying around such baggage or had it come to accept life for what it was— imperfect? Maybe if I sat here long enough, the answers to my own flawed existence might drop from the sky. I'd been given an impossible choice. Either the devil I knew, or the angel who'd risen from the dead. What was I to believe when the people who were supposed to love me the most had lied to me every single day of my life? What was wrong with these people? How was I supposed to choose a victor when both appeared to be the villain?

"Got any advice?" I asked my leafy friends. As predicted, they didn't have words of wisdom, nor did they offer me an ounce of sympathy. No doubt they'd heard their share of sob stories over the long years, and mine was just another one to add to the puddle of tears at the base of their trunks.

A gust of wind blew off my hat. In seconds, the cap had traveled far enough that it was no longer worth my time to chase it down. It was, after all, just band merchandise. There were thousands more where that came from. The winds had been acting up for days now and were expected to intensify. Evidence of their fury could be seen all around as I climbed over shredded white bark and discarded branches, some the size of small cars. I didn't want to imagine the damage that tonight's predicted eighty-mile an hour winds would bring to my personal oasis. The old majestic Eucalyptus trees were already whimpering from the effort as the punishing gusts tested their aging balance. But it wasn't until I heard the sound of splitting wood that I raced out of the grove. Of all the ways to die, getting flattened by a falling branch seemed the most undignified.

I spent the rest of the afternoon by the expansive pool. The unusually hot temperatures were great for sunbathing, but not so great for everything else. I alternated between lying out and taking dips in the pool, and for the first time in a long time, I didn't worry about paparazzi climbing over the shrubs to snap a picture. As I saw it, if the photographers were willing to scale the walls surrounding the fortress, they deserved a half-naked shot of me.

The wind eventually messed with my relaxation when a strong gust blew a lounge chair right into my leg. A welt appeared and, swearing up a storm, I gathered my stuff and ducked into the safety of the sprawling one-story mansion. Too bad my father hadn't pitched in extra cash for a wind-free week.

Still, I couldn't help but be impressed with how well the man knew me. He'd found a place that had enough stuff to keep me busy for weeks. The arcade beckoned me to the promised land of male-driven fantasy. But my stomach growled, so I headed off in search of food. Finding the kitchen in this place wasn't as easy as turning a corner.

As I ambled through expansive rooms and sweeping hall-ways, flipping switches along the way, I had to wonder why a house this large didn't come with an instruction manual or, at the very least, a map. Because if I was going to be here for five days, I needed to know where to drop a deuce.

The gleaming kitchen came into view a few blocks away, like a beacon of light calling me home. Starving from the hike, I grinned when I opened the refrigerator and found it stocked full of prepared meals. Of the healthy variety, of course. A clear sign from my father that I shouldn't consider my five-day break an excuse to slack off on my exercise routine or eat like shit. Although, I had to admit, the first thought that popped into my mind as I perused the wide variety of fruits and vegetables was the box of Twinkies I'd laid waste to last week. Something told me I wouldn't find any surprises like that in the pantry.

After heating one of the meals in the microwave, I plopped down onto a stool and scarfed down a large serving of spinach lasagna. Just as I was swallowing the last bite, a set of keys hanging on the wall caught my attention. I hopped to my feet and wandered over, immediately identifying the keyless remote hanging by the silver band. A Range Rover. Even more impressive was the fob, labeled with the word *Nanny*.

"They give their nanny a Range Rover?" I mused to no one. Impressive. It occurred to me then that I was holding freedom in my hands. Oh, the things I could do with the Nanny's Range Rover. Yes, I'd promised my father I wouldn't leave the premises without calling for a bodyguard, but that was only because I didn't think I'd have the means to escape on my own. Now... the possibilities were endless.

Grinning, I kissed the cool metal. "Well, hello Twinkies."

Not that I dared step foot into another grocery store. At least not while preteen girls still found me attractive. Twinkies were merely a metaphor for the wide variety of snacks that could be mine if I found this magical Range Rover. Hell, maybe while I was stuffing my face with tater tots and deep-fried apple pie, I'd drive to the coast and watch the waves roll in. Of course, if the winds didn't die down, I could just step outside and be blown to the beach, no car required.

"Don't let me down, nanny," I said as I took the keys for a walk. My strategy for finding the hidden treasure was simply to keep pushing the lock button until the beeping alarm gave away the car's location. When I stumbled upon the second of three garages and laid eyes on the gleaming SUV, I let out a whoop of joy. *Dayum!* The nanny traveled in style.

And first thing tomorrow morning, so would I.

———

As predicted, when the day turned to night, the winds intensified. But it's not like I really noticed the punishing gusts since I'd been down in the windowless basement for hours getting my fill of its infinite awesomeness. A movie room, a full-size bowling alley, and an arcade featuring no less than twenty video games and pinball machines all conspired to keep me thoroughly entertained. More than once I'd wished the guys were here, but that would completely refute my father's misguided assumption that I needed rest. I actually did need a break. But only so I could come up with new and ingenious ways to make his life miserable.

I was going on my third hour of total brain-zapping fun, when the lights suddenly tapped out, plunging me into inky darkness. There was always that moment immediately following a blackout where you waited for the lights to kick back on. And that's what I did. Helplessly gripping the side of the machine, I swallowed hard and waited for the electricity to return. It didn't.

Well, shit.

I wasn't so much annoyed by the blackout as I was by the sudden end of my game. I'd been on track to beat my own record from moments earlier.

Checking my phone to reassure myself that I was still connected to the world, I gasped in shock. Eighteen percent charge!

Double shit.

This was bad... really bad. Nothing induced panic in Millennials quite like low battery levels. Never mind that I was buried deep in the basement of some increasingly creepy-ass mansion. Talk about horror movie fodder.

"This blows," I muttered.

I had no choice but to use my remaining battery on the flashlight app just to get up the stairs. All I could hope for was that the power would be restored before my phone plunged me into total radio silence.

After a few wrong turns, I found my way to the master suite and settled in for a night of mind-numbing boredom. With no power, I really had nothing better to do than go to bed... at 9:25 at night. I hadn't retired this early since Kindergarten.

But as it turned out, mother nature had other plans. The howling winds kept me wide awake as they raced through the trees at highway speeds, sending tattered branches to collide with the windows at full force. The house groaned and creaked under the weight of the monstrous gusts. If Santa Ana had her way, I wouldn't get a wink of sleep.

Then I remembered the fancy airplane emergency kit complete with useless essentials that I kept in my bag. Well, useless until tonight anyway. Extracting the pillow soft sleep mask, I tossed it aside. And then I found them, tucked under the small bottles of lotion and mouthwash—earplugs.

"That's what I'm talking about." My voice echoed across the vast space. Here, alone in the dark, I was surprised to discover the isolation felt eerily familiar. It occurred to me then that, although people surrounded me on a daily basis, I never really connected with them. Even the security guards who'd been with us since the beginning were nothing more than strangers. Aside from their names, I couldn't tell you another thing about them.

The thought bothered me enough that after popping the earbuds in place, I laid awake pondering just how much of my life I'd wasted in the pursuit of someone else's happiness.

Enough is enough.

Tomorrow morning I'd do something positive for a change. Maybe I'd buy a bunch of sandwiches and pass them out to the homeless by the pier. Or I could just drive up the coast and stop at a roadside cafe and engage in conversation with real people. Yes, I liked that idea. Feeling positive about my future for the first time in a long time, I closed my eyes and, within seconds, was out like the lights.

5

BODHI: THE DEVIL WITHIN

A SUDDEN BOOM RIPPED ME FROM SLEEP. THE DREAM I'D BEEN residing in now dangled on the edge of my consciousness and, for a moment, confusion hung heavy in the air. I checked my ears, because surely the plugs had fallen out if I was hearing this kind of commotion. But no, they were still in place. Prying them out, I was shocked by the sudden increase in noise.

A series of popping explosions cleared away the haziness, and I bolted to my feet, the sheets sliding to the floor. An eerie orange glow pulsated off the dark walls. The shrieks of what sounded like a train barreled through the house, sent me racing to the window. But before I could get there, a punishing blast shook the house, flinging me forward toward the glass. At the last moment, I caught myself, bracing my hands on the window frame. Staring through the fragile glass, a flickering flame caught my eye.

"What the...?"

While I'd slept, nature had set a blowtorch to the landscape, bringing a raging inferno right to my doorstep. A blanket of red crested the mountain, fanning out across the dry and delicate terrain. The utopian forest in the back was now fully engulfed in flames. Embers, carried by unearthly gusts of wind, settled amongst the branches, turning the majestic trees into brittle victims of a cataclysmic wildfire.

Even through the window, I could feel the heat and smell the smoke. Or was it inside the house? Before I could fully wrap my head around the idea that the fire was closer than I'd first imagined, an explosion redirected my focus. As if doused in lighter fluid, the trees were detonating in fiery displays of rage. Nothing made sense. Where had the fire come from? When had it started? And why was it suddenly bearing down on me?

As I watched the scene unfold, too stunned to move, flames began to crawl up the windowpane. It took a moment for the enormity of the situation to hit me. But when it did, I whirled around and headed for the door. The steady crackling brought on a fresh wave of panic. The fire wasn't just confined to the backyard or the side paneling of the house. The devil had made its way inside... and it was coming for me!

Dropping to a crouch, I blindly searched for the clothes I'd discarded before bed. Finding my shorts almost immediately, I yanked them on before continuing my hunt. My shirt was nowhere around, but my feet found their way inside the leather Rainbow flip-flops with relative ease. Not the best footwear for outrunning a fire, but then I hadn't been expecting to awaken to Armageddon.

Yanking the pillowcase off the king-sized pillow, I ran into the bathroom to douse it with water, while trying desperately to remember what else to do in case of a fire. I'd never set foot in a classroom, so I wasn't present for any official fire safety training, but I had played the son of a firefighter once on a made-for-TV movie. That should count for something, right?

No, idiot!

Chastising my inner voice, I wrapped the wet fabric around my nose and mouth, tying the ends in a tight knot behind my head. The sounds of exploding glass hastened my speed. With flames fully draping the window, the only way out of the room was through the door. If I was met with fire on the other side, I wasn't sure I'd survive.

Maybe I hadn't made my intentions clear to the karma gods, but I really, seriously wanted to live. Suddenly the past three months of struggle seemed inconsequential. Faced with my own mortality, I wished I could take it all back. The tantrums. And the acting out. Because none of it mattered. Not the letter from my long-lost mother. Or the feud with my father. I just wanted to make it to sunrise.

After a useless search of the shadowy floor for my shirt, I decided it could be sacrificed, as well as my suitcase. But what about my guitar? My mind flashed back to the person who'd gifted it to me all those years ago and I knew there was no way I'd leave it behind. Finding the leather strap, I flung it over my shoulder, and then crawled along to the nightstand to retrieve my phone and wallet. But in the darkness, I knocked them both to the floor. With the mounting smoke, I conceded defeat. Dammit! My phone deserved better. I could only hope its demise would be quick and painless.

Knowing enough about house fires to stay low and check the doorknob for heat, I was somewhat relieved to discover it was cool to the touch. Maybe I'd been wrong. Maybe the crackling sounds and the breaking glass had been outside all along. But the minute I opened the door, I saw how wrong my wishful thinking had been. The beast was inside all right, and currently ravishing the entire right side of the mansion. Like a three-headed dog, the flames guarded the main entrance and exit to the home.

Every hair on my body stood at attention. I'd never been tested like this, nor had I ever been tasked with critical decision-making. I wasn't sure if I could trust my instincts, but what choice did I have? If I was going to survive, I had to become the man no one had ever allowed me to be.

Sprinting through the death tomb, I wisely headed in the opposite direction of the fiery savage consuming my five-day wellness retreat. Thankfully, my earlier quest for the nanny's car left me somewhat familiar with the general area of additional exits. With the guitar strapped to my back like a terrified turtle, I stumbled down the hallway, using my hands along the walls as a guide. An orange glow reflected in the glass, the only light in this part of the house. But it was enough to guide me to the safety of the courtyard.

Hope swelled the moment I flung open the French door. Yanking the pillowcase off my face, I drew in a healthy gulp of air. My relief was short-lived as I took in my surroundings. Instead of the safe passage I'd envisioned, I'd collided headfirst into the apocalypse. Not only was my vacation home on fire but so, it appeared, was every other house on the block. Some appeared to be in the very first stages of a scorching smackdown while others, like mine, had already been battered enough to have been assigned hospice care.

But it wasn't the burning structures that had me in a frenzy. It was the blanket of red creeping up the ridge. The fire's front-line had spread wide and was flanking both sides of the hillside road where I'd be expected to make my escape. As I weighed my options, embers whizzed past my head like flaming arrows aiming for their next target. This wasn't just a wildfire. It was an uncontrolled firestorm. With no passable way out.

I could try my luck on foot, but it was a long way down the mountain.

I might actually die.

Memorial shrines with embarrassing pictures of me would spring up everywhere, maybe even one on the exact spot where firemen would find my charred remains. Little girls the world over would mourn, all because their teen idol couldn't formulate a plan to save his own damn life.

I needed a car. *The nanny's car.* And it wasn't far away. The garage was on the other side of the courtyard in a structure that had yet to be touched by fire. Maybe I could save myself after all.

But all optimism faded when I thought of the keys on the counter in the kitchen – the part of the house that was currently up in flames. I looked down the street and then back at the house. There was no real choice. I wouldn't survive on foot. I needed a vehicle, which meant, I was going back in.

Reluctantly, I stripped off the guitar case and reaffixed the pillowcase back over my nose and mouth. Before the rational half of my brain could talk me out of it, I darted back into the house. With the flames now ominously bright, I had no trouble seeing the nightmare in front of me. In minutes the place would be fully engulfed and if I miscalculated, the coroner would be identifying me through dental records.

Zigzagging my way through the house, I headed for the kitchen, which was now probably just a liquefying pit of stainless steel. But if there was still an intact island counter that meant there was also a set of keys just begging to be spared. Sprinting through a cavern of flames, the blazing temperatures baked my unprotected torso and I felt the little hairs on my skin melting from the searing heat.

Emerging into the kitchen, I zeroed in on the prize— the shiny metal ring on the counter. The roar in my ears was deafening. It was as if everything the fire touched shrieked in agony. Goddammit, I hoped death's spindly hands didn't get a hold of me because there was no doubt in my mind I'd be a screamer.

Pushing the thought aside, I scooped up the keys. Holding the little lifesavers tight enough to cut off circulation, I retraced my steps. Somewhere along the way, the pillowcase had fallen from my face and was now just a useless bandana hanging limply around my neck. I tried to lift it back into place, but my arms were no longer functioning properly. The smoke. There was so much smoke. It seared my throat and with every step I took I could feel the thick fog closing in on my airway.

Still I forged on—each breath more labored than the last. The adrenaline rush had evaporated, and now I existed on sheer power of will. Although my dream destination had been the garage, I knew I couldn't make it there, at least not without some fresh air. The courtyard loomed ahead, and I longed for its saving graces.

Stumbling out the door, I dropped to my hands and knees coughing up billowy white smoke. Where was the oxygen? Why couldn't I get air?

Taking a series of shallow gulps, I finally drew in a deep breath, surprised when air filled my lungs. After securing the pillowcase once again, I grabbed my guitar and reentered the inferno for the last time.

The fire had now staked its claim on this half of the house and was swirling upwards in a powerful display. But I was no longer afraid of the bully. It could take the Eucalyptus grove and the house, but I'd be damned if it took me.

At the entrance to the garage, I searched for my salvation in the darkness. Fumbling with the buttons on the key, my shoulders sagged when the interior light flickered on inside the Range Rover. I tossed my guitar in the backseat, flipped on the headlights, and found the emergency tab so I could manually raise the garage door.

Once I was behind the wheel, I maneuvered the car out of the garage and down the driveway, only to come to a screeching halt at security fence. What the hell? How had I forgotten about the gate? With no electricity, I was stuck. Slamming my balled fists against the steering wheel, I swore as loud as my lungs would allow.

Think.

If the garage door had an emergency lever, the security gate was bound to have the same mechanism. A fail-safe for situations just like this.

Willing my body to keep fighting, I jumped out of the vehicle and headed straight for the breaker box. Frantically, I pulled and pressed everything inside until I heard a loud click as the lock on the gate disengaged.

I should have been ecstatic, jumping for goddamn joy, but my strength and resolve were zapped. The only fight I had left in me was being used to swallow back the vomit threatening to spew from my guts. Even though my body appeared to be shutting down, my mind was screaming for me to flee.

The fire was bearing down and, in a few minutes' time, the road would no longer be passable. My body would just have to wait its damn turn.

I'd just begun the arduous process of sliding the fence along the track when a series of loud cracks drew my attention to the house. Turning in time to witness the roof collapse, my jaw came unhinged. I'd been in there less than five minutes before. I could've easily been crushed under a pile of smoldering ash.

It wasn't so much relief I felt, but sadness for the place that had given me such comfort for the short time I'd been there. My therapy spot on the base of the twisted tree in the Eucalyptus grove was decimated, the arcade with my winning time – gone, and the little kids whose Nanny's car I'd just stolen, had lost their home. With newfound vigor, I made quick work of the gate, then climbed into the Range Rover and drove off the property without looking back.

6

BREEZE: THE PET SITTER

WE WERE AT A STALEMATE, SWEETPEA AND ME. I'D BEEN CARING for my canine charge for five days and we were no closer to an understanding now than we were upon first introduction. I tried not to take it personally. After all, I was the one who rescued strays off highways. And as a child, I'd insisted on only adopting the hard-to-place, physically challenged pets. Heart issues, missing limbs, or stinky skin conditions— the more debilitated, the better.

Perfection was overrated. And that included the human race. I drifted toward complicated companions. Maybe it was the nurse Nightingale in me, but I was a sucker for the bruised and battered. It was what had attracted me to Mason when we were only eight and I saw him crying on the sidewalk after being locked out of his house by his schizophrenic mother. And Brandon. He was all misplaced anger and resentment. But I was ready and willing to roll up my sleeves and get to work fixing the hell out of him.

The problem with these people, I'd since found, was they soaked up the nurturing like a sponge but weren't as good at giving a few drops back when I really needed it. Knowing when to cut the cord on the emotionally needy was what kept a compassionate, loving person like myself from becoming a door-mat. I'll admit it was a fine line, one I'd been walking my whole life, starting with my immature, non-committal father and continuing on with my cheating ex-fiancée. Certainly, it would've been easier to harden my heart and close it off to the wounded, but then I would've missed out on the hidden gems, like Mason and my poor sweet, old Hugh.

And in that same vein, I was convinced my current chal-lenge, Sweetpea, had a heart of gold buried somewhere deep within that itty-bitty bitchy body of his. Sure, on the outside he appeared to be the devil's spawn. There was nothing sweet, or pea, about him unless you counted the puddles of urine he left all over the house. But, the bleeding heart in me reasoned, even inappropriately named Chihuahua mixes were worth the effort.

Still, the short-tempered pup was depleting my reserves. Feeding time with Sweetpea was an exercise in survival. He was a carnivore with a taste for blood. When it was time to eat, I gingerly placed his bowl on the floor and pushed it over with a broom. I'd been warned about fingers near his food, and the loss of said digits, so I wasn't taking any chances with the miniatur-ized meat grinder.

Playtime with Sweetpea was about as fun as a bikini wax following a long, cold winter. Both scenarios usually ended with me quivering on a chair screaming for relief. My hero came in the form of Hercules, the family's enormous Saint Bernard, who was as sweet as his little brother was rotten. Herc was not only a peacemaker, but also a Chihuahua-whis-perer. He seemed the only one able to talk my nemesis off the cliff.

Nighttime with Sweetpea was reminiscent of a hostage situa-tion, with the diminutive dictator cuddling up next to me for warmth but not allowing me to move a muscle. If I had the gall to pivot in my sleep, I could expect a splinter-sized tooth planting itself deep in the tender flesh of my patootie.

Maybe I was just rusty in the pet-sitting arena. After all, I hadn't owned an animal since relocating to Southern California. My current landlord, a cranky, rules-oriented woman, didn't allow pets or the cooking of certain smelly vegetables. The veggies rule I could live with as I wasn't the biggest fan of leafy greens anyway, but I struggled with the other. There were times I missed animals so much that I snuck into dog parks under the guise of being a pet owner just to frolic with other people's pups.

So it was a no brainer when I was asked to pet sit for the Kufrin family. Cindy, the mother of one of my child clients, presented the offer to me after an animated conversation about a baby bird I attempted to return to the nest before getting browbeaten by his irritated mother. How was I to know the little guy was testing his wings?

Anyway, Cindy's proposal was one of those too-good-to-be-true deals and I should have known there was something fishy about it. But a hundred and fifty dollars a day to spend weekends and evenings with her family's pets in a multi-million dollar mansion while they were in Europe for twelve days was just too good to pass up.

And then I met Sweetpea. You know you're in trouble when the pet owner leaves a copy of his rabies certificate right next to the number for the nearest urgent care. Thank god he was up-to-date on his shots or I'd already be foaming at the mouth. It soon became clear that Cindy hadn't offered the job to me out of the kindness of her heart. She was offering it to me because Sweetpea was very likely blacklisted in the canine community, his mug shot hanging in animal establishments all along the coast as a warning to unsuspecting pet sitters like myself.

"Please, Sweetpea," I pleaded with the tiny Napoleon. "If you let go I'll let you spoon me tonight, no questions asked."

Our current deadlock was over a cat toy. He'd swiped it from Lucy, the mansion's cat, and she wanted it back. With both hands on the toy and the dog's teeth clasped securely over the sparkly mouse, Sweetpea and I began our stare down. It was going on three minutes, twenty-eight seconds and neither of us was budging.

Until the lights went out.

———

Time goes by so much slower in the dark, especially when sleep was off the table. Had I known I'd be spending the evening in obscurity, I wouldn't have taken a nap earlier in the day. Now I was wide-awake and bored to tears. With no television, and the Internet only accessible on the front porch with my arm lifted and tilted at a seventy-degree angle, my options for entertainment were limited. Since my mom and Terrance were teaching their evening couple's relaxation class, I took to texting or calling every human I'd ever known. In a moment of extreme weakness, I even dialed up my wayward father.

Four rings later and he was on the line.

"Hello?"

His intro was less a greeting and more reminiscent of a person trying to figure out how the strange talking device worked.

"Hi, Dad."

Silence filled the space between us. I pulled the phone away from my ear to make sure we were still connected but, sure enough, the call time was still ticking away.

Confused, I tried again. "Dad?"

"Who's this?"

Since I was the only one qualified to use the moniker, I was instantly pissed.

"It's me. Your daughter."

More silence as I held my breath, waiting for his reply. I'll admit, it had been a while since we'd spoken, but certainly not enough time to forget his own child.

"Breeze," I added quietly in an attempt to jog his long-term memory. This pretty much summed up our entire relationship. He had to be repeatedly reminded of my existence.

A long, relieved exhale. "Ah. Right ... Breeze."

"Who else would I be?" I asked, rolling my eyes. "Unless you have another daughter somewhere."

"Not that I'm aware of," he chuckled. "Sorry, I'm just a little distracted right now. Got some old high school buddies over for a few beers. You just sounded so old, baby girl."

"Old?"

"Yeah, like a woman. I got confused."

"You do know I'm twenty six, right?"

"Shut the fuck up! Are you shitting me right now?"

My shoulders slumped. Sure, he'd missed every birthday since I was seven. But still, this was a new low. "No, not shitting you at all. If you will recall, I was born back in 1992."

"Wait a minute! How old does that make me then?"

"Forty-five."

I didn't need a calendar to remember *his* age. John had become a father at the ripe old age of eighteen and had been forgetting his responsibilities ever since.

"Well, fuck!" My father paused a moment to address his buddies. "Do you guys know I'm forty five fuckin' years old?"

There was commotion in the background as all his friends replied in the affirmative.

"Okay, this sucks. Why didn't someone tell me I was old as fuck?"

My father was still engrossed in the far-off conversation while I waited on the line.

"Vic, get off the table," he yelled, forcing me to hold the phone away from my ear. The get-together sounded bigger than just a group of high school pals sharing a few beers. I had a sinking suspicion I'd just interrupted a smoke out.

"Who's Vic?" I asked, grasping at straws to hold the conversation together.

"Just some asshole I know. He thinks he can fly. Anyway, sorry, baby girl, what have you been up to? And don't tell me you've got some snot-nosed rug-rat of your own or I might just have a full on heart attack."

"No, no kids."

"Oh, whew. I so couldn't handle being a grandfather."

Right, like he couldn't handle being a father?

"So, what's happening?" he asked. "Why did you call?"

"No reason. Just thought I'd say hi. I'm sitting in the dark. There's a power outage."

"Really? That's weird. I have electricity."

"Right, but you live in San Francisco. I'm down south."

"What the hell are you doing down south?"

"Well, I've been living in Ventura County for two years now."

"Huh, really?"

I may as well have been talking to myself. Clearly he was preoccupied or just too wasted to offer me any attention.

"You know what, you sound busy. I'll just talk to you later."

"Okay, baby girl. That sounds good. Have fun."

And with that, he hung up on me. I stared at my phone in disbelief and then wanted to kick myself for being surprised. If I thought he'd fight a little harder to stay connected to me, I was sadly mistaken.

Stroking the silky fur of the cat curled up on my lap, I fought back tears. Why had I called him in the first place? People didn't magically change just because you needed them to. My father couldn't offer me any more solace than Sweetpea, who routinely bit my butt while I slept.

"It's his loss." I whispered the words my mother had used to soothe me when my father had skipped a weekend visit, or a birthday. *Or my entire life.* "He doesn't know what he's missing."

Lucy lifted her head, rewarding me with the affectionate attention I craved. I'd known this brown and white ragdoll cat for five days and she already appreciated me more than my own father did. That's why I loved pets. They didn't care what you looked like or how much money you made, all they required from their humans was basic necessities and a gentle touch.

I bent down and kissed the top of her head, and she purred her approval. Who needed a dad when I had my Lucy?

"I'm going to take you home with me," I mused. "Maybe your family won't notice."

A text pinged on my phone, and I shifted my focus to the message from Mason.

Sorry, just got your text.

With a sigh, I tapped out my response. *Took you long enough. I sent like four.*

Twelve, Breeze. You sent twelve.

I flinched at his reply, knowing how needy that made me sound. *Did I? It must have been a glitch in the phone because of the blackout.*

After a moment, he returned, *Whatever you say*

Fine. I'm bored. I have no one to talk to, Mace. I was so desperate I even called my father.

The dots danced on the screen and I imagined his surprise.

Your father? Jesus. What's John up to nowadays?

I wouldn't really know seeing as I had to spend our whole conversation reminding him of who I was.

Mason dropped a laughing emoji. *Sorry. He's a Dipwad.*

Yeah, a giant one. Anyway, why didn't you answer me?

I'm in Vegas. It's not like I can just drop everything to keep you company in the dark.

Ah crap. I forgot you were in Sin City. Are you sinning?

What do you think?

I think that was a stupid question. What are you doing now?

Shitting.

Ew, Mason, you disgust me.

You wanted me to text back and I am. Don't question my methods. Anyway, a friend of mine just told me there's a fire off the 150 highway.

I'm not surprised. The wind and the heat are brutal. Even without a bunch of pyromaniacs running around, the conditions are still perfect for a fire.

I know, but Breeze, what I'm saying is that could be the reason for the blackout.

Oh great. If the fire burned through the power lines then the electricity could be out for days.

Sucks for you. I'm in the City Of A Billion Lights. Even the hookers are lit up."

How nice for you.

Look on the bright side. If the electricity is still out by the weekend, you could always take your zoo to the Bay Area and go to the family reunion.

Oh right because nothing says, "I'm over you" like a woman arriving at a party with pet rats.

Yuck. That family has rats too?

Mason, they have everything. I wish you weren't in Vegas. You could come over and we could pretend to be on an awkward babysitting date. It would be so fun.

You are bored.

So, so bored.

Well, as fun as it is to be shooting the breeze with you, Breeze, I've got a Neon party to go to.

Nooo. You can't be done crapping already?
Oh, but I am. Goodnight, Breeze.
Goodnight, Mason.

I stayed put on the sofa, not sure what to do with myself until Hercules nudged me with his nose. He'd had enough of my hibernation and needed a little action. To drive home the point, the Saint Bernard stuck his snout up Lucy's backside causing a sudden and swift retaliation from the bundle of fur in my lap. Personality wise, Lucy was more like a dog, sweet and friendly with a tendency to follow me around wherever I went. But when pushed to the limits, as Herc had done with his 'nose to the butt-hole' bit, the mild-mannered kitty flipped to all fours and went into full on ninja mode, delivering a 'Me Too' movement beat-down for the ages.

Sweetpea wanted nothing to do with the current state of affairs, preferring instead to sit at my feet in a near catatonic state. It occurred to me then that I'd inadvertently stumbled upon the best method of emasculating the cocksure Chihuahua —turning off the lights on the whole damn city. Totally doable. Yep, the pup barked a good game, but that's all it was. Deep down, he was just an insecure little man compensating for his tiny package with belligerence.

Taking the long way around to avoid Lucy and her paws of fury, Herc dug his head into my shoulder, making me laugh at his antics.

"Okay, fine. You win."

With the animal parade following my every move, I wandered the house trying to figure out which light switches were in the up position because nothing sent panic through me like waking up to a house coming *alive* after a power outage. Shivering at the thought, the first feelings of uneasiness crept up the back of my neck and tingles fanned out over my skin. Something didn't feel right, like evil was lurking right around the bend.

Suddenly, I had an overwhelming urge to hide in a closet. Instead, I did the next best thing—I ate. It proved to be an appropriate distraction, and the dogs and I worked our way through the pantry with enviable precision. My phone rang, echoing through the darkness and startling me so badly I nearly choked on a mouthful of dried mangos. Lucy shot out of the kitchen like a bullet, Sweetpea peed where he stood, and Hercules dug his head into my leg, whining. I patted his wide, furry forehead. The blackout was getting to all of us.

"I know, Buddy. It scared me too."

I checked my screen before answering. Mason. "Hello?"

"Breeze!" he shouted my name, fear and anxiety threading his tone.

"Mace, what's wrong?"

"Get out!"

"What?"

"Listen to me. You've got to get out of there right now. A fire is coming your way."

"It's on the 150," I replied, confused by his urgency. "That's a good ten to fifteen miles away from me."

"Not anymore. The winds shifted. My buddy's up there. His house is on fire. It's coming straight for you and it's traveling fast. They're calling for immediate evacuations. You have five minutes. That's what they're saying for that area. Get in your car and get the hell out of there. Right now!"

"Okay. I'm... okay. I'll leave."

"Now, Breeze. Call me when you're out."

"Okay. Bye."

.   .   .

A few seconds later, an emergency alert alarm shrilled from my phone. This was no drill.

Jumping from the counter stool, a moment of panic forced me to take stock of the situation. *The animals.* I had to get them in the car. Swooping up Sweetpea, I ran with him into the foyer where I shoved him head first into his dog carrier. It was part of my new tough love regimen and so far it seemed to be working like a charm.

Seconds later I returned to the kitchen to find my trusty side-kick, Hercules, cowering under the table. I forced myself to calm down enough to communicate with him, even though what I really wanted to do was freak the hell out.

"Hey there, Herc, you want to play a game?" I cooed, forcing out an animated, baby voice to control the shakiness in my own. "Let's play." He lifted his head in cautious interest before deciding I was full of shit and lowering it back to the stone floor. Herc weighed in at a hundred and twenty pounds. If he didn't want to move, there was nothing I could do to make it happen.

"Mandatory Evacuation is in effect." The blare of the bullhorn penetrated the walls as fire trucks drove up the street warning residents of the approaching threat. "Leave the area immediately."

Fingers of dread clenched around my heart. "Please," I begged my four-legged friend. When he didn't move, I screamed, "Hercules!"

So much for my sweet voice. I now sounded like one of those evil Chucky dolls. But that didn't work either. So I plastered on a fake smile. "You want turkey, Herc?"

He lifted his nose in attention as I swung open the refrigerator and began flinging turkey slices all over the floor. That did the trick. The Saint Bernard's stomach took precedence over his survival instincts and he followed the processed meat like a duck waddling after a trail of breadcrumbs. I led him straight to the foyer where Sweetpea was waiting, and attached a leash to his collar. Ushering the boys outside and into my car, I caught sight of the fire, the orange glow closer than I could have imagined.

A firefighter entered through the front gate and jogged up the circular driveway.

"There's no time," he called to me. "You need to evacuate now. How many are in the house?"

"Just me."

"Do you need help?"

"No, I'm leaving in a minute."

"Alright, I'll open the security gate for you. Be quick."

"I will."

He slid open the fence for me before taking off for the neighbor's property. I shut the car door on the dogs and went back into the house in search of Lucy. I hadn't seen her since the phone rang and now she could be anywhere. If I thought Hercules was tough to lure out of hiding, Lucy would be nearly impossible.

I called her name repeatedly, checking the most obvious places first but the cat was nowhere to be found. With every bed I looked under and every closet I checked, the likelihood I'd find her before being forced to evacuate were diminishing.

"Lucy," I called to her, tears stinging my eyes. "Please don't make me leave you."

But she didn't answer or magically appear, and I'd run out of time. An explosion rocked the ground and smoke wafted through the house. The increased intensity of the situation no doubt had Lucy terrified. If she were determined to hide, I'd never find her.

Running to the ten-year-old boy's room, I grabbed the rat cage and carried it to the front door before making my way back into the kitchen for the last of my charges, a goldfish named

Winston. Checking the recycle bin, I found a large Gatorade bottle, rinsed it out and poked some holes in the top of the plastic before pouring the goldfish and his water into the bottle.

I took one last look around for Lucy, but she was nowhere in sight. The only thing I could do for her now was to leave the front door open and give the poor cat a fighting chance. Sadly, the indoor kitty had never stepped foot outside and this would not be a good night to start exploring.

I sprinted down the hall to the guest room, gathered up my clothes and iPad and tossed everything into my open duffle bag. An irritated meow sounded from the hollows.

"What the...?" I gasped, catching a disgruntled Lucy in mid-flight as she tried to jump out of my bag. "Oh no you don't."

Apologizing profusely the entire time, I aggressively shoved the squirming cat back inside the tote and secured the zipper. Although Lucy might not agree with my current methods, had she understood the alternative, which was a vigorous charbroiling, I'm sure she would've been totally cool with the whole 'kicking back in my undies' experience.

Over her aggravated howling, I shouted, "You can thank me later."

Slinging the bag over my shoulder, I ran for the exit.

———

My eyes fluttered open, confusion and pain swimming just beneath the surface. Touching my forehead, pain radiated from a large goose egg. I tried to recall what had happened... and why my car was now smashed accordion-style into a stone retaining wall mere feet from the opened security gate. The impact had deployed the airbag, now semi-deflated and billowing around me.

Warm breath and moisture on my face. Blood? No, it was

Hercules licking my face. His tongue bath had probably been what woke me in the first place. But why was he in the front seat with me? Had the intensity of the collision sent him flying over the seats or had he jumped over after the fact?

"Are you guys all right?" I asked, running my hand over Herc's floppy ears. Twisting around, I spied Sweetpea's carrier on the ground, wedged between the seats. His incessant yapping let me know the little dog was still alive.

Pieces of my memory abruptly resurfaced. Something on fire had crossed my path as I was driving off the property, maybe an animal, maybe a tumbleweed. Instead of hitting the moving target, I'd swerved, and that's how I ended up here—crushed up against a landscaping wall.

One by one, I moved my limbs, encouraged by the mobility and lack of pain. I was okay. Yes. Okay. But then I caught sight of the smoke and ash whizzing by at dizzying speeds. No, not okay. Nothing was okay. I was still in the middle of the nightmare— only now the flames were raging, having burned over the ridge and pushed their way forward through the backyard of the neighbor's place. I could feel the heat all around me.

"Oh god," I breathed out, turning the key in the ignition as I prepared to drive the mangled car to safety. But no matter how hard I tried, the engine wouldn't turn over. My Ford Edge was done for, determined to meet its end in a blaze of glory.

It was then that the full weight of the crisis hit me. When I'd first been loading up the animals, cars were still driving by, fleeing the fire, but as I sat unconscious in my totaled vehicle, the exodus seemed to have passed me by. Gone were the head-lights crossing through the dark. Gone were the firefighters going door-to-door canvassing. All that was left up here in this coastal mountain living community was me, a car full of animals, and a monstrous fire gobbling up the world around me.

If I was going to see another day, I had to make it happen myself. Opening the car door, I eased out from behind the wheel. Not waiting for an invitation, Hercules squeezed by my butt and was out the door. I half expected him to take off and save himself, but like the loyal teddy bear he was, my canine companion stood by my side, awaiting further instruction. He wasn't about to abandon me, and neither would I forsake him and his furry siblings.

Flinging my kitty filled duffle bag and Sweetpea's carrier over my shoulder, I grabbed the rat cage and balanced Winston on top of it all with my chin before leading my circus of sorts out the front gate and down the street. Had I been more mindful of my own perilous situation, I might have thought twice about saving my helpless charges. But I wasn't thinking of just myself. The animals were scared, and I wasn't going to just leave them to die.

Of course, that was before the choking smoke attacked my throat. Before the oxygen in the air began to evaporate. And before I realized I might just die on this windy, hilltop road with a gaggle of pets by my side.

I knew what needed to be done, even before the thought fully formed. In order to give myself a chance, I had to set the animals free. I hated the idea of them running terrified into the night, but consoled myself with the knowledge that they were faster than me and stood a better chance at survival free from their restraints.

Carrying my living baggage away from the road, I solemnly began to unburden myself of the weight that held me down. Setting the rat cage onto the ground, I pulled off the towel and opened the door flap, shaking the bars to jar them into action.

"Go." I urged, but the normally sociable rats cowered in the back of the cage, too afraid to move. They would, when they had no choice.

"I'm sorry," I whispered, and I truly was. I'd tried. I really had.

Placing Winston on the ground next to the cage, I said a quick goodbye.

Next came Sweetpea. Opening his carrier, I gently pulled him out and gave him a kiss between his Yoda ears. He seemed too disoriented to go for my jugular.

"Save yourself," I whispered to him. The Chihuahua stood transfixed looking to me for guidance. I had nothing left to give him. "Run, Sweetpea. Go."

As I unhooked Herc's leash, the Saint Bernard stared up at me with big brown eyes, so trusting in my ability to save him. I couldn't. Just as his brother was doing now, Hercules stood beside me, refusing to leave.

Tears rolling down my cheeks, I patted his head for what I assumed was the last time, then shoved him away. "Go!" I screamed. "Run!"

But he wouldn't leave. One look into his soulful eyes told me he'd be my companion to the bitter end. "Okay," I whispered. "You boys can run with me if you want but, just know, I'll only slow you down."

Pulling the duffle bag off my shoulder, I had one last pet to free. Lucy—my spirit animal. My heart ached knowing I'd be sending her to her death. She had no experience in the outside world and no real chance at survival without me. With dread, I unzipped the bag and reached in to pull her out. But as she emerged, her terrified crystal blue eyes dilated to a dark black, I just couldn't do it. Not yet. I still had some strength left in me for her. Keeping hold of her collar, I emptied my duffle bag of belongings until the only weight left for me to carry was the nine-pound cat. I zipped her back in and slid the bag over my shoulder once more before I started running down the sidewalk, Sweetpea and Hercules lapping at my heels.

We hadn't made it but one house down when I saw the lights of a car flooding through the smoke. I wasn't sure if I was imagining things until I heard the crunch of the tires against the asphalt. Screaming for the dogs to stay put, I dropped the duffle bag and ran screaming into the street, flailing my arms wildly in the air. The driver was moving fast, making me more determined to hitch a ride. But when it became apparent the car was barreling straight for me, my excitement waned. I hastily jumped out of the way as brakes screeched and the stench of burned rubber mixed with all the other scorching smells of the night.

As it worked to avoid me, the car's left tire ended up on the curb before coming to a complete stop. I searched for the dogs, hoping they hadn't been hit. In seconds they were once again crowding around my feet. The driver-side window lowered, revealing a man who looked every bit as traumatized as I felt.

"Are you okay?" he asked, his words heavy with remorse. "I'm so sorry. I didn't see you."

I nodded stupidly, staring at him with unblinking eyes. A thick layering of ash had settled into his hair, giving it the same grayish tint as my elderly fiancé, Hugh. My gaze dropped to his bare chest, and further to his washboard abs. In any other situation it might have been a nice touch to be saved by a half-naked Abercrombie model. But he was no model. My rescuer was none other than Bodhi Beckett, of AnyDayNow fame.

7

BODHI: LIKE THE WIND

I F I THOUGHT THE DANGER LEVEL WOULD DECREASE THE FURTHER down the road I got, I was wrong. It was coming at me from all angles as the tiny red ashes zipped by faster than my car could drive. It was because of this craziness that I almost missed the woman in the street, waving frantically for me to stop. I slammed on my brakes as she hurtled her body out of the way of my oncoming vehicle.

Reeling from the near miss, I rolled down my window to apologize, but the woman just stood there in a daze.

"Do you need a ride?" I asked. That was apparently the correct question to snap her out of whatever stupor she was in.

"Yes," she answered, her voice cracking with emotion. "I...I need a ride."

Along with a bleeding bump on her forehead, she had dried tear-trails etching lines in the soot on her face. Judging by her appearance and by the fact that she was escaping on foot, her evening probably hadn't been much better than mine.

"Get in, I'll take you down the road."

"Oh, thank you so much. I have my pets."

She motioned to the dogs standing beside her.

"Yeah, that's fine. Get them in too."

But instead of opening the back door she said. "I'll be right back." Before I could offer a protest, she told the dogs to stay put and took off up the street. The mutts didn't obey, giving chase as she called over her shoulder to me, "Just give me one minute, please."

One minute? In my newly acquired fire escaping experience, one minute was the time it took for a roof to cave in. "Wait! Where are you going?"

"I've got to get the others. Please, please wait."

The others? There were more people escaping on foot? Well shit! You'd think she'd have led with that information.

Pushing the door open wide, I jumped out and dashed after both her and the dogs. I found the woman bent over a cage. "Thank god." I heard her sigh before replacing the towel over the top and grabbing for a leash lying on the ground. After hooking it onto the big dog's collar, she handed me the reigns.

"Can you take Hercules back to your car. I'll get the others."

And when I looked down, I realized the *others* weren't human, which was currently the only species I was willing to risk my ass for.

"There's no time. We've got to go. Now!"

"Please," she pleaded, tears filling her eyes. "I can't leave them."

Something about her desperation kept me from bolting back to my car. Maybe it was that she was committed to a cause other than herself. That's more than I could ever claim. "Okay. Hand me another one. But hurry."

She picked up the tiny dog and unceremoniously dumped him into a carrier. "Here. He bites so don't put your fingers in there."

Yeah right. It wasn't like I was going to get all touchy-feely with the Taco Bell dog while the world around me burned to the ground. Besides, the little mongrel looked psychotic. The minute I grabbed hold of the handle to his carrier, he was growling and attacking the flimsy bars.

Reaching my car, I opened the door and the massive dog wasted no time jumping into my backseat. The nippy pup wasn't nearly as accommodating. And as I placed his carrier onto the seat, he attacked the crate, nearly biting my damn finger off.

"Fuck you, Little Dick." I retracted my hand in the nick of time. I was never a dog person, and even less so now that the shrunken canine was hell bent on mutilating me. "Watch it, Yappy. I'm not invested in you at all so keep that shit up and see where it gets you."

My eyes met Hercules's, and I was forced to do a double take. He was looking between his canine brother and me with an almost humanlike expression of frustration on his face.

"Are you seeing this too?" I asked him. "Is he always such a jerk?"

The big dog leaned toward me like he had a secret to share and, no joke, I met him halfway thinking he might actually have something juicy to tell. But then he morphed back into a regular, dumb dog and gave me the soggiest tongue lashing I'd ever experienced in my life. It was as if I'd left my window down at the car wash and the rotating mop reached in and took a swipe at my face.

"Oh my god, dude," I complained as I wiped the slobber off with the back of my arm. "Keep that thing in your mouth from now on, you hear me?"

The woman was already at the car trying to get the hatchback open. "Is it locked?" she asked, panicked eyes darting to mine.

"Wave your leg under the back bumper."

"Huh?"

I mimed for her the correct foot movement to open the trunk, but she just looked pissed by the technological advances keeping her from... well... advancing.

"I'm not a magician," she complained, thrusting the cage into my arms. "Here, can you wave the rats into your trunk?"

I would have laughed at her bitchy response had she not uttered the word rat. Like I said earlier, I wasn't a dog person, but if the choice was between a dog and a rat, I'd pick the canine every single time. Why would anyone keep rats for pets? And more importantly, why would anyone try and save them in a fire? Did she not realize how many of their rodent countrymen died every damn day in lab experiments? It's not like the world would miss two more. But with no time to argue, I waved my leg and the trunk immediately opened, allowing for the cage to be slid into the back with ease.

"Is that it?" I asked.

But she was already gone, sprinting back to the sidewalk where I'd nearly ran her down. "One more."

I checked the position of the fire, which was not only behind us, but to the side of us and down the road from us as well. We were in the center of a giant firepit that had breached its barriers. Under my breath, I unleashed a volley of swear words. If I died because of lab rats and Little Dick, I was going to be eternally pissed.

"We have to go!" I yelled.

"I know," she said, already running back in my direction. "I'm really sorry. Thank you so much for waiting."

She was carrying a duffle bag and in her right hand was a bottle of Gatorade. I reached out to take the tote, but she sidestepped me.

"I got it. This bag has claws."

Just as she was sliding the wiggling bag into the hatchback next to the rats, we both jerked our heads in the direction of an explosion. The house next door was blazing. After exchanging horrified expressions, we slammed the trunk and raced for the safety of the car.

"What the hell is happening?" I asked, neither expecting nor receiving an explanation to the nightmare raging around me. As if to drive home the danger we were facing, the dried brush directly beside the car sizzled before igniting with a pop.

"Go. Go," she called out, pounding on the glove compartment.

I put the car in gear and stepped on the gas. I hadn't even gotten my license until I was eighteen and I'll admit, I had a tendency to drive on the lower side of other drivers' sanity levels, earning me the nickname 'grandpa' from my band mates. But tonight, I'd be making the boys proud.

The woman held on for dear life as I maneuvered down the hill, avoiding a gathering of fire trucks pulled off to the side of the road. I wanted to roll down my window and inform them of the losing battle they were fighting. Any residents still in their homes weren't coming out alive. Although, let's be real, the firefighters were experienced enough to know this was no ordinary blaze. They might as well have been fighting the fire with garden hoses for all the good it would do them.

One fireman saw our approach and began to aggressively signal with his arms and point down the road in the universal sign of 'Hey Idiot! Get the hell out of here.'

My passenger and I sat rapt in our seats as we pushed toward safety. We hadn't made it two blocks before an unexpected bend in the road forced us deeper into the inferno.

"Watch out!"

Her scream pierced the cab, commanding my foot to brake

even before I knew the reason for her outburst. A tree, fully engulfed in flames, crashed to the ground two car lengths in front of us, sending embers cascading up and over the windshield. My sudden deceleration caused the backend of the Range Rover to fishtail and I struggled for control. We both screamed as the truck performed an entire rotation before coming to an abrupt stop within inches of the burning obstruction.

Breathing heavily, I looked to my passenger for encouraging words of wisdom, but she had nothing more to add to the stunned silence. It occurred to me then that the yappy dog in the backseat had actually stopped barking. Apparently he wasn't a fan of my Tilt-A-Whirl driving skills.

I placed the car in reverse to get us a safe distance from the burning blockage but with distance came clarity. This narrow road was our salvation, and now the downed tree was blocking us from deliverance. The only way out was through the punishing flames.

Slowly I turned toward my passenger, ready to explain the dire situation, but the minute our eyes met, an understanding passed between us. We were out of options. I knew it. She knew it. The sloppy-tongued canine in the backseat knew it. If we turned around and followed the fire trucks up, we would die. If we stayed put, we would die. Our lives lay on the other side of that tree.

Incredibly, the woman seemed to absorb every word I didn't speak. Gripping my forearm, she nodded, ready to meet the challenge head-on. Even if that challenge meant driving through a stone-fire oven.

"Wait, what's your name?" I asked, suddenly overwhelmed with the urge to know this stranger beside me, the woman who faced the possibility of death with stunning courage and strength.

Her eyes softened, the fear in them temporarily abated as she answered my question. "Breeze."

I wasn't sure I'd heard her correctly. "Breeze? Like the wind?"

Seeing the irony in her name, a tiny smile found its way to the surface. "Yes, Bodhi Beckett. Like the wind."

8

BREEZE: SYMPATHY PUKER

THERE ARE MOMENTS IN LIFE YOU KNOW WILL CHANGE YOU forever. The day Terrance had showed up, hand in hand with my beaming mother, carrying a bouquet of fresh flowers meant just for me, was one of those moments. Another occurred minutes before my beloved grandmother took her final breath. She'd opened her eyes, looked around, and asked why there were so many people gathered at her bedside. My mother and I had been alone with her at the time. And then there was *now*, staring into the eyes of the man I would face death with. I didn't know him before today, and probably wouldn't know him after. But for the rest of our hopefully long and prosperous lives, this would be a stitch in time that neither of us would forget.

A calm settled over me in the seconds before he leaned on the gas pedal and shot us into the flames. I'd never been known for my steely reserve, but when it counted and everything was on the line, I was brave. And so was he—more than I ever would have been if I had been driving. I just had to sit here and pray. Bodhi had to transport us through earth's fiery core with an entire pet store in the backseat. Mason could say what he would about defective former child stars, but mine had it all going on, and then some.

Hercules whimpered from the backseat, momentarily drawing my attention away from the path ahead. I reached back to soothe him when the realization dawned. This was all on me. If I hadn't insisted on saving the animals, we would've passed this spot *before* the tree fell and we wouldn't be trapped in a coffin rolling through hell. Why not take it a step further? Had Bodhi left me in the street back there, he'd already be at the ocean by now, safe from harm. If he died on this mountain road, it would be my fault.

I'm sorry, I wanted to say, but no way did this guy have time for apologies. He was busy keeping us alive. With a grimace of determination stamped on his chiseled profile, Bodhi maneuvered the car up and over the curb and drove us directly into the belly of the dragon. Heat penetrated through the surface of the vehicle and, almost immediately, I could feel the temperature rise inside the cab. We were being cooked alive. Sweetpea barked incessantly in his carrier, and Herc's long, sorrowful wail sounded like a baby's cry. I wasn't sure how much he understood about what was happening, but he knew enough to be terrified. Even Lucy got in on the action. With her angry meows muffled from inside the bag. I caught a glimpse of one of her paws reaching up through the small opening where the zipper and duffle bag met.

"It's not ending," Bodhi yelled over the roar. "I can't see the street."

"It's there. It has to be," I said, trying hard to keep the hope alive for the both of us. But with every second that passed, the chances of us getting back onto the road without smashing into a tree or light pole diminished. "Just a little bit further."

Although my words were paved more in wishful thinking than actual foresight, they seemed to be what he needed to hear.

"Okay. Hold on."

Tightening my grip on the 'Oh Shit' handle, I bit back my scream as Bodhi floored it, blindly navigating his way through the smoke and fire until a sudden sharp veer to the right set the tires back on cemented ground. And although we were free from the tunnel of terror, the Range Rover had emerged from the inferno on fire. The flames licking up the hood increased the likelihood that it wasn't the only surface of the vehicle currently sizzling. Since we were still surrounded on all sides, Bodhi had no choice but to keep driving. Stopping now was more dangerous than barreling down the two-lane road in a mobile barbeque.

Neither of us spoke as he kept his foot pressed deep on the gas pedal. The speed at which we were travelling actually worked to extinguish a fair number of the flames on the hood. Briefly prying his eyes from the road, Bodhi dared a glance in my direction. We were both breathing heavily, traumatized by the lengths it took to come out the other side.

And then it hit me. We were still alive! And more importantly, it looked like we'd stay that way as the world around us gradually returned to normal. Here, the trees were still standing. The hillside road hadn't been reduced to a valley of flames, and the stately homes weren't yet exploding. And world-renowned popstar Bodhi Beckett and me—we were still breathing.

I opened my mouth but no words could do any of this justice, so I held onto the silence. Without warning, Bodhi swerved over to the side of the road, put the car in park, and jumped out.

"The towel on the rat's cage," he said. "Give it to me."

Springing from the car, I opened the back door and, snagging the towel off the cage, I tossed it at Bodhi. He quickly went to work slapping out random flames still smoldering on the metal. He continued batting at the melted paint long after the threat had been extinguished. Clearly he'd gone someplace else in his mind, someplace fraught with danger and distress.

"You can stop now," I said softly. "The fire's out."

Bodhi turned toward me, blinking multiple times in what appeared to be an effort to clear his mind, then mercifully ceased his firefighting efforts. The towel was still wrapped around his knuckles and he held on tightly, seemingly unconvinced of lasting safety. Regardless, if a second wave was coming for us, his charred towel wouldn't have much fight left in it. I needed to pry it from his hands.

"Here, let me take that," I offered and, as if it were a loaded weapon, I cautiously extracted the towel from his steely grip. "We're safe now."

The reassurance surprised even myself. After the last hour, it seemed almost deceitful to speak such hopeful words. Bodhi stood, conflicted, his hands curling into fists. I could see in his body language that he wanted to believe me, but he'd seen too much to take my baseless predictions at face value.

Looking toward the orange hued horizon, a myriad of emotion passed over his troubled face. I felt nothing but sympathy for this man. Had he been anyone else, anyone ordinary, I might have wrapped my arms around him and given the guy a supportive pat on the back. But Bodhi wasn't just anyone, and that fact wasn't far from my mind. Celebrities, as a whole, shied away from the touchy-feely approach. From what I gathered, they treasured their privacy and what interaction they did have with the general public did not include hugging or light petting. Still, I had to wonder, now that we'd faced death together, where was the line drawn between strangers and Stockholm Syndrome survivors.

In the end, Bodhi made the call on the type of support system he needed, and it didn't include me. Shoulders slumped, he unexpectedly dropped onto the sidewalk, burying his head into his hands. Perhaps even more awkward than consoling a celebrity was consoling a crying one. At least that's what I assumed he was doing, even though he maintained a steely silence. All I could see of his internal turmoil was his quaking body. With each vibration of his broad shoulders, my own resolve weakened. Depleted myself, I took a seat beside him and allowed the tears to flow freely down my cheeks. There was a time and place for superhero strength and then there was now... the time to be human.

––––––

Sitting side by side consumed by our own harrowing memories, neither of us spoke. But it wasn't an uncomfortable silence. There was some solace in knowing I wasn't the only one who felt so gutted. Several minutes of parallel suffering passed before Bodhi slowly rose to his feet and offered me his hand.

"We should probably keep moving," he said, sounding more in control than he looked. Gesturing toward the growing smoke cloud on the horizon, he added, "It's still coming this direction."

Illuminated by the headlights, I got my first solid look at the guy who saved my life and, maybe it was a case of hero worship, but I was awestruck in his presence. Looks-wise, Bodhi Beckett had seen better days. Half-naked, hair wildly unkempt and covered in thick layers of soot and ash, the guy had a serious cro-magnum man vibe going on. And yet, props to him for being distracting enough to temporarily take my mind off the plume of fire and smoke currently gobbling up the landscape. Normally I wasn't into the whole 'hunter and gatherer' look, but I made an exception for famous popstars surviving their first apocalypse.

Staring back at me from behind long dark lashes, Bodhi's light blue eyes were as pretty as they were haunted. I wondered if this troubled expression of his had been with him longer than just tonight. Certainly he appeared wiser and more poised than his celebrity alter ego would suggest. The young guy mugging for the camera on the cover of magazines was a far cry from the subdued one standing before me now. Yet something told me getting to the bottom of his story would take longer than the handful of minutes I probably had left with him.

From my position on the sidewalk, Bodhi seemed larger than life... and I suppose he was. This was a guy worshipped by millions and now suddenly he was here with me, sharing a moment neither one of us could have foreseen. I blinked him in, my brain still catching up on the idea that my savior was also a pop music superstar. And for the first time since crossing paths with Bodhi, I felt wholly unworthy of sharing his space.

"Breeze?" he questioned, still offering a hand to me.

"Oh geez, sorry," I said, sliding my palm against his. "I'm trippin' out."

And like a weed peeking out from a crack in the sidewalk, a smile fought its way to the surface, instantly transforming Bodhi's serious expression into one of relief and amusement. "You and me both."

I allowed him to pull me to my feet but was unprepared to be planted inches from his imposing body. How had I, in a matter of an hour, gone from pathetic Breeze sitting on the sofa calling her deadbeat daddy for emotional support into the Lara Croft of firestorm survival? And more importantly, how was I now suddenly in a full frontal stare down with a guy whose face I'd seen staring back at me from the pages of a magazine?

His eyes burrowed into mine as if they were looking for a safe place to take refuge and, oh lord help me; Bodhi Beckett instantly became my newest obsession. It was like the heavens had opened up and handed me a dream come true. All those little, defenseless animals I'd nursed to health over the years had brought me here—to the wounded landscape of the man who stood before me now. In my mind's eye he was the flawless mix of beautiful but scarred. A man who was broken just enough that his fragmented pieces could still be painstakingly sewn back together again. Honestly, I had to keep myself from salivating. Oh, how I'd love to get my hands on him, not in the biblical sense... okay that too... but for a mender like me, Bodhi was the perfect project and I was convinced that, given half the chance, I was just what this guy needed.

Bodhi's eyebrows lifted as he continued to stare, and I wondered what his internal dialogue sounded like. It probably went something like this – *how do I get this googly-eyed dork to let go of my hand,* or *where can a guy get a restraining order at this late hour.*

Yes, it was times like this I was glad human beings weren't equipped with mind-reading capabilities, because if Bodhi had picked up on even an inkling of what I'd been thinking, he would have dropped my hand and run toward the flames. Certainly I was the last thing a guy like Bodhi was looking for. He was a shiny billboard of accomplishments and I was, well, one of those dull, brown corkboards you hang on the wall and cover with post-it-notes. If my lackluster brilliance hadn't been enough to hold the interest of a cheating ex-fiancé, there was little hope a gleaming superstar would find me fascinating.

Thankfully, Sweetpea and his incessant barking ended the awkwardly long stare down between the two of us. Bodhi wisely diverted his eyes away from my psychotic plotting and fixed them on my small charge. A grimace instantly hardened his features as he took in the ramped-up dog slamming himself into the sides of his carrier. Good lord, Sweetpea's anxiety levels were through the roof tonight, and even though he wasn't my pup, I was still embarrassed.

"That dog needs meds," Bodhi commented absently, not even trying to be funny, even though it sort of was.

I nodded my agreement. "Or chloroform."

"Yeah, I vote for chloroform."

I laughed but it died off quickly. It felt almost inappropriate, like we were at a funeral. And I suppose, in a way, we were.

"Hey, I'm really sorry about your house," he said, surprising me with his genuine concern. "But at least you got your animals out, right?"

"I'm not sure the house is actually gone. It wasn't on fire when I left it but... I guess its chances aren't real good, are they?"

"No, not good at all."

"Anyway, it's not my place. I was pet-sitting."

Bodhi's eyes widened as he glanced from me to the creature convention in the backseat of his car. "Wait. You were saving someone else's pets?"

I shrugged. "I take my job seriously."

"Well, shit," he said, as if stunned by the news. I couldn't tell if he was highly impressed by my work ethic or frustrated for being dragged into Animal Planet in the first place.

Encouraged by the smile that broke free from its confines, I relaxed and said, "I'm going to add it to my marketing flyers —'Saves animals from raging infernos.' If there are any houses left standing, I'll be the most popular pet sitter in the county."

"No fucking doubt. Shit, I'd hire you... if I had pets to save, that is."

Suddenly Bodhi didn't seem as intimidating as I'd made him out to be. Still flawed? Oh yes, that much I was convinced of, but he knew how to hide his inner turmoil well and transform himself into your average, everyday hot guy.

"I guess I should extend the same condolences to you," I said, employing my gift for gab to keep the conversation going. It didn't work.

Bodhi seemed confused, and eyed me questioningly.

"I'm sorry about your house," I clarified.

"Oh." He exhaled. "I was trying to figure out who died. No, it wasn't my place either. I was house-sitting."

Now it was my turn to gape in surprise. What were the chances of us both being supporting players in this natural disaster?

"Well check us out!" My voice tipped up in amusement. "We're a couple of squatters."

He laughed. "I guess we are."

"So... are you as good at your job as I am?"

"Huh?"

"Did you save the house?"

A mischievous grin swept over his face. "Do I *look* like I saved the house?"

The soot and grime clinging to his skin answered the question, and I couldn't help but laugh.

"In that case, my suggestion would be to omit that unsavory piece of information from your flyer."

"Ya think?"

Suddenly I was feeling pretty good about the burgeoning connection I was making with my survival buddy.

"Hey," he said. "Can I ask you a favor?"

A favor? Like I'd say no. Pretty much, at this point, he could ask me to wade through the LA county sewer system after Thanksgiving and I'd say 'pretty please.'

"Of course. Anything."

"Can you drive for me?"

It wasn't what I'd been expecting, but certainly driving him around was preferable to a sewer stomp. Still, I was slightly bummed I couldn't be of more service. "Sure, you okay?"

"I'm fine. Just not feeling real good."

Bodhi walked around to the passenger side while I took my place in the driver's seat, settling into the leather interior. Wow, my butt was instantly pampered in the plushness of my upgraded ride. Perhaps I'd been too busy escaping certain doom to have noticed the luxury before but now I was making up for lost time. I finally understood the hoopla surrounding this car. It was like a gigantic slice of billowy angel food cake cushioning my backside. Had Bodhi not been beside me, I probably would have groaned in pleasure like the vehicularly-deprived hillbilly I was. But thankfully I'd been given just enough upbringing to fake my way through upscale situations.

Reaching for the key, I quickly realized there wasn't one, just a 'start' button on the dashboard. Well, slap me cross-eyed! What the hell was this, black magic? First the 'fairy godmother' enchanted trunk and now this. Wide-eyed, I brushed my fingers over the button, marveling at the science fiction of it all.

Sidetracked by my new alien spacecraft, I hadn't noticed Bodhi staring at me questioningly from the passenger side seat. Clearly, he wasn't convinced of my ability to pilot the thing. I flashed him my most trustworthy smile letting Bodhi know that, yes, I could be counted on to deliver him safely to his desired destination. But much like a rescue pup exploring her new forever home, I just needed a few uninterrupted moments to acclimate myself to my new surroundings.

Skeptical but patient, Bodhi allowed me the benefit of the doubt and smiled encouragingly before covertly checking his seatbelt to confirm it was securely in place. If he was expecting fireworks, I didn't disappoint.

Reaching for the button, I confidently pressed it with my index finger as I stepped on the gas pedal. The engine revved with intensity, filling the cab with a high-pitched grinding noise. Cringing, I glanced over at my passenger hoping he hadn't noticed my blunder, but the smile on his face told me he had.

"It was already on," he stated, and there was no escaping the amusement in his tone.

"Yeah." I grinned through my embarrassment. "I got that."

"And, uh, foot on the brake when you hit the button. Not on the gas."

I flashed him a thumbs up as I put the car in gear and, without further incident, pulled back onto the road. Although I was looking straight ahead, I could see from the corner of my eye that Bodhi was still watching me with that entertained look on his face. I'm not going to lie, I soaked up the attention. I mean this was an epic moment in my otherwise uneventful existence. Popstar Bodhi Beckett and I had an inside joke. How weirdly awesome was that?

After all was said and done, maybe we'd become friends after all. I pictured Bodhi calling me up whenever he was in town and arranging for us to meet somewhere for lunch. We'd laugh about the chloroform joke and the hilarious moment when I revved the car engine in the middle of a firestorm. Okay, so maybe I was attaching too much meaning to our very brief conversation, but I really did want to know the guy, if only to satisfy my own out-of-control curiosity. How often did a girl like me get the chance to converse with a guy like him?

Still, forging a connection would be an uphill battle. What did I have to barter in return for inside information on his glamorous life—a really good shampoo and head massage?

Chancing another glance in his direction, I was disappointed to see the amusement had faded from his face and now Bodhi was staring intensely out the window. His sudden change in demeanor put an end to my make believe lunch date. Okay, so maybe I needed to be less ambitious. Lunch was a lot to ask for. I'd be totally cool with a backstage pass and a shout out from the stage. Sure I was a country music fan at heart, but I could be swayed over to the dark side for the right bare-chested hero.

Sirens in the distance brought me back to the present. I needed to focus on the task at hand, which was to put some distance between us and the end of the frickin' world.

Cruising quietly down the main road, we were no longer the only lost and displaced souls fleeing the blaze. As more upended people from the lower elevations joined our exodus, we found ourselves in a traffic jam rivaling even the most crowded of Los Angeles freeways.

Silence settled between Bodhi and me and the longer it went on, the more my optimism of a connection between us faded. At this point, I'd just be lucky to get a mention during one of the countless interviews he was sure to give about his harrowing near death experience.

"Pull over!"

Startled at his sudden outburst, the desperation in Bodhi's voice triggered an immediate reaction, and I swerved to the side of the road. He was out of the car before I'd come to a complete stop, stumbling to the bushes where he proceeded to retch.

Did I offer assistance? Let him be? What was the protocol for barfing celebrities?

"Are you okay?" I called out the window.

Please be okay.

"Do you need help?"

Please don't need my help.

Certainly, I wasn't insensitive to Bodhi's plight. On the contrary, I wanted desperately to assist him, but keeping my distance was somewhat necessary given my notoriously weak stomach. As a child, my mother had coined the phrase 'Sympathy Puker' and that summarized me perfectly. Even the sound of a hairball forcefully expelling from a pint-sized kitten was enough to send me to the toilet yaking.

"Can I take you to the hospital?" I offered, swallowing back an unflattering belch. I was already dangerously close to spewing despite not even being in his gag radius.

Bodhi lifted his head in an apparent bid to answer my question. Too weak and overwhelmed by nausea to respond, he bent back over the bushes and continued to vomit. My stomach churned, knowing what needed to be done. I owed him more than a shout through the window. If Bodhi needed my help I'd suck it up. Literally. He'd driven through a wall of flames for me, so the least I could do was hold onto my dinner long enough to help the poor guy back to the vehicle.

I gingerly walked around the car, already beginning to feel faint. Bodhi's audible soundtrack was getting louder and more intense the closer I inched. Once his convulsing frame was in sight, the queasiness attacked from all angles. And even though I tried to hold it back, my stomach proved to be a cowardly bastard.

In a most unladylike fashion, I let loose a series of loud retching burps. So obnoxious were the gagging sounds exploding from my esophagus, Bodhi had to interrupt his own puke party to interact with me.

"Go," he said, frantically waving me off. Apparently he didn't require any of my generous assistance. I choked and heaved my way back to the driver's seat. The second I was out of his earshot, the gagging subsided, my heated skin cooled, and embarrassment set in.

A couple minutes passed before the passenger door opened. Weak from his ordeal, Bodhi leaned in, one brow raised in my direction. What could I say to put a fun-loving spin on my escapades?

"I have no excuse," I blurted.

I often found full disclosure to be the best way to combat gaping disbelief.

Bodhi grinned. "Well, okay then."

I sighed. "The sights and sounds of vomiting trigger a gag reflex in me. It's kind of, you know, like a medical condition."

"Huh, wow, a medical condition even. That's wild, Breeze."

That face. He was mocking me. We exchanged amused glances. Dang, he was a cutie.

"You must be fun at parties," he said.

I laughed. "Surprisingly, I'm rarely invited to parties. I can never figure out why."

"It's a goddamn mystery."

Despite the fact that he was being adorably interactive, Bodhi still sported a sickly pale shade and I watched him wobble like a newborn colt taking his first steps.

"Dude, you need to sit down. I'm pretty sure you puked out last week's breakfast."

"I'm fine," he insisted. "I can probably drive now."

"Um, no."

"What do you mean 'no'? This is my car... sort of."

"What do you mean by 'sort of'?"

"Well, I might have *sort of* stolen the car." He was so matter-of-fact in his statement that I almost applauded his cool.

"So, here's the deal, Bodhi. There's no gray area when it comes to stolen vehicles. Either you have permission to drive them or you don't."

"I don't."

"You don't." Grimacing, I retracted my hands from the steering wheel like it was a hot potato. "Wonderful. I hope the owner has insurance."

"It's the nanny's. But I'm sure there's insurance. And anyway, without me, the nanny's Range Rover would be very dead."

"Wait, you have a nanny?" I asked. "That's...unexpected."

"Not *my* nanny. Jesus. How old do you think I am—ten?"

Pressing my lips together, I bit back a smile. "I was more insinuating you had kids of your own, not that you were the kid yourself."

"Oh." He laughed. "Sorry. Okay. Totally misinterpreted that. I'm used to people thinking I'm a teenager so I just... never mind. Okay, that was embarrassing. Anyway, no kids. The nanny's car belonged to the house I was staying at. I stole it to stay alive."

"Well then, I think you'll be forgiven."

It was clear Bodhi had been closer to the flames than me and, although I was more than curious what happened to him higher up on the hill, I instinctively understood he wasn't ready to talk about his trials with me, or anyone, just yet.

Misunderstanding my silence, Bodhi took it as ambivalence.

"Look, if you don't feel comfortable driving this car, I'll take over."

"Nah. What'll they do, sue me? I don't have anything to take anyway."

"That's the spirit."

We laughed together as he lowered himself back into the passenger seat. "It's just as well that you drive because, not only is this not my car, but I was driving without a license too."

"Of course you were."

"Again, not really by choice. My driver's license and my phone are both currently burnt to a crisp."

I eyed him with interest. "You've had quite the night."

"You have no idea."

The amusement faded at his solemn admission. I sought him out in the ambient lighting and, when our eyes met, an understanding passed between us. Choices had to be made tonight that neither one of us wanted to make but we'd survived and were stronger for it. Maybe I didn't know the extent of his ordeal, but I had an inkling of the terror. I touched the knot on my forehead. Yes, I could sympathize.

Bodhi set aside his own raw memories to attend to mine. "That looks painful. How'd you get it?"

"I collided with a retaining wall. Totaled my car."

"Shit."

"That's why I was running down the street in the first place. Lucky you."

"Yes," he said, his eyes fixed on mine. "It was lucky for me."

"How do you figure? I nearly got you killed."

"I almost died, with or without your help. It felt like the apocalypse up there... like I was the last human alive in a wasteland. When I saw you, I can't begin to describe the relief I felt just knowing I wasn't the only one left standing."

In the strangest way, I understood his reasoning. I'd never felt so alone as I made my way down that deserted street. Nothing about what we'd survived was within the norms of reality.

"And," I perked up, appreciating his viewpoint. "You wouldn't have had my valuable assistance while you were puking."

"Yes." Bodhi chuckled. "The worst help I've ever received."

I pulled out into the pile up of cars, and as we crept down the hill an easy camaraderie formed. Now that I understood he didn't blame me for putting him in harm's way, I was able to relax.

Bodhi pointed to the Gatorade bottle sitting in the center console. "Do you mind if I have a drink? My throat feels like I swallowed sawdust."

I winced, not wanting to reveal the truth about the silent passenger traveling in the adjustable cup holder. "It's not Gatorade."

"It's not?"

I shook my head. "It's Winston."

"What?" His forehead creased as he examined the bottle.

"Winston is a goldfish."

"A goldfish?" His voice was tinged in disbelief. "We saved a goldfish?"

I shrugged. There was nothing I could say to defend myself.

"I mean, I accepted the rats... and the bag with claws. Hell, I even get why you saved the yappy little shit in the backseat, but *a goldfish*?"

I held out my hands and shrugged again.

Bodhi didn't appear the least bit bothered by my admission. In fact, he seemed mildly amused if the lazy smile were any indication. Maybe he'd already learned to accept my peculiarities. I found it was easier that way, just dump all my weirdness on the floor and get it out of the way.

I watched as Bodhi opened compartments.

"What exactly are you looking for?"

"Something to drink that doesn't have a fish swimming in it. You don't by chance have a water bottle in the cat bag, do you?"

"No, just the cat."

"See, earlier today if someone were to say that to me I'd think it was weird but now, animals in bottles and bags seem entirely reasonable." Bodhi eased back in his seat, giving up the quest for liquid. "So, is your name really Breeze?"

"Breeze Marigold Cassidy."

"Jesus."

"Yep," I nodded my agreement. "Hippie parents. It could have been worse; their second choice was Lotus Windsong Cassidy. My mother thinks unique names make unique people."

"Well, she might be onto something because I've never met anyone like you."

There was no mistaking the inflection in his voice. He'd meant that as a compliment and my skin flushed accordingly. He had a mesmerizing effect on me. I felt like a schoolgirl sitting next to her crush.

"Nah," I waved off the compliment for some self-deprecating fun. "I would've been just as weird if they'd named me Lauren."

"I didn't say weird, I said unique. There's a difference."

"A very slight one but, yes, thank you for that."

He smiled, eyes twinkling in the dimming light. "Believe what you will but I like your name. It suits you."

More heat crawled up my neck. "Thank you."

Get it together, Breeze.

"Is Bodhi your real name?"

He seemed genuinely rattled by my question. "Why would you ask me that?"

"I don't know," I hesitated, sparing him a glance. "I thought maybe it was a stage name or something."

After a moment of silence, he replied, "No, it's just... sorry. Bodhi's my real name, yeah."

Whoa, what the hell was that? His adverse reaction to such a seemingly innocent question intrigued me. What was up with this guy and why couldn't I shake the feeling that there was more to him than met the eye?

Trying to stay as cool and unaffected as possible, I asked, "So, where to?"

He shrugged. "I'm currently homeless with no phone, no wallet, and no clothes."

I nodded before delivering what I hoped was a witty zinger. "So, I should drop you off at the pier then?"

9

BODHI: TASTE OF FREEDOM

Breeze Marigold Cassidy pulled up to a plain-looking one-story home and parked on the street. But instead of getting out of the car and heading inside, I watched her case the place with the efficiency of a burglar.

An uneasy feeling settled in the pit of my stomach. What the hell was she doing? What the hell was *I* doing? I should have known better than to trust a total stranger. I knew nothing about her and still I'd accepted her offer to stay at her place for the night. Chances were she'd tipped off the media and in a matter of seconds I'd have a barrage of cameras flashing in my face. How much would she make by selling me out? Dammit. Even after everything I'd been through tonight, sleeping under the pier sounded preferable to this crap.

Lips pressed in a tight line, I shook my head and contemplated the best way to get out of this mess. I wasn't pissed at her as much as I was irritated at myself. I knew better than to let my guard down. How many times did I have to pay the price before I finally got it through my dense skull that putting blind faith in strangers never turned out well? If Breeze's behavior was any indication, I had at least one more lesson to learn.

When she'd brought up the idea of bringing me home, I'd been in no position to decline. Actually, no, that wasn't true. I easily could have refused her offer. One call, and I'd have my choice of any five-star luxury hotel. But being alone in some sterile, impersonal space was the last thing I'd wanted. Even if my father arrived to keep me company, he'd never be able to fully appreciate the sheer horror of what I'd survived. But Breeze would.

I was in this situation now because I didn't want just any company—I wanted *her* company— the woman I'd survived hell with. Breeze got it. She'd lived the nightmare right alongside me. Years from now, when I retold the events of tonight, she would always be part of the narrative.

Suddenly I felt bad for my lack of faith in her. It's not like she'd had time to network and sell me out. And if I thought about this logically and not with my typical blustery arrogance, I'd realize there was nothing staged about our meeting. Nothing planned or predicted. Everything that had happened to us tonight had been the result of pure happenstance.

If I couldn't trust a person thrust into the path of my oncoming vehicle, then I had bigger problems than I thought. I'd always lived by the 'trust no one' motto but things were different now. *I* was different. Running through that burning house, struggling for every breath, a horrifying thought had popped into my mind: no one would miss me when I was gone. Sure, millions of fans would mourn my death, but none of them knew the real me. And they'd move on as soon as a new teen idol was crowned.

No one would truly mourn my passing. No one I loved anyway. And the reason was, I didn't really love anyone back. My life was bleak. There was no light. No connection. No passion. As horrible as tonight was, I'd been given the gift of foresight. Life was too short to be lived in the dark.

With that in mind, I was dedicating myself to a whole new beginning. A whole new me. Instead of being the same old Bodhi Beckett I'd always been, I was going to try something new. Be someone different. And lucky for me, I just happened to have a whole other identity—one I hadn't known about until three months ago. Today wouldn't so much be the death of my old self, but the rebirth of the person I was born to be— Alexander Easton. Son of Marni Easton, and god knows who else.

"Problem?" I asked, setting aside my reservation.

"A small one but I think we're good."

"What are you looking for?"

"My landlady. She's... how do I put this... *special*."

"Like 'good' special or 'what the fuck' special?"

"Well, she hates men, pets, and broccoli."

I had to smile at that. Breeze was all kinds of quirky. Most of the people I knew wouldn't run into a burning building to save their own mothers, and here she was shoving cats into duffle bags. Maybe this was what I'd been missing—the spontaneity that was life. The messy. The unpredictable. Like the wind.

Trying to calculate my odds with the veggie-hating shrew, I asked, "In that order?"

Breeze raised a brow, studying me in amusement. "Well, that's an interesting question, Bodhi. I mean I don't think it really matters in the scheme of things. My bet is she hates the thought of you, in *any* old order."

"Yeah but what you're not factoring in is my way with women. I'm fairly confident I can whittle her list of hates down to two."

She laughed, not the fake 'you're famous so whatever you say is hysterical' giggle. But the more natural 'I find you oddly humorous' chuckle. I had to say, I preferred the latter. Although, to be fair, the fake laugh hadn't bothered me until I heard Breeze's genuinely awesome one.

"Okay Romeo," She humored me. "I'd love to see you try."

Maybe it was the way we met, but I wasn't getting the fangirl vibe from Breeze at all. She obviously knew who I was given the fact she'd used my name well before we'd been formally introduced, but either she didn't care about my celebrity or the blow she'd taken to the head had altered her reaction time.

Whatever it was, I couldn't help but be impressed with the outlook of this girl. Both her disposition and her strength of character. It had been a long time since a person had caught my attention like she had. And, although I couldn't get a full picture of what she looked like under all the blood, sweat, and tears, I could see enough to know she was, at the very least, an attractive girl. Lively deep blue eyes outlined in long, fluttery black lashes accented her pretty oval face. Were those lashes real or fake? I couldn't tell, but they complimented the rest of her perfectly. Breeze was small framed and trim, yet had the body of a woman who still enjoyed the food on her plate.

Coming from an environment of required perfection, where starving yourself was the norm, it was refreshing to see a person comfortable in the skin she was wearing. Breeze was the real deal, the type of woman I wouldn't typically meet but one I couldn't seem to look away from.

"Oh, and did I mention my landlady looks like a grizzly bear and carries an arsenal of weapons specifically for your type of charming?"

Suddenly wooing the armed property-owner wasn't the fun challenge I'd expected it to be. My face must have betrayed me because Breeze looked me up and down in amusement before saying, "Clearly you aren't as confident in your wooing skills as you proclaim."

"That's not it at all, I'm just recalculating my approach."

"Uh huh. Anyway, I'm not so much worried about you as I

am the pets. They don't have your special swagger to protect them."

"This is true. So are we all just going to parade through her house and hope for the best?"

"We're not going through her place. I live in the granny flat out back."

"Well, then what's the problem?"

"I just didn't want us to become target practice, is all. Maybe I'm just being paranoid but, you know, her house is dark so she's probably asleep."

"Or... and I'm just throwing out a wild theory here... don't you think it's possible her house might be dark because the electricity's out in the entire city?"

"Crap! The full moon's so bright I forgot the damn power was out. Okay, that puts a slight wrench in things. We just need to be exceptionally quiet. Can you do that?"

"Well, I don't know, Breeze. I can try."

She laughed like I was some top-rated comedian. I liked that. And yeah, I could be quiet, but I had my doubts about yappy-pants in the backseat. Anything short of using actual chloroform didn't seem worth the effort. But Breeze was out the door before I could voice my concerns, kicking her foot all around the back trunk area while reciting a variety of different spells to make it open.

"Abracadabra. Wingardium Leviosa. Expelliarmus."

I hopped out and hurried to her side, eager to watch the show. "Come on," I said. "Everyone knows all the Expelliarmus spell does is disarm the opponent. You need to use the unlock charm."

"Oh, I'm sorry." She rolled her eyes. "I should have brushed up on Harry Potter before driving a frickin' Range Rover."

I shoved her aside playfully. "Let me show you how it's done. Alohomora!"

I waved my leg and the trunk's cover began to rise.

Breeze shook her head. "You shouldn't need a college degree to drive one of these things."

"I don't have one."

"Yeah, but you're rich."

"So?" I laughed. "What does that have to do with anything?"

"You're used to fancy things that make no sense. I mean, what's with the curtains that open and shut at the push of a button? You know how I do it? I walk over and manually pull them open. Voilà!"

"Sure, you could do it that way, but technology's the shit. Why wouldn't you want to use it?"

"It's not that I don't appreciate electronics. I'm just saying what's the point of push button curtains when it's quicker and easier to do it yourself?"

"They're remote controlled."

"What are?"

"The curtains, they're remote controlled and set on timers so no button pushing. Some are even dusk to dawn regulated."

Breeze stood there with her hands on her hips as I went on and on about curtains. Once I came up for a breath, she asked, "Are you finished now?"

"I... yeah, sure."

"Good." Breeze tucked a strand of hair behind her ear. Was it pink? I couldn't tell under all the fire debris. Then giving one last glance in the direction of the main house, she lowered her voice and said, "I'm going to have you carry Brangelina and I'll tackle Sweetpea."

What was she talking about? I wracked my brain trying to recall any previous mention of the former Hollywood power couple. I had nothing. Taking pity on me, Breeze filled in the blanks, as if it were a conversation we'd already had many times over.

"The rats? Brad and Angelina?"

No, that definitely wasn't communicated to me at any time during our miraculous escape or even during this special black ops mission. I considered arguing the point but decided it wasn't worth a comment or complaint since I'd be carrying the rats regardless. As I hoisted the cage into my arms, the celebrity rats scattered, sending dust and wood chips flying.

"Hey, Breeze?" I whispered.

"Yes?"

"This might be a good time to tell you I'm not a fan of rodents."

"That's not what I saw on TMZ. You seemed quite chummy with a squirrel last week." She blitzed me with a sly sideways glance.

"You saw that?"

"I did."

"And what about the full moon at the convenience store?"

She nodded. "That too."

"GI Joe?"

"Yep."

"Well, shit." I shook my head, smiling. "Stalker."

"No, I'm under thirty... and human. I think I can confidently say I've seen pretty much all of you now, Bodhi."

"Not everything," I answered with an arched brow. If she was going there, so was I.

Breeze laughed. "The night's not over yet."

And even though she was clearly kidding, my ears perked up anyway. Now, I was feeling way better about my decision to crash land at Breeze's place. Even if it meant tiptoeing my way through the backyard of the gun-toting enemy of the vegetable world.

Hercules ran up ahead and, assuming he knew where he was going, I took my rats and followed him.

"Wrong way, dork." Breeze giggled as she sped-walked in front of me cradling something bulky under her shirt. "Follow me, not the dog. He's never been here before."

I got a better look at her pregnant belly and it was wiggling. "Tell me that's not the Chihuahua," I said.

"Well, it's not the Saint Bernard."

In response to my questioning stare, Breeze elaborated. "He's afraid of the dark. I thought it would keep him from barking. It seemed like a good idea at the time."

"Huh, okay. And you're not afraid of disembowelment?"

"I wasn't until you mentioned it," she said, a tapestry of emotion passing over her quickly crumbling face. "Although now I'm worrying about disembowelment *AND* a double mastectomy so thank you very much."

Breeze didn't let the possibility of disfigurement get her down. In fact, she was even more determined to get us all to her place quickly. We'd almost made it too when the back door to the main house opened and, lit up by a 1950's lantern, the female version of the Brawny paper towel man stepped out on the stoop.

Breeze panicked, shoving both the rats and me into the shrubs. I toppled onto the cage, it's interwoven metal lattice sturdy enough to prevent me from diving head first into Brangelina's love den.

"Jesus H. Fuck, Breeze," I complained, pushing back the branch poking me squarely in the ass.

"Shhh, quiet," she said, using her pregnant dog belly to shield us from harm.

"Breeze, is that you?" A deep female voice called out.

"Yes, Pat, just me."

Then, under her breath, she whispered, "And everything you hate, including a carload of pets and a half naked man."

"I think we can all take solace in the fact Breeze didn't save the broccoli," I added quietly.

Breeze struggled to suppress a giggle as she reached behind the bush to smack me. "Shhh."

"What's going on out there?" the suspicious woman asked as she attempted to get her lantern light to shine in our direction.

"I wouldn't come out here, Pat. There's a huge fire up on the hill. So far we're safe in this part of town, but there's a ton of smoke and ash coming our way. It's super unhealthy. I need to get inside myself. If I were you I'd close all your doors and windows and even duct tape around any openings to keep the toxins from getting inside."

"Oh, okay. Good idea. Do you want to come in here with me?"

"You're so sweet. But no. I'm okay. I'll see you tomorrow, Pat."

We waited until we heard her door shut before Breeze helped pull me out of the bushes.

"You know," I said, righting myself. "Being a celebrity and all, I'm kind of an expert at ducking and hiding. I could've gotten the job done without the fucking shove into the shrubbery."

"I know. I'm so sorry. I can't believe I pushed you. I'm a horrible human being." She laughed while delivering her apology, which, in turn, made it sound less genuine. Still, I wasn't holding a grudge. Breeze had proven to be an unpredictable force of nature.

She opened the door to her small cottage and I was nearly knocked over for a second time as Hercules decided he wanted to be the first one over the threshold. Being famous, I was used to a certain protocol when it came to entrances. As in—I was always the first one through any door. But this was Breeze's world, a place where mammals known for licking their own butts had higher priority than me. And after a lifetime of being number one, I was sort of digging this unexpected kick in the nuts.

I followed Breeze into the darkened room.

"Just put the rats down there on the floor," she instructed before pulling the little dog out from under her shirt and shoving him into my hands. "Here, take Sweetpea. I'll go back and get the cat and the fish."

Of course, how could I forget about the cat in a bag and the fish in a bottle? Yesterday, I would have viewed that entire sentence with contempt, but today I smiled at the absurdity of it all. This was as close to an alternate universe as I was ever going to get.

Extending Sweetpea at arms-length as if he were an alien baby with a poopy diaper, I glanced him over, unsure what Breeze wanted me to do with the little killer. I didn't plan on holding him indefinitely while she went on a scavenger hunt for the cat and the fish.

The dog wiggled wildly in my hands, twisting his head like a possessed gremlin before employing his razor-sharp teeth to break free. I yelped as he made contact, dropping the vindictive pup into the kitchen sink. As he bared his teeth, growling viciously, I grabbed for the only weapon I could find to defend myself—a pink spatula—and I waved it around in a display of manliness I was glad no one was around to witness.

"Stay back," I warned, ready to either swat him silly or smear frosting over his elfin body.

As Breeze slipped through the front door, Hercules ran over to her, clearly ratting me out for dropping his nippy brother into the sink.

"Dude," I complained to the giant backstabber. I thought we were better friends than that but apparently not.

Breeze came straight for me and grabbed the pathetic

weapon from my hand. Clearly she was one of those types who didn't believe in corporal punishment.

"What part of 'remain quiet' did you not comprehend?" she asked, grabbing Sweetpea from the sink. "I could hear you squealing from the car."

"First of all, I don't squeal. And secondly, he bit me."

"Yes. He bites people on a minute-by-minute basis. Ouch, see. He just bit me too. Big deal. Bee stings hurt worse."

"That's not a selling point, Breeze. Maybe you haven't been stung recently but that shit lingers."

With the hint of a grin she said, "If you're afraid of a four-pound dog, go stand with Hercules. He'll protect you."

"I'm not scared," I grumbled, even as I took a step closer to the big dog.

Breeze securely locked the door before setting the duffle bag onto the bed and producing one very unhappy cat from the canvas depth.

"I'm so sorry," she soothed, petting the cat behind the ears. "I know you probably hate me right now, but I'll make it up to you, I promise."

"I think it's enough that you saved her life," I chimed in.

"I know that. And you know that. But Lucy here doesn't know that. As far as she's concerned I shoved her into a bag just for the fun of it. If I don't do a little groveling, our little feline friend here is going to pee on every square inch of my apartment."

"Fantastic," I grumbled under my breath.

Tears flooded her eyes, spilling onto her cheeks, and she hastily wiped them away. "Sorry. I'm a little emotional when it comes to these animals. I thought I was going to have to leave them for dead tonight."

Her hands shook as she related the story to me. Why she'd

initially chosen to put the safety of those animals over her own was a mystery, but it was clear Breeze operated in a whole other mind-set. It wasn't until I watched the cat, after being crammed in a bag all night, stretch up and touch noses with Breeze that I understood the power of compassion. The cat had forgiven her, not because Breeze had thrown money or resources at the problem, but because she'd proven her worth with nothing more than a kindness.

Breeze caught me staring and shifted uncomfortably. She probably thought I was judging her, when in reality I was judging myself. Maybe if a nurturing, sympathetic hand had been employed in my upbringing, I wouldn't find this whole scene so foreign.

"I'm sorry," I said, feeling every bit the emotional freak I'd just discovered myself to be.

"It's okay. I'm a little emotional, is all," she answered, brushing off the uncomfortable exchange. We were standing close, our faces lit by the phone screen. Suddenly, our eyes met and all reservations fell away. I was inexplicably drawn to her shine, a solar light in the darkness, attracting a convention of moths... me being the biggest one of them all. That positive energy of hers was like a messenger calling me home.

For the first time in my life I knew exactly where I was supposed to be. This meeting of the minds was no accident. Breeze and I had been brought together for a reason, and I was committed to finding out why.

"Anyway," she brightened. "Enough of the 'what ifs'. We're all alive because of you, and that's what needs to be focused on, right?"

I was no superhero. In fact, I'd stopped to help her more for my own sake than hers.

"It really wasn't..." I began humbly denying her assertions, but Breeze had already lost interest, and was off rummaging through drawers in her tiny, dollhouse-sized kitchen.

"I know I have a flashlight in here somewhere," she said, before suddenly pulling one out. "Boo-ya! Check me out! A flashlight *and* a battery powered lantern. It's from Halloween but that's okay, right?"

I shrugged. "I mean during blackouts I prefer Christmas lanterns, but I suppose that one will work."

"Okay, smartass." A smile illuminated her face as she flicked the lantern on. "I think I have just enough charge left on my phone for us to let our families know we're okay. My friend, Mason, has called fourteen times."

I thought about my own family, my dad and the guys, and how they probably had no idea what had happened on that ocean view hilltop. In fact, it might take days for the word to reach them since none of us were the types to keep up with the happenings of the world. That's when it hit me. They didn't know. In exchange for my near-death experience, I'd been handed a 'get out of jail free' card. I could go anywhere, be anyone, even go in search of long-lost relatives without the fear of being tracked down by my father's cronies. But in order for that to happen, no one could know where I was. At least for a couple of days.

"Breeze, before you call... would you mind not mentioning me, at least by name?"

She seemed confused by my request, so I was forced to elaborate.

"I just don't want the press to know where I am. They'll have cameras poking through the windows in no time."

"Oh, yeah. Sure. I won't say anything."

And she didn't. I listened to Breeze calm her family while ensuring them she was fine. She mentioned me in passing as a man who stopped to help, but never dropped my name like some less principled people might have done. When she'd finished her phone calls, she passed the device onto me.

"Here, your turn."

"Thanks," I said, in no need for her phone but not willing to share with her the reason why. I stood there staring at the screen.

"Oh, crap. Sorry. You probably want some privacy. I need to take a shower anyway."

Once Breeze left for the bathroom, taking the majority of light with her, I was suddenly alone... with my guilty conscience. I wavered on whether what I was doing was right, and if keeping my father out of the loop constituted cruel and unusual punishment. It wasn't like he was going to find out about the fires tonight anyway. I'd just be waking him up and needlessly worrying him. Although, that's what he'd want me to do... what I should do. But that was the problem. My whole life I'd always done what was required of me regardless of whether I'd wanted to or not. Being selfish was never an option.

Until now.

I wasn't doing this to make my father suffer, and certainly I didn't want him to think I was dead. But as with all difficult decisions, sometimes there was collateral damage. I'd been on the receiving end of Tucker's poor decision-making skills more times than I could count, so if I needed to carve out some time to myself, I would do it without guilt.

The decision made, I sank to the floor, my back propped against the wall. While I would have preferred the sofa, I didn't want the toxins clinging to my body to be transferred onto Breeze's couch. Looking around her place, I tried to get a sense of who she was but, aside from the outlines of furniture highlighted by the beam of the flashlight, Breeze remained a mystery.

A rustling sound caught my attention and I turned in time to lock eyes with the Chihuahua.

"Hey you, have you come to finish me off?" I asked before noticing a change in the small dog. He was worn to the bone. I could only imagine the fatigue that came with barking – *all fucking night*. And even though I wasn't a member of Little Dick's fan club, certainly I could sympathize with another living thing in need.

"Come here," I offered, patting my leg. To my surprise, Sweetpea jumped up and settled onto my lap. The pup had given me his trust and, I'm not going to lie, I'd never felt so worthy. He blinked at me a few times, his eyes heavy with sleep before he laid his head down and accepted me for what I was, a safe place to slumber.

Running my hands over his coarse fur, it occurred to me that comforting the dog had the same soothing effect on me. My body relaxed and a strange lightness filled me to the brim. Growing up, pets were not allowed, so I'd never understood what all the fuss was about... until now. Were they the calming force that kept people sane? No wonder dog walkers always seemed so damn cheerful. I needed to get myself one of these.

"You know what, Little Dick?" I whispered. "You aren't half bad after all."

10

BREEZE: TEAM EDWARD

I SLIPPED INTO THE BATHROOM, BURSTING WITH EXCITEMENT. Bodhi Beckett was here, in my cottage, *one wall away*, and somehow I had to pretend it didn't matter.

I'd never been good at acting. I was the kid in the school play who ended up in the back row dressed like a tree. And now I had to keep Bodhi's existence in my kitchen under wraps.

Pushing aside the intrigue, I held the light up to the mirror, illuminating my face so I could examine the knot on my forehead. The bump was tender to the touch, sporting a little heartbeat of its own. I could only imagine the color scheme I'd be working with in the morning. Although I'd planned on applying a little makeup to the area after my shower, it was clear that nothing short of spackle would do.

Not that it mattered, since first impressions had already been formed. If my whole damsel in distress bit hadn't been enough to electrify Bodhi, I was pretty sure the horn in the middle of my forehead would do the trick.

But who was I kidding? Bodhi hadn't accepted my offer to spend the night because he was eager to bang a mythical creature. He just needed a place to lay his weary head.

Sighing, I quit worrying about my appearance and turned toward the shower. Just as I was about to undress, the world swam out of focus, and a sharp pain lanced through my chest. A tremble shook my legs and spread like a tiny earthquake. Swallowing hard, I gripped the sink, gasping for air.

You're going to die.

Random thoughts flickered. My mom and Terrance. Mason.

Help me.

A scream exploded in my head—*mine*. And then the pounding—thump thump thump—and Bodhi's voice.

"Breeze?" More pounding. "Breeze! What's wrong? Are you okay?"

"I just... I c-can't breathe. I-I'm freaking out."

"Open the door."

I would if I could, but my feet were glued in place. Oh, god, was I paralyzed? "I-I can't."

A muffled curse, and then Bodhi's voice again. Calm. Reassuring. "Listen to me. You're probably having a panic attack. I can help you."

Yes, help me.

"O-okay."

"All right. Cup your hands over your mouth and take a deep breath. Hold it a second, then slowly let it out. Do it now."

Dutifully, I followed his directions. Once. Twice. Five times. Slowly but surely, the panic receded, the fog lifting by degrees. When the feeling came back in my legs, I stumbled to the toilet, closed the lid, and sank onto the unyielding plastic.

"Talk to me, Breeze."

But I couldn't. Words failed me.

Minutes passed and I wasn't sure if Bodhi was still with me until I heard his voice floating in from the other side of the door. Soft and melodic. He was singing. To me. Not some pop melody or top 100 hit. This was a lullaby. Closing my eyes, I let the words soothe me.

> *When you feel afraid*
> *When you lose your way*
> *I'll find you*
> *Just try to smile*
> *And dry your eyes*
> *I will bring back the moon*
> *Into your skies*

When he finished, I found the strength to wobble to my feet. And when I opened the door, Bodhi was there, sitting on the floor, his back pressed against the wood. Slanting his gaze to mine, he smiled.

"Hey," he said quietly as he climbed to his feet. "You okay?"

I didn't say a word, just walked into his arms and buried my face in the bronzed hallows of his neck. Had I given my actions more thought... or any thought at all, I probably wouldn't have forced my affection on him. But tonight was one of firsts, and I figured why stop at a panic attack when I could go for broke and cross the 'no touching the celebrity' rule.

Bodhi's arms banded around my waist, and he began to rock me.

"What was that song?" I whispered.

He was silent for so long I wondered if maybe he hadn't heard me. Lifting my gaze, I searched his eyes for an answer, but found only pain.

"Did I say something wrong?" I asked, appalled at my misstep even though I still wasn't sure what it had been.

"No. It wasn't you. I don't even know where that came from. You were scared and I wasn't thinking."

"The song helped me. It was nice, soothing... like a lullaby."

He nodded, his eyes far away as if lost in a memory. "When I was young someone close to me used to sing it when I was afraid. It's been so many years. I can't believe I even remembered it."

From his tone and the awkward tilt of his body, it was clear —this person was no longer in his life. Suddenly, I wished I'd paid more attention to him in the media. It might have helped me piece together the puzzle.

"Well, it must be the magic cure because it helped me recover. I honestly don't know what happened to me. One minute I was fine and the next, it felt like I was dying."

"Definitely sounds like a panic attack."

"Maybe. How did you know what to do to stop it?"

"I've had them before—a lot actually." The minute the words left his mouth, I could tell he regretted them. Tilting my chin with his thumb, he gazed down at me with serious eyes. "This is just between us, okay? Please don't share this information with anyone."

Just the fact that he had to ask was proof enough that we lived in separate worlds. No one would give me a passing glance if I admitted to suffering from panic attacks. But for Bodhi, such knowledge had the potential to be broadcast live to an overly eager audience.

"You can trust me," I said, wondering how many times he'd heard that hollow promise in his lifetime.

Bodhi held my gaze for a moment before finding whatever assurance he needed in order to continue. "When I was a kid I was pushed into things I wasn't comfortable with and panic attacks became my way of dealing with stressful situations. It was terrifying. My heart would race, my chest would constrict, and I felt like I couldn't catch my breath. All the symptoms you were describing to me."

His admission opened up so many more questions. I

wondered if he'd had someone to help him through the fear? I didn't think so.

Emboldened by his faith in me, I gently cupped his cheek. "Thank you for helping me through it."

Bodhi's expression softened as he brushed his thumb over my goose egg. "Maybe you should have that looked at. Does it hurt?"

"I mean it doesn't *not* hurt," I replied. "But I'll live."

He nodded. "We both will."

———

Handing the towel to Bodhi, I pointed him in the direction of the shower, but he remained rooted in place, conflicted. Was it just me, or was tonight's shower time particularly fraught with complications?

"Everything okay?"

"Sure." Bodhi grinned. "I was just wondering how you felt about nudity."

I stopped towel drying my hair and cast him a questioning glance. "I mean I'm not one hundred percent opposed. Why?"

"I don't have any clothes to change into."

"Oh." I let out a relieved breath. As dreamy as he was, I wasn't quite ready for dangling bits. "No worries. I've got you covered."

"Really?" He perked right up. "I just assumed by the looks of the dollhouse you live in, you didn't have any men's clothing laying around."

"Oh, that's what you wanted? Yeah, I haven't had men's clothes in an apartment of mine since I gathered up all my ex-fiancée's clothing and donated them to the homeless shelter."

"And when you say donate, did you have permission to give his shit away?"

"Technically, no."

"But un-technically, you had his permission?"

"Um, no. Not that way either. Let's just say he wasn't thrilled to find Dumpster Donnie wearing his leather jacket."

His mouth curved wryly. "I hope your ex deserved it."

"Oh, he deserved it, all right. My only regret was not getting my hands on the pieces of his wardrobe that had already been relocated to his lover's place."

Bodhi winced. "Ouch."

"Yeah."

"And he was your fiancée?"

"Yes, and she was my cousin."

He choked out a laugh before our eyes met and the smile faded from his face. "Wait, are you serious?"

"Unfortunately, yes. It was quite the scandal. But, you know, it was a long time ago and I'm over it. Let's go find you some clothes."

An awkward silence settled between us. Maybe he was trying to come up with an appropriate response but I wasn't looking for sympathy. That was an emotion I'd tired of long ago.

Rummaging through my dresser, I tossed t-shirts at him, but he vetoed every one of my choices. Either they were too small, too pink, or too form fitting. Finally I found a grey regular cut t-shirt in a size large and flung it over to him.

"This is it, Bud. Take it or leave it."

He held it up, grimacing when the beam from the flashlight revealed the slogan on the front. Team Edward. "Oh my god."

"What?" I asked, feigning innocence. "I got it on opening night."

"And you didn't pick a Team Jacob shirt? What's wrong with you? Werewolves beat vampires any day of the week."

I held my hand up to stop the blasphemy. "No. Just stop. Team Edward is where it's at. End of story."

Bodhi sighed before wadding up the t-shirt and tucking it under his arm. "I'm not going to like these sweatpants you speak of, am I?"

"Probably not."

After considerable effort, I found a pair of sweatpants in a larger size and walked them over to him.

He didn't even wait for the spotlight before he complained, "These are yoga leggings, not sweatpants."

"Same thing."

"No, so incredibly *not* the same thing."

Grinning mischievously, I shoved a pair of flowered panties into his hand. "For you."

Bodhi barked out a laugh and tossed them back in my face before disappearing into the bathroom with his Team Edward t-shirt and a very flattering pair of butt enhancing yoga pants.

"So, is that a 'no' on the panties?" I called out.

Silence was the only response.

————

Bodhi emerged from the shower a new man. Not only did he appear relieved to have the ash and soot gone, but the decontamination proceedings had given him a surprisingly cheery disposition. Instead of sulking about in his unflattering post-catastrophe outfit, Bodhi fully embraced it, modeling his new body positive wardrobe on the makeshift catwalk he'd created smack dab in the middle of my tiny living space. Careful to keep my voice to acceptable landlady-levels, I whisper-hooted my approval as he whirled around in his skin-tight sweatpants.

"Universe," I lifted my arms to the heavens. "Hold me back."

You would have thought he was swinging from a stripper pole the way I was carrying on. If I'd had cash readily available, it would have already been tucked inside his waistband.

After the show, Bodhi collapsed onto a kitchen chair, a wide smile splashed across his face.

"You seem to be feeling better," I said, fanning myself for effect.

"I could say the same about you."

"Me? No. I always perk up when hot guys strut their stuff in my living room wearing Twilight memorabilia."

"How often does that happen?"

"You know, not as often as I'd like."

We smiled, a comfortable camaraderie settling between us.

"Damn, I feel good." Bodhi slapped his hand on the table. "Like I can take on the world."

"Don't you take on the world on a daily basis?"

"I wish."

"You're a pop star. I hardly think you lead a boring life."

"I didn't say it was a boring life, just highly structured and hectic as hell. It just feels good to have nothing to do... nothing to worry about. I'm free."

I studied him a moment, not sure what he meant by 'free', but it certainly seemed a weight had been lifted from his shoulders. I wondered what the burdens of a person who lived a sun-kissed life with money, talent, and unlimited women at his fingertips looked like.

"So, this free world you speak of... do you mean free as in 'liberty and justice for all'?"

"No, free as in 'I almost died so now I'm really going to live.'"

"Until the sun comes up and life goes back to normal," I said, not realizing how pessimistic I sounded until Bodhi's sails deflated. Deep in thought, he traced lines on the kitchen table with his finger.

I touched the moving muscles in the back of his hand, surprised by the quiver that sizzled up my spine. "Hey, I'm sorry."

"I get where you're coming from, I do, but here's the thing, Breeze. I don't want things to go back to normal. I'm done doing the same old shit. Why can't we just be whoever we want to be?"

He could. There was nothing holding him back. Bodhi was an adult with loads of cash to make any dream a reality.

"I already am who I want to be," I answered honestly.

Bodhi stared at me like I was some rare white tiger. "Really? You're happy with your life?"

"Yes. I mean of course I hope there are surprises along the way, but overall, I'm happy. Why? You're not?"

Pondering, his brows drew together. "I don't hate my life, if that's what you mean. I'm lucky to have experienced everything I have. But in the process, I think I've sort of lost myself. Tonight was a wake-up call for me. If I don't take control now, I never will. So, no I'm not going back to normal... not until I've tasted a little bit of freedom anyway."

Oh damn! Where did I sign up to be included in his liberation? Somehow I just knew it would be epic. "Damn Bodhi, you were only in the shower for ten minutes."

"I know." He shrugged. "I think fast."

"Okay then. If you had unlimited freedom and no time or money restraints to hold you back, what would you do?"

"You mean like a bucket list?" Even as the question left his lips, he appeared to be giving it serious thought.

"Yes. For example, someday I want to rent a motorhome and drive across the states, visiting all the famous road trip attractions, like the world's largest fork or the 30-foot long corndog."

"Wh... wow, okay. That doesn't sound fun at all - but good for you."

I smiled at his diss. "Hey, you asked what was on my bucket list and that's it. So tell me, Popstar, what could you possibly desire?"

"I want to go camping."

"Camping?" I gawked at my handsome companion. "That doesn't require time or money... hell, you could even get by without toilet paper for that one. I thought bucket list items were big, grand dreams fulfilled."

He raised a brow at me. "And a 30-foot long corndog is a grand dream?"

I shrugged.

Appearing reflective, Bodhi admitted. "Every day for me is big and grand. I want to experience the small stuff."

"Like?"

"I don't know. I've been working my whole life, so sometimes I feel like I missed out on being a kid. I've never run through a sprinkler or flown a kite or even been on a swing. That's what I want... the simple things in life."

My smile wilted as I stared into Bodhi's pretty eyes. While I was looking ahead to a future I hoped would come, Bodhi was looking behind at a past that never was.

Suddenly this guy who appeared to have everything might possibly be the least privileged of us all.

"What about your parents? They never did those things with you?"

Shifting in his seat, Bodhi looked away. "I never had a mom."

Pain shrouded his features. And longing. This was the wound he carried, the one I'd sensed earlier and had wanted to heal. Had she died or was she merely out the picture, like my father? In the end, I guess it didn't matter. Gone was gone.

My heartbeat quickened at the thought of helping this guy through his hurt. This right here... this was what I was born for.

Before I got the courage to form a follow-up question his frown deepened.

"And my dad... he wasn't really into giving me a traditional childhood."

"That's..." I was about to throw him some pity but he must've sensed it, because he was out of his chair, digging in my fridge before I could speak the words. Clearly he was as uninterested in my sympathy as I had been in his.

11

BODHI: A MATCHING PAIR

SHIT. WHAT HAD I BEEN THINKING, SHARING MY FAMILY DYNAMICS with Breeze? For as long as I could remember, the subject of my mother was off the table, in both my private and public life. Not only had I never been allowed to question my father about her, but the topic was also off limits to interviewers. I suppose if I were someone more important than a boy band member, reporters might try digging into my past. To be perfectly honest, I'd welcome the intrusion. As a child, any mention of my mother was met with resistance and the same regurgitated story was spewed out for me to chew on. The underlying message had always been that she'd died giving me life, basically strapping me to a burden of guilt I'd carried with me until the day that letter arrived, exonerating me from all blame.

But the twenty-four years before she'd made contact had been fraught with questions. Because my father had made mention of her such a taboo subject, her loss hit me hard. Growing up, I'd not only felt singled out, but also crippled by her absence – which was pointless seeing as plenty of kids grew up without a parent and functioned just fine. Hell, I functioned just fine... until the abandonment of my past crept its way into the present day and I did something stupid like sharing my issues with a person I'd nearly reduced to road kill.

Like my father had drilled into my head a hundred times over, our business was no one else's business. I'd never really understood the significance of his insistence on discretion until just recently. All these years, Tucker Beckett wasn't muzzling me to protect my privacy; he was hiding me... from my mother. No doubt it had to be tricky to lie about something as huge as a dead parent when your kid was a goddamn celebrity. Keeping me from talking ensured she'd never figure out who her son really was. Only somehow she had found me, and now here we were.

Sometimes I wondered how different my life would have been had I not been forced to operate behind a veil of secrecy. Would I have been a more loving person? It didn't take a therapist to point out the survival mechanisms I had in place to hold people at bay. My reluctance to share my life with women in general wasn't just a reaction to my upbringing, but also a form of self-protection. Bad things happened to women I loved. My mother had made the ultimate sacrifice, or so I'd been told. And then there was Beth.

Retrieving her face from my memory bank, I forced myself to remember. She was my live-in nanny, hired by my father to take some of the burden off his shoulders of raising a kid on his own. I was five when she first appeared in my life and nine when she was gone for good. Although my memory of her had faded some over the years, the impact she'd had on me was still felt far and wide. Losing her decimated my young life and left me bleeding in her wake.

Beth had been widowed at twenty-five. Her high school sweetheart and soldier husband died in combat the same year she'd come to live with us. I could still remember the sadness in her eyes and the way she tried to hide it from me by only crying behind closed doors. But I'd always been an intuitive little kid, probably because of the responsibilities placed on my shoulders so young, and I worked hard every day to bring smiles to her face. I like to think I healed her, but maybe that was just the wishful thinking of a child.

Over the years we became as close as any mother and child could be. When my father insisted on work and more work, she fought for fun. When my father turned his back on a comforting hug, Beth was always there with open arms, and when I went in search of answers to the mystery of my dead mother, Beth was the one who came through.

But the closer Beth and I got, the more fractured her relationship with my father became. He routinely accused her of trying to undermine his authority and threatened to fire her. I just never thought he'd actually do it - until suddenly she was gone.

While watching her pack for the 'vacation' she never came back from, Beth presented me with two gifts. They would both become my most prized possessions. The first was a photograph she slipped into my hand of a woman she claimed was my mother. She'd made me promise to keep it safe and never let my father know of its existence. The second gift she gave me was the guitar I'd learned to play on, a memento belonging to her late husband - the same one I'd carried on my back to safety a few hours earlier when the world was crumbling around me.

Glancing over at Breeze from the protection of the refrigerator, the Halloween lantern creating a halo effect around her, I studied the look on her face. Yes, there was pity, but what struck me was she didn't seem surprised by my drama. And how could I blame her? I had, after all, just played right into the stereotype of the broken child star. Breeze was probably calculating in her head how long it would take me to implode. I hated to break it to her, but she'd be waiting a long time. I might be emotionally stunted, but I'd been dealing with this my whole life and I was no shitshow.

Standing with the refrigerator door opened wide, I groaned in displeasure at Breeze's measly offerings.

"What the hell, woman? Were you raided by a raccoon?"

"No, but I was planning on spending the next two weeks at the house in the hills and didn't see any reason to stock the shelves. In hindsight, I should have kept better track of Nostradamus' Doomsday Calendar. Forgive me. Anyway, you're welcome to the condiments."

She wasn't kidding. Ketchup, a tub of butter, and a jar of hamburger pickles were the only edible things in there.

"Shut the fridge to keep the cold in," she complained.

"For what? You have nothing to keep cool."

Still, I did as she asked before heading over to the cupboard in search of even the slightest morsel, yet aside from a few cans and a box of crackers, it was as bare as the refrigerator had been before it.

At this point I wasn't picky, shoving a cracker in my mouth only to rush to the sink to spit it out.

"Good god, Breeze. How old are these things?"

"Not that old. Maybe a couple of months."

"Well, in cracker years, that's like twelve."

Her giggle was nearly irresistible, and I had a sudden urge to smother her neck in kisses just to hear more of it. But I was much too controlled for such a chick flick moment.

Begrudgingly, I slumped back into the seat opposite her. "I should have saved a sous chef."

. . .

After Breeze and I shared a jar of pickles dipped in ketchup, our conversation returned to its earlier track. Thankfully, she was wise enough to keep the dialogue light and far away from the pity party I'd escaped from earlier.

"So, about your bucket list," she began. "If you give me an hour, I can probably help you cross half the items off your list."

Her smile put me instantly at ease. Instead of being embarrassed by my catalogue of preschool desires, I was strangely excited to tackle them. With Breeze. Although I had people to attend to my every need, the things I wanted to do couldn't be attempted with hired help. I needed someone as dedicated to my mission as I was. "Yeah, okay. That would be cool. Thanks."

Sweetpea wandered into the kitchen and stopped at my feet. He blinked up at me and I scooped him up with a confident grin.

Breeze's mouth dropped open and I shrugged. "Little Dick and I came to an understanding. You just need to show him who's boss."

As if on cue, Sweetpea sunk his teeth into my hand. Not deep enough to break skin, but with enough gusto to let me know I was talking out of my ass. Obviously, he was still firmly in charge of our relationship.

"Dude, you're such a slime ball," I whispered shaking loose of his clutches. "You were supposed to be my wingman. Way to make me look bad in front of the lady."

"Impossible," she answered, her liquid eyes meeting mine. I held her gaze as if seeing her for the first time. Breeze was beautiful, and not in that plastic perfection sort of way that I'd come to expect, but in a lived in, comfortable-with-herself style that couldn't be bought. This girl knew who she was and, coming from a guy who was still searching for his identity, it was an attractive quality.

Reaching over, I twirled a lock of her blond hair around my fingertip, examining the pink tips. I smiled because it was distinctive, and edgy, and exactly like the woman herself— a breath of fresh air. My eyes drifted up to meet hers and I was relieved to see amusement there.

"What are you doing, Bodhi Beckett?"

I'd never been the most playful guy, but I was in a mood tonight and nothing was going to squash it.

"Okay so, I'm just going to put it out there. I'm super attracted to you."

Her eyes widened. "Seriously? Wow...so... do you think it has something to do with smoke inhalation or maybe survivor's guilt?"

"No, I don't think so. I'm just... like... into you."

Breeze snagged her bottom lip between her teeth. "Huh, okay. Well that's— shocking."

"Is it?"

Those eyes of hers, so beautiful and expressive, grabbed hold of mine and wouldn't let go. As we stared at one another, she turned my hand over and began tracing lines into my open palm. I was no stranger to foreplay, but it had never felt quite so innocent.... or so blazing hot. I was glad for the table between us because it hid the hardness brewing in my girly yoga pants.

"Where did you come from?" she whispered, her gaze still locked on me.

I wasn't sure how to answer. Three hours ago I didn't know she existed and now I was worried about how much time we had left. How could I have been sucked in so quickly yet not feel in the least bit confined? It was possible I was all worked up after our near-death experience, and this strange throbbing attraction was just a result.

"Wherever led me to you," I replied, trying not to wince at

my own words. I sounded like stage-Bodhi. But that was okay, because Breeze appeared to be swooning.

Still holding my hand, she stood and then pulled me to my feet. I barely managed to catch Sweetpea before he tumbled to the floor.

"Quick with the hands, I see," she quipped as she led me to the bed.

I dropped the mutt on the mattress and then pulled Breeze flush against me, her back to my chest. The minute my lips brushed the exposed skin above her collar, she spun around.

"Wait?" Her palms landed flat on my pecs. "This...I can't do this. I'm so sorry. I'm just all over the place with my emotions right now and as much as I want to be with you, I think it's best to slow it down."

Slow down?

My brows drew together as I tried to remember the last time I'd been brushed off. *Never.* I was the prize. The guy you bedded just to prove you could.

But Breeze was nothing like the women I hooked up with. She lived in the real world, with real life expectations. And standards. The girl was looking for a boyfriend, or at least something more than a one-nighter.

If I wanted her, I had to be on the same page—which I wasn't. A relationship was never part of my master plan. But one look in her soulful eyes, and I couldn't figure out why.

Plastering on a mask of indifference I said, "No problem. I get it. Plus, Little Dick and I are a package deal anyway." The minute 'Little Dick' and 'I' were combined into the same sentence, I knew I'd just misspoken. "That didn't sound right at all, did it? I meant—"

"I know what you meant." Levering up on her tiptoes, she gave me a quick peck on the cheek before flopping down on the bed. I shifted my feet, unsure of what to do until she patted the space beside her. "What are you waiting for, Bodhi? Come over here and get to know me."

————

We spent the next hour talking... and touching. Lots of touching. If this was her definition of 'get to know each other' then sign me up for the extended Q&A session. Though Breeze's tight little body was a worthy distraction, I'd managed to stay on track well enough to give her what she'd wanted—the small pieces of me I kept hidden from view. The girl was like my truth serum, extracting from me my true, unfiltered self.

"What happened to you tonight?" she asked. "Can you tell me?" Sliding her fingers along my forearm, waves of pleasure spread from the place we were connected. I'd tell her anything as long as she didn't stop. "Just exactly how close did you get?"

My hand crept to the smooth skin on her stomach as I gathered the strength to bring the nightmare back to life. "I woke up to an inferno. No joke, by the time I figured out what was happening, I was running for my life."

As she lay riveted on the bed, I went on to describe the scene. From the exploding trees to my sprint through the burning house to retrieve the car keys, I didn't leave anything out. Even my fear of death at the hands of the vindictive monster.

"It was the oil," she said, after I'd come to the part of my tale where our stories converged.

"What?"

"The explosions you heard. Eucalyptus oil vaporizes in the heat and the gas it emits is highly flammable. Those trees can turn into fireballs if embers touch them. The explosions that woke you up were probably the oil in the crowns detonating."

"How do you know that?"

"My stepdad is a naturalist. He knows everything about the environment. We used to take long nature walks every weekend when I was growing up. Boring stuff for a preteen girl, but obviously I retained the info dumps."

"That's like the opposite of what my father did with me. Our weekends were all about auditions and business lunches. When they put out crayons, he wouldn't even let me color because he said it wasn't professional." I let my head fall back. "I was six-years-old."

I could taste the bitterness on my tongue. I'd have given anything to grow up like Breeze—carefree. But instead, I got schedules and meetings and work. If anything, our little talk only solidified my decision to keep my father in the dark. The only way to move forward with Tucker Beckett was to leave him behind. For the moment, at least.

———

"I've got another one for you." Breeze was lying on her back, pinkish-blond hair fanning out around her as I stretched out at her side on one elbow. We were closer now, our bodies fused as we settled into a comfortable camaraderie. Enthralled, I was glued to her every word, genuinely excited to hear the next outlandish thought coming out of her mouth.

Based on past experience, it was sure to be entertaining.

I'd never been so engaged in a conversation with anyone, much less a female. While most women were a means to an end, Breeze was more like a means to a beginning.

"Hit me," I answered, sweeping a stray hair off her bruised forehead. A small gathering of freckles drew my attention and they were so adorably positioned that, without thinking, I placed a tiny kiss on the tip of her nose.

Her eyes sparkled as my carefree act reverberated through her female brain. No doubt she placed extra meaning on the intimate gesture.

"What were you saying again?" I asked, attempting to jog her memory and take the heat off.

A shiver ran through her and she shook her head. "Oh, right. I hate watching interviews with people who are out of breath. Like when a reporter asks an athlete a question right after he finishes swimming the 1,500-meter freestyle."

"Yeah, that sucks. Who wants to hear panting unless it's porn?"

"Exactly," she said, chuckling.

"Okay, how about this one? I hate seeing one shoe on the side of the road. How does that even happen? I mean to those people I ask, what's the rest of your life like?"

"Preach," she said, running her fingers along my jawline. "We're like a matching pair of socks."

"Or Mac and Cheese."

"Peterpan and Tinkerbell."

"Eeww... I like SpongeBob and Patrick better."

"Or..." She eyed me coyly. "Here's one you are particularly familiar with—Ken and Barbie."

I laughed out loud. "Is that a dig at my action figure?"

"Of course not." Dipping her head to my chest, she giggled in the most endearing way. "But can I just say... your Barbie's so dang pretty."

"I hate everyone," I complained, but without an ounce of irritation. I pulled her closer, holding on with an exuberance I hadn't felt in years.

Her laughter was contagious, and I was willing to catch her disease. I wanted so much more from her than just a quick lay. I could have that anytime. But this feeling of being close to someone who knew how to turn the light on inside me even during a blackout—I owed it to myself to see where it might go.

I was convinced Alexander Easton, the person I was born to be, would've taken a chance on a girl like Breeze. And so would I.

Better late than never.

Closing the final inches between us, my lips hovered unwaveringly close to hers.

Breeze accepted the invitation, leaning into me, a response I hadn't expected but welcomed with the wonder of a small boy sampling his first piece of candy.

Was this what people meant by chemistry?

I gently stroked the baby soft skin of her cheeks, not sure if I'd ever felt something so inviting. And when my fingers sank into her hair, Breeze gripped the back of my neck and pulled me in. My lips crashed into hers, my whole body sizzling as the current pulsed between us, every nerve in my body firing in rapid succession. If this was how a kiss was supposed to feel, then clearly I'd been doing it wrong all these years.

A seductive little moan parted her lips and, as she tipped back, the radiant glow of her hair created a halo, prompting me to lose all perspective. I was officially her slave, willing to do whatever it took to keep this feeling alive forever.

I made another go at her mouth, and she yielded, our tongues jockeying furiously for position. For dominance.

This feeling. This connection. This is what I'd been searching a lifetime to find.

And then suddenly I was on top of her. Were we doing this? She hadn't wanted sex. That's what she'd said. But those sexy legs wrapped around my waist begged to differ. She was a tornado, an unstoppable force.

My mouth slid from hers before I got sucked into the vortex. "Breeze...tell me what you want."

She had to say it. Because as much as I wanted her, I needed to know she felt the same.

A moment passed. And then another. And just when I was about to pull away, her lashes fluttered and she met my gaze with soft eyes.

"You."

12

BREEZE: THE MORNING AFTER

Morning light streamed through the window, rousing me from sleep. I took a few moments to orient myself and figure out the tangle of bodies, human and otherwise. On my left, Bodhi Beckett, international popstar – yes, I was still trying to wrap my brain around that one - lay sprawled on his stomach, arms and legs stretched in every direction. Reaching behind me, I found the shirt I'd forcibly ripped from his body.

Nice work there, Breeze. So much for self-control!

He'd found the yoga pants sometime during the night. Probably to keep from getting ogled if I happened to wake up first.

Good call.

Heat flooded my cheeks as I recalled our brief, yet intense moments together. He'd worked me up into a frenzy of lust so by the time he'd posed the sex question, I was too far gone to offer anything more than a yes.

We'd barely gotten the condom in place before it was all tangled limbs and soft moans as he thrust wildly. Faster. Harder. More intense than anything I'd ever felt. I'd never felt more connected or more reckless in all my life. Quaking fury pulsed between us until we'd both collapsed in a spent tangle.

As weirdly disturbing as it sounded, I now understood what my lovemaking guru of a mother was talking about when she went on and on about the health benefits of good, unhinged fornication. Typically I just tuned her out because, number one, who wanted to hear that crap coming out of their mother's mouth? And, number two, I'd never had an experience to match what my mother droned on about at length, so why bother listening?

See, Brandon had never been what you would call interactive. He was my first and I didn't know any differently, so I'd accepted his 'when he was done, we were done' version of sex at face value.

But last night, I finished before Bodhi. Twice. And I was still enjoying the effects a full five hours later.

My gaze continued to skim Bodhi's body before finally landing on his face. It was framed by dark, messy hair that touched down to his shoulders. At present, it was carelessly flipped over his forehead like a wave ready to be surfed. And although his show stopping eyes were sealed in slumber, I was certain the memory of their brilliance would be etched into my brain forever. So blue, like an arctic pond.

The man was blessed with beauty, all right.

No wonder his Barbie was getting so much action on YouTube.

Bodhi shifted, drawing my attention to his sculpted back and muscled arms. I was about to scoot closer and get a better look at my brand spankin' new celebrity screw buddy, but Hercules, with his hundred plus pound body, was lying across my feet, essentially trapping me in place.

And I wasn't the only human to become an animal pillow during the night either. Lucy had taken up residence at the small of Bodhi's back, her head actually resting on the dips and swells of his impressive rump. Such a smart cat. I wished I'd thought of that first.

Rounding out our interspecies orgy was Sweatpea, lounging in his spot of honor on the pillow between Bodhi and me. The furry jerk stretched happily in his sleep, face to face with his newly discovered favorite person. I, of course, got the butt end of the deal.

I smiled at the absurdity of the situation I found myself in now. Women plotted a lifetime to spend the night with the guy currently dribbling on my pillow, and all I had to do was fling myself in front of his fast-moving vehicle during a firestorm to get in his pants. Not a bad trade off if you asked me. When it came right down to it, a full body cast wouldn't have been too steep a price to pay for my current view.

I mean, let's be honest here, Bodhi wasn't just famous... he was smokin' hot famous. So much so that I was never going to wash these sheets again. He was worth the cost of buying a new set. And this view, right here, was worth every penny.

I wasn't exactly sure how Bodhi had gone from an untouchable heartthrob to an actual human being in such a short period of time, but I was sure it had something to do with the way he'd opened up to me so effortlessly. I suspected it took a moment of vulnerability for someone like Bodhi to distinguish himself as one of us common folk. That was the downside to celebrity. They were forced to hide behind a wall of fame to protect themselves from the overeager interest of fans that didn't see them as people. The fire had forced Bodhi out into the open, exposing him for who he really was... just a man with a knack for taming out-of-control dogs and impressing females with goose eggs on their foreheads.

It made me wonder what else was everyday and ordinary about him. Certainly, he had the same desires as any man. He'd proven that last night in every way that counted and if I dialed up the sexy this morning, I knew I could have him again. I mean what guy would turn down a free invitation for morning sex? I'm talking the kind that occurs *before* the trip to the bathroom.

Unplanned. Unbridled. Unsanitary.

Oh yeah. He'd be into it. And judging by the way my body was heating up, so would I.

But then what? Where did we go from here? Was he going to stick around now that I'd already played my trump card? Of course not. Bodhi had probably slipped on those lady sweats in the middle of the night in order to have a head start out of my life the moment his eyes opened for the day.

I wanted to be more than just his one-night stand, yet that's what I'd relegated myself to by acting like a horndog humping my way through a citywide blackout. I was now going to have to pay the price for my embarrassing lack of impulse control because, if there was one universal truth about rock stars, it was that you didn't ask one of his caliber, a guy who had his pick of pretty much any eligible female of childbearing age, to actively engage in the wooing process. They weren't boyfriends. They were bed buddies – nothing more and nothing less.

So then why was my brain not believing that? Why did I expect more from him despite the fact that all indicators pointed in one shaky direction? I'll tell you why. Because my mother and stepfather had always made me feel I was special enough to alter the very fabric of the universe. There was nothing I couldn't do, and that included changing the whoring ways of big name celebrities. I'll admit the altar-dumping had dampened my resolve but it didn't change the core of who I was inside, and that was a woman who believed I was worthy of the very best. Ugh, the curse of high self-esteem. Thanks Mom!

Still, if I thought logically about this, there were some indicators that blinked positive. The first was we hadn't met at a concert or passing on the street. Thrown together during the scariest moment of both of our lives, our connection had been accelerated into overdrive. There was nothing like surviving countywide destruction together.

Sure, to an outsider, it sounded ridiculous to pin my romantic hopes and dreams on a popstar with teen dream hair, but there were exceptions to the rule and I planned on being one of them.

Staring up at the ceiling, I played the night back in my mind, sifting through the memories —the good, the bad, the terrifying and the orgasmic.

I hadn't been imagining our connection. It was there and with every touch and every word spoken, Bodhi had shown me who he was. If I were just a throwaway girl, why would he risk his privacy on me? Something had kept him here last night and the hopeless romantic, undying optimist in me wanted to believe it was more than just a warm bed.

The flashing light on the microwave snagged my attention.

What the...?

Was that...?

Oh my god!

The electricity was back on!

"Herc, move!" I demanded, struggling to get out from under him. He was dead weight and it took a fighting spirit just to free my feet enough to sit up. "Jesus, dog, you take 'bed hog' to a whole other level."

Nudging Bodhi, I whispered in his ear. "I have a surprise for you."

He grunted but remained in his prone and groggy state.

"Guess what's back on?" I said in a sing-song voice. "The power, baby!"

Bodhi's eyes flew open and he blinked at me. "Wha ...? The power?"

"Uh-huh. Come on, sleepyhead." I bounced in my spot.

"Wake up so we can flick all the light switches on and off repeatedly just because we can."

He shifted, then went stone still, his petrified gaze finding mine. "What's on my back?"

"Lucy."

"Remind me what animal that is again."

"The cat."

"Oh, fuck. Thank god."

"Why? Did you think I let the rats loose on you?"

He groaned, his eyes drifting shut once more. Apparently, the cat, the lights, and me weren't enough to keep Bodhi's interest. Yep, this was going to take a little charm on my part. Bending down to within an inch of his face, I hummed a happy little tune until he could no longer ignore my bumblebee like presence.

This time when his lids fluttered open, I assaulted him with my biggest brightest smile. "Hi again. In case you forgot, my name is Breeze and I'm your fire buddy from last night."

"Yes, I remember you." He smiled. "The girl with the forehead boner."

My hand flew to the bump. After all the gushing I'd just done in my head for him, the first thing he remembered about me was my protruding knot?

Way to make an impression, Breeze.

Jumping out of bed, I stared down at him with a condemning glare.

"Was it something I said?" He shifted onto his side. I watched the cat slide off his back. Propping on his elbow, he treated me to a nice view of his impressive rack of firm, defined abs.

Oh yeah, that was... wow. Yep.

My gaze inadvertently dipped lower, and I was visually assaulted by the party in his skintight pants. Momentarily losing my train of thought, I couldn't recall why I'd jumped to my feet so quickly in the first place.

"Can you please put that away?" Confused, he looked around. "Your dick, doofus," I huffed. "It's all up in my face."

Bodhi laughed. "I think you would know if my dick was up in your face. Besides, this is your fault."

Mine? Well, damn he did remember me. Way to go, Girl! I was super flattered. I mean, even with a pregnancy pouch between my eyes, he still found me attractive enough this morning to create a pup tent in his pants.

"I told you these leggings were too tight. I've got no room for my junk."

Wow, okay. He still had room to grow. I mean last night I hadn't stopped to consider size, but okay. Impressive. Focus, Breeze... on something other than...

"You alright there, Pinocchio?" he asked with a smirk.

My cheeks ignited and I spun for the bathroom so I could examine my forehead erection, but Bodhi caught my wrist.

"I'm kidding. Where are you going?"

"Where do you think I'm going, jerk?" I shook loose of his hold. "Now that you've made me aware of the monstrosity on my forehead, I need to see for myself what I'm dealing with."

A mischievous smile stretched wide across his face. "I wouldn't do that if I were you."

"You think this is funny?"

"No." He pressed his lips together, trapping a chuckle.

"All right, go ahead and have your fun but we'll just see who'll be the last one laughing, because this right here," I pointed to my knobby knoll, "is street cred. What do you have to show for last night? Huh? Yoga pants?"

Bodhi looked down, checking for battle wounds and imperfections. But even the singed ends of his hair looked like a hip new fashion statement. Satisfied he'd come out of the night unscathed, he shrugged.

"Just what I thought, poser. You've got nothing."

"Damn girl! You're all spicy this morning," he said, grabbing me again. Only this time his grip was like iron and he pulled me on top of him. "Are you always like this or is the extra blood flow to your brain altering your personality?"

That's it.

Scowling, my fingers found the sensitive skin on the sides of his stomach and I dug in. Bodhi giggled like a schoolgirl and I'd nearly managed to get an 'Uncle' out of those full, sexy lips when the hunk of a man turned the tables, pinning me to my back. I squealed my approval and soon we were both panting and laughing. Then, out of nowhere, the silly kindergarten fun shifted into something decidedly more sexual. His lips found mine, tongue sweeping inside my mouth with urgent strokes.

Digging my fingers into his cloth-covered ass cheeks, I yanked him against me, drawing a loud moan from deep in his throat. Our bodies were a single stitch, united in desire. Pure, unbridled instinct took over.

This was happening again and, afterwards this wouldn't be considered a one-night stand anymore.

Perhaps it was my third eye taking over the pleasure center in my brain, but my view of reality was warping fast. Tunnel vision had become my finest friend, because Bodhi was all I could see. He was my every desire, the focus of all my mind-numbing lust.

His fingers threaded my hair, and I tilted my head to allow greater access as he slid his tongue to the hollow of my neck. And all the while I rocked against him, whimpering my encouragement. His free hand found my panties, deftly sliding them over my ass and as far down my thighs as he could reach. I took over, wiggling until I was free of the constricting lace.

My hands slipped into the waistband of Bodhi's pants. He hadn't been kidding about the skin-tight sweats. I could barely wedge my fingers inside, but I managed. The second I freed him from the spandex, Bodhi's dick sprang to attention and he wasted no time patting the nightstand for the pack of condoms.

"Breeze," he panted. "I can't find—"

"Side drawer," I said, distracted by the feel of defined abs and muscled biceps.

Bodhi ripped open the foil and started to roll the latex over his shaft, but I pushed his hands away and took over, never breaking eye contact. I was in charge now, so I pushed him on his back, and lowered myself onto his formidable erection.

Flexing my internal muscles, I arched my back and prepared for the ride.

His hands molded my hips, guiding me, although it hardly seemed necessary. I knew just where to go and how to make this a rewarding experience for the both of us.

Bodhi shuddered, biting back a soft moan. The sensuous sound reverberated through me and I tingled. Somehow, he managed to pull the shirt over my head, exposing my breasts. Bodhi cupped one soft mound, circling my nipple with his thumb. And just when I thought it couldn't get any more intense, he sucked the pebbled peak between his lips.

Groaning, I continued to meet his thrusts as his hand slid from my hip to my ass where he massaged the quivering flesh.

"Bodhi..."

My head fell back, teeth sinking into my bottom lip to keep from screaming.

Meeting his heavy-lidded gaze, I watched his face contort, a warm glow spreading through me. I was doing this to him. *Me.*

The world shimmered around the edges as he picked up the pace.

"Breeze... Jesus... I'm gonna..."

He came before the thought fully tripped from his lips. As the spasms rolled through him, his fingers found their way to my center. And then I was there, chasing him over the cliff and racing him to the bottom.

When the storm passed, and there were no sounds but our ragged breath, I collapsed against his chest.

"Oh my god," I whimpered.

He stayed silent, just held me tight as his lips found that spot on my neck that he liked to nuzzle. But even without words, I knew how he felt. I sensed it in his touch. His kiss. This wasn't just *nothing* between us. It couldn't be because *nothing* had ever felt so right.

Bodhi gently pressed a kiss to my tender forehead.

"I was only kidding about your extra appendage," he said huskily. "You're beautiful. I hope you know that."

My lips found his. Warm. Inviting.

This was what I'd been looking for all along. I nestled into his comforting embrace, not realizing how much I'd been holding onto until the burden was lifted from my shoulders. All the stress of cancelled nuptials, of uprooting my life and starting over from scratch. It had all been worth it for this singular moment. This tiny smudge in time.

An oversized tongue caught us unaware, coating our flesh in a giant helping of slobbery affection.

"Hercules," Bodhi complained. "Way to ruin the moment."

As Bodhi's strong hands settled me at his side, a curious little head poked its way out from between the pillows. Sweetpea. Had the little voyeur been watching us the whole time? Apparently, Herc wasn't the only perv of the animal kingdom.

———

While Bodhi was in the bathroom, I took the dogs out to do their business, careful to keep the furry beasts as well hidden as possible.

From my brief time outside, it was clear the fire was still raging. The air was thick with smoke and, although I couldn't see flames through the haze, that didn't mean the blaze wasn't headed in our direction.

Sinking onto the couch, I hastily flipped through the stations to find coverage on the fire. I gasped as video footage of house after house burned to the ground flashed on the screen. The fact that I'd been inside of that firestorm was almost incomprehensible. I could still feel the heat on my skin and taste the soot on my tongue. My lungs constricted from imaginary smoke.

Fearing another panic attack, I breathed deliberately into my hands, my eyes glued to the coverage. A map of the burn zone brought some relief since it appeared the fire was travelling north and away from us, but fires, spurred by the heavy winds, sprung up all over Southern California. Our little ocean community was surrounded from all sides. If the winds changed direction...

My thought trailed off when the coverage shifted to a reporter close to the scene.

"We've been told by officials there are upwards of forty people still unaccounted for. As reported earlier, singer Bodhi Beckett from the popular boy band, AnyDayNow, is still listed among the missing. He was said to have been staying in one of the homes affected by the fires and his whereabouts are unknown at this time. We will, of course, update you as new information becomes available."

My head spinning from the unexpected information, I paused the report.

What. The. Actual. Fuck, Margaret?

How was Bodhi still considered missing if he called his father?

Unless...

"Bodhi!" My voice rose when he didn't answer. *"Bodhi!"*

Emerging from the bathroom, he looked at me curiously as he towel dried his unruly hair. "What the hell? Can you scream any louder? I don't think they heard you in Hawaii."

I motioned to the tv. "You need to see this."

Once he was at my side, I pushed play so he could listen to the report. It was no less shocking the second time around. For me at least. But Bodhi was strangely quiet, rubbing his fingers over his stubbled jaw.

"Bodhi..." His eyes found mine, only to dart away. I swallowed hard, growing more disillusioned by the second. "Bodhi, what have you done?"

Rather than answer, he walked toward me with his arms outstretched.

"You told your family you were safe, right?" I pressed, narrowing my gaze. "You called them last night, didn't you?"

He stopped dead in his tracks with a look reminiscent of a dog who'd gotten into the trash and had no way of denying it because the frickin' can was wrapped around his neck.

I was getting madder by the second. He'd put me in a terrible position. I'd inadvertently been harboring a dead guy... and not just any dead guy. Oh no, mine had to be important enough that people actually gave a fuck. "Bodhi?!?"

"No, okay," he admitted with a sigh. "I didn't call them."

"Why? What were you thinking? This is bad. They think you're dead." I grabbed my phone and pressed it into his hands. "Call them, now."

He stood there staring at the screen. And then he lifted his gaze, resolute.

"I can't," he said dully, dropping my cell on the table. "Not yet."

I blinked at him, unable to comprehend a world where you allowed your loved ones to suffer such a crushing loss.

As I made to stalk past him, he grabbed my arm. "Please, let me explain."

The desperation in his eyes gave me pause. Something was motivating him to deceive everyone who meant anything to him. People didn't just do that for fun. Bodhi had a reason and I owed it to him to shut my mouth and hear him out.

Sinking back down onto the sofa, I folded my arms over my chest. "I'm listening."

There was a long pause as Bodhi gathered his thoughts... or came up with a plausible lie... I wasn't exactly sure. His fingers grazed the back of his neck.

"Okay, so here's the deal. I need a few days. There's someone I need to find."

Incredulous, I gaped at him. "A few days? They'll be conducting your funeral in a few days."

"All right then." He lifted his chin. "Just give me a day and then you can out me to the press, whatever."

I blinked at him. Once. Twice. "I'm not going to out you, Bodhi. You're going to out yourself."

"Not yet, I'm not. I just really need this time. Please understand."

"Who could you possibly want to find that is worth this?"

His gaze dropped to the floor. "My mother."

The word fell from his lips, almost hesitant. Like he wasn't used to saying it. During our game of true confessions, he'd hinted that she was deceased.

"But..."

Guilty eyes found mine. "Up until three months ago, I

thought she was dead, and then I received a letter. From her. I haven't told anyone about this, Breeze. Not even my father."

"Why?"

"Because if it is really her, he's the one who created the lie. And he'll stop at nothing to keep us apart. The fire... it gives me the opportunity to connect with her without being followed. Nobody knows where I am. I'm finally free... at least for a day or two."

Willing away the headache brewing behind my eyes, I kneaded my temple. "This is seriously crazy, Bodhi. How are you going to explain where you've been when you magically resurrect yourself? Have you thought of that?"

"I'll just say I lost everything in the fire, which is true, and that I couldn't call. Hell, this is California—I'll just tell them I was meditating through the trauma. I'll keep you out of this, I promise. All you have to do is look away."

"Look away?"

I slumped in the cushions. Maybe I'd been wrong. Maybe there was no connection. I was just a safe place for him to hide.

"So that's it then?" I asked thickly. "You're just going to up and leave?"

No doubt Bodhi picked up on the disappointed tone of my voice. I knew it was stupid of me to want more, especially when he had big things like a reunion with his undead mother to worry about. But I did. I'd grown attached to him over the course of the time he was hiding out in my granny flat, and I wasn't sure if I could just look away anymore.

Bodhi pulled me to my feet. Banding his arms around my waist, he nuzzled my neck. "I don't know what you want me to say. I'm trying to make this easier on you... and not put you in a bad spot. But hear me, Breeze, I'm going in search of my mother with or without your cooperation."

Backing out of his hold, I searched his face, finding steely determination. Nothing I could say would persuade him to clear his name off the missing list.

"Where is she?" I asked, "Do you even have an address?"

"Yes. I hired a private investigator. She lives in East Palo Alto which is—"

"South of San Francisco, I know. I'm from the area."

"If you just let me get out of Ventura County, I give you my word, I'll stop somewhere along the way and call my father. I won't let him worry more than a day, I swear."

I could feel him wearing me down. And really he didn't need my approval. Bodhi had lived the first twenty-four of his years, months, days, and minutes without me. In the scheme of things, I was only a blip on his radar. Why was he trying to sell me on this in the first place? What did he care what I thought?

The fact of the matter was if Bodhi was determined to do this thing, it wasn't my place to stop him. But that didn't mean I couldn't negotiate a better agreement for myself.

"I'll go along with your plan on one condition."

Bodhi hesitated for a good ten seconds. "Okay, what?"

"Take me with you."

"What? Why?"

"First, I want out of here. Fire is surrounding us, and I don't feel safe after what happened last night. And second, I can't stay here with the pets. I'm not going to be able to hide them much longer and when my landlord sees or hears them, she's going to freak. I messaged the family while you were in the shower and they're trying to get a flight home but realistically they aren't moving back in for a while, even if their house is still standing. I've got to come up with somewhere to go. My parents live in the Bay Area and they love pets. If you drop me off there, I can get my mom or stepdad to drive me back next week."

"Or you could take them to a shelter and let the family deal with it when they come back."

"Not going to happen. The shelters will be bursting with displaced pets. I'm not parting with these guys—not after everything that's happened. Besides, you need me to help you hide."

"I do?"

"Have you even considered the fact that, dead or alive, you're still Bodhi Beckett? And now that you're presumed dead, your face will be everywhere."

He pondered for a second. "So what do you suggest?"

"A makeover – nothing outrageous, just enough to give you a fighting chance. And lucky for you, I'm just the girl to make it happen. You may have magic powers when it comes to luxury trunks, but I'm a magician when it comes to hair."

"Hold up. You want to cut off my hair?" Bodhi took a giant step back as if he feared I was running at him with scissors. Once he was a safe distance, he took to pacing the floor. "I don't know, Breeze. It's sort of my signature look."

"Exactly my point."

Bodhi spent even more time chewing over my words and I couldn't help but smile. It's not like he was making some life or death decision here. It was hair that was going to grow back.

But then it occurred to me that maybe Bodhi wasn't used to making his own decisions. From what I gathered, his father had been calling the shots his whole life.

I was about to retract my offer when a smile spread wide across his face and he said, "You know what? I actually like the idea. Let's do it! In fact, shave it all off if you want to."

"Whoa, pull back on the crazy, Dude. I'm not suggesting full on baldness here, just a new look – something that will stop up your fans and maybe keep them from immediately recognizing you. Get it?"

"Got it. Do with me what you will."

I raised a brow. "So you're sure, then? Road trip with me and the animal brigade?"

"Damn, right." Bodhi looked genuinely happy.

"Okay then. I'm in too, as long as you promise me as soon as we cross the county line, you're calling your father and letting him know you're not a pile of ash and bone. Deal?"

"Um, yeah, that's not going to work for me. No calls will be placed until I get to see my first live sea lion. Once that happens, I promise to call him. That's non-negotiable."

So that was his game. No communication until we were all the way to Pier Thirty-Nine in San Francisco. I smiled as only a northern California native could. Because Pier Thirty-Nine wasn't the only place to see a pack of seals on the California coast. I wasn't about to tell him that, though.

Instead, I held out my hand. "All right Bodhi. You drive a hard bargain. But you've got yourself a deal."

13

BREEZE: THE MAKEOVER

THE SALON WAS EMPTY, JUST AS I'D EXPECTED IT WOULD BE. Though my work wasn't in the direct path of danger from the fire, it was close enough that a bunch of women weren't going to brave the elements to get pampered.

I held the door open and Bodhi peered inside. "You sure no one will come in?"

"It's doubtful. But if someone does, I'll just throw a towel over your head. This is a hair salon. No one will think twice about it."

Satisfied, Bodhi stepped over the threshold, scanning all the stations. "Let me guess which one is yours."

"Okay," I smiled, confident that, of the ten booths scattered around the room, he wouldn't figure out which one was mine until his very last guess. We all decorated our stations differently. Those with kids had shrines built up of their smiling faces. The older ladies might have a picture of their grandchildren or a photo of their dog. The newlyweds had honeymoon shots and the candy lovers had heaping bowls of mini chocolates at their stations.

"This one," Bodhi guessed a workstation displaying dog

pictures. Given what he knew about me so far, it was a valid choice.

"Nope."

He snagged a candy out of a bowl. "Okay then, this one and, might I add, my personal favorite."

"You like candy?"

"Doesn't everyone?"

"Are you the type of celebrity who makes your assistant pick out the red M&M's before giving them to you?"

Bodhi wrinkled his nose. "Of course not." From his tone, he appeared hurt by the joke. "What kind of person do you think I am?"

"I was only kidding," I backtracked. "I'm sorry. Bad joke."

"Yeah, I'd say so." A grin broke wide across his lips. "All M&M's are served to me separated by color, of course."

I smacked his chest. "Don't do that to me. I thought you were mad."

"It's called acting, Breeze," he said playfully before grabbing for more chocolate minis from my coworker's bowl. "This candy is frickin' amazing. How can you work here with this stuff lying around all day?"

"It's called making a living, Bodhi."

Ignoring my dig, he continued his exploration of the salon.

"Okay, so I know the kid ones aren't yours and unless you have particularly bad taste in guys, which you disproved this morning," He paused to offer a self-assured smirk. "Then this one here can't be yours either. I give up. Which one is it?"

"The one with the roses."

Bodhi wandered over to my station where a flower overload was underway. Pictures of the dainty blooms were pasted to my mirror and little rose trinkets littered the counter. But it was the tall vase filled with buds that caught Bodhi's attention. He ran his fingers over the petals. "Wait, these are fake. What's the point in that?"

Yes, they were fake roses and not even pretty ones, but they held a special meaning. These were my proposal roses, eleven in all. Before sneaking out to ask for my hand in marriage, Hugh would always swipe one rose out of the silk arrangement from the lobby of the nursing home.

The first rose had come only a week after I'd started working at the salon, well before I'd had time to decorate my station, so my coworkers took it upon themselves to help me along by bringing me rose related items for fun until the point where it looked like I was a contestant on The Bachelor television show.

My roses and I had become a running joke at work and as funny as it was, my Hugh was no laughing matter. He was sincere and loving and, like no other man before him, Hugh had chosen me... over and over and over again.

As I told the story of my suitor to Bodhi, he laughed in some spots and seemed moved by others. By the time I was finished, he was fully vested in the saga. Lingering in the same spot, he stared at the flowers.

"You okay?" I asked.

"Oh, yeah. Sorry. The story inspired me. I was writing a song in my head."

"You write?"

Maybe there was too much surprise in the way I asked the question, but I wasn't prepared for Bodhi's adverse reaction. I'd unintentionally stumbled onto a sore spot... or he was still acting, I couldn't tell. That's how good he was.

"You don't think I can write songs?" He cocked his head. "Why? because I'm in a boy band?"

"No. I didn't know you wrote songs because I don't listen to pop music."

His irritation morphed to curiosity. "What do you listen to then?"

"Country."

A slow smile hitched one corner of his lips. "Seriously?"

It was my turn to be defensive. "Yeah. You got a problem with that?"

"No," he said, then backtracked. "Actually, yes I do have a problem with that. You listen to country music? Really?"

"Yes, really. And by the end of our road trip, so will you."

He chuckled. "I beg to differ. My car, my rules."

"No. Your stolen car equals no rules. I get fifty percent of the radio play."

He stared at me for an exaggerated minute before executing the most pathetic whine imaginable. "Breeze, don't do this to me."

"Oh, it's on, Buddy. I already have an entire playlist ready to go."

"Alright then. Two can play this game. I hope you like Justin Bieber."

I gasped. "You wouldn't."

"Watch me."

Bodhi and me stood firm in our pissing match until both of us dissolved into laughter.

"Dammit! I knew you were too good to be true. Country music, really?" he said, shaking his head in disbelief.

"Ahh. You think I'm too good to be true? Thank you."

"*Did...* as in past tense."

"Oh, okay, well I guess our road trip won't feature any rest area booty calls for you then."

"Nothing would make me happier than *not* having sex with you at a nasty-ass truck stop."

He had a point there. I patted my chair. "Whatever. Sit and let me make you look pretty."

Bodhi plopped down into my chair, a smile still gracing his handsome face.

"What?" I asked.

"Nothing. You're fun."

Our eyes met in the mirror and, in that moment, I knew there was more to us than one night...one event.

"So," I cleared my throat still a bit shell shocked by the connection I felt for him. "Is that how it happens? You see or hear something that inspires you to write?"

"Pretty much, yeah."

"Have any of your songs made it on albums?"

"Yes, but not in the way they were intended to sound."

"What do you mean by that?"

"I just hear them differently in my head. Softer. Acoustic. But by the time the powers that be get their hands on it, the song becomes something I don't recognize."

"And you don't like that?"

"It doesn't matter what I like."

"Sure it does. It's your song."

"It's more complicated than that," Bodhi said, brows drawn together. "People expect me to be a certain way even though it's not really who I am. I've been playing a part for so long, sometimes I don't know where the character ends and I begin."

"And you're hoping this trip might answer some questions for you."

He nodded, but it was a cautious gesture. "That's why I have to find her. I need to know where I come from. Why she left."

I understood his pain better than he knew. "My father left me too. It's not easy knowing you weren't important enough for them to stick around."

"No, it's not."

"But, I think some people just aren't mature enough to

nurture a tiny soul, and maybe I was better off not having him in my life."

"That's what scares me most about meeting my mother. I've played her up so much in my mind that it will be near impossible for her to live up to expectation."

It didn't take a clairvoyant to read the future for Bodhi and based on my own experience, I feared he was in for a massive disappointment. If his mother had stayed out of his life for this long, there was a reason, and it probably wasn't a good one.

"Okay," I said, changing the tone. There was no room for heavy conversation in the middle of a makeover. "Let me show you the style I had in mind."

He settled back into the chair, appearing completely comfortable with the idea of my chopping off his iconic hair.

"Here," I said holding up a picture on my phone. Bodhi diverted his eyes before he got a look at the hip new style I was suggesting.

"No. I want to be surprised."

When it came to new hairstyles, surprise was never a good idea. Although, with Bodhi's strong facial features he could pull off just about anything.

"Are you sure? I don't want you to be pissed if you don't like it."

"I told you Breeze, I trust you."

And shockingly, I believed he meant every word.

———

I spent the following thirty minutes bleaching strips of blond into his naturally dark brown locks. Although his strands were free from highlights at the moment, Bodhi was no stranger to color as he related to me in hilarious detail. His hair had been all shades of the rainbow during his rise to fame and he had old pictures of himself on the internet to prove it.

We chatted effortlessly throughout the process and I realized that this easy camaraderie had been lacking on the few dates I'd had since my break up. Despite our vastly different lives, we were just a guy and a girl finding our way in an upside-down world.

"Okay, let's get you to the sink," I said, absently running my fingernails the length of his neck. Why I felt comfortable enough to touch him with such confidence, I didn't know. I just was. From the look of lust in Bodhi's smoldering eyes, he didn't mind.

A few miles away, the fire continued to tear its way through the coastal mountain range, yet even that roaring inferno wasn't as hot as the intensity between us. Bodhi grabbed my hand, pulling me into his lap and, as it had been earlier, we were all over each other again. Our mouths collided, lips working furiously as our tongues danced to the beat of a pop-country song. Nimble fingers slid under my shirt while I cradled his face, rocking against him.

"Oh god, this is... are you sure no one will come by?" he asked, hands poised at the tiny hooks on my bra.

"No, not sure at all."

"What about the window? Do you think people can see in?"

The entire front of the salon was a giant window. "Yes. It's glass, which is typically see-through in both directions."

Bodhi's laughed died when I ground my center against his burgeoning erection. Then an image popped into my head of his fried hair falling out in clumps at my feet.

"What about the bleach?" I asked, enthralled by the hand that had mercifully appeared between my legs.

"Fuck the bleach."

"Okay," I panted, so far out of control that I wouldn't even have cared if Hugh walked through the door with the final rose. "Fuck the bleach."

"Although," he hesitated. "What exactly will happen if it stays in for too long?"

I dipped my hand into his yoga pants. "Your hair will fall out."

It was then that we came to our senses and laughed at the absurdity.

Nudging me forward, he adjusted his erection. "Sorry, Breeze. You lost me at clumps."

"Really?"

"Yep."

Untangling our limbs, I hopped to my feet, and ushered Bodhi to the shampoo bowl. Once he was in the reclining chair, getting him to focus proved difficult. His hand slid to the back of my leg as I worked my fingers gently through his hair. And then that talented mouth clamped down on my nipple through the thin fabric of my shirt.

"Bodhi," I said, jumping back. "Focus. Clumps, remember?"

"Yeah, okay but don't shampoo me like that then."

"Like what?" my fingers returned to his locks, kneading his scalp in a circular motion.

"All erotically and shit."

"I shampoo everyone this way."

"And your clients don't have multiple orgasm per day?"

"Not that I'm aware of, no."

Bodhi spent the next couple minutes of my sexually charged head massage moaning seductively under his breath, and every celebrity fantasy I'd ever harbored seemed to be coming true. It took everything in my power not to climb on top of him again. Did he know what he was doing to me? Did he care?

It wasn't until I had him back at my workstation that my professionalism kicked in. I went to work on Bodhi's signature mane, clipping it short and tapering up the sides. I left some length on the top so he could wear it slicked back, messy all over, or spiked to the heavens. Streaks of caramel blended seamlessly into his dark locks, subtle enough to give his hair texture and shine without making an overt statement.

When I was finally done, I swung Bodhi's chair to face the mirror. Getting the first view of his newly chopped hair, his eyes bulged. "What the...?" He tugged at the strands. "I don't even look like me."

A flush of panic gripped my insides. He hated it. Oh god.

"I'm sorry," I said, rushing to force more words of apology passed the lump in my throat. Bodhi probably had a high-end stylist. Why had I ever thought I could compete with that? "I wanted you to look at the style first but you told me to surprise you... so... um *surprise.*"

"Relax, Breeze," he said, angling the hand mirror to check himself in different angles. "It's a sick haircut. I love it."

"You do?"

Grabbing my hand, he pulled me to him for a kiss. "I do. Thank you."

I pretended to faint on top of him. "You scared the heck out of me. I thought you were going to be so pissed."

"Of course not. Even if I hated it I wouldn't have been pissed. After what happened last night, I'm done sweating over the small stuff."

"I like your thinking."

"Yeah?" He stared up at me with an irresistibly sexy smile.

"Yeah," I whispered back, twirling a strand of my own hair because I just honestly didn't know what to do with myself in the vicinity of such hotness.

"Breeze?" The smile on his face faded.

"Yes?"

"I know this is a horrible thing for me to ask, but can I borrow some money? I promise I'll pay you back with interest."

A multi-millionaire was asking me for money? What had the world come to? "What do you need money for?"

"Uh, clothes, of course. I'm not meeting my mother looking like Richard Simmons." He pulled at the fabric of his loaner wardrobe. "Neiman-Marcus or Macy's will be fine."

I coughed out a laugh. As if. "Yeah, that's a little rich for my blood. You need to shop like the penniless dead guy you are. I have just the store for you."

———

We had to drive to an adjacent town to find a discount clothing store that wasn't closed.

As I parked, Bodhi examined the sign over the store. "Marshalls? Is it a men's store?"

"It's an everything store."

"Like Macy's?"

"Um...sure," I lied. "Like Macy's."

I grabbed the hoodie I'd packed for him. Bodhi had lost interest in Marshalls and was again marveling at his transformation in the rearview mirror.

"Here, put this on and cover your head."

He scoffed. "Yeah, I don't think so."

"Why?"

"First, I don't want to mess up the do' and second, that sweatshirt's baby blue."

"So?"

"And it's a woman's cut. Not a chance I'm putting that on. I draw the line at Twilight attire. Besides, no one's going to recognize me with shit clothes and short hair."

"I didn't give you a face transplant. It won't take much for you to be recognized. If you won't wear the sweatshirt then, here, at least put this on." I handed him a surgical-style facemask I'd grabbed from the salon, the kind we used for smelly perms. Today it would double as both a disguise and protection from the smoky elements.

"Fuck me," he exclaimed. "This just keeps getting better. I honestly embarrass myself."

I watched in amusement as he secured the mask over his mouth.

"Now I look like Michael Jackson... if he were an unfashionable white guy. Hey Breeze?"

"Yes?"

"On a scale from one to ten, how attracted are you to me right now?"

I laughed. It was true, Bodhi Beckett had seen better days. But his flirty banter was doing a number on my insides and, even looking like he did, I still found him indescribably hot. "Eleven point five, baby."

"Hot damn, let's go shopping!"

———

There are apparently two ways to shop. One was for rich people and the other was for average Joes.

"This is not Macy's," Bodhi said as he got his first look at the bargain aisle.

"I never said it was."

"But you implied as much."

"That was just to get you in here and now that you are, I'm giving you that taste of the normalcy you crave. Now, do you want to complain or do you want to shop?"

Suppressing a smile, he stomped his foot like an insolent toddler. "Shop."

I laughed, pointing him in the direction of the shoe department. But first he needed a cart—*to ride*. What he didn't factor into the equation was the tip radius of the smaller than average shopping cart. The minute his weight was added to the bar below the rolling contraption, the opposite end popped up and nearly toppled over on top of him.

I took control of the navigation from that point on. Which was a good thing, because the minute he got to the shoe aisle he lost track of reality.

"Oh my god. Can you believe the prices?" he asked, perusing the labels in the higher price range.

I peeked over his shoulder at the $49.95 tag. Good lord! What was it made out of —whale penis?

"So damn cheap," he marveled, ignoring my obvious shock. "This place is the shit!"

Obviously, we had different definitions of cheap. After trying on a dozen pair of shoes, Bodhi dumped four boxes into our cart and started off to the clothing section.

"Not so fast, big spender." I grabbed his arm. "Here's how it works on a budget. You have to pick your favorite pair and that's all you get."

"Really?" he said, giving me the side-eye. "That sucks."

"Yes, it does."

"How do you pick just one?"

"When you don't have a choice, it becomes easier."

"Huh. Okay." Rubbing the back of his neck, he stared longingly at his cart full of shoes. "Well..."

He spent the next five minutes agonizing over his choices. In the end he went with a pair of boat shoes and, pleased with his selection, we were off to the Men's department where the process repeated itself until he had a modest pile of clothing he could be proud of.

While Bodhi was in the dressing room, I wandered the store

and found the perfect item to kick off his childlike bucket list.

"Hey!" I called and when he turned in my direction, I blew a wand of bubbles into his face.

He batted at the soapy mess. "What in the hell?"

"Bucket list, baby!"

"You don't think I've blown bubbles in my life?"

"Have you?"

"Well, not directly, but I've walked through them on stage a thousand times."

"That's not blowing bubbles. Here."

I dipped the stick back into the canister, then handed him the wand. Pulling down his mask, Bodhi blew the entire load of soapy water into my face. His grin was infectious as he reached for the bottle. But this time, when he loaded the wand, he tipped forward and blew the bubbles straight into my cleavage. Yelping, I ducked behind a rack of clothes. Dropping to his knees, Bodhi sprayed the next assault before grabbing my shirt and dragged me out of my hiding place.

"Did you know there's no angry way to say bubbles?" I asked as he dipped his head to give me a soapy kiss.

"Bubbles," he bit out, attempting a hostile tone. But then a wide smile curved his lips and we both laughed.

Until a manager strolled up with a sour expression.

"Off the floor, please," he ordered, glancing us over with disdain.

"He needs to say bubbles," Bodhi whispered to me.

I lost it then, squealing with laughter. The manager wasn't amused.

"Up, now, or I'll have security escort you out."

I'd seen their security on the way in—one lowly dude with a crossing guard vest on. I wasn't too concerned. But then I caught sight of Bodhi's fully exposed face, and my humor faded.

Motioning for him to replace the mask, I nudged him toward the row of registers where we paid as quickly as possible.

I wasn't sure if Bodhi caught the look of contempt as we scooted by the manager, until he whispered close to my ear, "He must be on Team Jacob."

On his way out of the store, Bodhi was already stripping off his Twilight tee and changing into a bicep hugging Hurley shirt. I'd barely managed to get him into the vehicle before the yoga pants came off. Clearly he was comfortable with nudity. With his bits and pieces fully exposed, Bodhi took his sweet time removing the tags on his board shorts. My embarrassed giggle was a source of great amusement for the flasher.

Next, we stopped at the pet store to buy a proper cat carrier for Lucy, as well as food and supplies for the rest of the pack. Rounding out our shopping trip, we grabbed some snacks for the road before heading back to my place to pack.

Coasting to a stop in front of the house, I spotted the landlady standing at my front door.

"Oh shit! Wait here," I told Bodhi as I jumped out of the car.

I made it to her side in time to see her turning the key in my lock.

"What are you doing?" I asked, panic rising in my tone.

She swung her irritated gaze my way. "Dogs, Breeze. The barking hasn't stopped for two hours. You know they aren't allowed."

"I know. I'm sorry. I was pet sitting when the fire hit. You've seen the news. I couldn't leave them to die."

"Take them to the shelter now," she ordered. "If I hear that dog bark one more time, I'll chuck him in the garbage."

Bodhi skidded to a stop at my side, shoving the pet carrier and food into my hands. And then, as if he wore a bodysuit and cape around his neck, my hero stepped valiantly in front of the landlady. "We're leaving in a few minutes. If you think you're going to trash that dog, you'll be going through me first."

Pat's eyes narrowed to slits. "Are you threatening me?"

"No. I'm telling you — no one touches that dog."

And so began the most awkward stare down I'd ever witnessed. Bodhi in his quarantine mask and Pat in her sleeveless flannel button up. Neither budged as they glared at each other. Rather than step between them, I decided to take the opportunity to duck inside the house to give Bodhi the chance to lay on the charm he claimed as his superpower.

It took me all of ten minutes to feed the animals and get everything packed and ready to go. Mentally preparing myself for the fireworks, I opened the door and found ... nothing. Had Pat taken Bodhi hostage? In a panic, I jogged to the main house. Slipping through the door unannounced, I was totally prepared to find Bodhi bound and gagged in her living room. Instead he was bent over the kitchen table signing an AnyDayNow collectible magazine.

Bodhi flicked his gaze to me when he noticed me standing there. "Hey, Breeze."

"H-hi." I took a couple steps. "What is happening here?"

"Girl, why didn't you tell me you were harboring Bodhi Beckett in my granny flat?" Pat asked, her cheeks flushing pink with excitement. "Oh my goodness, this is the most thrilling day of my life. I'm just speechless!"

I cast a questioning glance in Bodhi's direction.

"Turns out you were right," he said with a smile. "The haircut isn't foolproof, nor is the mask. Pat here is a big fan. She recognized me the second you shut the door."

"I sure did," she crowed. "You can't fool old Pat. I'd know you anywhere. You've always been my favorite 'Dayer'."

Dayer...

Was my lumberjack landlord really using the tween terminology for the band? Apparently there was no age limit for idol worship. More importantly, was she aware of Bodhi's missing in action status? No way was the fifty-eight-year-old fangirl going to keep her mouth shut about Bodhi's whereabouts. Suddenly I had a bad feeling about our road trip. Pat's favorite Dayer was about to get a one-way ticket back to La La Land.

"I've been crying all day thinking sweet Bodhi was killed in that terrible fire and then, as if by some miracle, he shows up at my house... my house, Breeze."

"You're the best," Bodhi said, sliding the magazine in Pat's direction as he laid on the charm and reduced my landlady to a pile of liquid goo.

It was an impressive show indeed. I'd never question his magnetism again.

Sidling to my side, he slipped a reassuring arm around my waist. "I told Pat how the band was keeping my whereabouts a secret from the news outlets until I could get safely home. She agreed to keep quiet and in return I promised to send her an *AnyDayNow* gift box in the mail with all the guys signing a personal message just for her."

"*Ohhh,*" I said, sporting a fake ass smile that matched Bodhi's. "What a wonderful offer. I'm so happy you two were able to meet, but we should probably hit the road now. You don't want to keep the band waiting."

Bodhi nodded, taking my landlady's trembling hand in his and kissing the backside. "It's been a pleasure."

Pat's body sagged under the weight of her giggles. "Isn't he just dreamy, Breeze?"

Oh yeah, he was dreamy all right. In fact, I was *this* close to buying the two of us matching posters for our walls.

14

BODHI: PINNIPEDS

"What?" I finally asked, cutting my gaze to Breeze, who'd been wearing the same expression since we pulled away from the curb. Shock. Maybe a little awe. Not that I minded. Much. There were plenty of things I wanted to do to earn that look in her eye. But none of them involved my celebrity.

"What exactly happened back there?"

"I was protecting Little Dick, and seconds away from getting axed in the nuts, when Pat slapped her hands over her mouth, mewled like an animal with a mangled limb, and started jumping in place. I honestly wasn't sure if she was having a medical episode or if a swarm of bees was fleeing the burn zone. I can tell you one thing, it never once crossed my mind that a woman who wears Timberland boots would be an AnyDayNow groupie."

Breeze playfully hopped in her seat. There was so much enthusiasm in that simple twist of her body. How could I not smile? Since she'd come into my life my energy had been different. I felt happy and so damn alive.

"Here's a creepy thought," she whispered, her eyes wide with the promise of a story to dazzle me. "Do you think she's got a shrine of you in her bedroom?"

A shiver ran through me as I pictured the lumbersexual with a full-blown AnyDayNow fetish. "Honestly?" I winced. "Yes."

If I thought Breeze would sympathize, I was sadly mistaken. Her smile widened. "She probably sleeps with one of your Barbie dolls and kisses it goodnight."

"Breeze, please be respectful. It's an action figure."

She laughed, leaning closer to me. The feel of her breath against my neck nearly did me in. If she kept up this flirty behavior we were never getting out of town. "I owe you an apology, Bodhi. You told me you could charm a snake, I just didn't believe you and I'm sorry."

"We all make mistakes," I conceded. "And you're forgiven."

"Speaking of mistakes, are you sure you should be driving? What if we get pulled over? You don't have a license."

"The reason I insisted on driving is two-fold. First, you still can't open the trunk even after being given ample opportunity to learn. Until you master that skill you don't deserve to drive."

"Whatever, Jedi master. What's the second reason?"

"I don't want you driving a stolen vehicle."

Arching a perfect brow, she sat back in her seat, sizing me up. "Well, how gentlemanly of you."

"Yes." I smiled. "You're welcome."

"And what happens if we get pulled over? What if the police are looking for this car?"

"They're not. As far as they know, it burned up in the fire."

"Okay, smart stuff, but what if they just pull us over because the car you're driving looks like it survived a riot?"

I sighed dramatically. She was totally overthinking this.

"Hey, it's not that far-fetched," she insisted. "The paint is charred and peeling. The sunroof is sealed shut. Even the wind-shield wipers are melted to the frame. I mean, Bodhi, what happens if a bug hits the glass and we can't wash it away? Huh? What then, genius?"

"Stop being so extra, girl. Damn. Remind me not to take you along on a bank robbery. Look, you saw what happened with Pat. That should tell you never to underestimate the scope and size of my fan base. Maybe the cop that pulls us over because a bug has committed suicide on our windshield has an action figure of me too."

Breeze cleared her throat and said in a low, deep tone, "Barbie doll, but yes. I get it. Your band is the future. I hear it's prophesied to one day unify all the nations on earth and usher in a new age of peace and groovy prosperity."

My jaw dropped as I cut my gaze to hers. No frickin' way! "Tell me you didn't just quote Bill and Ted's Excellent Adventure, my favorite movie of all time?"

"Why yes, Bodhi. I totally did. Wyld Stallyns, all the way!"

We did a simultaneous Wyld Stallions hand signal salute, which only solidified my attraction. Now I was absolutely convinced this meeting of the minds was meant to be. It was as if the universe had chucked the girl into my path just so we could share this exact moment.

I was still marveling at my good fortune when she shrieked, "Oh my god! Pull over!"

"What is it?" I slammed on the brake, still a little twitchy from last night. "What's happening?"

"Oh, sorry. Sorry." She soothed my tattered nerves with a kiss when we rolled to a stop. "Nothing bad, look!"

I followed her gaze and saw nothing out of the ordinary.

She snorted, patting me on the arm. "A sprinkler, Bodhi. And not just any sprinkler but the old-school rotating kind. What are the chances?"

"I don't know," I said truthfully. "Depends on what the hell you're talking about?"

Breeze didn't wait for me to catch up. She was already out of the car, leaving me to ponder her words while watching her from the rearview mirror as she skipped down the sidewalk.

"Come on!"

She signaled me forward with the exaggerated wave of her hand as if I were a dog she'd wanted to come. My gaze shifted to the sprinkler, then to Breeze, then to Hercules' reflection in the rearview mirror.

"Goddamn Herc, is she crazy or the girl of my dreams?"

The big dog didn't answer. But that was okay because I'd already formed my own opinion of Breeze Cassidy and it was decidedly awesome.

Pushing open the door, I jogged up to her side then took Breeze's hand and let her lead me to my first frolic through the sprinklers.

———

A couple of hours into our trip, Breeze directed me off the beaten path and onto a scenic coastal road. I welcomed the detour. With every mile we traveled, I felt the noose tighten around my neck. The longer it took to get to San Francisco, and the inevitable phone call to my father, the better.

When she pointed to an area just past Morro Bay, I dutifully parked the car, then turned to her with an exaggerated sigh. "Another surprise?"

The boredom I tried and failed to telegraph was just for show. There was nothing boring about the adventures Breeze had already brought to life. If this was what constituted a normal life, then sign me up.

A smile played on her lips. Coy. "It's a good spot for the dogs to stretch their legs and I want to show you something."

Spying the tourists, I took care to don my hoodie and keep

my head down. Until constipated barking drew my attention to the waterfront. Hundreds, maybe thousands of seal-like creatures with large hanging noses basked in the sun, occupying every square inch of the prime beachfront real estate. I'd never seen such a sight.

"What the hell are those things?"

"Elephant seals. The males can weight upwards of 5,000 pounds."

"I should say so."

When I cut my gaze to hers, the smile went from coy to downright smug. "And that, Mr. Beckett, satisfies your seal requirement. I think someone now owes his father a phone call." She finished her little display by pantomiming wiping her hands of me and my sea-lion inspired ultimatum.

"I don't think so," I said, resolute. "Those slabs of baloney are not what I call sea lions. Mine are cute and brown and clap their hands and waddle around like fat guys with swim flippers on."

"No, you're right. They're not exactly the same. Sea lions and elephant seals are like second cousins because they belong to the same family of mammals called the pinnipeds. So what I'm saying is – since they're similar enough to share family holidays, in my book that means Bodhi Beckett's about to come back to life."

As much as I wanted to argue the point, I couldn't. It was time to concede defeat. It wouldn't matter if I called now or once we got to San Francisco because I was already far enough away from the burn zone to evade detection from my meddling father.

I nodded, sullen. Because even though I was doing the right thing, that didn't mean I was happy about it.

"Yes." Breeze woot-wooted, her whole body coming to life at my surrender. There was a little dance, and even a fist pump. For her this was good news. For me... not so much.

"So, you'll call your dad now?"

A tiny speck of doubt shone in her eyes as she waited for my confirmation.

I sighed. "After I get a better look at these big blobs of blubber. Why are they all here?"

"The elephant seals come every year. The winter months are when they have their babies. The females will get pregnant again before going back to sea and won't give birth until they come back here next year. Wild, isn't it? There's a pup there. Do you see it?"

She pointed out the babies littering the beach. Even though they weren't much to look at, the pups were undeniably fascinating. I particularly enjoyed the two males fighting for supremacy while the females egged them on with fart-inspired barking cheers.

My attention back on Breeze, I swept a lock of hair out of her face. "Do you think that's considered a sexy sound in the pinniped world. Are the male seals like 'ooh baby, give me more of the 'rip ass' bark.'"

She beamed, and it was sexy as all hell. "I'm sure. Check out that big stud over there. He's more popular with the ladies than you are." A giggle parted her lips. "He has his own harem of females and everything."

"Yes, but does he have an action figure modeled after him? I don't think so."

After fifteen minutes of seal watching, Breeze somberly pressed her phone into my palm.

Tipping her chin to the car, she offered me a sympathetic smile. "I'll wait here. I think you're going to need the privacy."

15

BODHI: STILL ALIVE

"Tucker here."

For as long as I could remember my father had answered his phone with the same brisk announcement. It was almost as if he couldn't be bothered with the word 'hello'. But there was something different about the greeting today...something heavy and laden with effort. Was he...crying?

"Dad."

"Bodhi?" That word, my name, it was spoken steeped in disbelief. "Bodhi! Oh god, Bodhi." His voice broke, that strangled sob shaking me to the bone. "Is it really you?"

Shame pooled in my belly, spreading to my limbs. What had I been thinking?

"I'm okay, dad."

Heavy breaths marked the conversation. "Your belongings were found in the rubble. I thought... they thought..."

He didn't need to finish his sentence. I knew exactly what he'd thought because it's what I'd chosen to make him think. Even as pissed as I was at my father, no one deserved that misery. "I know, Dad, I'm sorry you had to go through that but

I'm alive. Everything happened so fast I had to leave my stuff behind."

As I waited for my father to regain his composure, I wracked my brain for any occasion that I'd heard him cry. There were none.

"Can you tell me what happened?" he finally asked. "How you got out?"

I related the story, not sparing any details. I owed him that much. By the time I'd finished, his breathing had returned to normal.

"Are you hurt? Burned?"

"Um, no, maybe some smoke inhalation but otherwise I'm okay."

"I can't even tell you, Bodhi... I can't even... I've never been so scared in all my life. Thank god you're safe. Where are you? I'll come and get you right now."

Tucker's concern struck a chord and my conviction wavered. Maybe it was best to call this whole trip off. My dad may be a controlling asshole most of the time but at least he was a devoted one. Did I really need to know my mother? It's not like she'd done a damn thing for me in life. Except stay away.

I was about to crack when I glanced over at Breeze, on the bench getting brutalized by my furry-assed best friend, Sweetpea. And suddenly I remembered why I needed the time away. It wasn't just about my mother. It was about me finding out who I was and where I'd come from. Bonus points would be handed out if I could also figure out where the hell I was going.

"I'm not coming home yet. I have somewhere I want to go first, but I'll be back for the show Friday night."

"What do you mean you aren't coming home?" An authoritative edge crept into his tone. "Where are you going?"

"I can't tell you that."

"Well, where are you now?"

"I can't tell you that either." I tracked my finger on the steering wheel, ready to move on. "Look, last night I thought I was going to die, and it caused me to reevaluate my life. I need this time for myself. I'll be safe and, like I said, I'll be back for the concert."

"The concert? Jesus Christ, Bodhi, five minutes ago I thought you were dead. There wasn't going to be a concert... ever again."

"And now there is." I blew out a breath. "Listen, I've got to go."

"Bodhi, wait. How can I get in contact with you? Let me send you a phone."

"No. I don't need one right now."

"But *I* need you to have one," he insisted. "I need to know where you are at all times."

"No, Dad, you don't. I'm not a kid anymore, and if I say I need to take a few days to myself, that's what I'm going to do. And don't bother calling this number back because I just borrowed it from a random person. I'll call you in a couple of days to arrange a flight back to Los Angeles. In the meantime, let the guys ... the media ... let everyone know I'm fine. I'll talk to you soon. Bye."

His objections raced across the line, but I hung up. Maybe it was cruel to freeze him out so soon after the fright he'd suffered but if I gave Tucker too much power, he'd use it against me, and I'd already decided that wasn't acceptable to me anymore. My dad was no longer calling the shots. I hadn't saved myself to become a slave all over again.

Nope.

I was taking back my life.

16

BREEZE: ROAD TRIP

"EVERYTHING GOOD?" I ASKED, CURIOUS HOW ONE TACKLES A conversation centered around the sensitive issue of resurrection. "Was he surprised?"

Bodhi arched his brow. "Nah, I mean he was kind of like, 'crap you again'?"

I laughed nervously at his sarcasm. "Sorry, that was a stupid thing to ask."

Sighing heavily, he let the mask slip. "No, I'm just testy right now. And to answer your question—yes, he was surprised. For some strange reason he thought I was dead."

"Gee, wherever did he get an idea like that?" I ducked to catch his gaze, "You know, Bodhi, I hate to say I told you so but..."

"Oh, I know you told me so, but here's a fun fact about me that maybe you didn't know. I'm a fucking idiot."

I hauled to my feet and wrapped him in a hug. "It's okay, at least you have a nice ass," I offered, patting his butt.

"Well, yes, there's that."

After a long moment, Bodhi broke our connection. Scooping up Sweetpea, he offered me his free hand. "You ready?"

"You're not going to tell me what he said?"

"Was I supposed to?"

We hadn't even known each other a day, yet for some unknown reason, I expected to be filled in on his conversation.

"I mean if you don't want to tell me that's fine too." The pout on my lips was unmistakable. I was giving him an out, yes, yet all while still expertly conveying my disappointment. Damn, I was good at this communication stuff.

His lip tipped up slightly as he watched me with curiosity as we strolled. "You can barely contain your curiosity, can you?"

Was I that easy to read? For him, I guess. I side-eyed him, prepared to deny the accusation. But I couldn't. "I'm truly dying here. Even just a tiny morsel would help."

Brows drawn together over troubled blue eyes, he kept his gaze on the ground. "He was crying, Breeze – like really crying. I'd never heard him like that and now I feel like a total dick. Then to make matters worse, when he wanted to come get me, I said no."

When I reached for Bodhi, Sweetpea bared his teeth and I retracted my hand. "It's not too late. You can go back if you want. I can get someone to pick me up from here. We're only a few hours from San Francisco now."

"And leave you and the animals deserted out here on Blubber Beach? I don't think so. Besides, this doesn't change what I need to do. I'm still going to find my mother. And at least now everyone will know I'm alive and I won't need to hide anymore."

Relief washed over me. Selfish, considering Bodhi's turmoil. But if he thought his life was going to be smooth sailing now that he'd miraculously come back to life, I feared he had another think coming. "Are you sure you won't still need to hide? I mean there's the matter of hordes of preteen and teen girls who will see right through that nifty new hairdo of yours."

Producing the little mask from his pocket, he affixed it over his nose and mouth. "Problem solved."

"Except there's no fire here. In these parts the facemask will be more of a fashion statement than a health requirement."

"Well, what can I say? I'm a trend-setter. Oh, and by the way, while I was in the car, I logged into my iTunes account. I have a playlist on your phone all ready and waiting for the final leg of our trip."

"Ahh, damn. I thought you liked the country playlist."

He grimaced. "I did not."

"Liar. You said, and I quote, 'actually, this isn't too bad.'"

"So, naturally you mistook that for 'like'?"

"You're missing the boat, dude. I keep telling you— country's the new rock. There's a gold mine to be had there."

"I already have a gold mine. Now who's ready for Bieber?"

————

We were about an hour into his playlist when an acoustic song came on. Bodhi stealthily reached over and pressed forward without taking his eyes off the road.

"What was that?" I asked, my gaze fixed on his chiseled profile. "I actually liked that."

"Really?"

A small smile curved his lips so I picked up the phone to investigate. "Ahh, it's yours."

Two spots of color stained his cheeks. "And that's why I skipped it."

"Why is it on the playlist if you didn't want me to hear it?"

"Because, and I know this might be hard for you to comprehend, Breeze, but before we met *yesterday*, I actually had a life unrelated to you. My guess is I added that song weeks ago and forgot it was on this particular playlist."

"Or," I mused. "You rushed to add it just for me and then skipped over it to get my attention."

His sigh was all for show. "Sure. Yes. That's what happened because I had so much time to plan between breaking my father's heart and right now."

I pressed the back button. "Well, anyway, I'm going to listen to it and you're going to be quiet while I do."

Bodhi shook his head, but I didn't fail to notice his smile. "And you don't have a boyfriend? It's mind boggling."

"I know, right? It's always puzzled me too. Anyway, lucky for you, the position is open and I'm currently taking applications, just, you know, FYI."

"Cool. Thanks."

"And Bodhi? Keep in mind that although being a country music fan isn't required, it might bump your application to the top of the pile."

"So it's a big pile, huh?"

"Fairly large, yes. Now be quiet so I can hear your song. I need to see what we're working with."

The track wasn't a typical *AnyDayNow* song, focused on girls and partying and hip hop dance beats. This song was raw, stripping away all pretenses. Just a boy and his guitar. And that voice. He sang of love and loss with haunted lyrics that spoke to my wounded heart. Whoever he'd written it for caused him pain, and I wanted to be the one to ease his suffering.

Bodhi focused on the road while I listened, then re-listened to the tune. His numerous sideways glances told me he was interested in my opinion, but he had just enough fear of my answer not to ask. Before I could play the song for the third time, he covered my hand with his.

"I didn't know you could sing like that," I said once I could formulate a thought. "You've got a little of that raspy tone to your voice but at the same time it's so smooth. And what was the high pitch thing you did toward the end? I got goose bumps. You're super talented, Bodhi."

He blushed at the compliment, though I wasn't sure why. I'm sure Bodhi heard praise all the time.

"Thank you." He smiled and I smiled back. The energy passing between us fortified me with the courage to say out loud what was screaming in my head. "She must have been pretty special, the girl in that song, for you to have loved her so much."

Bodhi's hand shot to his hair, nervous fingers sifting through the strands. When a good minute passed without a response, I added, "Anyway, it was a beautiful song. I'm assuming you wrote it."

He nodded jerkily.

"Do you have more like this?"

"Enough to fill an album."

"So then why haven't you... filled an album?"

"I told you before, it's not what people are expecting from me."

"So? What's good is good. And that song, Bodhi, it's good. No, it's great. And I'm not just saying that because we slept together. I'm saying it because I truly believe you have a gift. In fact, I'm going to go out on a limb here and say you've been wasting your talent in a boy band. You could be the next great country-rock star."

———

We were still on the coast when the sun began to set. Since we weren't bound by the clock any longer, we pulled over to watch the day turn to night from one of the many sand dunes lining the beaches.

"This isn't your first sunset, is it?" I asked, leaning against him, the heat of his body warming me in places he couldn't touch.

"No." He hummed low in his throat, drawing my gaze. The sun's filtered rays cast his face in an orange glow, and I wasn't sure I'd ever seen a more handsome man. Until he smiled a soft smile. "But it's the first time with a pretty girl."

And then it was quiet, just the sound of the surf and his brilliant blue eyes on mine. Trembling inside, I slowly leaned forward and pressed a kiss to his lips. We sat there for a moment, connected. To each other. And the sea. And the sunset. And then his arms banded around me and he pulled me closer. This was a new feeling, tender and sweet, yet no less erotically charged than the knock down wrestling matches of last night and this morning. My body tingled in response to the sensitive side of Bodhi. I'd glimpsed it in the song he wrote. But now I could feel it, our bond, to the tips of my toes.

Easing me onto the sand, he shifted, and we were face to face. His hand slid up my arm, past my shoulder, and landed on my cheek. Then his mouth was on mine again. Tasting. Exploring. All against the backdrop of the brilliant sky.

"Are you for real?" I asked, a swarm of butterflies taking flight in my stomach as his hand continued to roam. Everything about us felt urgent. Intense.

Maybe it was the fire, but each moment seemed more precious than the next. Whether Bodhi was on board or not, when all was said and done, I'd have no regrets.

"Don't be fooled by the fancy packaging, Breeze." His gaze fell to my lips. "Under everything I'm just a screwed-up guy trying to find his way in this world."

Fully embracing his troubled soul, my fingertips skimmed his cheek. "I see you, Bodhi."

He jerked back, brows drawn together. "What did you say?"

"I see you," I repeated hesitantly. "Why?"

After searching my face for a long moment, the smile returned. "It's just a line I use during my shows to slay the elementary school girls. But coming from you, it doesn't sound nearly as cheesy."

"Thanks, I think."

"You know what I meant."

And I did. That was the weird part of our connection. It was like I'd known him forever. Like his heart spoke to mine. A tender beat I wanted to hear forever.

17

BREEZE: A FIST FULL OF NICKELS

BODHI DROVE SLOWLY DOWN THE STREET, TAKING IN ALL THE stately mansions. "Damn, these are nice houses. Which one is yours?"

Sinking deeper into the plush leather, I chewed my lip. "The single story on the left."

A moment later when the house in question came into view, Bodhi swung his gaze in my direction and gaped like a fool. "That's your house?" I jerked a nod. "You have got to be shitting me right now?"

Yes, I lived in Cliffside Estates, an exclusive enclave nestled on a cliff overlooking the Pacific. The mini mansions lining the street were well lit, gleaming masterpieces of architecture. Except for ours.

"Not shitting," I said with a sigh. "That's my house. Just pull into the driveway and don't say a word."

Before we'd even rolled to a stop, Bodhi collapsed into a fit of laughter. I'd thought about warning him beforehand. But what was the point? The reaction would've been the same. Laughter. And it was kind of funny. Though our neighbors probably wouldn't agree.

You see, in every upscale development there was always one house that pulled down real estate prices. That was ours. My family home may have been located in Cliffside Estates but it was no majestic manor. Surrounded by multi-million dollar estates, our ramshackle dwelling was often referred to as 'The Black Hole'.

The house had been in my family for sixty years. A throwback to another era, the modest split level boasted outdated bricks and a funky shaped roof. Blanched and weather-beaten, the house was the singular eyesore in a land of giants.

Once upon a time, all the houses on the street looked like ours, back when we'd lived a quarter of a mile walk to the cliff's edge. But erosion from powerful storms destroyed the homes closest to the bluff, forcing the removal of those residences in danger of crumbling into the surf. Suddenly, our humble abode had become prime real estate.

Investors took notice and came knocking. They offered virtual fortunes and one by one our neighbors fell. Their homes were bulldozed to the ground to make way for new, stately mansions. We were the holdouts, the ones who didn't bow to the pressure. What the stakeholders hadn't bargained for when they were making their offers was that not everyone had a price tag and that *everyone* was my mother. She was the frustrating home-owner with an aversion to all things materialistic. Money meant nothing to her, although admittedly she inherited a nest egg from her own parents which allowed her to live comfortably the rest of her life.

"My parents are... How should I put this...?"

Bodhi shook his head, grinning. "You know what? No explanation needed. This place speaks for itself. It's like something out of a time warp. Wait, is this the Brady Bunch house?"

"I wish. Then at least there would be an excuse to preserve a historical landmark. I think I must warn you that my parents are every bit as eccentric as the place they live in."

He rubbed his hands together. "Oh yes! This is going to be epic!" And with that he hopped out of the car like an eight-year-old on his way to a birthday party at Chuck E Cheese.

Joining him at the bumper, I offered a wry smile. "I wouldn't get too excited. We might not be able to find them inside the place." When his brow knit, I lifted a shoulder. "They aren't big on cleaning, so the house will probably be a mess. "

Before Bodhi could respond, or dive back in the car, the light flicked on. My mother appeared from behind the ivy lattice wall, smoothing the ends of her pixie haircut. One strap of her overalls slid off her shoulder as she sauntered toward us in clunky Doc Martens.

"Are you giving the boy disclaimers, Breeze?" Mom asked. "Please. We aren't heathens."

Blinking, she stopped in her tracks as she got a good look at the 'boy' in question. Clearly, she recognized him. Which, in turn, shocked the hell out of me. I assumed my parents wouldn't have a clue who Bodhi was seeing as they didn't approve of any pop culture occurring *after* the seventies and eighties.

My mother came out of her coma and let out a whoop, clapping her hands. "Terry!" she called to my step-father. "Get out here! You've got to see this!"

"Mom?" Jerking my head in Bodhi's direction, I widened my eyes and mouthed, *"Stop."*

She didn't and a second later my stepfather wandered out of the house in a pair of rubber ducky board shorts and nothing more. Black tufts of chest hair migrated down his belly, over his shoulders, and blanketed his back. Really? He knew we were coming. He couldn't at least slip on his favorite Ninja Turtle t-shirt?

"What are you yelling about?" he asked.

Mom pointed at Bodhi. Not a gesture to respectfully announce his presence, but a full-on finger point. I'd warned him they were eccentric but this...

"Holy Mary, Mother of Jesus!" Terrance exclaimed, tipping forward to examine Bodhi like he was an exhibit at the museum.

This was a new low for both of them. Yes, Bodhi was a celebrity, but certainty he deserved some level of respect.

"I called it!" My mother squealed as she pivoted to Terrance to give him a high-five. "Did I not call it?"

"You called it all right, woman. I'm just privileged to know you."

My stepfather offered an exaggerated bow while Bodhi and I exchanged confused glances.

"What's happening?" I asked.

"I'm just so smart. We saw on the news that Bodhi was missing and I told your dad... I said, watch he's probably Breeze's mystery man, the guy who saved her on the hill and holy crapoli – I was right. Damn, I scare myself sometimes."

"You scare us all," Terrance agreed before addressing Bodhi. "Nice to meet you, son." And then me. "How's my favorite girl in the world?"

He couldn't just hug me. That would be too simple. Instead he scooped me up, shook me like a ragdoll, then twirled me around. Bodhi received a cuddle too, but his was merely a giant bear hug and thankfully his feet remained on solid ground.

"I can't tell you how relieved Mom and I are to see you... both of you. What a terrifying experience. We're so happy you're finally home."

Sweetpea picked that moment to make his presence known, erupting into a series of annoying yaps.

"I see we have other guests." Terrance said and, peeking into the car, he smiled broadly. "Ooh, rats. My favorite."

Bodhi's eyes couldn't have been wider. My stepfather had a

gift for captivating an audience. Just not the way he might have hoped.

"I didn't get my hug," my mother said as she squeezed me silly, peppering kisses all over my face.

Once I was free of her clutches, her eyes fixed on Bodhi and she opened her arms wide. "Do you mind?"

Without waiting for an answer, she folded him into her embrace. "Thank you for helping our daughter and bringing her home safely to us," she whispered. "We're beyond grateful."

"Oh yeah, of course," he said, sliding his arm around my waist. "But your daughter has helped me as much as I've helped her."

"Oh, I'm sure she has." Mom winked, then her eyes darted back and forth between Bodhi and me. What? No. She'd better not start with the innuendos or I might just have to die. "Did Breeze cut your hair?"

He grinned, his hand raking his freshly shorn locks. "She did. The idea was to make me less conspicuous."

"Right. I see where she was going with it." Mom tilted her head, tapping a finger to her lips as she surveyed my handiwork. "Only, I think it might have the opposite effect." Her gaze shifted to me and she smiled. "If you're going for unremarkable, Breeze, maybe don't make him look so hunky."

"I worked with what I had," I complained, throwing my hands up. "What was I supposed to do, give him a mullet?"

Before my mom could get in another jab, Bodhi rocked back on his heels and said, "I feel like I'm not even part of this conversation anymore."

"Welcome to my world, bud," Terrance said, shouldering past us with the rat cage in his arms. Enthralled by the rodents, he dipped his head and mumbled to his new friends, "Aren't you gorgeous little fellas?"

"Pretty sure your rodent friends are a boy and girl, Pops," I said. "I was told their combined Hollywood name is Brangelina."

"Well, I can't be sure until I check their underbellies but, from first glance, I think we're dealing with BradAngelo." Terrance said as he trudged toward the door. At the last minute he stopped and looked over his shoulder at Bodhi. "You can come help me if you want."

Bodhi wrinkled his nose. "Will we be checking for rat testicles?"

My stepfather considered the question for a moment before admitting, "Probably, but I've got beer in the fridge."

After a moment of contemplation, Bodhi shrugged and followed Terrance.

Mom tore her gaze from their retreating backs and shifted her focus to me. "Oh my god!" she mouthed, her eyes twice their normal size.

"Right?"

"Uh...yeah. What were the odds of you getting saved by... *that*?"

"I can't imagine them being real high."

"Probably not. And the odds are even less of the two of you going to pound town, but look at you! You go, Girl!"

I crossed my arms over my chest. "How could you possibly know whether we slept together or not?"

"You brought him home."

"So what?"

"Breeze. You've only brought three men home. One was Brandon. One was," she waived her hand dismissively, "I can't remember his name, the one with the mohawk who cried a lot."

"Troy."

"Oh, that's right, the Weeping Warrior. Anyway, that brings us to number three." She inclined her head toward the house like I didn't know who she was talking about before adding, "See, honey, you're like a pigeon. You only come home to breed."

I just choked out a laugh. "You're ridiculous, Mom. I hope you know that."

"Ridiculously intuitive. Don't even try to deny you and Bodhi aren't doing the bowchickawowwow."

She swiveled her hips in an exaggerated motion that made me wince. "Until you speak in age-appropriate slang, we have nothing more to say."

"And the best part of this whole thing is now that you have your Jon Snow, you can come to the family reunion."

"Mom." I lowered my voice to barely a whisper. "Don't you dare bring that up to Bodhi. That's not why he's here."

Mom's face flashed with surprise at my abrupt tone. Then she wisely closed her mouth. Not that I hadn't expected her to bring it up. Just not so soon. Any illusions about my celebrity bed buddy would be dashed when she found out Bodhi was heading back to Los Angeles the day before the reunion.

But now that I was in town, there'd be no getting out of my family obligation. The firestorm, and subsequent road trip, had dumped me straight into the lap of my ex-fiancée. I was going to have to play nice - alone.

"What did he come here for then?" Mom asked, leaning a hip against the singed paint on the quarter panel of the Range Rover.

"Not for me, if that's what you're thinking."

Before she could respond, Terrance and Bodhi joined us, beers in hand.

"Thanks for letting me stay here tonight," Bodhi said, raising a bottle to my parents.

"Oh, of course," Mom replied. "I so enjoy harboring fugitives."

"You heard about that, huh?" he asked, with just the hint of a smile.

"It's all over the news. I think people in Mongolia have heard about it."

"So what's the verdict now? Am I dead or alive?"

"First you were dead. Like candlelight vigil dead," Mom said. "But now you're alive and the world can rejoice once more."

"She's mocking me already?" He laughed.

Before I had a chance to answer, Mom mused, "I'm warning you, though. You may want to lay low for a few days. Maybe go to a movie in a darkened theater or a family reunion with people you don't know. Stuff like that."

I flashed her a warning glare. Thankfully, Bodhi had no idea what she was babbling about. Still, he seemed amused by the whole exchange with my parents. Which was encouraging. At least he wasn't running away.

"Anyway, I made up the bed in Breeze's old room. I assumed the two of you would want some privacy." She winked at Bodhi. "And fresh sheets."

"Mom? Not cool. Boundaries, remember? Is it too late for us to book a hotel?"

"Don't be ridiculous. Anything you can do in a hotel, you can do better here. Terrance and I don't judge, do we sweetie?"

"No, we do not," he replied. "The two of you can feel free to—"

"Nope." I covered Terrance's mouth with my hand. "I think you've said plenty. Bodhi gets it. Now, can we change the subject please?"

"I'm actually thoroughly enjoying this conversation," Bodhi said.

"Oh, I'm sure you are. But I'm also convinced it's getting close to bedtime for these two chatter bugs."

"Are you kidding?" Mom said. "We're just getting started.

Terrance and I are binge watching Orange is the New Black. Very informative. Lots of lesbian sex." She tossed us a smile. "You really should watch it."

My cheeks ignited with the fire of a thousand suns. *Kill me now.*

As Terrance took care of the other animals, Mom grabbed Bodhi's arm and steered him toward the front door. "I'm sure you're starving. I have dinner all ready. Come in. Oh Breeze, wave to the Ring."

"The what?"

"The doorbell."

"You have a Ring doorbell? What do you need that for?"

"Packages I get from online shopping. It records thieves. Very useful."

"Huh, that's high tech for you, Mom."

She laughed me off before leading the two of us through the house. To my surprise, the place was spotless and the typical nonsense clutter was nowhere in sight. I did a quick scan for the bobble-headed plastic turtles and the Mario Kart toy collection, but... nothing. Even the blue Aladdin genie Terrance insisted was modeled after him was gone.

What happened to my McDonald's Happy Meal living room?

Shabby chic coastal designs had replaced the bric-a-brac, and on the wall—no way—I took a step closer to examine the smart TV.

"What happened to all your .... stuff?" I ran a hand over the fabric on the sofa. "And the old suede couches? And the black and white television set?"

Mom beamed. "I hired an interior designer. You like?"

I loved! But that wasn't the point. Who was this materialistic woman and where had she been when I really needed her?

"The exterior is next," Terrance chimed in, cradling Lucy in his arms. "We're having it completely redone after the winter months."

All these years of ridicule for being the black sheep of the neighborhood and now they decide to update—at a time when I get absolutely no benefit from it?

"You alright there, Sweetie?" Mom asked, patting my shoulder.

"Sure. Just shocked."

"It's not a big deal. Your dad and I just needed a change."

After she called Terrance my dad, I knew what was coming. My stepfather never passed up a teaching moment. "In case you're wondering," he said to Bodhi. "Breezie and I aren't blood related."

He loved the shock factor of that line. Every single one of my friends meeting him for the first time got the same ridiculous salutation. See, there was no reason for clarification because it was clear by the lily-white color of my skin and the chocolate brown flavoring of his that the two of us weren't a perfect DNA match.

Holding back a snicker, I smacked my stepfather. "Must you."

"What?" Terrance shrugged, grinning mischievously. "He seemed confused."

"Bodhi, were you confused?"

"Not really, no."

"There you have it."

"She's so testy," Terrance whispered conspiratorially to my companion.

I rolled my eyes. "Whatever, Pops."

"You know, Bodhi," he said. "If there's one thing I've learn from raising a daughter, it's that there's always a little 'fuck you' in every 'whatever'."

That got him a laugh *and* a fist bump from a bona fide celebrity. My stepfather beamed with pride.

"So, what do you really think?" Mom asked, opening her arms to the new living space.

"It's beautiful. It just doesn't seem like you."

She shrugged, appearing a little let down by my reaction. "The older I get, the more I appreciate functionality."

Now I felt bad. Mom was looking for reinforcement not eye-popping shock. "I love it," I said, embracing her.

My cell phone dinged so I pulled it from my pocket.

"Oh no, honey, that's mine." Mom held up a nearly identical phone, only hers was the newest model. "I just need to answer this text really quick."

"You have a smart phone now? I can't believe you swapped out that ancient flip phone? Whatever happened to 'if it ain't broke don't fix it'?"

"It broke." Of course it did. "Besides, Breeze, I got tired of people thinking I was a time traveler."

"Well, that was bound to happen."

"And now, the best part is, I have all my apps at my fingertips."

"Oh god, Mom, you're blowing my mind. You have apps?" What was happening here? When had my earth mother, the woman who'd forgone carpools for the more eco-friendly 'bike-pools' become the futuristic matriarch of the Jetsons?

"Oh my god, Daughter," she mimicked me. "Stop acting like I've been abducted by aliens. So I like a little technology in my life. Big deal."

Mom proceeded to snap a selfie of the two of us, and add the dog-ear filter before sending it off to cyberspace.

"You have Snapchat too?" I nearly fell to the ground in shock.

"Of course. Who doesn't?"

"I'll tell you who doesn't – *you!* The woman who refused to own a microwave because you thought it would damage our DNA and cause genetic mutations?"

Mom cringed.

"No?" I gasped. "There'd better not be a microwave in that newly remodeled kitchen of yours."

Although she tried to block me, I slipped past her and into the kitchen. And there, sitting amongst the updated stainless steel appliances, was my mother's lifelong nemesis— a microwave.

My mind was officially blown.

———

"Okay, so, here are the towels," Mom said, handing me a stack. "I added some extra sheets just in case, you know..." Her eyes twinkled as she sent off the most awkward nod in Bodhi's direction.

"Oh no," he stumbled over his words. "That's not... um..."

She patted his shoulder. "Right. Right."

"No, really..."

But mom was out the door before he could reassure her that he had zero plans of banging her daughter in her childhood bed.

He sank down on the mattress. "Wow, your parents are..."

"Oh, trust me, I know."

"It's just, is it weird that I feel like I'm letting Betsy and Terrance down by not having sex with you tonight?"

I laughed, wedging between his knees so I could get close enough to steal a kiss. "If I had a nickel for how many times I've heard that in my life..."

He wrapped his arms around my waist, playfully asking, "Oh yeah? How much money would you have?"

My shoulders slumped. I had nothing to show for my bravado. "Honestly? I'd be a very poor woman."

"Really? Like how poor?"

"Let's just say a quarter would be too rich for my blood."

"Huh? How many guys have you been with?"

"I started dating my ex back in high school. We were together for six years. After the split, I dated a few guys."

"How many is a few?"

"Two."

"So, based on the number of guys you've slept with you'd have fifteen cents?"

"A dime, actually."

"A dime?" He laughed. "Wow, Breeze, you can't even buy a gumball with that."

I giggled, smacking his chest. "And how much would you have, Popstar? A hundred dollar bill?"

"Please. Do you have any idea how many nickels it would take to earn me a hundred smackers? I'd be physically exhausted."

"Oh, I'm sure you earn a nickel a night on tour."

"No, actually I don't." he said. "That's RJ's thing. Not mine."

"So you're saying RJ Contreras is more prolific than you?"

"Uh, yeah. He even has one of those coin counters and little brown paper wraps to bring his nickels into the bank."

I was starting to get a bit antsy. I needed to know the dollar amount I was working with here. My smile melted as I swept hair off his forehead and demanded full disclosure from money-bags. "How much, Bodhi? Give me a ballpark figure."

And so began the longest, most drawn out calculation I'd ever encountered in my lifetime. Bodhi tallied under his breath, even employing the assistance of his fingers to come up with an acceptable dollar amount. Finally he met my eyes, appearing confident in his answer.

"Before I give you the total," he said. "I want to voice my objection to this line of questioning."

"Duly noted."

"And I feel like whatever I say will be used against me in a court of law."

"Bodhi," I blurted out. "The bottom line?"

"Fine $1.65."

"Wait, is that per person or per time?"

"Same thing."

He was right. I was using his admission against him. Even though I didn't know him well enough to judge, my response was still borderline 'jealous bitch'. "You've slept with thirty-three nickels?!"

He shrugged. "Give or take five cents here or there."

"Bodhi, Jesus. Did you even have time to reload between nickels?"

"I thought this was a judgment free zone. I'm supposed to be safe in the love shack. That's what your mom said."

"Yeah, well, she's full of shit."

"See. I told you this wasn't a good idea, but did you listen to me? Nooo... you kept pushing for my bank account numbers."

"Because I didn't realize what a slut you were before we started counting money!"

"You're looking at this in the wrong way. The point I was making is that none of those nickels were spent on the same woman."

"And that's supposed to please me?"

"It should."

"How do you figure?"

"Because, Breeze, you're my first dime."

———

I was a dime! A dime.

Bodhi's admission, however unorthodox, warmed me from the inside out and left me all gooey and starry-eyed.

Okay, sure, maybe it wasn't the most romantic thing to come out of a manwhore's mouth, but I was batting off the butterflies anyway. Bodhi Beckett could have whoever he wanted, as many times as he wanted, but I was the one who'd changed his spending habits.

Once we were in bed, I couldn't even think about sleep. "Bodhi?"

"Yeah?"

"We could make it fifteen cents, if you want. My parents wouldn't mind if we fornicate."

Choking out a laugh, Bodhi shifted in bed and pressed his finger to my lips. "Babe, normally you'd have me at fornicate, but this is a special circumstance. As we speak, Terrance and Betsy are on the other side of this wall— - your stepdad still in his rubber ducky shorts— with a notepad and pen in hand, eagerly waiting to critique my performance."

I scrunched my nose. The sad part? He was probably right. I could picture my parents sitting us down after breakfast to give us our score.

"Maybe we should just call it a night," I suggested.

He laughed, settling onto his back and pulling the sheets up to his neck. "I'm thinking that's best."

"Although..." I said, drawing out the word to add a touch of sexy.

Bodhi shifted again, throwing off the sheets and rolling onto his side to face me. He'd heard the suggestive tone in my voice and despite the obvious pitfalls of sex in a hippie household, my guy was still willing to entertain any avenue that might lead to some booty. What a keeper.

"I was just thinking how fun it would be to give my parents a little dose of their own medicine."

A conspiratorial grin materialized as he wrapped his brain around the inner-workings of my evil mind. At this point, it didn't matter what I proposed because Bodhi Beckett was all in — and then some. "You're not suggesting what I think you're suggesting, are you?"

Bodhi reached up and slid his hand through wayward stands of hair on his forehead. My eyes tracked his every sexy move.

"Oh, but I am," I said, a conniving smile curving my lips as my fingers followed his into his luscious mane. "And all it will take from you is some painful dialogue, a little bed rattling, and a whole lot of faked orgasms. What do you say, Bodhi, you ready to prove how good an actor you are?"

"Bitch, please. I'm at least as good as a porn star. Let's do this thing!"

18

BODHI: QUICKSAND

I AWOKE THE NEXT MORNING TO SUNLIGHT POURING THROUGH THE curtains. Throwing an arm over my face, I chuckled. Maybe last night's performance wasn't worthy of an Oscar nod, but it was certainly enough to earn a nomination at the adult film awards. I was fairly convinced that if Breeze hadn't overacted her third mind-blowing orgasm in less than five minutes, we could have fooled her parents into thinking I was a super stud.

But as it was, Terrance and Betsy knew a thing or two about shitty acting and turned the tables on us, faking their own love-making session by turning up the television in their room during a particularly racy scene in their favorite binge television program.

Still drowsy, I thought about catching a little more sleep. But Breeze wasn't next to me, which was probably what woke me up in the first place. I sensed her absence. The girl was quickly becoming a staple in my diet, a necessity I couldn't live without.

I was fully vested in her now... in *us*. My mind was officially blown. Breeze was everything, all wrapped up in a shiny pink package. I was quickly falling into a place I'd never imagined myself going. If there was such a thing as love at first sight, I was pretty sure it felt like this. She consumed me and, when she was near, I felt this freakish pressure in my chest. And then there was the smile that refused to leave my face, and the boner reserved specifically for her.

At the very least, I was intensely attracted to this woman. At the very most, I was already gone. She made it so easy to fall. There was something drawing us together, as if we were meant to be. What happened up on that mountain... there was a reason for it. Maybe we were meant to meet, meant to protect each other, meant to fall in love.

If I let Breeze slip through my fingers...

I banished the thought when Sweetpea stretched, his little legs using my skin as a yoga mat.

"Good morning." I tickled the pup behind his ears. Wrong move. The little jerk jumped to his feet, bared his teeth, and growled menacingly at me.

Damn this dog had some real issues. I mean, come on. What trials could a pampered dog, raised in a luxurious mansion, have endured to turn him into such an utter asshole?

Feeling secure enough in our relationship to get to the bottom of the mystery, I asked, "What the hell is wrong with you?"

I thought we were getting somewhere when he tilted his head as if pondering. But then Little Dick dropped the pretense and attacked, snapping and snarling and going for my moneymaker.

"Dude! Not the face. Never the face!"

I pushed him back behind enemy lines, but the cocksure Chihuahua kept advancing, chomping those pint-sized teeth at me. A full-on civil war in a nice warm bed was not the way I wanted to start my morning. Luckily, I had what my nemesis didn't—the gift of size. Scooping him up in one hand, I swiftly dropped him onto the floor. "Now try to disfigure me, shithead."

It was then I noticed Breeze leaning against the door frame, with her arms folded lazily over her chest. That sleepy smile of hers grabbed hold and shook me awake. Disheveled hair sat atop her head in a messy bun and just the slightest hint of bare skin peaked over the waistband of her flowered sleep shorts. And just like that—I was hers.

"Dude," she said, amused. "If I were trying to disfigure you, I wouldn't do it wearing moose head slippers."

She lifted one leg to reveal her footwear.

"I was talking to Sweetpea but damn, girl, horns and everything?"

"Of course. Would you expect any less of me?"

I thought about it for a moment, finding it telling of the relationship we were building. No, I didn't expect anything less from her. Ever. In fact, it was Breeze's unpredictable nature that had me groveling at her feet.

Maybe it was a side effect of growing up in a cynical environment, but I never thought people had the capacity to surprise me. Then Breeze came along with her fake medical conditions and horny moose slippers and slapped me upside the head with her quirkiness. Every so often a person dropped into our lives, changing our path. But I had a strong suspicion Breeze was altering my course for good.

"You like what you see?" she asked, performing a little hip swivel that was fully appreciated by my ever-expanding woody.

I removed the sheets to reveal just how much I liked what I was seeing.

"Oh crap, Bodhi, you really like moose."

"Uh-huh. Are you coming over here or what? Because I've got a half-torqued chub that's not going to beat itself."

She flicked her gaze over me, tongue sweeping seductively along her lower lip. "What's in it for me, hotstuff?"

"You will be fully compensated, I promise."

It was a meeting of the minds. Moose slippers and parental proximity weren't enough to dampen our spirits. If anything, last night had proven even vigorously performed fake sex did nothing to rattle those people. If we wanted to have a little fun in Breeze's childhood bedroom, there was absolutely no one offended enough to stop us.

Breeze grabbed Sweetpea and ushered him out the door before flicking off her snazzy slippers and starting my day off with a bang.

———

"Good morning," Betsy said, greeting us each with a kiss on the cheek. "Sit. I'm making omelets."

"Oh, yum," I replied, plopping myself down in the chair and rubbing my hands together in anticipation. There was nothing like banging her daughter down the hall to work up an appetite. I kept that tidbit to myself although, honestly, the extra information probably would have earned me a high-five.

"Did you sleep well?" she asked, the hint of a smile playing out over her lips.

"Oh yeah, I was exhausted."

"Yes," Betsy giggled. "I'm sure you were."

Breeze grabbed a piece of toast, ripping small pieces off the corner instead of taking a bite. "Mother, you're goading. Bodhi has no filter and I'd rather not start a discussion about your and Terrance's rather unorthodox bedroom practices."

"Us?" Terrance wandered in still wearing his rubber ducky shorts. Breeze and I exchanged a knowing glance. "Airports are quieter than you two."

———

"So, you are... I am... it's... I'm so nervous... sorry."

My mother's stammered apologies raced down the line. Maybe ringing her up out of the blue wasn't the smartest choice. She was so flustered she had trouble stringing words together into legitimate sentences.

"How about we meet somewhere?" I asked.

But it wasn't a question. More like a gift. And one I hoped I wouldn't regret giving.

"Okay." She sounded more hesitant than excited, which surprised me given that she'd been the one to reach out to me in the first place. Regardless, I quickly gave her an out. "Unless you don't want to. That's fine too."

"No, it's not that, I just don't have a car that can make it to Los Angeles, but I can try and borrow one."

Once I understood it wasn't about our meeting, I let go of the breath I'd been holding. "I'm in the Bay Area."

"You are? Why?"

To find out who the fuck I am, that's why?

"To see you."

The truth spilled out, thick enough to coat the silence that swelled between us. It was so quiet, I thought she might have hung up.

"Hello?"

I hated the fear edging my tone. We were strangers. It didn't matter if...

"Oh, Alex, I'm sorry. I..."

Too stunned by the name she'd used, the rest of her sentence was lost on me.

"Don't call me that," I snapped. "My name is Bodhi."

To my surprise, she was quick to reply, and rather forcefully, "No, your name is Alex."

A duel of wills played out in the silence that ensued. I

wanted to counter her argument but didn't have enough background information to make a draw.

"I don't mean to be harsh. Of course, I'll call you Bodhi."

Her concession confused me, but a win was a win.

"Um, okay, when can you meet?"

"Can we meet tomorrow morning? Or if that doesn't work, I can try to rearrange a few things today."

Rearrange? She hadn't seen me in over twenty years. You'd think she'd clear her calendar. But then, what did I know about her life? Maybe she had a big deadline looming or a pressing nail appointment.

"Tomorrow morning's fine."

After firming up the arrangements, we said an awkward goodbye and I sat back, staring at the screen with my stomach coiled into knots. Was I making the right choice by going into this blind? Maybe I should read the report provided by my investigator with the background information he'd gathered on her. I'd specifically chosen not to look at it after he'd pasted a post-a-note on the report.

Remember what I said about expectation.

Talk about a disclaimer. Whatever truth lay within those papers, he felt the need to warn me. But I didn't want her misdeeds smashed into my face before I'd had a chance to form my own opinion.

Or did I?

———

Sidestepping the conversation in the kitchen, I headed straight to the bedroom. It only took a minute before a light rap on the door forced me to shake off the haze. Since my back was pressed against the wood, I was face to face with Breeze in under five seconds.

She blinked at me. "Whoa, that was fast."

"I used to be a doorman."

Confused, she wrinkled her nose. "Really?"

"No." Chuckling, I gathered her in my arms.

"Ah. Sarcasm. Got it. You okay?"

"I think so. Second guessing myself."

"Well, why didn't you say so? Second guessing is my specialty."

"Really? I didn't realize. In that case, I had an investigator look into my mother and he found stuff on her. But I chose not to read the report because I don't want my opinion of her tainted before we meet."

Breeze didn't have to say a word. Her very visible cringe was proof she thought I was crazy.

"You think I'm making a mistake?" I asked.

"Um, well, how thick was the report?"

"Pretty fucking thick!"

More cringing.

"Stop." I laughed. "You're not helping."

"Sorry. Look, I don't think it's wrong to give her a chance to explain herself. If you know her background going in, you'll be biased. At the same time, knowing will keep you from getting duped."

"What would you do?"

"I'd find out everything I could about her, right down to her favorite Disney villain—but that's just me. I like to be thorough."

———

Since the reunion with my mother would be taking place the following day, it ruined Breeze's plan for not only a surprise camping trip, but also 'Bucket List Wednesday.' However, it proved not to be a problem because Breeze knew how to roll with the punches. Scraping the camping fun altogether, she effortlessly retitled the day 'Bucket List Tuesday' and within an hour of my phone conversation, we were pulling up to a park.

A very public park. Sweat broke out on my brow as I took in the scene. For all her good intentions, Breeze hadn't experienced AnyDayNow pandemonium levels yet and just because the last couple of outings had been a success didn't mean we should push our luck. I should say something, warn her. But that happy smile on her face, one that was full of promise for the great day she had planned, kept me silent.

"You all right?" she asked, a little of the light fading from her eyes. "What's with the pouty face?"

"There's no pouty face. It's just my regular one."

"Not when you're with me, it's not. Now, turn that frown upside down and let's go roll down that hill."

She jumped out of the car before I could protest. Hill rolling hadn't been on my list of things to do. But, as with everything since meeting this girl, I couldn't bring myself to say no. So once again, I let her take the lead.

Grabbing ahold of my hand, Breeze sprinted up the hill, dragging me after her. Once at the top, she planted her hands on either side of my face and said, "Now, this isn't usually part of the childhood experience, but I can't help myself."

The kiss that followed made the trip up worth it. I smiled against her lips, allowing the anxiety to melt away as I lifted Breeze off her feet. Her legs wrapped around my waist and we kissed, lost in our own little world. There were no demands on my time, no screaming fans, and no hiding behind a wall of fame.

"Are you ready?" she asked, breathless.

No. But did it matter? Whatever made her happy, that's what I'd do. Heart pounding, I eased us onto the lush grass and let gravity propel us down the hill.

––––––

Medieval paper kite flying was next on our list, but getting lift off was near impossible, even after Breeze added her own puffs of air to the rickety contraption. She assured me that *failing* to fly a kite was a common childhood experience, so we crossed that particular activity off my list as well.

The park proved an effective location for a myriad of childhood activities. After catching a bug, splashing in a puddle, and jumping in the world's smallest leaf pile, I felt lighter, happier, than I had in years. Breeze and I had earned this day. No rules, no expectations, no worries. We were safe, unharmed, and free from the smoke and ash cloud now large enough to be seen from space.

Best of all, there were no curious onlookers lurking in the bushes. The park Breeze had chosen was nestled against the hills in an affluent area where the only people wandering around were a few retired dog walkers and a group of moms with babies in strollers, their preschool age kids climbing all over the playground equipment. No one was expecting to find the wayward member of AnyDayNow swinging from the jungle gym.

That's not to say my presence didn't attract some attention. Eager four and five-year-old kids flocked to Breeze and I the minute we took over the equipment. The munchkins followed us around like we were the most fun they'd had since birth. With our band of merry mini-men sticking to us like glue, Breeze and I climbed the jungle gyms, tumbled down the slides, and scaled the monkey bars.

"Okay, we're going to jump now," Breeze instructed as we soared through the air on a pair of side-by-side swings. "Hands on the other side of the chain. Now jump!"

Following her example, I let go of the chain a good five feet in the air. While Breeze got a nice arch and landed gracefully on her feet, I became tangled in the chain and face planted in the soft sand.

"You were supposed to land on your feet." Breeze snorted a laugh.

"See, you could have made that clear."

The Lego gang sprang forward, dog piling on top of me as if I'd orchestrated the entire belly flop for their pleasure. Mothers descended from every direction, peeling their unruly charges off my back. As I pushed to my feet, flashes of recognition shot through the eyes of the mommy brigade.

"You know who you look like, right?" one woman asked, her eyes rounded balls of wonder. No matter how I answered the awkward query, I always sounded like a douche. But I couldn't ignore her.

"Um... I have a pretty good idea."

"So you are..." Her voice lowered to a whisper. "Him?"

I nodded, adding a grin. Cue the douchebag.

Several other mommies squealed their delight and chattered amongst themselves. But there was one outlier—there was always one—who felt the need to question.

"Wait, who is he?" she asked, rubbing her belly. She was the type of pregnant that created shade for those below.

"Bodhi Beckett," came the resounding response from her friends.

The expectant mom glanced me over critically. "No, I don't think so. Bodhi's got long hair. You got ID on you?"

I shook my head. Even if I had an ID, I wouldn't show her. It wasn't up to me to prove my identity. Running my fingers through the locks in question, I watched as the two moms traded barbs over who had a better eye for pop stars.

While I waited for the verdict, I took the opportunity to glance over at Breeze, who'd been especially quiet during the exchange. We locked eyes and hers were doused in guilt. I grabbed her hand in a silent bid to reassure her. She wasn't responsible for this, I was. I could have kept our day low-key. But it was a trade-off I was willing to give. Besides, this was an everyday occurrence. And let me tell you, lactating mommies were the least of my problems. In the white water rapids of fame, this was just a dribble.

But being that this was Breeze's first experience with my life-style, I wanted to make it a positive one. Maybe if she saw that having an enthusiastic fan base could still be worked into the fabric of her life, she might be willing to take a chance on me. Draping my arm over Breeze's shoulder, I nuzzled her hair. There was no mistaking her importance and the other women took notice, awarding her the respect she deserved.

———

After our brush with the fans, Breeze and I decided to bypass the picnic in the park and opted for dive-bombing seagulls on the beach where the asshole birds forcibly removed food from our hands. Because of the chilly temperatures, we didn't linger for long. A hastily built sand castle, a toe-dip in the frigid Northern California surf, and half a sand dollar plucked from the sand concluded our beach adventures.

Safely tucked inside our stolen vehicle, I made one last request of my companion.

"Please don't make me have any more fun today."

Although 'Bucket List Tuesday' was arguably a rousing success, after taste testing being a kid, I could objectively say that shit was exhausting. I now understood why naps were built into the ecosystem of childhood and why tantrums were a real and constant threat to public safety. Hell, I was one Nerf gun war away from a full-on nuclear meltdown.

———

With Breeze, it was easy to forget the world I came from. As we went about our day in near obscurity, I could have been anyone — a college student on winter break, a soldier on leave, a young lover spending quality time with his girl. Of course, I knew it was all a mirage, and that life would return to normal in a few short days, but that didn't dim the light flickering inside me. After today, I was convinced there was more to my story than a teen idol shuttled from one venue to the next under the protection of burly security guards. I wanted a life away from the crowds, the screaming, and the cameras. I wanted to live in this parallel universe where people were fully in control of their senses and went about their daily lives with nary a passing interest in those around them. I could see myself here blending into life as an equal... with Breeze by my side.

But as the old saying goes, all good things must come to an end... and it did... in crushing fashion. Item number twenty-eight on my bucket list. It hadn't been there at the start of the day, but I'd added it on our way back to Breeze's house, having a sudden hankering for an ice cream cone. Of course, she'd wanted to take me to her favorite local place, but what we hadn't factored in was the ice cream parlor was near a high school, which had just been let out for the day.

It started innocently enough with a group of three, a boy and two girls, spotting me despite the dark glasses and baseball cap. It was that inevitable moment of contact, eyes meeting mine, yet still I thought I could handle the situation. But kids with cell phones were a far cry from moms with breast pumps and, before I knew it, they'd called in reinforcements.

The three multiplied into six, then those six mutated into twelve and that was before the mitosis began spitting out carbon copies of teenage girls all wearing Uggs and sipping on Strawberries and Crème blended Frappuccinos. Within minutes, we were fully surrounded.

"One at a time," I pleaded, trying my best to appease the crowd bearing down on us.

"Bodhi?" Breeze scooted closer, her confidence in my ability to handle the situation seeming to waver. I got her concern. I was starting to feel overwhelmed myself, and that usually signaled the onset of stage four fangirling. As more bodies crammed together in the small space, the oxygen level decreased and I had an eerily similar feeling to being caught in the middle of the firestorm. Having been in this position before, I'd seen things spiral out of control. Even with security, it was always a harrowing experience.

I grabbed her hand. "Stay close."

Abandoning our ice cream cones, we pushed our way toward the exit. Like concertgoers in a mosh pit, bodies jostled against us, hands ripping at my clothes, scratching my skin, and pulling Breeze's hair.

"Don't let go," I warned as we made our way down the sidewalk, the mob of bodies propelling us forward.

"Bodhi?"

Something had changed in Breeze's demeanor. We'd escaped a firestorm, driven through a wall of flames, but even then I hadn't seen this look of panic in her vibrant eyes.

I should have warned her or, at the very least, prepared her for such a scenario. But instead I'd faked who I was because I didn't want her to see the real me. I was the guy who'd grown up in a bubble and who couldn't go for a walk with a dog, or dash into a grocery store for a carton of milk, or get a damn ice cream cone without the threat of being mauled by a large subsection of the population.

I'd purposely deceived her because I knew damn well that

me thriving in Breeze's world was entirely different than her thriving in mine.

Someone like Breeze, easy-going and earthy, could never flourish in an environment where people were routinely slurped up by the fame machine and spit back out, bloodied and bruised.

"You're going to be okay," I said, trying to ease her distress even as mine soared. "Just don't let go of my hand. We're almost there."

I could see the car ahead, but the crowd was like quicksand, and the more we struggled, the faster we were being sucked down. Suddenly, her hand was ripped from mine and no matter how hard I tried to claw my way back to her, I couldn't.

"Get to the car," I called to her, lifting the key to unlock the door. The battered Range Rover had delivered us to safety before and I had faith it could do it again. "I'll come to you."

But that was a tall order seeing as I was being swept up in a sea of girls. A storefront window stopped our forward motion but did nothing to improve my situation. I was now trapped with a press of bodies sealing me against the glass.

I could no longer see Breeze over the crush of bodies. If something were to happen to her because of my own damn stupidity, I'd never forgive myself. Why had I insisted on ice cream? What was I, five?

Scanning the area, I tried to figure out the best approach when I spotted a girl struggling for air. This wasn't just about me. If I couldn't get this under control, people were going to get hurt.

"Back up!" I shouted, trying to be heard over the screams. "If you want pictures you have to move back."

And while those in the front tried to follow my order, they were losing ground to the fans pushing forward. Surprisingly, over the roar of the mob I could hear Breeze's frightened voice calling 911 for help. Although minutes earlier I would have balked at involving the police, I now saw no way out of this without help.

Before the police arrived to take control of the situation, a concerned group of passersby, led by Breeze, managed to break up the crowd enough to free those in the heart of the melee. Including me.

Sore ribs, police intervention, and a hundred selfies later, we'd finally made it back to the safety of the car. Breeze twisted in her seat, buried her face in the crook of my neck, and burst into tears. Holding her tight, I rubbed her back, soothing her as best I could. With every sobbing breath she took, I knew this carefree woman could never survive under the oppressive blanket of my fame. I was losing her.

19

BREEZE: BIG GIRL PANTIES

I'D NEVER CONSIDER MYSELF A WEEPY GIRL, BUT THE LAST FEW DAYS had tested that long-held belief. As if the firestorm didn't forge enough bad memories, now I had the ice cream stampede embossed in my brain forever. I wasn't naïve. I knew Bodhi was famous. But I guess I hadn't realized the extent until it nearly killed him.

Dropping him into the middle of a perilous riptide was something I'd never intended to do. How could I have known timing was everything in the life of a teen idol? In some ways I felt deceived by Bodhi. He knew something like this could happen and, while I was laying out the plans for the day, he'd said nothing. Bodhi should have warned me, outlining the dangers that came with frenzied fan behavior. Had I any inkling that something like this could occur, I never would have put him in that position in the first place.

How quickly the tides had turned. Just this morning I'd been dreaming of our future together. Bodhi really was the perfect guy in every way... except one. And sadly, that one way threatened to destroy us both. How could he and I make this work with millions of fans vying for his attention? And how could I maintain any sense of normalcy in my life if it was attached to his?

Bodhi and I had driven home in silence, escorted by three squad cars. An uncomfortably quiet dinner followed, the two of us struggling to make small talk with my parents or eye contact with each other. I'd had every intention of pulling him aside as soon as dinner was over, but Bodhi blindsided me, announcing he was tired and going to bed early.

No doubt being manhandled by an unruly mob took a lot out of a person, but I suspected Bodhi's sudden onset of fatigue had more to do with the uncomfortable conversation he knew was coming his way.

Finding a quiet spot on the patio, I sank into a chair and dialed up Mason. We hadn't had a chance to talk since the night of the fire and I needed to get his take on things. Of all people, he understood how my mind worked and I hoped he'd have better luck coming up with a solution to the Bodhi problem than I did.

Mason answered on the first ring. "Okay, so I just saw the raw footage on TMZ and can I just say, girl, you're looking spot on."

"Thank you." I laughed. "I especially liked the part where I was standing on the sidewalk alone, screaming his name."

"I agree. That was some academy award worthy shit right there."

Maybe I would have found the whole thing humorous had I not felt this was the beginning of the end for Bodhi and I.

"And for your information," Mason added. "I'm pissed that I had to find out about you and Bodhi Beckett on social media. I feel robbed."

"I know. I'm so sorry. I promised him I wouldn't say anything but, now that it's all over the web, there's no reason to hide anymore. What do you want to know?"

Turns out he wanted to know a lot, and I spent the next half hour answering all of Mason's questions. When he was finally caught up I said, "You have no idea how scary that was. I've seen stuff like that on television but, up close and personal, it's a whole other story. I'm not kidding when I say someone easily could have been seriously injured. The whole boy band adoration thing is out of frickin' control."

"AnyDayNow fans are crazy. I'll give you that," Mason said. "I went to one of their concerts last year and the screaming was so bad they were handing out earplugs to anyone who looked old enough to still use Facebook. But look on the bright side, at least life with a pop star isn't boring, right?"

"No, it's definitely not boring." I sighed. "But, I don't think it's for me."

"What do you mean? You'd better not be breaking it off with him before I get to meet the dude... or get a backstage pass to one of his concerts. You're not doing that to me, are you?"

Him? It wasn't like this was a calculated attempt to make Mason's life unhappy. This was about me and my own misery. "I hate to say this, but if I'm going down in flames, so are you."

"Ah dammit, Breeze. You couldn't hold it together for one week? With Bodhi rising from the dead, this weekend's AnyDayNow concerts are going to be epic."

"Can we focus on what's important?"

"That is important."

"Okay, let me rephrase it—something less materialistic."

"Oh, you want me to get deep with you? Fine. I don't get it at all. I thought you liked him. Hell, this morning you texted me and said you were falling in love. And now you're talking about leaving? It was one incident, Breeze, chill out!"

"That's the thing, it's not one incident. This happens to him all the time. Am I just supposed to stand on a street corner like Jane calling out to her Tarzan for the rest of my life?"

"Here's the thing. I've listened to you bitch and complain for over two years about not being able to find a man who makes you feel... I don't even want to say this, but I suppose I must... all *gooey* inside. And now that you've found the Pillsbury Dough-boy, he's not good enough because *he's frickin' loved by millions!* Boo-fucking-hoo, Breeze. Ugh, I want to murder you right now."

"Wow, tell me how you really feel," I said, not sure if I should laugh or cry at his brutal assessment.

"You can't deny it, Breeze. Because of what Brandon did to you, you're scared of rejection so you push men away before they can hurt you. I get that—Brandon caused you a lot of pain. But it's also why you're perpetually single, and if you continue this pattern you'll be all alone at thirty-five and I'll be forced to bang you in order to give you the kid you always wanted."

"You don't want to bang me?" I whined.

"Not particularly, no. In case you forgot, I'm gay! And besides, that wasn't the main point I was making."

"Yeah, I get it. I'm a mess of human emotions. What's new?"

"Look, I'm going to give it to you straight, Breeze. You're a pretty girl. I see the way guys look at you. You shine. But every time someone shows an interest, you find some ridiculous excuse for why you can't date. Then, as if by some miracle of god, a gorgeous pop star is dropped into your lap free of charge and what do you do? Oh, yeah, you find a reason to drop kick his ass right back up to heaven."

Neither of us spoke for a moment as I let his words sink in. Although I didn't much care for his delivery, Mason was right. I was afraid of rejection. And Bodhi with all his beauty and talent and nickels, he was the biggest risk of all. What would happen when someone else came along, someone better at surviving fires and flash mobs than me? Then what? I'd never fallen this fast or this hard and it was a terrifying feeling to know Bodhi had the potential to destroy me.

"Shit, I'm sorry," Mason backtracked. "That was harsh. I'm not in the best place right now. Don't listen to me."

I instantly picked up on the defeatist tone. "What do you mean? What's happening?"

"Just... nothing."

"Mason?"

"I can't, not now." He sounded so exhausted, like he hadn't slept in a week. Why hadn't I heard this earlier? I'd been so consumed by my own drama that I hadn't stopped to consider he might have some of his own.

"Talk to me."

A quiet rumbling low in his throat. "I'm on the ledge, Breeze."

"What does that mean?"

He didn't respond but I could almost hear his heart beating through the line. Whatever he had to say was breaking him in two.

"I overdosed the other night in Vegas."

"On drugs?"

"No, on love," he answered, despair overlapping the sarcasm. "Of course on drugs."

His admission was like a stab through my heart. Not only was I shocked by his news but there was an unbearable feeling of guilt. I was Mason's best friend, yet he hadn't felt comfortable enough to confide in me that he'd started using again. I'd suspected it, even asked him point blank once, but he'd come up with plausible excuses for his behavior, so I pushed my worries aside. I suppose the fact that he was able to hold a job and function in his everyday life was enough validation for me to take his word at face value. Now, I wondered why I hadn't dug deeper, fought harder.

"What did you take?"

"OxyContin, mostly."

"Mostly? Was it deliberate?"

"I wasn't actively trying to kill myself, no."

"That doesn't sound encouraging."

"It wasn't as bad as last time, I promise."

A couple of years ago, he'd almost lost the battle. It took two doses of the opioid reversing drug naloxone to revive him. A stint in rehab followed and, as far as I'd known, he'd been clean ever since.

"I'm so sorry. I wish I was stronger. For you. For me. I didn't want you to be disappointed in me. But, Breezie, mentally, I'm barely hanging on. I think I'm going to end up just as crazy as my mother. I can feel her disease growing inside me like a weed. It's only a matter of time."

The turmoil coursing through Mason could be felt across the divide. I knew well his fear of becoming like her, but if he continued down this path, that's exactly where he'd end up.

"They wanted to send me to a rehab facility straight from the hospital but there were no open beds. So I checked myself out yesterday."

"Oh, Mason."

"I know. Rehab's still in the works. I'll get help."

"Why didn't you tell me? I would have come."

"You were dealing with your own stuff. Besides, I didn't want my drug habit to ruin your chance with Bodhi. That's how badly I want a ticket."

I gave him the required chuckle but was still worried sick. "You know I would have dropped everything for you?"

"I know, and that's why I wanted you to stay put and focus on yourself. If there's anyone who deserves love, it's you."

No, *he* deserved it—the little boy who craved affection, but never got any. If only Mason could find the peace that had always been lacking in his life. "I can't let you be home alone after an overdose."

"I'm not home alone. I have a caretaker."

Aside from me, Mason rarely had people over to his apartment. He was weird about stuff like that. "You do? Who?"

"Curtis."

"Curtis? As in 'pees sitting down', Curtis?"

"Yes, Breeze, one and the same. He was in Vegas too. He's the one who called the ambulance. He stayed at the hospital with me. Curtis has experience dealing with people like me."

"You mean hot guys with mommy issues?"

Mason laughed and the sound was like music to my ears. "No, withdrawing drug addicts. Listen, can you do me a favor?"

"Yes, anything."

"Pull up those big girl panties of yours, and go tell Bodhi how you feel."

"I don't know. I feel like I need to come to you."

"No...you need to stay where you are or I'll never speak to you again."

"Are you sure?"

"Yes, I'm sure. Curtis has this covered."

"All right then. When I get back, we'll figure everything out. You're going to be okay, Mace. I promise. Love you."

"Love you too, Breeze. And don't forget about those backstage passes."

———

After changing into my t-shirt and sleep shorts, I tiptoed to bed and slipped under the covers as quietly as possible. Bodhi was on his back with one arm resting over his forehead. His bare chest exposed, it was as if he were taunting me with his perfection. Had he not gone to slunk off to bed to avoid our talk, I might have been more adventurous. But since I wasn't entirely sure where we stood, I kept my greedy hands to myself.

The bed creaked, then the bedside lamp unexpectedly switched on. Bodhi rolled to his side and his arms tucked around my chilled flesh. Drawing me into his warm body, he buried his face into my neck and peppered small kisses over my shivering skin.

"I thought you were asleep," I whispered.

"I can't sleep. I heard you talking on the phone."

"With my friend, Mason. Oh, and before I forget, he's requesting a backstage pass to one of your LA shows. I don't know if you can make that happen, but I figured I'd throw it out there."

"Yeah, I can make it happen."

"Thank you." Running my fingers along the muscled curves of his back, I asked, "Nervous about tomorrow?"

"Not as much as I'm stressing about today. I'm so sorry, Breeze. What happened this afternoon, it was just insanity."

"Hey, it wasn't your fault."

Bodhi's miserable eyes met mine. "Actually, it was. I shouldn't have put you in that position. If something had happened, I never would've forgiven myself."

"But nothing happened and I'm fine." Why I felt the need to lie to him, I couldn't say but, by minimizing the impact the day had on me, I'd squandered the chance at an open and honest dialogue.

"I think sometimes I forget who I am when I'm with you. You just make me feel so good—normal—and I forget about my limitations."

"So what happened today, that level of fan worship, it's normal?"

As the seconds slipped by, he squeezed me to him a little tighter and then sighed heavily.

"Pretty much, yes."

I nodded, gutted by his admission. This wasn't something

that would magically go away. If I wanted to be with him, I'd have to learn a new normal.

"You're so nonchalant about it, like it's no big deal."

"I've been famous my whole life, so I don't really know any different. Even when I was five, before I even knew how to write, I'd get stopped on the street and asked for an autograph. It's normal for me."

"But getting stopped on the street isn't the same as what happened today. It was pandemonium, and that's not normal by anyone's standards. This was bordering on assault. You have to see that simple fan encounters don't include suffocation."

"I know, but typically when it gets out of control like that security is there to control it."

"Typically? What happens when it's not typical?"

"Today happens, that's what."

The tightness in my chest spread as dread filled my lungs. As much as I wanted to stand by his side, I wasn't sure I could give up my autonomy. I respected my laidback lifestyle enough to want to protect it from Bodhi's feverish one.

"Can I ask you something?"

I felt him stiffen. "Sure."

"You say you've been famous your whole life. How did it all start?"

He pondered for a few beats. "I was discovered at a mall when I was two. Did some modeling, commercials, and then I got my first television series at four and that's when it took off."

"So you were juggling work and school?"

"I had on-set tutoring."

"You didn't go to school?"

"Not the traditional kind, no."

"Huh, so you never had teachers telling nerdy math jokes, or prom, or Friday night football games?"

"No, no, and no."

"Do you ever feel like you missed out?"

His granite jaw appeared to tighten and I wondered if I'd hit a sore spot.

"Maybe sometimes, but I didn't hate growing up on television, or at least I didn't until my star burned out. Then it became the opposite of fun."

I gently ran my finger along his arm, encouraging him to continue. By his jittery disposition, I surmised this was a truth he wasn't used to sharing.

"There's a black hole that opens up when a child actor gets too old to play little kids but too young to play teens. Actual teens are generally cast aside for 'Hollywood' teens—twenty to thirty year olds. Once I hit sixteen and started puberty, I was done for. I couldn't get a job in a mouthwash commercial, that's how thoroughly I'd been tossed away."

"It must have been hard on your self-esteem."

"It was, but even harder on my father's. He'd made a name for himself in Hollywood and it wasn't a good one. Let's just say he was the stage dad from hell. You would've thought he was the star the way he carried on about every little thing. People only put up with him because I was popular and, in order to keep me around, they had to deal with his shit. But having Tucker by my side was like carrying around two hundred pounds of baggage. Once I'd grown out of being cute, Hollywood couldn't dump me, and him, fast enough."

"I can't imagine you not being cute."

"Oh, you'd be surprised. Have you ever heard of that Chinese guy who sued his wife for giving him ugly kids—and won? He claimed she'd deceived him by having plastic surgery and not disclosing her ugly duckling status from the beginning. Well, Breeze, you've officially been warned."

My mouth dropped open. "I don't believe you were ever an ugly duckling."

"Well, okay, not by most people's standards, but certainly by my father's. See, I'd had the audacity to go through puberty in a less than attractive manner. A growth spurt left me tall and gangly with a spattering of pimples and unacceptably crooked teeth.

Tucker decided my lack of job opportunities was because I wasn't good-looking enough so he went to work fixing my outside. I went through six months of the acne treatment that required monthly blood draws and minimal contact with the sun. I was put on a regimented weight gain diet while working out with a trainer two to four hours a day. I spent nearly two years in braces, after undergoing a surgery to align my back teeth because apparently, celebrities weren't allowed to have a slight under bite. And the icing on the cake came when my father deemed my post-puberty nose too wide at the bridge and arranged for a nose job on the day I turned seventeen. Happy birthday to me."

Bodhi's story blew my mind. His father's maniacal insistence on beauty was like Munchhausen by Proxy for the Hollywood crowd. What Tucker had subjected him to constituted abuse and Bodhi didn't even realize it. I was beginning to get a better picture of a father-son relationship that was no partnership. Tucker was the king and Bodhi his loyal subject. No wonder he felt the need to deceive his father. Freedom for Bodhi did not come for free.

"But even after he'd fixed my physical issues, I was still unemployable in the business because my father was like kryptonite in the casting circles. That's when he decided to switch gears and tackle a different avenue toward fame and fortune... music. The idea was to turn me into a pop star and, in turn, make both of us matter again."

"Did you even want to be a musician?"

"I hadn't really thought about it before that, but I'd been in both music and voice lessons since I was five, so it wasn't such a farfetched plan. I'm no Freddie Mercury but I have a fairly decent singing voice. Pair that with the 2.0 Bodhi upgrade I'd gone through and Tucker had stumbled onto a legitimate business plan.

He handpicked four other teenage boys to join me in forming AnyDayNow. Several producers jumped in to provide the capital when it was determined that my father might have a winning hand. And he did. Within a year of forming the band, Tucker had morphed from an overbearing stage dad into a music industry power player."

"And you became a teen idol by no choice of your own." I realized I was sounding like Debbie Downer but there was nothing inspiring about a story where a full-grown man filtered his dreams through his son.

Bodhi nodded. "The funny thing is, back then, it never occurred to me to mind. I'd been groomed for stardom, so it was a natural process for me."

For the first time, I saw Bodhi's life for what it was— manufactured. Everything that had happened today at the ice cream parlor was just the after effect of a father living vicariously through his child.

"So how do you feel about it all now? Do you like being a teen idol?"

"Uh, I didn't mind in the beginning. It was flattering, all that attention. But as our star status exploded, it became more difficult. Now, I just feel like I'm playing a part, you know?"

"So why don't you leave?"

"It's not that easy. Everything I am and everything I'll ever be has his signature written all over it. He not only owns me, he owns the band. Every step we take, every decision that's made, goes directly through him. Managing AnyDayNow put him on the map, and Tucker Beckett won't settle for anything less than world domination."

Gripping his chin, I turned his face toward mine. "You do have a choice. It's your future and no one has the right to dictate it for you. If I were you, I'd hire an outside lawyer and figure out exactly what your obligations are."

"You want me to leave the band?"

"It doesn't matter what I want or what Tucker wants. What matters is what *you* want. Whether that's as a member of AnyDayNow or not, you owe it to yourself to find out what your rights are so you can go into the decision informed."

I could almost see the wheels turning in his head. Whether he'd thought of this before or not, I couldn't read, but certainly he was giving my advice some consideration.

"And does the same go for us?" he asked, a sly smile displacing some of the gloom. "What matters is what I want?"

I laughed. "Oh, no. In our relationship, think of me as your overbearing manager."

"Hypocrite."

I tucked back into his side, my head in the crook of his arm. God, how I wanted to be all in with this amazing guy. Like 100% in. "I really like you, Bodhi."

"But?"

But... even setting aside my fear of rejection could I really see myself changing my entire life for him? That was the question I couldn't answer.

"But, your fame—I'm not going to lie. It scares the shit out of me. You see the way I am. I like country western bars and shopping at Marshalls. I'm afraid that big ball of energy that hovers over you is going to swallow me whole."

"Why do you have to make it difficult? You could've stopped before the 'but'."

"I could have, except the 'but' is a really big deal for me. If I can't see myself thriving in your life, isn't it better for me to walk away now before our feelings get all tangled up?"

"I don't ever want you to walk away from me. I won't let you." Bodhi hooked his arm around my waist and pulled me backwards on top of him. Enveloping me in his strong arms, he kissed my neck while his fingers skated over my ribs. Waves of desire and giggles swept through me.

"Let me up," I demanded with absolutely no conviction.

"Would you please stop squirming?" His hands slipped further down my body. "You're like a worm with arms."

"Then stop with the torture fingers." I said, reaching back and making contact with his balls.

"Oh no you don't." Displacing my hand before I had a chance to latch on, he pinned it against the mattress. "You're mine."

"Dream on."

"No dreaming required."

And he was right. Bodhi's hand continued the seductive descent, sliding into my pajama shorts. I gasped when he touched my most sensitive spot, teasing with lithe fingers. Releasing my wrist, his free hand roamed lazily over my breast. Once his fingers found my nipple and circled the pebbled tip, I had no fight left. I gave myself over to him to do as he wished. And he knew just what to do. My breathing intensified with each stroke of his capable hands and I found myself moving smoothly to the rhythm of his beat.

"Bodhi," I whispered.

"Shhh."

"I just... we need to... oh god."

The sensations were building so fast that words failed me. I was acutely aware of his brawny body curved into me from behind, his hardness pressing into me. Lips like silk danced skillfully down the back of my neck setting my tingling skin on fire. Yes, whatever the obstacle, we could work through it because I'd be damned if I let him find himself another dime somewhere down the road. He was right. I was his.

Bodhi shifted, his warmth leaving me but only momentarily so he could change our position. He was on top of me now, his powerful body dwarfing me in both size and need. I opened my legs, wanting him inside. Slowly he entered, my body trembling, reigniting. The heat was back and I was flushed with need. He was mine.

Like slow moving torture, his measured, deliberate thrusts held me rigid on a sword's edge. I wanted to scream at him to go faster, but I trusted him and his ability to take me where I needed to go.

Driving my hips up to meet him, I urged him on. Bodhi groaned, no longer able to keep up his methodical rhythm. Frantic in his need, Bodhi increased the pace. I looped my arms around his neck, slick with sweat, then pulled him toward me.

"Kiss me," I said.

His gaze dipped into mine a moment before our lips met.

Moving as one, we climbed to dizzying heights. His hand slipped between us, fingers searching for the magic spot that would send me flying.

"You feel it?" he rasped.

And I wasn't sure if he was talking about the sex or the warm glow occupying every square inch of my chest.

Either way, it didn't matter. The answer was yes. Always yes.

So I nodded.

And then his lips were on mine again. He swallowed my gasp and the moan that followed. And when he met the end of me one last time, I let go.

20

BODHI: MOTHER'S DAY

WE PLANNED TO MEET AT A GATHERING OF ROCKS OVERLOOKING the beach. I'd insisted on a wide-open space so I could easily escape if need be. Although I'd thought about asking Breeze to come along, in the end, I decided this was something I needed to do alone. And I was glad, because the minute I laid eyes on my mother, the emotions surging through me were more than I wanted to reveal to the girl I was falling in love with.

Marni Easton—*my mother*—was already there when I arrived. She'd been easy to identify since I'd kissed her photograph every night before bed until I was probably fourteen years old. But the woman sitting before me was not the same fresh-faced girl of years past. Life had taken its toll on Marni, and each year she'd lived without me had weathered her beyond expectation. I suspected hers was an aging that had more to do with unhealthy lifestyle choices than the natural process by which the body matures.

Still, she made a valiant effort to spruce herself up for our meeting. Make-up clung to her skin, settling in the deep lines bracketing her mouth. Dark brown hair touched her shoulders, pulled back in the front and secured with colorful clips. Her bright and cheerful clothing appeared carefully selected, as if she were trying to disguise her true self behind a perky facade. If not for the cigarette shaking in her right hand, I might have bought what she was selling.

As I closed the gap between us, she stood on unsteady legs. After one last furtive puff on her smoke, she dropped the butt and smoothed a hand down the front of her blouse. Any lingering doubt that Marni Easton was my birth mother was put to rest the minute our gazes collided. Our eyes were the same shade of blue. The frosty hue didn't translate to the photograph I'd cherished for years, but in the early morning light they were truly striking.

She stepped forward, her hand extended in greeting. I stopped, fists clenched and buried deep in my pockets. She hadn't earned the right to touch me. Not yet.

Marni's arm dropped limply to her side and she shifted her feet. "You cut your hair," she observed, a small smile curving her lips.

I nodded, not even trying to hide my grimace. All the years of silence and that was the best she could do? "I needed a change."

"Well, with your looks I suppose you can make anything work, can't you?"

It was one of those awkward questions that didn't require an answer, so I just shrugged.

"You were always the cutest baby. People used to stop me on the street to tell me how adorable you were. And now look at you, all grown up— a star."

Her dreamy expression unsettled me. It was like staring into the eyes of a gushing fan, not my flesh and blood. Who exactly was she seeing when she looked at me— her son or a member of AnyDayNow? Though my guard was already up, it sealed tighter.

"I heard about the fire and was so worried. Were you hurt?"

"No. I'm fine. Look, I don't want to sound rude, but I have a lot of questions. Can we just skip the banter and get to it?"

Clearly 'getting to it' stressed her out. Clasping her hands, she knotted her fingers, eyes darting around to avoid my gaze. When she finally looked at me she swallowed hard, then nodded tentatively.

Now that I had her undivided attention, I jumped into the deep end without floaters. "Why did you leave me?"

She seemed stunned. Why, I wasn't sure. Wouldn't that be the first question you'd expect to be asked if you hadn't seen your son in over twenty years?

"Is that what he told you, that I left you?"

The way she emphasized *he* with such bitter contempt, I imaged we were in for a rough ride.

"No, I drew my own conclusions since you've been absent my whole life."

She pressed her lips into a thin line. "I hope you understand that Tucker Beckett is not who you think he is. His real name is Eddie Watts. And where I come from, he's a nobody."

Indignation rose up on my father's behalf and I wasn't sure why. Probably because he was there. He'd stuck around. Which is more than I could say for the woman in front of me.

"He's not your father, Bodhi," she said flatly. "You're not even blood related."

I'd heard it before. She made sure to put it in her letter. But did she think that made a difference? Excused her in some way?

A scowl coated my features. "Tell me then. Who is Eddie Watts?"

"He's my stepbrother. After you were born, I was struggling financially and I went to him for help. He took us in."

"Sounds like a nice thing for him to do." So far my father was the hero in this story.

"That's what I thought, but when you were about a year old, I had an opportunity for a job in a different city and I left you with him. When I came back a couple of days later, he refused to let me in. Accused me of abandoning you. You have to understand, I was trying to do right by you. Get clean."

Her eyes widened as if she'd revealed too much. I half expected her to slap her hands over her mouth.

"Were you a junkie?"

She pulled her shoulders back. "I had a drug problem, yes."

"Do you still have a drug problem?"

The slight twitch of her lip didn't escape my notice. "I'm clean now, but I'm not going to lie to you. I've struggled my whole life with addiction. I'm trying, but it's not always easy."

I had a feeling it was the most honest thing to come out of her mouth, and I was not without sympathy for the woman. She seemed truly beaten down by life, and I had no doubt it had been a difficult one. It also explained why Tucker was so militant with me when it came to alcohol and drugs. If I had a strong family history of abuse, it made sense he wouldn't want me around the stuff. Which was no easy feat given the environment I grew up in.

She waved a dismissive hand. "Despite my problems, Eddie didn't have the right to steal you."

"What do you mean he stole me?"

Marni's lip curled, her eyes distant, as if she were lost in another place and time. "He took you away from me, Bodhi. I came home one day to an empty apartment. Eddie disappeared and took you with him. He stole you. You were mine and he fucking stole you."

Taken aback by her hostility, I glanced her over. She wasn't the 'clean' mild mannered woman she pretended to be. At least I knew where I got my acting talent.

Her eyes widened in response to my quirked brow. Suddenly

she was left to soak up the spill with a series of carefully selected words.

"Maybe I sound bitter," she conceded. "But you have to see it from my point of view. Eddie made a choice that changed both of our lives. He shouldn't get off scot free."

"Did you go to the police?" I asked blandly. "Report me missing? I mean, am I on one of those missing kid sites?"

Marni shifted uncomfortably. Then lifting her chin, she sniffed. "The police had it out for me. They only saw me as a junkie. They didn't care that I was your mother or that I loved you. No matter what Eddie's told you, Alex, I've always loved you and I never hurt you. I promise you, that wasn't me."

What the shit? If someone stole my kid - hell if someone snatched Little Dick out of my hands - I'd make a fucking report.

Warning signs were going up all over our bumpy road to reconciliation. Had something happened to me when I was a baby—something bad enough that Tucker felt the need to hide me from my mother? Sure, Marni had been an addict, but plenty of questionable people raised offspring. Not always well. But they did it. Tucker could have left me in her care and went on his merry way. But he hadn't. Instead he'd chosen to take the drastic measure of hiding me... *in plain sight.*

"Did someone hurt me?"

The color drained so drastically from Marni's face, she looked like a wrinkly corpse. "No."

"You said that it wasn't you who hurt me."

"I... I meant in general."

"No, you didn't."

"Bodhi, please. I'm here to get to know you. I want to reestablish a connection with you. I know I'm probably not the mother you hoped for, but I have never stopped loving you. Ever. Haven't you ever made mistakes in your life that you regret?"

Honestly, no, I thought to myself. Tucker had never allowed me to become a man who could make those mistakes. He'd kept me sheltered. Under his wing. And as much as I resented him for it, had Tucker not stepped up all those years ago, my life would have been completely different. I wouldn't be Bodhi Beckett, teen idol and member of one of the biggest boy bands in the world. And I wouldn't have the money to live comfortably for the rest of my life.

She took a step forward, but I dropped my gaze.

"Just give me a chance, Bodhi," she pleaded. "Please. If not for me, then for your half-brothers."

My head shot up, a lump forming in my throat. I had brothers? Siblings were something I'd wanted my whole life, and now she was handing them to me on a silver platter.

Detecting the change in my demeanor, Marni rushed to take her phone from her pocket. She turned the screen in my direction and every dream I'd ever had of being a big brother came to life.

"Evan is sixteen and Jonah is thirteen."

I nodded, magnifying and moving the picture around to get a better look. Like me, Evan had dark hair and angled features, but that's where the similarities ended. His eyes were ink black and his smile didn't reach his eyes. Jonah, on the other hand, couldn't contain his grin if he tried. He was pure joy and contentment. Of mixed race, his skin was darker than mine, but his eyes... they were blue like Marni's. Like mine.

I marveled at this incredible find, feeling a surge of anger toward my father. He'd done this to me. Kept me from the one thing I'd wanted my whole life— brothers. A family.

"Do they know about me?"

"They know about Alex, but they don't know Alex is Bodhi Beckett. I only just found out myself. Eddie changed your identity. I watched you grow up on television but never knew you were my son."

Her shoulders slumped and, for the first time, I saw the toll my absence must have taken on her.

"I'm sorry," I said, touching her for the first time as I rubbed circles on her back soothingly. "I didn't know any of this. He told me you were dead."

"He told you I was dead? I thought you just didn't want to see me." All traces of vulnerability vanished and she muttered under her breath, "Oh, I'm going to bury him just like he buried me."

Her comment was troubling enough that I questioned her story. Was Marni already in contact with Tucker? Was he paying her off to stay away from me?

The question was too troubling to risk asking now that my brothers were involved. I had to play nice if I ever wanted a shot at a relationship with them.

Settling on a more neutral inquiry I asked, "How did you find us?"

"About four months ago, I saw a picture of you and Eddie together. He's gotten older and richer, but I'd know him anywhere. And then when I saw you beside him, it all fell into place."

And that explained why my father never wanted to be photographed with me. The picture she'd seen must've been taken by paparazzi because he'd never willingly allow that to happen. He always kept his distance when cameras were around, claiming he wanted it to be about me.

Who wants to take pictures of my ugly mug anyway? he'd say.

Pushing aside the memory, I met my mother's gaze.

"So, what is it you want from me?"

She placed a hand on my shoulder. And I let her.

"I want to know you, of course." She smiled. "Be a part of your life and have you be part of ours."

"And what about Tucker?"

She shrugged. "What about him?"

"Are you going to press charges against him?"

Had it been my kid that someone had stolen, I'd want justice. Or at least some sort of police intervention.

"I think there's a way we can come to an understanding, Eddie and me."

Wrong answer.

21

BREEZE: ROUND TWO

SITTING BY THE PICTURE WINDOW IN THE FRONT OF THE HOUSE, I anxiously waited for my man to return home from the visit with his mother. Every scenario had passed through my mind. It could go either way. Bodhi's expectations were high, but so was his doubt. How did one wrap their brain around twenty-four years lost?

After last night, I was more conflicted than ever. Ever since Bodhi had barreled his way into my life, wrapping himself around my heart like twine, I couldn't imagine existing without him. We had it all— white-hot chemistry, teamwork, and the playful camaraderie I'd always dreamed of in a partner.

But Bodhi was a marked man, hunted by the very people who claimed to love him. My mission, if I chose to accept it, was to bring love, peace, and a sense of normalcy to his crazy life. And I could do that. But at what cost? How much was I willing to lose in order to gain the man of my dreams?

The Range Rover rolled up to the curb and I perked up. A minute passed, and then two, but Bodhi remained inside the vehicle. Imaging the worst, my pulse raced.

Dammit! What was with those luxury vehicles and their

dramatically tinted windows? It made gauging the emotional stability of the driver inside near impossible. The longer he stayed put, the more convinced I became that the mommy dearest reunion had not gone well.

Holding back nervous jitters, I braced myself and walked outside. I'd just stepped onto the grass when Bodhi rolled the passenger window down. He was smiling. I let out the breath I'd been holding as I raced to greet him.

Ducking my head inside the car, I grinned. "Hey there, handsome. I take it the meeting went well?"

"Ehh." Bodhi shrugged. "I think she's blackmailing my father."

I searched his face, waiting for the punchline. But there wasn't one. He was serious. And a little too chipper. "You seem fairly okay with that, so good for you."

He laughed, clearing up the confusion with three little words. "I have brothers."

The place in my heart reserved for Bodhi stretched out a little wider. Despite the circumstances, his capacity for love was astounding. "What are they like?"

"I don't know yet. I'm meeting them tonight at six. Their names are Evan and Jonah. Can you come with me?"

I struggled to keep up with the blur of information. "Of course. Wow, that's fast."

"Well, it had to be tonight since I'm leaving for LA tomorrow."

As his words sank in, I felt the color drain from my face and a pitiful sob catch in my throat. This couldn't be right. Not once did he mention that he'd be breaking my heart on a Thursday. "You're leaving... tomorrow?"

He frowned. "I... yeah, I thought you knew."

No. No. That was definitely not made clear. Thursdays had once been my favorite day of the week. I mean what was there not to love? You were over the hump day and sliding into the weekend – so much to look forward to. And now, Thursday sucked worse than waiting to press that 'skip ad' button on a YouTube video.

Without a word, I turned and slunk off in the direction of the house.

"Breeze?"

Holding up a hand, I kept walking. "I can't right now, Bodhi." Before the sob exploded from my throat, I added, "But I'm super happy for you."

"Breeze, stop!"

He was behind me now, closing the gap between us in record time. I picked up the pace but, before I could make my dramatic exit, Bodhi sprang like a cheetah and caught my arm.

I spun around and, even though I had the urge to knee him in the nuts, the 'oh shit' look on his face tempered down my resentment. Instead I slapped his chest.

"Why didn't you tell me you were leaving tomorrow?"

"I have a concert Friday," he said, brows knit together over uncertain eyes.

"Friday. Not Thursday."

He scratched the back of his neck and looked at me like I'd just landed from another planet. "Right, but there's a lot of preparation that goes into a show. I can't just pop in ten minutes before the concert starts. Maybe I didn't make that clear."

It made sense. Of course it did. Still, I didn't want to hear it.

Frustrated tears sprung to my eyes at the thought of him being out of my life, and bed, for good.

"Your communication skills suck," I grumbled, swiping my cheek with the back of my hand.

Bodhi grinned as he tucked a strand of hair behind my ear. "I'm sorry." He brushed his thumb over my bottom lip. "I should have communicated better. But, I'll be clearer right now. I want you to come with me."

My sagging body perked up at the thought of flying to Los Angeles in some private jet, then standing stage side and watching my sorta-boyfriend perform in front of an audience of thousands of fans who wouldn't crush us against a store front window. How refreshing.

I wanted to say yes—and would have said yes—if the image of my mother's disappointed face hadn't overshadowed the concert fantasy now withering out in my head. Instead of watching my man sweat his way across the stage like a Greek god, I would be the one perspiring profusely when my ex-fiancé's perfectly domesticated life was dangled in front of me like a bad luck charm.

"You have no idea how much I want to, but I just can't. We have a family reunion this Saturday. I already promised I would go and if I back out now my mother will be so disappointed."

"Oh." Bodhi's optimistic expression faded before my very eyes. "You never said anything about a reunion."

"Well, since you were leaving on *Friday* and weren't going to be in town, I didn't bother mentioning it. Why?"

"Is *he* going to be there?"

Inclining my head, I examined Bodhi's face. Furrowed brow. Pursed lips. And yep, a ticking jaw. He was jealous...of Brandon?

Perhaps it hadn't been the wisest choice to fill Bodhi in on all the sordid details of the breakup. Even though there were points in my story where he'd been clutching the steering wheel until his knuckles turned white, I never saw this coming.

"He's married to my cousin, so yeah, I assume he'll be there."

"You should have said something."

"Like you should have told me you were leaving on a Thursday?"

"I'm serious, Breeze. He'd better not mess with you."

"Do I look like I can't take care of myself?" Parking my hands on my hips, I hoped it would convey how incredibly badass I was, even though I could feel the Lara Croft awesomeness beginning to fade the more I thought about the reunion.

"I *know* you can. I just don't like the idea of some dude making you feel like you're somehow... less."

Less? Yes, that was an excellent adjective to use when it came to the love triangle I'd unwittingly found myself in. It didn't matter how far removed I was, or how much Brandon now repulsed me, my self-esteem had taken a hit and all the memories were still fresh in my mind.

Tipping my head back, I swallowed the dread and flashed Bodhi a brilliant smile. "I'll be fine. Let's go inside. I want to hear all about your brothers."

Before we'd taken a step, four cars came to a screeching halt on the street. Startled, Bodhi let go of my hand, sliding in front of me. It wasn't until the window slid down on the first vehicle that I breathed a sigh of relief. It was just the teenage boy who lived down the street. I knew him on sight but couldn't for the life of me remember his name.

"I told you it was her," Neighbor Boy crowed to someone in the car. The back window slid down, and giggling floated through the air, along with a couple of gasps.

"Jeremy?" I asked, taking my place at Bodhi's side. "No...it's Jacob, right?"

"Josh," he corrected. "Dude, are you dating Bodhi Beckett?"

"Josh, listen..."

Before I could finish my plea for privacy, car doors swung open and an entire pack of teens piled out, heading straight for Bodhi. We were surrounded in an instant.

Taking the interruption in stride, Bodhi said, "Listen, I'm happy to take pictures with you guys, but please keep this quiet. Can you do that?"

Although everyone nodded, snapchats were released into cyberspace and within moments their phones were chirping. It was only a matter of time before our little black hole of a house would be inundated with Dayers from all over the state.

Not that it mattered what I thought, because I'd been unceremoniously pushed to the side. Literally—as some girl had actually shoved me out of the way to gain better access to her idol.

Muscling my way back in to the inner circle, I grabbed Bodhi's hand. "This is getting out of control. We need to go inside. *Now.*"

He nodded, and together we broke through the crowd and jogged to the porch where my mother was waiting.

"What's going on?" she asked, concern painting her features as she eyed the squealing fangirls descending on the house.

"Josh, that kid down the street figured out I was the girl in the ice cream parlor yesterday. He brought his friends."

Her lips flat lined as she stepped aside, motioning to the door. "Get inside." With that she marched down the driveway, fingers balled in fists at her side. "Josh McGregor, get your ass out of here right now or I'm calling your mother!"

A moment later, my hundred and ten pound mother stomped inside the door, growling like a Yeti. She bore no resemblance to the mild-mannered flower child of yesteryear.

"Ugh... that kid... " She rubbed her forehead. "I forgave him for the whole Ding Dong Ditch episode when he was ten, and I even laughed it off when he circulated a petition to have our house declared a historical landmark, but this— messing with my daughter and my favorite pop star —he's gone too far this time. Now, you know I'm against waterboarding, but maybe if someone just holds Josh down, I could dump a little gutter water onto his forehead and..."

Mom stopped talking when she caught sight of my droopy face and trembling lip.

"We'll be right back," she announced to the guys before grabbing my arm and leading me down the narrow hallway to her bedroom. Once the door was securely shut, she folded me into her embrace. She'd always known just how to sooth my tattered soul.

I was a fixer. That was my thing. Bring me your poor, your unstylish, your damaged. Bodhi had been my perfect landscape — a man wounded just enough that fixing him would be my pleasure. But what I hadn't counted on— what hadn't been factored in to the final project —was, at the end of it all, I would be the one in need of therapy.

Mason was wrong. This was about more than just fearing rejection. It was about losing myself. Bodhi's life sucked the energy right out of me. I could almost feel my anxiety rising to unhealthy levels. I couldn't be the girl who cried after every encounter.

Loving Bodhi was one thing. I could do that effortlessly. What I couldn't do was spend my life being pushed aside and sucked dry by outside forces beyond both of our control.

Mom only allowed me a minute of self-pity before pulling away. "Okay, now that you've had your cry, let's find a solution, shall we?"

"There's only one solution, Mom. I have to break up with Bodhi Beckett."

22

BODHI: AN UNLIKELY HERO

THE KNOCK AT THE DOOR CAME LESS THAN AN HOUR AFTER THE neighbor boy sold Breeze out for a chance at some post-euphoric tail. Josh didn't fool me. He was just in this to do the dance with no pants with as many girls as he could fit into his pimped-out Mercedes. It made me wonder what he got for his efforts aside from a swift kick in the ass from Betsy.

I know what it got me—a puffy-eyed girl who'd been avoiding me like I had an aggressive case of crabs since we stepped into the house. After two unexpected fan encounters, it was clear I couldn't handle this alone. I needed help and, of course, the last person I wanted it from was the one person who knocked on the door.

Strangely enough, I knew who it was even before I heard his voice. For all the bitching and complaining I did about my father, he'd been the one constant in my life. Never far from my side, I could sometimes predict what he'd say or do before it even happened. And that was why I hadn't been surprised by his sudden intrusion. It had been expected. After all, Tucker would have spared no expense finding me the minute I'd hung up the phone at Blubber Beach.

Still, I was impressed. He slid into home plate an impressive forty-eight hours later. Although, to be fair, the breadcrumb trail I'd left was the size of Connecticut. But still, to pinpoint my exact location was astute indeed. Sure he'd received a little help from TV and social media. Our freedom dash had made the local news as well as a variety of entertainment shows. A picture of Breeze and I escaping the horde was accompanied by the uber helpful news snippet, 'Bodhi Beckett and unidentified female chased down in a Northern California coastal community by a stampede of female fans.' Yep, with that valuable tidbit, it wouldn't have taken a good investigator more than an hour to track me down.

"Tucker Beckett here. I'd like to see my son."

Jesus, he made every greeting sound like an ultimatum. Even when he wasn't trying, my father still came off like a douche. From my spot on the couch, I saw Terrance fidgeting in response to Tucker's curt request. Poor guy. No doubt he rarely ran into uptight Hollywood dipwads who bossed him around in his own home. With my father no doubt dressed for success in his expensive business casual wardrobe, I wondered if Terrance was regretting his choice of the yellow Minion board shorts and wife beater combo right about now.

"Oh, um," Terrance fumbled with his words before doing the worst thing possible if you were trying to conceal a fugitive... he turned and made eye contact with me, the runaway prisoner. Dude, come on!

That was all Tucker needed to overpower the situation.

"Bodhi!" His big, booming voice cut through the hallways of Breeze's childhood home, ricocheting off every wall as it pierced my ears. "No more games. I need to see you now."

I glanced in Breeze's direction, trying to gage her reaction. She hadn't been the same since being dropkicked into my world but, after last night, I thought I'd at least eased her worries some. Until the Josh incident stirred thing up all over again. I knew Breeze had feelings for me, but were they strong enough to weather my constant storm? It was a lot to ask of a person to give up their privacy for the sake of a guy she'd just met.

As I pushed off the couch, I checked Breeze's phone for another message from Marni. We'd made plans to meet at six and, no matter what came out of Tucker's mouth, I would not be missing my time slot.

Breeze grabbed my hand, locking eyes with me. Infusing me with strength.

"Relax, it'll be fine," I told her as I leaned in to steal a kiss. It was meant to be a quick peck, but Breeze cupped my cheek, holding the kiss for longer than expected.

Before I could fully appreciate the number it was doing on my insides, Tucker rounded the entry way and we came face to face for the first time in five days. His eyes darted to Breeze, confusion lining his brow.

Terrance stood off to the side, irritation flashing across his features for the first time since I'd met him. As usual, I was embarrassed by my father's behavior. Looking every bit the urban professional with slicked back hair and a Bluetooth affixed in his ear, he wore his standard uniform— a fashion forward button down shirt and expensive slacks.

Betsy emerged from the back room, exchanging a whispered word with Terrance before she approached my father with an outstretched hand.

"Hello, I'm Betsy, Breeze's mother."

Tucker took her hand, flashing his winning smile before turning his attention back to my girl.

"And you are Breeze, I presume?"

Pushing to her feet, she smoothed her shiny hair before sliding her palm against my father's. "Yes. Hello."

"Sorry, but I'm a little confused about how the two of you met. Did you know each other previously?"

"No, Bodhi rescued me from the fire."

Shock deluged Tucker's features. "He did?"

Obviously, he didn't think I was capable of such a feat. Or... more likely he was formulating a plan to spin our tale of woe into a press opportunity. If that was his angle, he'd be sadly disappointed because Breeze would never become band publicity fodder.

But then, to my surprise, Tucker took a turn toward the unexpected as his bottom lip began to tremble. It only took a second before he regained his composure and, clearing his voice of sentiment, he replied, "Well, it's very nice to meet you, Breeze. You seem like a lovely woman." Shifting his focus my way, he smiled tightly. "Can we speak in private?"

"Why don't you take your dad to the covered patio?" Betsy suggested. "I'll bring you some cold drinks."

"That won't be necessary," Tucker shot back. "I sincerely apologize for putting you out. Please let me know what we owe you."

I cringed, as did every other person in the room *not* named Tucker. Why did he always assume everything had a price?

"They weren't babysitting me, Dad. Jesus."

He seemed taken aback by my reaction, and uncharacteristically contrite. "You're right it was a stupid thing to say. I'm sorry, Betsy. Yes, we'd love something to drink. Thank you."

Admitting he was wrong? What in the fresh hell was happening to this man? It was like he was a software program committing to memory each new interaction and then learning from his mistakes. Something had changed in him since the fire. Something significant enough that it was altering the very fabric of his being.

I gave Betsy a tight smile, then ambled toward the patio with

Tucker a few steps behind. Was he dragging his feet? Did he suspect the turn our conversation was about to take?

Once outside, I turned toward him and was shocked when he pulled me into a surprise hug. I don't think we'd done that since I was a child. "Thank god you're safe."

"I'm fine, Dad."

"Are you sure? You're walking stiffly, like you're hurt?"

"No, it's from yesterday. I'm sore. I was flying a kite and falling off swing sets."

"Why would you do that?"

"Because it's fun. Haven't you ever done something just for the fun of it?"

"When I was young, I guess."

"Well, that's where we differ, because my father never let me do things like that."

It was the equivalent of a slap to the face and Tucker recoiled. Shifting his feet, he finally found his tongue a good minute later.

"You don't think I already know I was a shitty father?"

"Do you?"

"I've done a lifetime of soul searching in the past few days. It hasn't been real easy for me either, Bodhi. When I thought you were dead, I can promise you, I had an avalanche of regret."

"Well, then that should make my next question easier. Tell me about my mother— the one you claimed died twenty-four years ago."

Horror. Absolute gut-wrenching horror. It was painted all over his face.

"How did..." He swallowed hard as if his tongue were too thick to push the words out. "What do you know?"

"I met her this morning."

His face crumbled. "No, Bodhi. Why? Why didn't you come to me first?"

"Because you lied to me. What makes you think I'd trust a word out of your mouth?"

"Oh Jesus. Oh no. This is…" Stumbling backward, the color seeped out of his normally bronzed skin. "Bodhi, please, you have to hear me out. There's so much you don't know—about her, and about me."

"Like you're not my real father? I already know that, asshole."

He dropped to the edge of a wicker loveseat, teetering back and forth and, for the first time, concern for his health sidetracked my need to make him pay for a lifetime of deception.

"Are you okay?"

"I think…" He grabbed my arm. "I think I need that water Betsy was offering."

"Wait here."

I ran into the house and straight for the kitchen where Betsy was filling a pitcher with lemonade. Her normally placid demeanor shifted into panic mode the moment she saw me. I wasn't even finished explaining the situation before she'd taken off down the hall, calling over her shoulder for me to bring the water.

Arriving back on the patio, I was stunned to find Betsy embracing Tucker, his forehead pressed to her shoulder.

Was he… crying?

Speechless, I held his glass of water with a shaky hand.

Pulling his shoulder back, Tucker blinked at me with frantic eyes. "I'm so sorry. You have to believe me, everything I did was to protect you. I swear."

"Protect me from what? My own mother?"

"God yes, Bodhi, from your own mother."

Betsy took the water and turned it over to Tucker before addressing me in a calm voice, "I know you feel you've been wronged, but just remember there are two sides to every story. You owe it to yourself to hear him out."

She glanced back at Tucker before patting my cheek and slipping into the house.

"Tell me," I said flatly.

Resigned, my father stared into his glass. "How far back do you want me to start?"

"As far back as it takes to explain why you made me think it was my fault my mother was dead."

"I never meant for you to think that."

"Well, I did."

Tucker buried his head in his hands. "I screwed everything up so badly."

There was no disagreeing with him on that front. And as much as I wanted to feel sympathy for him, he hadn't earned it yet. I flopped in the chair opposite him and waited for my truth. And, finally, after an over twenty-year wait, it came.

"I was eighteen when my mother remarried a man named Andrew Easton. It was her third marriage. Needless to say, because of her track record, I wasn't real optimistic about this one lasting either. So, before they married, I moved out. I had no interest in a new daddy.

"Anyway, he was an okay guy, I guess. But he came with a lot of baggage. His ex-wife had taken off with a former flame, leaving him to raise two daughters alone. The older one was sixteen and her name was Serena. The younger was Marni—she was fourteen. I think he married my mom to be a good influence on his girls, but she was a timid lady, had struggled with depression all her life, and was also a gigantic pushover. Andrew's daughters ate her alive.

"From the start, those girls were nightmares. Both had drug and truancy issues. They were rude and never listened to my mother. The words they called her..." Tucker shook his head, anger tinging his tone.

"Anyway, mom sunk further into depression and, a year after she married Andrew, she reached the end of her rope and hung herself with it."

It was the first time he'd ever discussed his family with me, and now I understood why. Tucker had always been about perfection, and to have something so devastating, so messy, in his past would have been viewed as shameful. His hand shook as he lifted the glass to his lips.

"I blamed those girls," he admitted. "And aside from seeing them occasionally at the restaurant where I worked, we had no contact. I learned a few years later that Andrew had a heart attack when Marni was sixteen. After that, she just ran wild.

"I was twenty-five the day she walked into my work six months pregnant and begging for my help. She claimed she wanted to get healthy, for you, so I took her in. It was the first time I'd ever seen her put someone else first, and I was hopeful that you would be the thing to turn her life around.

"Anyway, Marni lived with me those last three months. She got a job as a waitress and was doing great. Until you were born and things began falling apart. Friends, parties, drugs... they came back with a vengeance. Bad things started happening. Some days I'd come home from work to find Marni and her friends passed out on my couch while you were lying on the floor, needles scattered all around. Other days, I'd come home and find you alone in the crib, diaper full and crying from hunger. Soon she was disappearing for longer and longer stretches of time. I wasn't your father or even related to you, but suddenly I became your primary caretaker. I never signed up for that, Bodhi. You were just dropped in my lap and I did the best I could."

As I listened to the story, I had newfound respect for Tucker.

He'd only been a little older than me when all this went down, and I had to wonder how well I would've handled a drugged-out Marni... and a baby.

Tucker sighed, and then continued, "When you were about four months old, Marni was arrested. I'd been working with social workers and they were fully aware of the situation. When they confronted her about abandoning you, she signed away her parental rights and suddenly I was being given the option to adopt you or let them place you in foster care until they could find you an appropriate family. The thing is, I'd grown attached to you." His gaze found mine and held. "I loved you, Bodhi. And I thought that would be enough, but clearly I had no business being a father. I realize now how selfish I was. I should have let them place you with a loving family instead of turning you into a circus animal. I'm so sorry, kid. I really am."

Tears spilled down his cheeks, and the sympathy I never thought I'd feel hit me full force. He looked...broken. Not larger than life, like he'd always appeared. Today, Tucker proved he was only human.

"You did the best you could," I said quietly. "There's no telling whether I would have gotten that loving family."

It was the closest thing to forgiveness I was willing to give him at this point in his story.

Appearing grateful for my small concession, Tucker nodded and continued with a sigh, "Anyway, after Marni spent time in jail or rehab, she'd just randomly show up on my doorstep unannounced, crying and asking to see you. And I allowed it. She seemed like she was getting her shit together. I trusted in her sobriety. She promised me, Bodhi. She promised I could trust her."

He paused, pain and regret etched deep in the lines on his forehead. I leaned forward, wanting—*no*— demanding more. Was this what Marni had let slip in our meeting this morning?

"I let her move back in with the contingency that she stay off drugs and watch you during the days while I was working," Tucker said dully. "It was working for the first few weeks and it saved me the childcare costs. But then one day when you were just over a year old, I came home and found her knocked out on the couch. Some guy was in there. You were screaming in your crib. I knew something was wrong when he tried to block me from going to you, saying you wouldn't shut up and that he was just trying to get you to be quiet."

Tucker broke down as if reliving a physical pain. Rising to my feet, I gripped his shoulder, offering what solace I could. I had no memory of the incident, no stake in the horror playing out in his mind.

"You'd been badly beaten. Broken ribs. Fractured jaw. I pressed charges and both the guy and Marni were arrested. I didn't wait for her to work a plea deal and arrive back on my doorstep. I was never going to allow her to hurt you again. That's when I packed us up and moved to Los Angeles. I changed our names to keep her from finding us. And, yes, once you were old enough to start asking about your mother, I didn't want you tainted by the past. So I lied to you—told you she was dead. I figured it was better for you to think of her as an angel than the devil I knew her to be."

"And Beth? What happened to her?"

"Beth." Tucker released a weary breath, shaking his head. "Would you believe me if I told you I fired her because I was jealous? She was just your nanny, but you began to see her like a mother. The plain truth was, I hated that you loved her more than me."

The two of us sat silent for a long while, caught up in the story of our shared past. For the first time in my life, I under-stood Tucker— maybe even admired his devotion to a baby that wasn't even his. He'd given up his life in San Francisco to keep me safe. He may not have been a traditional father but at least he had kept me alive and healthy and gave me a future I wouldn't have had with my mother.

"Are you paying her off?"

Tucker cringed. "Yes."

"For how long?"

"About seven months."

Of course, Marni hadn't disclosed that piece of critical information.

"But if I'm legally adopted, she really has nothing to hold over you."

"She has you, Bodhi—her trump card. I was paying her to spare you the truth."

"Then, why did she reach out to me? Wouldn't that end her paydays?"

"See, the problem with blackmail is, once you give it up once, the price goes up. She was squeezing me for more. I could see the writing on the wall. It was never going to end, so I had a 'take it or leave it' agreement set up for $5000 a month. She agreed to it and was cashing the checks, so I thought you were protected. Apparently not."

"You think she's looking for money from me too?"

Tucker hesitated for a long moment. "I'd like to say she's changed her ways, but I've been dealing with her for the past few months and what you need to understand about Marni is that she's the most important person in her life. I do think she loves you, I really do, but she'll never be able to put you first, no matter what she promises. Just remember that."

"By not telling me about her, you put me in a vulnerable position, you know that, right?"

He nodded. "Yes. I know. It was stupid. I haven't been thinking like a father for a very long time. I sort of lost myself in the Hollywood trap."

"Sort of?" I gaped. "It was a little more than 'sort of'."

"I know." His lips fell into a deeper frown. "When you first started out in the business, it was a fun little pastime, but then real offers materialized and it became a job. Not only for you, but for me too. I got all caught up in the power. It wasn't until you started pushing back a few months ago that I took a hard look at my behavior. I didn't like what I was seeing. And then the fire." He shivered. "I thought I'd have to live with that crushing regret forever, and it felt like a just punishment."

I detected only remorse in my father's words. The remorse that came with seeing the light under the worst possible circumstances.

"I'm firing you as my manager," I said quietly. But for a slight twitch, my father remained stone faced and silent. "It's not to punish you," I was quick to assure. "But it's a conflict of interest to have you managing me and being my boss. And my father."

And Tucker was my father. He'd raised me. Sacrificed for me. All the things a parent should do.

He jerked a nod. "I get it. I do. It's just a tough pill for me to swallow. You're my life. I don't know what to do with myself if I'm not micromanaging you."

"Don't I know? No offense, but you're the stage dad from hell."

Tucker's gaze shot to mine and I smiled, the dark cloud lifting as the seconds passed in silence.

"I know," Tucker finally said with a bereft sigh. "Sometimes I can't stand myself. Remember the time when you were like ten and I was bossing around the television crew and you said, 'Dad, Jesus wants you to stop being a dick?'"

I remembered well. The whole crew clapped for me. Tucker and I had a good laugh at the memory. It had been so long since we'd connected on a personal level, I'd forgotten he was an actual human being under all the expensive clothing.

"Will you come back with me?" he asked. "I've got a jet waiting."

"Not tonight." I clapped him on the back. "But I'll be there tomorrow."

"Will Breeze be coming too?"

Breeze…

I frowned at the thought of her at the family reunion with her ex. "No."

Tucker's brows shot up, but he didn't press for details. Instead, he blew out a breath and sat back in his chair, lacing his fingers behind his head.

"Well, I guess I'll have to find myself a new client to suck the life out of."

"That's the spirit." I laughed. "Just because you won't be suffocating me anymore doesn't mean you can't find scores of other young hopefuls who'd jump at the chance to be throttled and deprived of oxygen by the one and only Tucker Beckett."

Smiling, he pointed a finger in my direction and winked. Were my eyes deceiving me or had Tucker just tagged himself out of the game? Maybe my presumed death had actually been the wake-up call he needed to finally unfurl his fist and let me go. It gave me hope that, in the near future, we could come out of it as father and son.

23

BODHI: MY OWN EDDIE

"ARE YOU SURE THIS IS THE PLACE YOU WANT TO BE DROPPED OFF?" the driver asked, craning his neck to get a better look out the windshield. I followed his gaze to the duplex, taking in the slanted garage door, the patch of dirt in the front where grass may once have grown, and the barred windows and doors.

Well shit.

Breeze and I exchanged identical disconcerted expressions before I confirmed to the driver we were indeed in the right place. I realized rents were high in the Bay Area, but my father was paying Marni five thousand dollars a month, and this drug den was the best she could do?

It was just that kind of day. Not only did I have showdowns with both my parents, but I also had to say goodbye to Betsy and Terrance, the pets, and one very bruised and battered Range Rover.

And then there was the matter of the growing herd of minia-ture humans grazing outside on Breeze's front lawn. Now that the Where's Waldo of the boy band world had officially been spotted, a migration of sorts began. An ever-growing influx of Dayers flooded in, with more on the way as scores of metal-mouthed adolescents hopped in the back of their moms' mini-vans and began their pilgrimage.

Touted as the new pop music mecca, Breeze's outdated family home had gone viral and was unexpectedly thrust into the twenty-first century. Suddenly, the 1960's eyesore had an Instagram account, and also a GoFundMe campaign. Stories flourished on the Internet, everything from Breeze's trending hairstyle to my *supposed* life-threatening burns—which I illogically chose to have treated in the Brady Bunch home instead of the sterile environment of a hospital. No one said fake news had to make sense.

Staying at the Cassidy-Bening house was no longer an option for me, at least not without an army of security personnel stationed around the perimeter.

And that's where Tucker came in. Even though I'd fired him, he continued to work his magic. Watching as things seamlessly fell into place made me appreciate my father's special brand of over-parenting. Flights were booked, hotels were reserved, security was strategically put into place, and a black SUV appeared in the driveway ready to take Breeze and I here, to the *Breaking Bad* drug shack.

Tank, our bodyguard for the night, hopped out first and took a look around before ushering us out of the car and up the cement slab that served as a porch.

Marni swung the door open before we even knocked, then took an immediate step back when she spotted the bodyguard.

"Is this... is he a cop?" Her eyes darted back and forth in a way that indicated her home was absolutely *not* police-proofed.

"He's security."

"Security?" Marni scoffed. "You need security to visit your own mother?"

Before I could answer, Tank interjected, "No, Madam, he needs security because he's Bodhi Beckett from AnyDayNow."

Oh yeah, that was unnecessary. I was pretty sure Marni didn't need to be reminded of who I was. Way to make me sound like a cataclysmic asshole, Tank. It went without saying that my bodyguard was a few tacos short of a fiesta platter. However, as evidenced by his nickname, he did win the contest for most massive and that was all that was required for his position. I grabbed his arm and pushed him back.

"It was Tucker's idea," I explained. "Not mine. The big guy will wait outside."

Tank shook his head. "Not my orders. I go where you go."

"Actually, you go where I tell you to go. You work for me now, not for him."

Clearly the steroidal monster hadn't been informed of the changing of the guard and, while he chewed over my proclamation, Breeze and I stepped inside.

At the last moment, Tank took a step but I held up my hand. "Stay!"

Breeze barked out a laugh as I closed the door. "He's not a dog."

My thoughts immediately turned to Little Dick, and I smiled.

"I know, Tank listens."

Our laughter caught Marni's attention and she looked between us, clearly curious about the woman I'd brought to her home.

"Um ... yeah... Marni, I'd like you to meet my..." A variety of options floated through my head, but I settled on something neutral. "Friend."

Marni tilted her head to the side, amused, "Uh-huh, and does *Friend* have a name?"

Breeze stepping in to introduce herself and, as they went through the pleasantries, I took a look around. Two sets of eyes locked onto mine.

Drawn to my brothers, I moved blindly, my hand outstretched. "Hey, I'm Bodhi." The older of the two, Evan, slumped against the wall, dropping his gaze to the floor.

Marni's sharp voice cut across the room, "Evan, don't be rude."

Surprised by her flash of anger, I took a step back. "Hey, it's okay," I said. "This is awkward for all of us."

My mother lifted her chin, fighting to regain her composure. "Oh, sure. I know. Evan's just shy. It can come across as bad-mannered."

Evan glared at his mother, the muscle in his jaw clinched tight. He said nothing, but the contempt was there for all to see.

The room descended into silence, tension like a thick fog rolling in from the ocean. Seeking a ray of sunlight, I turned my attention to Jonah, who'd been a bright, ball of energy since the moment I'd arrived. Unlike his brother, there would be no need to win him over. He was already there. Offering my fist, Jonah readily bumped his against it.

And without an ounce of restraint, my youngest half-brother and I chatted each other up like old friends. Jonah's paternal grandfather, Marcus, was by his side throughout the entire exchange. I wasn't sure why he was here, but it was clear the two were incredibly close and that the older man played an active role in my brother's life.

After a moment, we all took our places around the table and ate pizza straight from the box. As I continued my lively conversation with Jonah and Marcus, I watched Breeze from the corner of my eye, as she tried to coax Evan out of his shell.

He proved no match for Breeze's easy charm, and soon a smile tugged at his lips and the tension in the air evaporated.

Even Marni seemed to relax, dropping her mother of the year act in favor of some light-hearted banter. All seemed right in the world. I had everything I could ever wish for - a family, a career, and the girl who took my life to a whole other level.

I tapped Breeze's thigh under the table, and she turned, her eyes sparkling like jewels, her smile wrapping itself around my heart with ease. Our fingers threaded together like the notes of my favorite song.

This was our fate. The reason we'd come together up on that mountain. We belonged together and, in that moment, I knew I was falling in love.

Caught up in my own thoughts, I didn't notice the detour the conversation had taken. Instead of just leaving the kid be, Marni felt the need to call attention to Evan's many 'gifts'.

"Evan's an artist."

"Evan's best subject is writing."

"Evan's popular with the ladies."

It wasn't clear whether she was truly proud of him or just touting her own superior mothering skills. Either way, there was no need for the up-sell. Evan was my brother and, good or bad, I'd make sure he and Jonah were taken care of.

Instead of being pleased by his own accomplishments, Evan seemed to be shrinking further into himself.

Oblivious to her son's discomfort, Marni shifted her focus to Breeze. "Evan's at the top of—"

"Stop trying to make me sound like something I'm not!" Evan bellowed, slamming his hands against the table. His eyes found mine, pure hatred glowing in the angry slits. "You want the truth? I draw deviant art 'cuz I like death and destruction. Writing is my best subject, not because I'm good at it, but because it's the only one I'm not failing. The only girls that look my way are the ones who slash their wrists after class because they're as miserable as I am. Oh, and the only place I'm top of my class is in detention!"

Stunned, I watched as he stormed from the room with Marni

on his heels. A moment later, muffled voices drifted from a room down the hall.

"Don't take it personal," Jonah said with a shrug. "He hates everyone."

"That's encouraging," I replied grimly.

"Well, not everyone," he added. "He likes me."

"I take it he and your mom don't get along well?"

The boy's smile dimmed. "He doesn't like living here."

"What about you? Do you like it here?"

"He doesn't live here," his grandfather interjected. "My wife and I have raised Jonah since he was an infant. A few years ago we tried to get custody of Evan too, but Marni wouldn't allow it. I do what I can for the boy, but it's a slippery slope and he's sliding fast."

My hope dwindled. "Meaning what?"

"Meaning he's on his way to becoming his mother's son."

―――――

Evan never returned. And after Jonah left with his grandfather, it felt as if we'd worn out our welcome. Marni seemed tired and fidgety. Something had changed in her demeanor since coming back from Evan's room, and it didn't take a genius to see that she'd taken something.

I leaned toward Breeze and whispered in her ear, "Are you okay if I leave you a minute to find Evan?"

When she bit down on her lip, I took that as a no and walked to the door to let Tank in. He'd been a good boy, sitting right on the porch where I'd left him. While he occupied my mother, I strode down the hall, determined to forge some bond with Evan.

After knocking twice and getting no response, I let myself in.

Evan was on the bed, earbuds firmly attached. He jumped

up when I crossed the threshold, his headphones sailing across the room.

"What the hell are you doing in here?" he demanded, hands curled into fists at his sides.

I took a step back... and lied through my teeth. "I was looking for the bathroom."

Evan stared at me, his face a bottomless pit of distrust and anger. "Next door."

"Okay," I said, not moving from my spot. "Sorry if I scared you."

"Like *you* could scare me."

Ignoring his obvious taunt, I shoved my hands into my pockets. "Look, I'm not really sure what's going on here, but maybe if you talk to me I can help. Jonah said you don't like living here."

"Yeah, well, Jonah's an idiot."

"We both know he's not."

"You don't know anything about us."

"Because no one told me, Evan. It's not like I was purposely avoiding you your whole life. I only found out you existed about eight hours ago. I'm sort of playing catch up here."

"I wish I could say the same about you."

"What does that mean?"

Evan's fists unfurled and he sat down on the edge of his bed. "All I've ever heard my whole life is Alex this and Alex that. My bedtime stories were about how Eddie stole you... how evil he was and how perfect you were. No matter what I did I could never measure up to you. So excuse me if I wasn't super fucking excited when she told me she'd tracked you and Eddie down."

"How long have you known about me?"

"Months." Evan's voice transformed into a high-pitched nasally number as he imitated Marni. "Oh, and by the way, Evan, just so you know Alex is actually Bodhi Beckett. So yeah, fuck you!"

I stood transfixed by his rage and resentment. He hated me and, honestly, I didn't blame him. If I were measured up to a ghost my whole life, I'd probably feel just as bitter.

"And you want to know the twisted part of it all?" Evan angrily swiped at the tears slipping from his eyes. "I used to pray for Eddie to come steal me in the night, like he stole you. When I was little I'd be in here hiding from her 'friends' while she was out there smoking crack. And I'd pray so hard for Eddie to come save me. But he never came. And Marcus never came like he did for Jonah. And you know why? Because I don't fucking matter!"

Evan brushed past me, barreling down the hall. I skidded to a stop in the living room in time to see the front door slam and Evan disappear into the night.

24

BREEZE: GLAMPING

AFTER SPENDING THE PAST HOUR AND A HALF LOOKING OVER MY shoulder, preparing for the drug deal I was certain was about to go down, I breathed a sigh of relief as I ducked into the car ahead of Bodhi. The evening played out like a Mexican soap opera, only with worse actors. There was dysfunctional and then there were Bodhi's kinfolk. And that was coming from a woman whose fiancée slept with her cousin.

It was possible that Bodhi had just forgotten to mention Marni's tendency to nod off and itch like a dog battling fleas. Or maybe Bodhi had unconsciously rejected the warning signs because he needed this family connection enough to overlook the glaring inconsistences. I'd learned enough about Bodhi to know he craved simple human contact. I feared that Marni had figured this out and was using it against him.

Tipping my head back against the plush, leather seat, I closed my eyes. The full day of spontaneous weeping had tuckered me out, but watching Bodhi navigate his way through a familial landmine had tipped me over the edge. I was exhausted.

I was there by his side offering support where I could, but it wasn't lost on me that I'd become the token female in his action flick. Of course, I knew that Bodhi respected me as an equal, but he wasn't the problem – the world that revolved around him was. And as far as I could see, the writing was already on the wall. If I stayed with him, I'd forever be in his shadow, the woman who walked a few steps behind. And although that might be acceptable for some, my parents hadn't raised me to be invisible. I was the flamingo in a sea of black and white.

Bodhi's hand covered mine, and I felt long, strong fingers wrap around my own. When I turned my head to engage, I nearly melted at the vision smiling back at me. He was beautiful, and damaged, and talented, and thrilling.

"Hey," he said, his thumb stroking over mine. "A nickel for your thoughts?"

A laugh rumbled low in my chest. "Oh, you'd be quite wealthy after an hour in my head."

"I'm sure. So, what did you think of my ma? She's a keeper, huh?"

"As long as you 'keeper' in the basement."

Bodhi laughed, the tension of the day rolling off him like beads of sweat. "God, Breeze, what a crapfest. That was more cringe-worthy than the time Ryan Seacrest tried to high-five a blind guy."

I scooted closer to him. "You know, one time I went to this girl's house after school and she and her siblings ate butter slices for their afternoon snack. That was only slightly less awkward than tonight."

Rubbing his eyes with his palms, Bodhi's body shook with laughter. He laid his head back on the seat. "Ugh... sometimes I feel like we're the only two sane people left."

"We may be."

"Well, then thank god I found you." Bodhi squeezed my hand, holding it like it was the only lifeline he had left. Avoiding his gaze, I fought the tears threatening to give me away. I wouldn't be his much longer. What happened earlier had sealed the deal. I couldn't continue in this relationship knowing his lifestyle wasn't for me. It was best to break this off now before our hearts got any more invested. Knowing what was in store for us, I rubbed my belly, feeling the sickness brewing inside. By tomorrow morning, we'd again be walking this world alone.

Bodhi was quiet for the longest while and I wondered if perhaps he sensed the coming storm. Had the screaming voices inside my head somehow burrowed their way into his own thoughts?

"Marni lied to me this morning. She's not clean."

My heart hurt for him, but sadly I knew he was right. "No, she's not. And from what Marcus hinted, neither is Evan."

"You know what he told me in the bedroom? He prayed for Eddie to come steal him in the night. I mean how fucked up is that, right?" Bodhi groaned, shifting his gaze to the window before muttering, "At least we know where the $5000 is going... into her bloodstream."

"I'm so sorry, Bodhi. I know you were hoping for a miracle."

"Not even that. I just wanted a mom. She didn't have to be perfect, just functional. What I don't get is why she'd bring me there in the first place. Why not just meet at a restaurant... or even a seedy back alley?"

"I'm just taking a guess but maybe she wanted you to see how she lived, so..."

"I'd give her more money. Dangle my brothers in there to ensure I'll feel obligated to help out."

"Hey." Burrowing against his side, I rested my head on his shoulder. "It's just a theory – not fact, so don't take it that way."

"If she's using all that money on drugs, then giving her more will only perpetuate the problem. How do I help Evan without adding to her addiction problem? I mean the poor kid has nowhere to turn."

"Until now."

"If he'll even accept my help. He hates me, Breeze."

Slanting my gaze to his, I stared into his frustrated eyes. Marni had already managed to beat Bodhi down and she'd only had her claws in him for one day.

Evan had to be saved before it was too late.

"He's sixteen years old, living in a drug den and dreaming of being kidnapped by a guy named Eddie. Trust me, he'll accept your help."

————

Bodhi and I stepped out of the SUV in front of the most glamorous hotel I'd ever laid eyes on. I wished someone had warned me of its splendor before I'd dressed in blue jeans and cowboy booties for my walk through the lobby.

Although, who was I kidding? Tucked under Bodhi Beckett's arm, no one would bother to spare me a second glance.

As we stepped off the elevator, wandering hand in hand toward our palatial suite, Tucker's imposing frame came into view. Bodhi's gaze dipped to the keycard in his father's hand and he groaned.

"What?" I whispered.

"Nothing, it's just... he's not allowed to have a key to my room. I've been over this with him before. The man just doesn't respect boundaries."

Tucker eyes locked onto Bodhi with a pleading kind of intensity.

"How did it go?" he asked, as hopeful as one could be when dealing with the aftermath of a train wreck.

Bodhi flinched, and Tucker's shoulders drooped. "That bad?"

"Worse."

No gloating. No 'I told you so's'. Instead, Tucker squeezed Bodhi's shoulder sympathetically. "I'm sorry."

Bodhi nodded. It was an awkward exchange, but encouraging nonetheless.

Tucker plastered on a fake smile. "I think I can make your evening a little better." And like a blackjack dealer, he flipped the keycard around with deft fingers, offering it to his son.

Bodhi blinked at the piece of plastic before settling his wary gaze on his father. "Goddammit. Have you been in my room?"

"I have but, hear me out, it was for a good cause. Don't worry, it's the last time I'll let myself in your room."

"The last time should have been the last time," Bodhi grumbled.

Ignoring the outburst, Tucker nudged the key in in our direction. "You and Breeze have had a rough few days and I wanted to do something special for you, especially since you didn't get that camping trip you were both hoping for. Take the key. I promise you won't be disappointed."

Father and son stared each other down, but Bodhi was the one to finally cave, snatching the card from his father with a terse 'thanks'.

Much to my surprise, Tucker gave me a quick side hug. "Nice to see my kid has such good taste in women. Have a great night you two."

Without waiting for a reply, he turned on his heel and walked away.

"Well, that was weird," Bodhi said, scratching the patch of scruff on his jaw.

"Not really. You do have great taste in women."

"I know I do, but I wasn't talking about that. I'm just not used to him caring what I think. I need this whole day to end."

I grabbed the keycard from his hand. "Not before I see the surprise. What do you suppose it is?"

"I don't know. As long as it's not a clown, I'm good."

"Or spiders."

"You think he'd fill our room with spiders just to surprise us?" Bodhi asked, laughing. "That's messed up."

"You think he'd fill it with clowns?"

Bodhi grabbed me from behind and lifted me from the ground. "You're such a lively cowgirl." His lips found the curve of my neck and I squealed my approval. This was bad, really bad. I needed to dial down the flirty behavior. It was just too easy with him. Too natural. But, of course, I knew it was absolutely criminal to encourage such behavior when, by the end of the night, Bodhi and I would be no more.

Just a little extra time, that was all I was asking for. Just a little more of his hands up my... no! Focus. Wiggling free, I yanked down my shirt, dislodging his wandering fingers, before playfully shoving Bodhi away from the door. "Move it! I've got to see this surprise. Something tells me your dad doesn't do anything half-assed."

And I was right. I pushed through the door with Bodhi on my heels and stopped dead in my tracks. Right smack dab in the middle of the luxury suite sat a camping tent.

"You've got to be kidding." Bodhi breathed.

Even for a pampered popstar, this was a special treat, and not anything like the camping I was used to. No clingy dirt or sticky marshmallow residue. No sleeping bags. And best of, no ant trails or late night dances to the public restrooms.

Bodhi took my hand and we ducked inside the canvas teepee where a plush queen-sized bed waited, made up with Egyptian cotton sheets. And past that, the flap on the back was pulled aside, revealing an oval shaped Jacuzzi bathtub with candles lining the ledge

"Wow," Bodhi said as he peeked his head out the back. "You gotta see this."

To my amazement, the patio had been done up like a camp-site, with a wood burning fire pit. Unlike the raging inferno we'd survived, these flames were submissive and firmly under control. Yet, that didn't stop my pulse from quickening as the memories flooded back. Bodhi seemed to sense my fear and, lifting my chin, he rested his forehead against mine.

"It's all right, Breeze. Just breathe."

Tears slipped down my cheeks at the irony. We'd started with fire, and now we'd end with it as well. Except I didn't want it to end. Not ever.

Wrapping my arms around his waist, I held him tighter than I think I'd ever held anyone before. Surviving the fire had reworked our wiring, forged a connection that transcended the physical. And even though I'd made the decision to say goodbye, I wondered if we'd ever truly be separated.

"Look," he whispered, and I followed his gaze to the vastness of the ocean. Water as far as the eye could see, shimmering gold and silver beneath the low hanging moon. I'd lived a stone's throw from the Pacific Ocean my whole life and never seen it so tranquil. It was as if the universe was conspiring against me. Whispering promises of forever, when forever wasn't meant to be.

"Tucker thought of everything." Bodhi broke the quiet reflection. "He even dropped off my guitar so I can woo you with my music."

My heart sank. Now I had to listen to him sing, that melodic voice that had worked its way into my soul.

I might as well give up now. Maybe it was best to just enjoy tonight and deal with the tough stuff in the morning. One more idyllic night with the man of my dreams and then the sun would rise and it would be Thursday. My favorite day. Only it wouldn't be. Not ever again. Not after I broke us to pieces.

Sinking into the oversized chair on the spacious patio, I

wiped away the last of my tears and made peace with the hypnotic flames dancing before me while Bodhi tuned his guitar.

Slotting his thumb on the neck, he cradled the instrument against his body like a father would his child. Did Bodhi want kids someday? And who would they call mommy?

As the music floated to my ears, I let my head fall back. But then Bodhi began to sing, effortlessly drawing my gaze. He didn't notice, fingers gliding over the strings and eyes shut tight. Music healed him, righted all the wrongs. Even though I couldn't survive in his musical world, he belonged there. And I'd rather leave him than ask him to give it up.

A sweet melody drifted through the night sky and I melted in my seat, smiling at the familiar chorus.

"The song from the car," I said softly. "I love this one."

He nodded without missing a beat. And in that moment, I knew he was a talent far beyond the world his father had created for him.

I could see him in a smoky bar, on a small stage, with just his guitar. In my mind, I was there too, sitting in the first chair below the microphone, cheering him on.

That's how I envisioned life with Bodhi. Him and me and music. In a perfect world, that could be us. But if today had proven anything, it was that perfection was impossible to find.

Bodhi played two more songs before propping his guitar against the sliding glass door and squeezing into the space beside me. Once he'd rearranged me so I was partially on his lap, I settled in and laid my head on his chest. "Who's the girl from the song?"

Bodhi lazily rolled strands of my hair through his hands. "Her name is Beth."

"Are you still in love with her?"

A hum low in his chest vibrated against my ear. "I was never in love with her. It's not a romantic song."

"I beg to differ. It gives me chills every time."

"You heard what you wanted to hear, Breeze. The song isn't about a lost love. It's about someone who I loved and lost. There's a difference."

"Okay, then who is she?"

"Beth was my nanny, but I kind of thought of her like a mother. She was with me for a few years during my childhood."

"Did she die?"

"No. My dad fired her. One day she was there, the next she was gone. This guitar, it was a gift from her. It once belonged to her soldier husband who died a few months before she came to live with us. She's the one who gave me my love of music. You know how sometimes you meet a person who makes such an impact on your life that it changes who you are forever? Well, that was Beth. I was so young and impressionable when she left. It just decimated me – left me distrustful of women in general. That's the reason I only had nickels."

"Until me," I whispered, my heart grinding to a halt.

"Yes, until you."

Bodhi's fingers sank into my hair and, with a gentle tug, he tilted my face to his. And then his mouth was on mine, tongue sweeping in. Teasing. Tasting. He deepened the kiss, and I cupped his cheeks, holding onto this moment. This perfection. But we weren't perfect. And tomorrow it would all end. But tonight, if I held on, kept us locked together, maybe...

Breaking the connection, Bodhi's lips moved down my fevered skin, past my jaw to my neck. And lower.

I guided his mouth back to mine for another searing kiss. Because in the end, that's what I'd miss most, taking his breath as my own. And when I was all full up, and I couldn't take any more, I found the strength to gently push him away.

"Stop."

It was a plea from the depths of my soul.

Stop. Please stop.

Tipping back, he looked down at me with unfocused eyes and lips swollen from our kisses. Our goodbye.

"What's wrong?"

Everything.

My fingers followed my gaze to his mouth—I'd miss this mouth—and then up to those beautiful blue orbs. An endless sky. And I could almost see tomorrow. Just not mine.

And then I smiled. Because that's what I wanted him to remember.

Always remember.

"We have to talk."

———

It felt like the walk of shame. But instead of Bodhi kicking me out, I'd done the deed myself. There was no point in staying any longer. I'd said what needed to be said and there was nothing more to do but leave.

I couldn't remember all the words, the tiny truths that tore us apart, but each one felt like I'd buried a knife deep in Bodhi's heart. Even the apology that followed seemed to bring him pain.

And then the anger. I saw it there too, along with the shock.

"It's not your fault."

But he didn't believe me. And how could I blame him? Bodhi had spent his life being left behind. How could I explain that this was for the best? A clean break. Someday he'd thank me. But not now.

Tucked inside the taxi, tears raced down my cheeks, blurring my vision. Like the fire, we'd burned hot. But now a chill settled deep in my bones. And I wondered if I'd ever feel warm again.

"Up there on the left," I instructed the driver, swiping the tears dripping from my chin.

"The one with the Maserati in the driveway?"

"No, the next one."

"Ah, the one with the lion statues."

"No, the one that looks like it was spit out of a time capsule."

The driver had no trouble pinpointing the correct house after that. I was relieved to see no one but my parents standing in the yard. Whatever had happened to Bodhi's fan club, I'm glad they were gone.

A sob wracked my body as I stepped out of the taxi. And then I was running, straight into the arms of the man who'd shaped me into the person I was today.

"Come here, sweetheart."

I melted in my step-father's embrace. But didn't feel the usual warmth. Only safety. And that would have to be enough.

For now.

25

BODHI: ON REPEAT

PAPERS LITTERED THE FLOOR, PAGES OF LYRICS ON HOTEL notepads. Scattered thoughts in the margin of the complimentary newspaper. Even the back of the room service menu wasn't spared. And when I'd run out of room, I'd taken to writing on my skin. Her brutal words, memorialized on my flesh and etched into my brain for posterity.

"I think I'm falling in love with you, Bodhi. Only you. The other part of your life I just don't think...."

She'd stopped then, the rest of her thoughts trapped behind tight lips. But she wasn't finished.

"Maybe we can try again when we're both in different places in our lives."

And the dreaded, *"I hope we can still be friends."*

Hell no, I wouldn't be her fire buddy, the guy she was content to see a couple of times a year in a public place. I didn't do friend zone. And no thank you to being her safety net somewhere down the road. If I wasn't good enough now, she couldn't have me as a last resort.

Defeated. That was where I stood now, but I'd gone through

the spectrum of emotions since she'd left. Anger. Frustration. Embarrassment. I looked around at the mess inspired by Breeze's fear. Her refusal to consider a life with me. Hell, not even a life. Just a day. One more day. Maybe if I called her and told her that.

Maybe...

No. Because the things that scared her, they were part of me. My fame. My music. The life I was born to lead. Where did I go from here? I couldn't just flick a switch and turn it all off.

And did I want to?

It didn't matter. There was no ultimatum. No choice. She'd taken the decision out of my hands by removing herself from the equation altogether.

I see you.

That was what she'd said the first day we'd spent together. And I'd believed her. Trusted in the fact that when I was at my lowest, stripped down to my very core, she'd see me.

And maybe that was the problem. She *did* see me. And she couldn't handle it.

Breeze didn't want to be my sidekick, following me around while I chased my dreams. How could I fault her? Why would she be content to be a bit player, when she was bright like a star?

Still, plenty of people dealt with issues like this. Maybe not on such a grand scale, but we could have worked out a compromise. If she'd been having misgivings about my life, at least we could have tried to talk it out.

Not that it would have mattered. Breeze had made her choice long before coming to the suite. I hadn't even been given the option to fight for her, and that's what pissed me off the most.

Another rejection.

First my mother. Then Beth. And now Breeze.

I had it all—fame, money, talent—but the thing I craved most always seemed just beyond my reach.

Suddenly, I couldn't wait to get back to the life Breeze hated. Maybe it wasn't what she considered ideal, but it was mine and I wouldn't make excuses for it.

Ducking into the tent, I rolled my exhausted body onto the mattress and closed my eyes on the day I wished had never been.

———

Sleep provided no relief. I tossed and turned for hours, nightmares tormenting my subconscious mind. A patchwork of traumas. Dogs nipping at my ankles. Fangirls carrying Breeze away.

And the fire.

More than once I'd slipped beneath the veil, only to come to with a start, flames licking my skin.

I hadn't had one distressing dream until now—the night her warm, honeyed body wasn't pressed up against mine. Breeze was my security blanket. The reason I wanted to wake up in the morning and smile. Reaching over, I touched cool sheets where Breeze should have been.

If that's how she wanted to play it, fine.

I had stadiums full of admirers ready and willing to take her place. Women who were comfortable in the spotlight and would proudly stand by my side even when things got a little hairy. My nickels. They'd been there since the start. Did it really matter that they'd fallen in love with the character I played on stage?

I grimaced, sullen.

Yeah, it mattered.

I wanted my dime. Breeze. The woman who, in only a few days' time, knew me better than anyone before her... and I'd just let her walk out of my life.

I could no longer deny the similarities between Breeze and Beth -not only in their impassioned energy and blinding light, but also in their dual, crushing abandonments. Both had claimed to love me – no, both *had* loved me. That much I was certain of, yet both had left for reasons beyond my control.

The difference was I'd been only nine-years-old when Beth left. Powerless. She'd disappeared from my life simply because I'd lacked the maturity and strength to bring her home. But I wasn't that helpless child any longer. It was time to fight for what I wanted.

History would not repeat itself.

———

My father did a double take as I strolled toward him in the hotel lobby with Tank in tow, but no Breeze.

Before he could ask, I held up my hand. "She dumped me."

His reaction was swift and comical, like a cartoon character with eyes popping from the sockets. I patted his shoulder. "You alright there, bud?"

"Are *you*?"

"Yep." Pinning on a smile, I snagged a banana from the gigantic fruit bowl in the lobby. "Fine."

Because I knew it wasn't the end for Breeze and me. Not by a long shot.

"All right, well, that's... surprising." Tucker rubbed the back of his neck, eyeing me carefully. "You just seemed so hooked on her. Maybe I was misreading things."

"No, you weren't. I think I might actually be in love with her."

I peeled the banana, then chomped down while my father continued to gape, further imitating the caricature I imagined in my head.

Through a mouthful of mushy fruit, I asked "Can you please not make eye contact with me while I'm eating a banana?"

Tucker looked away, chuckling. "So, let me just see if I have this straight. You might love this girl, but she dumped you, and now you're eating a banana without a care in the world. Am I missing something?"

"Yeah, you're missing the part where I vowed to get her back. Trust me, old man, I'm not going down without a fight."

My father finally returned to his human form. "Honestly Bodhi, I don't know who you are anymore... but I kinda like it."

The private jet landed in Los Angeles and, the minute my feet hit the pavement, we were up and running. Welcome back to the grind. The paparazzi. The army of security personnel. The screaming fans. All for me—the guy who, two days ago, was crawling around the floor of a Marshall's clothing store blowing bubbles down my girl's shirt. That's where I wanted to be. Not here.

Sometimes this world made me feel like I was floating in zero gravity.

In the heat of the melee, with hands ripping at my flesh, I turned to my father. "Do you know there's no angry way to say bubbles?"

Brows furrowed in frustration, Tucker pushed through the crowds grumbling, "Fuck that. *Bubbles.*"

I'll be damned. You could remain angry. I laughed, wishing I could call Breeze and share the news, but she was gone.

Not for long.

Security protected our heads as they ducked us into a vehicle that whisked us away from the circus. Tipping my head back on the seat, I exhaled. "Dad."

"Yeah?"

"I hate this shit."

With a sigh, Tucker let his head fall back as well. "I know."

————

Because of my headline-making week, interview requests had poured in and, to my surprise, my father actually asked my opinion on the matter. He was trying, and I gave credit where it was due. In the end I agreed to an interview, but only if it was focused on the entire band and not just me alone. The fact that AnyDayNow had become the Bodhi show was never far from my mind, and I didn't want resentment to become the wrench that pried the five of us apart.

My father and I, accompanied by a small contingent of body-guards, met up with the other guys at a television studio. I was instantly surrounded, heartfelt hugs and unnaturally hard smacks on the back were the name of the game for all but RJ who stayed back, nursing a disgruntled scowl.

I slid to his side and tried whacking him in the nuts for old times' sake. He was quick to react. And retaliate. Before I knew it, he had me down on my knees, my arm twisted behind my back.

This wasn't playful fun anymore.

"RJ!" Hunter warned, heading into the fray.

The pressure in my joints eased and he let me up.

I spun around. "What the fuck?"

"That was for making me think you were dead, asshole!"

"Well, it was a traumatic week, dickhead. Maybe I just forgot."

"Right, so the ice cream, that was therapy?"

He had me there. "I'm sorry, okay? I should have called."

His shoulders hunched and RJ exhaled. He was worn out... beaten down. "Yeah, you should have."

Grabbing the broody bastard, I pulled him into a hug. "I'm sorry. I wasn't thinking. It's been an insane few days. I'll tell you everything as soon as we have a quiet moment. Say we're all good or I'll tell the interviewer you own a man purse."

A reluctant smile formed on his lips. "It's a satchel, dickweed."

I'd been forgiven.

———

While we waited for the crew to take their places, the five of us stood off to the side, conversing. Shawn placed his hand on my shoulder.

"Just so you know, I wrote a whole eulogy to speak at your funeral."

"That's nice."

"Uh-huh. I planned on telling the congregation what a good sport you were the time you found out I replaced your pocket-sized hand sanitizer with KY Jelly."

Confusion furrowed my brows. "What are you talking about? I don't remember that?"

"Oh well, then... never mind."

Eyes narrowed, I took in my nemesis. "Shawn, I swear, you'd better be kidding."

Not only did he not appear to be kidding, but that smirk told me he was proud of his prank. "Remember a couple of months ago when you kept getting sick? Like one cold after another?"

"Yeah?"

"It was then."

Grabbing his jacket, I shoved him back. "You asshole! I had no protection."

"Technically you did. I used spermicidal lubricant."

Raising his hands in surrender, Shawn patiently waited for the beatdown he deserved.

I didn't disappoint.

And while holding the prankster down in a headlock, I listened to Dane's idea on how he'd planned to celebrate my life. Unsurprisingly, his send-off would have been heartfelt and unique.

Always the sentimental type, Dane spoke of dividing my ashes into tiny urns and placing them in necklaces to distribute among our closest allies. These trusted few would then take my ashes on adventures around the world before releasing me into an ocean or sprinkling me over a mountain.

"I have a question." RJ chimed in as Dane was finishing his inspiring send-off. "If Bodhi had burned in a fire, how would you know what were his ashes and what were —say—that of a kitchen table? You know what I mean?"

Dane made a face, perhaps considering for the first time the flaws in his plan. He ran his hand over his jaw. "Yeah. Huh. That could be a problem."

"Right? Because you might think you are spreading Bodhi's ashes in the Amazon but, in reality, it was just some junk from Ikea."

"You guys are horrible." Hunter cringed. "I hope you know, Bodhi, I took this seriously. I wrote a eulogy that meant something... because you were one of my best friends and you deserved so much more than dying the way you did."

"Uh," Shawn cut in, still gagging under my chokehold. "News flash, idiot, Bodhi's still alive and currently suffocating me to death."

Satisfied Shawn had paid his dues, I let him up.

"What about you, RJ?" I asked, curious what my best friend had to say about me. "How did you plan for my funeral?"

RJ shifted his feet. "I wasn't going to go."

"Seriously?" How could RJ, of all people, not show up? "You weren't going to show up to my funeral?"

The other guys exchanged odd glances before RJ headed over to the row of chairs and took his seat at the end. I narrowed in on my friend. Something had happened in my absence that had him avoiding me like the plague; which, incidentally, I might actually have, since I'd apparently been sanitizing with lube for some time now.

———

The cameras started rolling and we took our seats, side by side, as we'd done a thousand times before. As musicians and friends, we melded perfectly into the characters we played on stage, ripping into each other to the delight of our overflowing fan base. Muscle memory kicked in and I went through the motions, even mugging for the camera as I'd done countless times before. It was all so familiar yet, at the same time, I could feel change was in the air.

I was like a ghost, looking down on the guy who used to be me. It struck me that I'd already closed this chapter of my life and had moved on to the next—the one with Breeze and my guitar and the songs that actually meant something to me.

Running my hands over my arms, I felt the words I'd written for her burning me through my long-sleeve shirt. These lyrics, they were my future and, before they faded from my skin for good, I needed to absorb their influence and learn their meaning. Breeze had been my teacher, opening my eyes to a new way, free from the trappings of celebrity. Our time together was a tiny stitch in the fabric of my life, but her impact had been monumental, proving to me I could be happy without the spotlight, the fortune, and the fame.

"Okay, I'm just going to put this out there, so please don't judge," Shawn whispered, his head partially concealed by a mannequin's billowing skirt. "But is anyone else as turned on as I am right now? I mean I know they're plastic and all, but these are some high-class dummies."

The five of us were in hiding. Minutes earlier, we'd been driven into a women's clothing store after thousands of fans descended upon the television studio, overrunning our security detail as they'd been attempting to herd us into the waiting vehicles. Hands had been everywhere—grabbing, scratching, and pinching. It was like running barefoot on a beach filled with crabs.

With our path forward blocked by bodies, a sideways trajectory became our only course of action and that's how we ended up here—hiding behind a group of mannequins— until the police managed to cordon off the area and free us from the horde.

Shawn popped his head up, peering at the fans banging on the storefront window. He groaned. "If they break through that glass, we're all toast. Police need to get this under control. It's dangerous. Now I know how Bodhi felt escaping the fire."

Yeah right.

"I'd take this every day of the week over a flaming roof collapsing on my head."

"Dude." Dane nudged me. "Now that you've been through it yourself, any advice on what steps we should take in the event of a fire?"

"What steps? Big fucking ones!"

All five of us dissolved into a fit of hysteria and had to be shushed numerous times by the guards tasked with getting us out of this mess in one piece. I looked around at the absurdity of the situation, seeing it for the first time through fresh, unfiltered eyes. Through Breeze's eyes.

A flash mob of preteen girls prepared to shatter the glass and bleed all the way to the hospital for just one special moment with their boy band idols. Full grown, ex-military men speaking frantically into their phones using words like 'Under Siege' and 'Extraction Point.' Roads being cordoned off as everyday citizens were physically removed from public streets under the threat of arrest.

All for us.

Five unassuming, unremarkable, and unworthy twenty-something guys just trying to find their way in the world like everyone else. It was pure and irrefutable insanity. And very soon, it would no longer be mine.

"Guys?" I whispered. "What the hell are we doing here?"

Not understanding the true meaning of my question, Hunter replied with an entire rundown of the situation.

RJ punched him in the arm. "He means, in this place in life, half-wit. Hunkering down like combat soldiers in a war zone."

I nodded, pointing at RJ. "What he said. Look, I don't want to let you guys down, but these past few days, I've really had some time to evaluate my life, and what I've concluded is—this shit sucks. I need things to slow down or I'm gonna go fucking crazy. I hate to do this to you but, after the tour is over next month, I think I'm done."

Silence. My gaze jumped to each of my bandmates—hoping and praying that they'd understand. We were family. To my amazement, nobody seemed surprised.

"So, I haven't said anything yet," Hunter whispered, "but Daisy and I are getting married."

We all jostled him around, congratulating him.

"Why didn't you tell us you were going to propose?" I asked, truly surprised he'd keep something like this a secret. He was the TMI guy of the group, and had even been known to confess rubbing one out in the tour bus shower.

Color rose in his cheeks as he replied sheepishly, "I just wanted it to be between the two of us. But now that she's said yes, I'm so stoked and I wanted my best friends to know."

"Of course she'd say yes." Dane said, ever the optimist. "You're a catch."

RJ nodded. "Exactly. And what woman wouldn't want a virgin? Now Daisy can mold you into her very own sex-puppet. Good for you, man."

"Well, since we're sharing confessions," Shawn chimed in. "I'm going to be a daddy. Shoshanna is four months pregnant."

Dane's eyes widened. "You? *You're* going to be a father?"

Shawn nodded, his grin spreading from ear to ear. "DNA tests pending, of course. But yeah, call me Daddy, boys."

RJ rose to one knee, setting off a volley of screams from the crowd so intense a security guard was forced to drag a rack of clothes over to shield him from view.

"Bodhi, you asked me why I wasn't going to come to your funeral. It's not that I didn't want to honor you. It was because I wasn't going to stand next to all the hypocrites mourning your death when they were the ones who put you in the coffin. When I heard they found your stuff and you were presumed dead, I lost it. I wish you would have called or something. I mean I almost drank myself to fucking death over it."

A lump settled in my throat the size of a boulder. "I'm... ah, shit, RJ. I'm so sorry. I wasn't thinking. Or maybe I was just thinking about myself."

"Yeah, ya think?" His lips flattened into a thin line. "Dick move, dude. Anyway, I beat you to the punch because I quit the band three days ago."

"You what?"

"You heard me."

"What the...?"

The others nodded in confirmation.

"I quit and flew home to Idaho. I only came back for you, but, as far as I know, they were making plans to cancel the remainder of the tour and end AnyDayNow for good. Trust me when I say, I'm ready to walk out the door with you."

Tears pooled in Dane's eyes. "Am I the only one who wants to stay on this ride forever?"

I gripped his shoulder. "That's the thing, Dane. It's not going to last forever. We're getting older. Trust me, there are five guys waiting in the wings, ready to knock us off our pedestals. Let's go out at the top of our game."

"I'm with Bodhi." Hunter sighed. "I don't want to become a joke."

"Exactly." RJ flashed me a wicked smirk. "We don't want to be the pubescent child star who can't even book a mouthwash commercial."

I delivered a swift punch to RJ's arm and then turned to my brothers. "Here's the deal. We can spend the rest of our lives with our heads up a mannequin's ass, or we can be out there." I pointed to the great outdoors. "It's a big, wide world out there, boys. Let's go live in it."

Adding our fists to the circle, we noticed one missing. Our heads swiveled in Shawn's direction. Had he seriously not been paying attention to our life changing conversation? Only a wicked grin revealed his true intentions.

"Sorry guys, I was just checking my Twitter status," he said, grinning as he made a show of putting his phone away. "So, what did I miss?"

———

While still hunkered down under maximum security, the guys and I made plans for our mutiny. Once the decision had been made, a weight lifted from my shoulders. I was one step closer to the life I wanted to live. An authentic life. Since we were all on the same page, no one person would take the heat for the breakup and we could all emerge untainted by drama.

Maybe someday we'd work together again but, for the foreseeable future, the five of us had agreed to go our separate ways. Professionally, at least. Privately, we were still brothers. Family.

Tucker took the news better than expected. After the conversation we'd had on Breeze's patio, he probably expected the exodus, although I'm not sure he was anticipating it times five. But true to his word, my father stood by me, negotiating a settlement with the handlers. Because we had only four months left of our current deal, it was agreed upon by all parties that after the end of the tour, they'd let the contracts burn out. In return, we promised to make the final thirteen shows a farewell event for the ages.

In two months' time, AnyDayNow would officially be no more.

———

Tucker stretched out on the couch in the suite, glancing over the notes I'd left on the table. "Are you sure, Bodhi?" His eyes flicked to mine.

I wasn't sure about anything. Except that Marni had agreed to sign over her parental rights to Evan in exchange for an all-expense paid trip to a luxury rehab where sobriety went hand-in-hand with massages and mani-pedis.

And that was only the beginning. More treasures would fall at her feet once the program was completed. A lump sum payout, overseen by a trust that would regularly administer funds. Contingent on Marni passing random drug screenings. And a nice three-bedroom house in a quiet neighborhood.

Despite everything I knew about the woman, I had to make the offer. If Marni was serious about getting clean, I'd give her the shovel to dig her way out. If she wasn't, she could use that shovel to add more dirt onto her grave. Because that's where she was heading. But the agreement I forged ensured that she wouldn't be taking my brother along for the ride.

"It's something I have to do," I said with a grim smile. "I don't expect you to understand, but I do need you to help me with the legal side of things."

To my surprise, Tucker nodded. No hesitation. I didn't even have to use my canned speech to convince him.

Inside, down deep, he felt something for Marni. She was my mother. And if there was one thing I knew, Tucker loved me. And that love extended to her.

Tucker pushed to his feet, his phone and my rudimentary contract with my mother in hand.

"Don't worry, son. I'll get it done. And, I know I'm probably the last person you want around Evan but... anything he needs, I'm here."

I nodded, thankful for his offer. There was still so much I needed to figure out but my immediate concern was for my little brother's safety. All the other details could be ironed out later.

Once Tucker retreated into the bedroom to contact my attorney, I sank onto the couch and stared at the screen on my phone.

Anxiety churned in my belly. For me. For Evan.

What if he didn't agree? What if he was too far gone? What if...

Pushing the doom and gloom aside, I swiped my finger over Evan's name.

He answered on the third ring. "Bodhi? What do you want?"

Curiosity replaced the venom that had laced his words during our last conversation. I took that as a sign.

Infusing cheer in my tone, I replied, "Today is the day, Evan."

One beat. Two.

Come on, little brother.

"For what?"

I smiled, relief washing over me like cool rain. "For you to matter. I'm your Eddie."

26

BREEZE: THE HIGHER GROUND

"Are you sure you'll be all right to go today?" Mom asked, joining me in the bathroom as I finished curling my hair. "Under the circumstances, maybe it would be best if you stayed home."

I couldn't blame her for giving me the out, considering what she'd witnessed.

Thursday was 'sob' day, featuring big, nose-stuffing episodes interrupted only by periods of rest when I'd replenish my reserves in order to continue on with a fresh torrent of tears when I woke. Just to up the misery ante, I watched every weepy dog movie I could possibly stand—death after doggie death.

Sobbing was the rule of order in the Cassidy-Bening household and I was its crown princess.

Not to be outdone, Friday was 'fuck day'... and not in the super fun, tangled in the sheets kind of way. No, Friday was the day the f-word was used as a sentence enhancer. Verbs, adjectives, nouns, and yes, I think maybe even adverbs, although I wasn't a hundred percent certain what they were. Since breaking it off with Bodhi, I was becoming quite the skilled linguist if you liked your communication on the offensive side.

Scrutinizing myself in the mirror, I was comforted by my

righteous hair, but the rest of me was going to require some extensive retooling. Red, puffy eyes, bloated cheeks, and the nastiest little smirk a day of f-bombs could produce. Brandon would not be impressed.

Brandon.

Why the hell did I even care what he thought? It wasn't like I still had a thing for him. But my need to demonstrate to my ex that I was doing fantastic was strong. Was I trying to prove my worth to him or to myself? I wasn't some spinster. Hell, I'd just reeled in a big-time hottie—a popstar with a rock star voice. Granted, it would have been more impressive had I actually gotten him into the boat. But that wasn't how I rolled. Oh no, this girl threw her perfectly fantastic catch back in the flippin' ocean.

Wait, why in the hell did I do that again? What was my reasoning?

Oh yeah, because I was dumb. Dumb, dumb, dumb.

"You look a little constipated, sweetie," mom noted as she fluffed up my curls in the back.

And I had to smile, because she knew just how to put the sweetest spin on average, everyday insults.

"Thanks for noticing. I was thinking about Brandon."

"Oh, well that explains it then. That man should come with a warning label and a box of laxatives."

No disagreement here.

"Okay, how's this?" Meeting her gaze in the mirror, I pinned on a smile. "Do I still look like I'm straining to have a bowel movement?"

"Well, I mean, now you just look like a sad clown going potty."

Laughing, I bumped her with my hip, knocking her off balance.

"There she is." Mom grabbed my cheeks and shook my face like I was a seven-year-old. "My happy, gorgeous girl."

"I'm getting there. Sorry about the past two days."

"Eh, no apologies needed. I actually learned quite a few new swear words, so thank you."

"Ha, you don't fool me. You're a lot savvier than I ever gave you credit for, Ms. Bowchickawowwow."

Mom performed a little curtsey before focusing her laser stare back on me. "You doing okay, for real?"

I let out a long, frustrated groan. "I suppose."

"You made your choice, Breeze. And now it's time to live with it."

The subtle reminder reinforced my feeling that Mom wasn't on board with my decision.

"I know. I guess I just wish I felt better about it. I can't shake the feeling I've made a huge mistake."

Mom dropped her gaze and I swear I saw her shrug.

"What was that?" I asked.

"What?"

"That little noddy-shrug. You think I made a mistake, don't you?"

"It doesn't matter what I think. It's your life, Breeze."

"It matters to me."

I stared her down until she finally caved. "Okay, fine. You know I'm a big believer in fate. What happened to the two of you, and then the instant connection it forged—things like that don't happen by chance. Have you ever considered the two of you were meant to be?"

My mouth dropped open. "And you didn't tell me this *before* I shoved a boot up his ass and went on my merry way?"

"It's not fate if you have to be convinced of its otherworldly powers. Take a deep breath and breathe it in. If it's meant to be,

Breezie, you'll find your way back to him. Have a little faith that things will go your way."

Mom slapped my butt. Pep talk over. "Now, get yourself ready and let's go kick some ass for real. How does that sound?"

"Strangely appealing. And now that you mention it, I *am* in the mood to beat someone silly."

The plan was to elude Brandon and Jenna for as long as possible. During the car ride over, I went through all sorts of avoidance techniques, most involving large objects to hide me from view— plants, tables, Uncle Raymond.

My little plan hit a snag the moment I walked through the door of the banquet hall and into my worst nightmare. Standing before me was Brandon and his happy family, all freshly scrubbed and eager to rub my nose in their perfectly sanitized world.

Brandon was bigger and buffer than before, his freshly tatted arms bursting from a shirt two sizes too small for him. Where did he shop? Baby Gap? His black hair was slicked back and the beard-goatee number was surprisingly well-trimmed. When we'd been together, Brandon kept things on the scruffy side. Now he looked like any other tool whittling away his extra hours pumping iron in the gym.

Jenna appeared radiant in a yellow wrap dress, shiny blond curls cascading down her back, and the most perfectly rounded baby belly. Of course, she had to be gorgeous. It was all part of the master plan to drive me into the ground. No doubt my cousin had received word of my presence at the event. Because it looked like she'd booked every beautifying procedure possible to make her dazzle.

It worked.

There was no competition. And who was I kidding? There never had been. She'd always been extra. Taller, thinner, with better skin, nicer clothes, and a mom who owned a microwave. Still, she'd always copied me. Whatever I could do, she could do better. It was an endless circle, even as children. We were the best of friends and the worst of enemies. As of late, we were only enemies and that made me sad. I hoped he was worth it.

A toddler with impossibly big brown eyes and bouncy, hairdresser-dream curls stole my attention away from her equally attractive parents. Her hand gently burrowed into Jenna's as she tucked her head into her mother's leg and peered up at me with curiosity.

Suddenly there wasn't enough oxygen in the room. In the world. Oh, the deception this little girl's creation had caused. I felt it in my bones as if it were only yesterday. How naïve I'd been - trusting in a future that would never be mine.

I wanted to run and hide—where was Uncle Raymond when you needed him —but my legs were riveted in place. It was then I noticed that all fifty-plus of my relatives were holding their breath, anticipating my reaction. Even the music from the live band had ceased.

What the hell? Had this whole day been choreographed for my humiliation?

Terrance's hand molded to the small of my back, providing me quiet comfort and the assurance I wasn't alone. My eyes collided with my mother's and she lifted her chin, a small smile curving her lips. Although no words had passed between us, I nodded my understanding.

How I responded would define me, and also go down in the annals of our family history. I could either kick up a shitstorm and ruin the day or take the higher road, swallow my wounded pride, and pretend seeing the two of them didn't make me want to drop a bag of dog shit on their porch and set it on fire.

The higher ground – I would take it – not for Jenna's sake, and certainly not for Brandon's, but for the sake of their little girl who was the innocent handiwork of two backstabbing cheats.

"Brandon." I nodded my uncomfortable greeting.

"Breeze." He nodded back.

Continuing the pathetic pattern, I turned my attention to my cousin. "Jenna."

"Breeze."

We stood there shifting our feet, the awkwardness on par with seeing someone you know in a grocery store and then running into them again in the next aisle. And the next aisle. And the next.

Perhaps not knowing what else to do, Jenna pulled her daughter in tighter, a fiercely protective gleam in her eye.

What did she think I would do, grab the child and toss her out the window?

What had happened to us? How could a loser like Brandon tear us apart so thoroughly that we couldn't be in the same room together without referees?

It hit me then that losing Brandon wasn't what hurt most. I could replace a man. Hell, I could even upgrade to a luxury model like Bodhi-frickin'-Beckett. But in Jenna I hadn't just lost my cousin, I'd lost my friend, my confidant, and my very own flesh and blood.

In a perfect world, I would have wowed the crowd with a witty catchphrase or even a snappy dance number but, sadly, that wasn't me. I was just Breeze, the girl who'd spent way too long beating herself up over a relationship that was never meant to be.

I shifted my gaze back to Brandon. He wasn't my fate.

Bodhi's my fate.

What had I been thinking? Life with Bodhi's fans might be hard but life without him all together would be excruciating. It took these two cheats to finally wake me up to what had been in front of me all along. Bodhi wasn't just any guy. He was my guy. My destiny.

Cementing on a smile, I turned to my cousin. "You look like you have it all figured out. I'm happy for you. Congratulations on the new baby."

And then I walked away, determined never to allow those two to drag me down again.

Interestingly enough, it wasn't the awkward interaction with Brandon and Jenna that nabbed the top spot on reunion gossip. Our old drama was but a spark in a firestorm compared to my news-making brush with fame. Word of my connection with Bodhi had not only spread through social media but also through the ranks of my increasingly internet-savvy family. Even the relatives with 'great' before their names seemed to be dialed in.

Suddenly, I wasn't the girl with egg on her face, but the dazzling star of the party. Instead of dwelling on the past, my relatives welcomed me back with open arms, inspired and encouraged by my tale of survival. I realized that it had been me who'd cast myself out of the inner circle. My shame at being cheated on had kept me from moving forward.

No more.

After telling and retelling my story a dozen times, I managed to slip away from my table full of admirers. My stomach had started to let out the most unladylike growls, so I headed straight for the buffet line.

I'd barely managed to scoop a helping of potato salad onto my plate when I heard a frustrated little sigh. And when I turned, I found Brandon and Jenna's little girl, levered up on her tiptoes, reaching for a brownie on an elevated tray.

"Do you need help?" I asked, smiling down at her cherubic face.

She blinked, and then slowly lifted her toy for me to see.

I bent down to her level examining the tiny stuffed Chihuahua in her chubby hand. "Look at that." Envisioning Bodhi in my kitchen fending off Sweetpea with a pink spatula, I smiled. "I know someone who loves these little guys."

"Oh yeah, who?" My smile melted, and I slanted my gaze upward—to Brandon, eyeing me with a wicked grin. He crossed his arms over his chest when I straightened, then tipped forward into my space. "Because you know I only like my dogs big —like me."

I snorted a laugh. "In your dreams."

"You never had any complaints before." His eyes danced with mischief.

Was he... flirting with me?

Taking a giant step back, I scanned the room for Jenna, but she was nowhere to be found. Not good.

Don't engage. Do Not Engage.

"Only because I didn't know any better."

Dammit! Why did you engage?

Brandon chuckled wryly, then caught one of my curls, twirling the strand around his finger. "You're looking fine, Breeze. There's something different about you. I can't quite figure out what."

Before I could disentangle myself, Jenna appeared. The look on her face left little doubt: she'd heard everything.

Turning her white-hot gaze on Brandon, she spat, "What. Are. You. Doing?"

Before my eyes, my ex transformed into the guy I knew and didn't love. "I'm having a conversation. I didn't realize I had to clear everything with you first."

Keeping her voice low, Jenna replied, "Normally you don't, but when it's with your ex, at a family reunion, then yes – clearing it with me is a mandatory requirement."

I glanced around for an escape. Any way to extract myself from their conversation. But I was penned in, my butt against the buffet table and them in front of me.

Still, I attempted to slide past my cousin. "Excuse me, I—"

"And after everything she's done to you?" Jenna growled, her eyes flicking to mine.

What the hell?

I felt the smile curve my lips. Yeah, I was in it now. "Um, really? You want to remind me again what I did?"

She had the nerve to look at me like she was the aggrieved party. "You made him feel like a monster, Breeze. For following his heart. And you gave his clothes away to the Goodwill."

"Hey, that last part was for charity." I chuckled at my own joke. Or maybe it was the absurdity of the conversation.

"See, this is the problem," Jenna whined. "You're so spiteful. Brandon's not yours anymore. Get over it!"

I pressed my lips together to keep from laughing in her face. "Trust me, I'm over it. A certain popstar saw to that."

Scoffing, she slapped a hand on her non-existent hip for emphasis. "*Oh please.*"

But Brandon hadn't taken the news with as much abject disbelief. Titling his head, he surveyed me with narrowed eyes.

"*You*..." He laughed, not sounding the least bit amused. "*You are boning Bodhi Beckett?*"

Jealousy dripped from his tone, landing at our feet with a thud. I expected some perverse satisfaction to follow. But it didn't. I felt...nothing.

"Well, not at this very moment, no," I quipped.

He poked his tongue in his cheek, and looked around like he couldn't believe it. But why the hell did he care? His penis had been making house calls to my extended family.

Jenna appeared equally perplexed, turning her attention squarely on her husband. "What does it matter who she's sleeping with?"

"It doesn't, I was just asking a question," he said, his voice rising with every word. "You got a problem with that?"

"You know I've got a problem with that."

Clearly things weren't as perfect in their relationship as they'd made them out to seem. Suddenly, I wondered why I'd wasted so much energy on this man. He wasn't a catch. He wasn't even a dropped ball. Brandon was a cheat and a liar and if he'd done it to me, chances were Jenna would be next in line.

Itching to escape this unconventional lover's spat, I considered crawling under the table to get away.

"Look, I'm going to leave you guys to it. I've got to... um... eat."

Brandon's attention shifted my way. "You don't have to go just because Jenna's being a bitch. I can have a conversation with whoever I want."

Great. Now I was a pawn. Because there's no way those words were meant for me.

"No offense, Brandon, but you're the last person I'd ever want to talk to again."

He blinked, a vein popping out on his thick neck. Anger. Dejection. Disbelief. It was all there. Had Brandon been feeding off my perceived misery?

And then he smiled.

"Come on, Breeze." He grabbed ahold of my forearm. "You're not over me, and we both know it."

I was about to reply when a voice came from somewhere behind me.

"Oh, but she is."

Bodhi?

I turned and found him stalking toward our little trio. All eyes were on him. And I had to smile. There was a reason the guy was a star. His mere presence commanded attention.

His fiery gaze flicked to my arm before locking on Brandon like a heat seeking missile. "I'm going to need you to take your hand off my girl."

Eyes wide, my ex jerked his hand away as if I'd burst into flames. Bodhi slid between Brandon and Jenna and looked down at me.

"There you are." His hand found mine, lacing our fingers together. "Let's dance."

Too stunned to protest, I followed Bodhi to the center of the room. And then his arms were around me, and I was off my feet,

"I see you," he said, a second before his lips found mine.

I didn't have time to ponder. To wonder why he'd come for me after I blew us apart. Because there was nothing in the world but his taste. His scent. And the feel of his body against mine.

Heat pooled in my belly, spreading to my limbs.

"You came back," I said in a breathy whisper.

"Of course. I never should have let you go."

His mouth descended once again, and this time there was no urgency in his kiss. We had forever. Bodhi hadn't said as much, but there was no way I was letting him go. Not again. Not ever.

The room erupted into a series of hoots and hollers, bringing me back to the present.

Eyes dancing with amusement, Bodhi broke away from my lips and then turned to our audience, lifting our joined hands over our heads like we'd just won a competition.

The crowd erupted in applause as we took a bow.

Embarrassed, I shuffled to the side with Bodhi in tow, but I'd only made it a few steps before he ground to a halt.

Cupping my cheeks, he stared deeply into my eyes. "Before you try to hustle me out of here, I've got something to say. What we have is a once in a lifetime deal. And the reason I know that is because I'm surrounded by people all the time— coming in and out of my life at a dizzying speed. Every once in a while, I might connect with someone, but to actually like the person." He shook his head. "Breeze, that just doesn't happen. Not to me. You're so pretty and smart. You fascinate me. That quirky personality and all your positivity. It just bubbles out of you... I just... It blows my mind. *You* blow my mind. As farfetched as it sounds, I think I might be in love with you, and I'm not afraid to say that because I truly believe it."

My heart swelled to twice its size as I blinked up at him.

Doubt crept into his eyes. "Say something, Breeze."

Before I could respond, a lovesick squeak drew our attention. I'd been so engrossed in Bodhi's heartfelt declaration that I hadn't realized my relatives had formed a circle around us, waiting on my answer. Smack dab in the middle was Uncle Raymond. Well dammit. Where had he been when I needed him?

"Are you crazy?" asked the squeaker, Reese, my nineteen-year-old second cousin. "What's there to think about?" She turned her attention to Bodhi. "Yes. She says 'yes'."

"Reese." I waved a hand at her. "My conversation."

This wasn't going to work. We needed privacy.

"Come on," I said and, grabbing Bodhi's hand, I took a step, but got nowhere.

Rooted to his spot, Bodhi smiled. "Actually, no. This is your family, right?"

I nodded.

Scanning the crowd, Bodhi's eyes landed on my stepfather.

"Terrance, I see you put on some pants."

My stepfather puffed out his chest. "I did. Thanks for noticing."

Bodhi's focus shifted to my mother. "Thanks for giving me the address to this place."

She lifted her glass. "Of course, sweetie."

Swiveling my head in her direction, my eyes narrowed to slits. "You knew he was coming?"

"He called me last night when you were making up pet names with the f-word in them."

I cringed, hoping Bodhi hadn't heard me in the background screaming out "Sweetfuckingpea" at the top of my lungs.

"So, when you were giving me that pep talk this morning about destiny and all that crap, you already knew he was coming?"

She shrugged. "Yes."

I shook my head. This woman. "Unbelievable," I muttered.

"Breeze, eyes up here." Bodhi tipped my chin with his index finger. "You're sort of ruining my declaration of love."

"Oh, sorry. Please continue."

"First. I want to introduce myself to your family." He waved. "Hey, everyone. I'm Bodhi. Most of you probably heard what happened to Breeze and I and how we escaped a fire together. But what you might not know, is how I fell head over heels for the girl. Our time together. The romantic connection. I'm telling you, people, it just doesn't happen. I mean, I love everything about her. Her smile. Her beauty. Her heart. Oh, and she does this really cute clapping thing with her hands when she's excited, and it's the cutest shit I've ever seen in my life. Like it's better than those kitten videos on YouTube."

A group of my great aunts giggled as they nodded in agreement.

"Anyway, I'm telling you all this because I'm trying to win her over and, if she doesn't choose me, I'll honestly be devastated."

My knees shook from the force of his confession. In what world was I allowed to choose him?

Bodhi swallowed hard as he took my hand. "Breeze, I don't want another night to go by where I don't know if you're mine."

Sighs echoed off the walls. Bodhi had laid himself bare in front of the people I loved. That was him. He lived his life in the open. In front of crowds.

But not me. What I had to say was for his ears alone.

I pressed a kiss to his lips. "Let's go somewhere more private."

This time he didn't balk when I took his hand. My family wasn't as agreeable.

The minute we took a step boos erupted.

Bodhi looked a little crestfallen as I led him to the far corner of the room.

"What the hell?" His eyes darted back to the dispersing crowd. "They're booing me."

"No, they're booing me. You, they're swooning over."

And then, as if he realized why we were here, he squared his shoulders. "There's only one person I care to swoon and that's you, Breeze Marigold Cassidy."

Oh boy. That charm again. Like Pat, I was putty in his hands.

"Before you say anything, I have to ask. How are my animal peeps? Little Dick? Is he still being a dick?"

"Yes, of course." I laughed. "Would you expect any less?"

Bodhi shook his head. "God, he's such an asshole. I love that dog. And the family?"

"They landed yesterday. And you want to hear something amazing? Their house was only one of three on the block to survive the inferno! It'll be a while before they can move back in but at least they still have a home."

"Damn. That was unexpected. Honestly, Breeze, fuck the

county! You're the best pet-sitter in the whole state!"

"Yep, I'll be adding 'saves homes' to my flyer too."

Suddenly serious, Bodhi gripped my arms, staring all the way to my soul. "You amaze me. I'm in awe of everything you do. I want you to know that whatever scares you about us, I will find a solution."

My heart soared. Bodhi was ready to fight. For me. For us.

But there was no need. I'd already chosen him. Now all he had to do was be quiet long enough for me to tell him how I felt.

"How can I help you see that we're perfect for each other? You and I, we're not meant for anyone else. You're my tailor-made princess."

He buried his face in my neck, placing feather-like kisses onto my flushed skin.

"And if you're worried about the Dayers, don't be. In a little less than two months AnyDayNow will officially be over."

The gasp that burst out of me startled us both. "Oh no." I shook my head, panic sweeping through me. "Oh Bodhi. You didn't do that for me, did you?"

He cupped my cheek, thumb skating over my quivering bottom lip. "It's not because of you, I promise. Remember what I told you before— what happened when I was a child star who'd worn out his welcome? Well, boy bands have expiration dates too. I'd rather take myself out of the game now while I'm still at the top than to end up somewhere down the road on Dancing With The Stars."

"So what does this mean?"

"It means..." Bodhi pressed a chaste kiss to my lips. "You'll be seeing a lot more of me. If you stop playing so hard to get, that is."

"I wasn't trying to be difficult, Bodhi. I was just scared."

He frowned. "Of me?"

"No, not you. Just the idea of you. We're so different. You've never even been in a relationship before. How do you know I'm the right woman for you if you haven't tested the waters?"

"I've tested the waters. Remember the nickels?"

"I'm not talking about sex."

He sighed. "Listen to me. The reason I've never been in a relationship is because I've never met anyone I wanted to risk my heart on. I'm not looking to waste your time. I want the whole thing—proposal, engagement, marriage, kids. But I only want to do it one time. That's all I have in me."

"And you think the person you want to do that with is me?"

Bodhi touched his forehead to mine. "I know it's you. And it sounds crazy to even say, but I believe there's love at first sight and I'm pretty sure it feels like this. There's no one like you, Breeze, and there never will be."

My insides caught fire, spreading a warm glow throughout my body. "You're a poet." I brushed a lock of hair out of his eyes. "You need to write this stuff down."

He grinned, rolling up his sleeve to reveal lines of fading ink. "Way ahead of you."

I ran a finger over the smudged edges. "What is it?"

"The story of us."

I took a few moments to read the words before I tore my gaze from the tribute. "I guess what scares me most is falling in love with someone who gets me so well he has the capacity to destroy me."

Twining our fingers, he brought our joined hands to his heart. "And you know what scares me? That I'm never going to meet someone like you again and I'm never going to feel what I've felt in the past few days. I've got a dozen more concerts to go and then I want to lay low for a while. Maybe go on vacation with my woman."

Dipping his head, he slid his tongue along my collar bone.

"Uh-huh. I'm liking where this is going. Continue."

"Okay, so I was thinking after I buy the Range Rover and have it repainted..."

"You're buying our Range Rover?" I cooed, clapping my approval.

"Of course. Anyway, after that maybe we'll rent a small trailer and start knocking things off your bucket list – like the world's largest tater tot."

"Corndog," I corrected.

"Same thing. Anyway, shush. I'm making my pitch. We could then find a farm somewhere, away from the crowds, where I can work on my music, even become a solo artist. And you can give horses hip new hairstyles."

My lips curved into a smile. This was a life I could get behind. "Ooh yeah, talk dirty to me."

"You like that?" Hope gathered in his handsome face. "For you, I'd even be willing to get one of those disaster dogs you're always going on and on about."

"They're not disasters," I said. "They have conditions that make them less likely to get adopted."

"Whatever. Bring it on. I'm not scared of missing limbs."

"My hero."

Bodhi tipped my chin with his thumb and leaned so close his breath became my air. "I could be."

Wrapping my arms around his neck, I pressed a featherlight kiss to his lips. "You already are."

"What do you say, Dime? You wanna make a beautiful life with me?"

I kissed him again, tasting only the promise of love.

"Where do I sign?"

Bodhi lifted his shirt revealing a patchwork of lyrics and there, etched into the flesh over his heart was my name.

Breeze

"On the dotted line, baby."

27

EPILOGUE: BODHI

THE BEST PART OF LIVING WITH A FEMALE WAS FREE FOOD ALL DAY, every day. Sometimes, when I got really lucky, like today, I'd have my pick of an elaborate culinary spread. Going from tray to tray, Terrance and I popped appetizers into our mouths like dogs swiping food off the counter before our owners had a chance to swat us away.

"Maybe you two could leave something for the guests," Betsy suggested.

Showing no mercy for the soon-to-be-arriving visitors, Terrance shoved a stuffed olive into his mouth. "I suppose we could."

I grinned, high-fiving my mealtime buddy. It was always smart to surround yourself with like-minded people, and Terrance and I... we were beginning to morph into one.

"Besides, Betsy," I said, "you need us."

"Yeah? How do you figure?"

"No leftovers."

"Perhaps you two forgot what happened on Thanksgiving."

"Oh, yeah." Terrance grimaced, the memory now fresh in all our minds. "That was not a good day to be in my pants."

"No," Betsy confirmed. "It definitely was not."

Breeze blew into the kitchen, her hair a gush of auburn curls and her skin highlighted in a sunny glow. I always admired the beauty in my girl, but today – oh, man, she had me awestruck. How was it I could fall deeper and deeper in love with her every day?

Gulping back my appreciation, I spoke between mouthfuls of crackers. "Damn, woman, you're a smoke show."

Her lashes fluttered ever so flirty-like, and when she stretched up in her slip-on Vans and planted a kiss on my willing lips, I was a goner. Everything about her was a cool, crisp wonder. God, I was so lucky.

"Are these jeans too tight?" she asked, rearranging them on her hips. "The struggle was real."

"Babe, in my expert opinion, they're not tight *enough*."

"Good answer." She laughed. "Of course, I'm not sure how much weight I can give your opinion. You did get turned on last night when I was wearing that green facemask."

"Hey," I countered. "You looked sexy... in a gangrene sort of way."

"Ah, true love," Terrance mused.

"They remind me of us when we were young," Betsy sighed, before drawing her daughter into her arms. "Sweetie, you look like you're smiling from the inside out."

"I am," Breeze replied, beaming as she settled her gaze on me. "I never thought I could be this happy."

Nor had I. The past year with Breeze had surpassed expectations. After the end of AnyDayNow, life had taken one unexpected turn after another. Since I'd been coming from an environment where every last minute of my day had been accounted for, Breeze had been the sorely needed shock to my system. Being by her side was like living in a Technicolor movie.

Everything was brighter and more in focus than ever before... and ours was a show I never wanted to end.

True to my word, Breeze and I traveled across country in a rented motorhome. Touring the world with the guys, I thought I knew everything it had to offer, but that was before I got to experience it through Breeze's spirited eyes. Suddenly, the Banana Museum seemed as interesting a place to visit as Buckingham Palace.

"Oh, crap!" The meatball Terrance had been preparing to consume had taken an unexpected death plunge to the ground, and as he bent down to pick it up, he was met with snarling and snapping as a set of menacing two-millimeter teeth prepared to devour him whole.

Delivering hushed instructions, I bravely stepped between the two warring factions. "Terrance, do exactly as I say. Slowly back away from the dog. That's it, nice and slow."

As Breeze's father retreated to safety, I narrowed in on my tiny nemesis – Satan's cocksure Chihuahua himself – Little Dick Beckett.

"You really want to do this?" I asked him, more as a challenge than a question.

His demonic growling told me oh yes, he really did. To my archenemy, the tasty meatball was worth a bloody round of combat. But I'd learned a thing or two about dealing with His Furry Highness, and all of it included protective oven mitts.

"LD..." Breeze began to reason with the canine. "You're on a strict diet..."

"No offense, Breeze, but it's a meatball. Any chance you had of making a deal with the devil went away when it hit the floor. Now, step aside. Let the pro handle this."

She laughed and waved her hand. "By all means. Please, handle as you see fit."

Grabbing the oven mitts, I advanced, ready to scoop him up

and deposit him into the dog crate that had become his kingdom. But Little Dick wasn't going down without a fight, and grabbing hold of the top of the gloves, he shook his head back and forth like a big cat violently shakes its prey to a bloody demise. Suddenly the idea of my severed fingers crammed inside his vindictive mouth wasn't so appealing, and I scrambled backward. Little Dick took advantage of my hasty retreat to gobble up the meatball, and then casually walked away as if our confrontation had meant nothing to him.

"God, he sucks," I complained. "Why can't we get a normal Breeze-type dog? You know, like the ones that crawl out of manholes with a single eyeball dangling off their foreheads. Because, seriously, dealing with a mixed-breed Cyclops would be easier to handle than that shithead."

Breeze gave me that look – the one that said I had no right to complain. It was, after all, my fault we were now Lucifer's next of kin. Just before Breeze and I set out on our cross-country motorhome trip nearly a year ago, we'd received a frantic call from the Kufrin family, pleading for us to take their little menace in. Even though their home had not sustained fire damage, it would take months for the utilities to be restored to that area, so the family had been forced to move into a rental.

As expected, the arrogant Chihuahua, formally known as Sweetpea, immediately made the wrong impression on... well, every living soul he came in contact with, and suddenly, those teeth of his were sending him on a collision course with euthanasia.

There had been no question in our minds that we'd give the pup a home. Little Dick was a part of our story, and for better or worse, he'd always have a safe haven with us. Besides, at night, tuckered out after a day of diabolical plotting, Little Dick would always curl up on my lap just like he had the night of the fire and fall fast asleep. And then I loved him – more than I cared to admit.

———

Breeze knocked me in the leg for the twelfth time since Mason and Dane had started in on a conversation that looked like it might end with a visit to a Motel 6. That smug I-told-you-so expression on her face said it all. Since that first concert when I'd gathered Breeze, her parents, Mason and my newly resurrected family in Los Angeles for one of AnyDayNow's last performances, she'd insisted the two were meant to be. And yes, they'd hit it off at the first concert, but Dane was busy with the tour and Mason was struggling through withdrawal. Both had gone their separate ways – until now.

Since finding love myself, I was all for spreading it around, and certainly there was no one more deserving than loyal Dane. But I wasn't as excited about their connection as Breeze was, because even though I had nothing against Mason, he was a troubled dude, and I had a sinking suspicion it would be my friend on the losing end of this uneven pairing. Still, the chemistry between the two was electric enough that there was no way either one of them was getting off the train at the next stop.

Dane wasn't the only Dayer in attendance. Hunter, married and with a baby on the way, had made the trip too. As had Shawn and his current baby mama. I only say that because the last one had proved to be a fraud, passing off her groupie baby to more than one potential pop star papa. And once the first round of DNA testing cleared him of paternity, Shawn celebrated with a fresh new round of women, only to find himself right back where he started.

RJ was the only former band mate not at my place, and that wasn't for lack of trying. We'd originally planned our get-together for the week before, but we'd been forced to rearrange at the last minute due to unforeseen circumstances. And since RJ was days away from launching as a solo artist, his schedule didn't allow reshuffling.

Although RJ would be the first to branch out on his own, the rest of us weren't sitting around idly. The year I'd taken off from concerts and touring had been a crucial one. Little by little, I'd been working my way toward the goal of singing the songs that meant something to me. And now, without my father pushing his agenda and without the hitmakers shoving their fluff songs down my throat, I was finally in the position to choose.

Our cross-country trip had solidified my vision of a rock career. Stopping at open mic nights as often as we could, I'd hide under a disguise, strum my guitar, and often sing for twelve hammered assholes. And yeah, sometimes I was booed off the stage, but sometimes... sometimes magic happened. That was the feeling I was going for; the reason I loved music. And the reason I would never stop singing.

I turned toward my father, who was deep in a discussion with Betsy. What a difference a year made. Tucker was no longer the demanding dictator with a boner for world domination. Seeing the error of his ways, he'd gone to work not only fixing himself but also making amends for his earlier mistakes. Out of nowhere, the uptight man who'd raised me was learning to laugh again. The change in him was profound, and I wasn't sure how much of it had to do with our heart-to-heart on Breeze's patio or the counseling he was now receiving to deal with the unresolved feelings of his mother's death.

More likely, his sudden transformation had everything to do with Evan. In a bizarre turn of events, Tucker became Evan's 'Eddie' after all. He'd stepped up for Marni's second son just as he had for me, and with one look at Evan, it was clear the profound effect he'd had on my little brother. Evan was no longer an angry teen on a downward spiral. With Tucker's support and guidance, he was thriving in school and learning to play the bass guitar. Music was something that flowed through our blood. After all, Marni had once been a competent shower singer before addiction brought her to her knees.

But Tucker had seen to it that Marni's life would not be mine, nor would it be Evan's. He'd taken two boys who were not his own, and not only did he provide for us a safe haven, but he gave us a future. I thought about everything I had; everything he'd given me in life. Without him, I wouldn't be here today. I wouldn't have Breeze. I wouldn't have...

Choking up, I called to him. "Hey, Dad."

Tucker turned in his seat. "Yeah?"

"Thank you."

His confusion was understandable. "For what?" he asked.

I swallowed back the lump forming in my throat. It had taken me time to fully grasp what Tucker had done for me, but now that I knew, I'd never forget. "For saving me."

My words hit him hard, and his bottom lip quivered as tears flooded his eyes.

"Yeah," Evan pitched in. "Ditto for me."

Too touched to respond, Tucker rose from the couch. Evan and I did the same, and right there in the middle of the living room, the three of us sealed our bond. I only wished Jonah could have been there to share in the moment, but earlier commitments had kept him at home.

Feeling the emotions right alongside us, all our guests were dabbing at their eyes. Well, everyone but Shawn.

"Why are you crying, Bodhi?" he asked, nodding toward me in a knowing manner. "Is it because of your haircut?"

The room erupted, tears morphing into laughter, and I jumped onto Shawn and delivered a playful beatdown.

"So, Tucker, is Evan going to be your new superstar client?" Hunter asked.

Evan laughed. "Not unless I suddenly grow some talent."

"Don't listen to him. He's a natural. But no. All I want is for Evan to focus on school and be a normal teenager."

"Wow, such a novel concept," I said, with no contempt attached to the jab.

"Right?" Tucker smiled. "Besides, I already signed my next star, and he's going to be huge."

Every Dayer in the room swiveled their head in Tucker's direction. "Really? Who?"

"Well, it's a band called Sketch Monsters, but it's the lead singer who's going to bring the house down."

"That talented?" I asked, intrigued by this new information.

He nodded. "But it's not just that. He's also got a pedigree that's just out of the frickin' world."

Barely able to contain himself, Dane abandoned Mason altogether to get the inside scoop. "Who?"

"You ever heard of Jake McKallister?"

I deflated. Tucker was just playing with us. "You're so full of shit. Why would Jake join a band? He's a superstar."

"Not Jake... my new client is Quinn McKallister, his youngest brother. Mark my words, boys, that kid is going to put me back on the map."

"God help him," I replied.

A sudden commotion sounded from down the hall, and Breeze jumped to her feet.

"Finally," she said.

"You want me to go?" I asked, as eager as she to get to the source of the escalating noise bouncing off the walls.

Braiding her fingers into mine, Breeze pulled me to her. "Together?"

Always.

And the glittery rock on her ring finger proved it. During a stop in Vegas, Breeze and I had impulsively tied the knot. One minute we were tooling down the interstate and the next, we were standing at the altar with a tuxedo-clad Little Dick standing in as my best man.

When you knew, you knew, and we saw no reason to wait. Of course, our impromptu decision hadn't been a popular one in the parent circle, so we appeased them with a more traditional ceremony a few months later. But that didn't change the fact that, two months after we met, Breeze and I were married.

And now, just eleven months after our Vegas nuptials, she and I were walking hand in hand down the hallway of the home we owned together. As we reached the door, I drew Breeze into my arms and kissed her.

My wife, and now... the mother of my child.

Walking into the room, we gazed down at our five-day-old baby boy.

"Hey, Alexander," I said, stroking my finger over his smooth cheek. "We've got some people we want you to meet."

The End

———

NEW!

Ripple Effect is the second book in the AnyDayNow series and features RJ Contreras in this enemies to lovers tale with an earth-shaking twist!

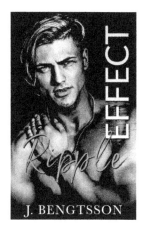

She's living next door to a superstar... and doesn't even know it.

When his mega-famous boy band AnyDayNow breaks up, international pop star RJ Contreras strikes out on his own. But when his solo career flops, RJ retreats to a no-frills apartment where he can hide out from the world and lick his festering wounds.

But when the girl next door starts slipping 'good neighbor' contracts under his door and complaining about his behavior through strategically placed Post-it-Notes, RJ snaps out of his self-absorbed melancholy to wage war.

Nothing short of an act of nature could repair the relationship between these two strong-willed enemies. But guess what Fate has in store?

DISCOVER THE BESTSELLING CAKE SERIES

Ten years have passed since Jake survived a stranger abduction.

He now finds himself on top of the world, a singer famous for the music that helped him heal. He thinks he's put his past behind him. He thinks he's okay. It isn't until he meets sweet, quirky Casey at his brother's wedding that he realizes all he's been missing out on.

Casey Caldwell has never had grand plans for her life. She's perfectly happy with the idea of meeting some nice nerdy guy after college and settling down near her family. But once she meets Jake, she can't remember why she ever wanted a simple life.

Whisked away into a world of music, riotous fans, tour buses, and movie-worthy shopping sprees, Casey is introduced to a life she could only have dreamed of.

But every fairytale has a villain ... and theirs lives inside Jake's head.

Together, Jake and Casey fight to keep their love alive, battling both the physical and emotional scars of Jake's abduction.

Each book in the Cake Series delves deeper into how that

one terrible crime continues to impact everyone in Jake's life and how their quest for love will set them free.

Exploring different points in time, we come to know the extraordinary McKallister family as intimately as we might know our own.

Start the beloved Cake Series at book one. Casey and Jake. Cake A Love Story.

Join my newsletter jbengtssonbooks.com/newsletter and Facebook reader group, J. Bengtsson's The Banana Binder

ALSO BY J. BENGTSSON

Made in the USA
Middletown, DE
02 July 2022